D1084756

THE
HOUSE OF CARDS

THE
HOUSE OF
CARDS

——————:——————

Leon Garfield

ST. MARTIN'S PRESS
NEW YORK

Library of Congress Cataloging in Publication Data

Garfield, Leon.
  The house of cards.

  I. Title.
PR6057.A636H6 1983   823'.914   82-10727
ISBN 0-312-39259-1

First published in Great Britain by The Bodley Head Ltd.

10 9 8 7 6 5 4 3 2

For
Helen and Brian

I

There was a baby crying. A very tiny baby, no more than four weeks alive. It was lying in a rough wooden cradle in an obscure corner of an obscure village somewhere in Poland, that began with a W and ended with a Z and was pronounced like a sneeze.

Commencing with a short series of 'Ahems!' after the manner of a public speaker, it soon launched upon an address of complaints and self-importance that went through the air like a saw. Although it could not speak a word of Polish—or of any human language for that matter—its meaning was perfectly plain:

'There is a disagreeable sensation of emptiness inside of me. Come at once and put it right. You—you with the large blurry face and enormous hands I have got used to! Come here and pick me up and feed me. At once, I say! It is no concern of mine what else you might be doing. Please don't bother me with such trifles. Come at once and feed me. Directly! Now! Now!'

And its voice rose to a piercing wail that mingled with the wind that blew through the empty village.

The empty village. Although the baby knew nothing of the kind, it was the only living soul in that place. Although it knew nothing of the kind, its mother lay dead, a dozen yards away. Next to her lay its father, also dead. In an angle of the wrecked window, a brother, dead. Out in the street, grandparents, dead. Uncles, aunts, cousins, dead. Neighbours, dead; and the village itself burned to a blackened skeleton along whose charred ribs crawled little worms of fire, looking for more to eat.

Such was the state of affairs one wild March evening in the year eighteen hundred and forty seven, when a gaunt, grey man tramped into the still smoking village and heard the baby crying.

The sight that met his eyes did not particularly surprise him. There was, he supposed, a war going on or an uprising, or a rebellion; though for what reason he neither knew nor cared. It was no business of his.

He paused, listened for a moment to the tiny wailing, then tramped on, a ruin among ruins. As he walked, he divided his looks between the stony ground and the lowering, wind-torn sky; and if looks were anything to go by, he was more than a match for both of them. His face, under the flapping brim of his dark, greasy hat, might have been described as a curse with a beard. It was as if once, long ago, he had fallen into a black mood and given a black scowl, when the wind had changed and fixed it; and all the winds that had blown thereafter had only served to bite it in more deeply. The very wrinkles round his sharp, suspicious eyes, that, on any other face might have suggested laughter lines, on his suggested laughter that had died and been buried there. It was a graveyard of feelings.

He carried a stick on his shoulder to which was tied a filthy bundle; and from a rope around his waist there hung a tinker's kettle, an old saucepan and a tankard, all so battered from banging against each other that they seemed to have dented themselves into faces almost as disagreeable as their owner's. An outcast, a scavenger, a rag-bag of rubbish blown in off the road, it seemed, by the wild March wind.

'You can't last much longer,' he grunted, irritably shaking the baby's crying out of his ears as if it had been a flea, or a louse—familiar companions both. 'Take my advice and die!'

Even as he spoke, there came a soft crash and a furious flurry of sparks as a wall, or a beam, collapsed. The crying ceased.

'That's an end of it, then. All over.'

He shrugged his shoulders, thrust out his lower lip, and went on trudging among the burnt-out ruins, looking for something that might be of use to him. His kettle, saucepan and tankard banged against each other like a doll's funeral.

Here and there the wind had succeeded in re-kindling embers that revealed, in their dull glow, motionless faces, motionless hands and fidgeting hair. Cautiously the tramp skirted the quiet forms as he poked about in cottage after shattered cottage. Sometimes he paused and looked down, when an attitude or an expression particularly caught his fancy.

'And what were you up to, friend?'—to a man lying across a doorway with a pitchfork clutched in his outstretched hand. 'Defending your castle, eh? Pitchfork against a sabre? Tell me, friend—' squatting down with a tinny peal of kettle, saucepan and tankard—'was it Cossacks who did all this? Or was it those mad Hungarian Hussars I passed on the road? I only ask, you understand, out of curiosity. It's no concern of mine.'

Receiving no answer but a stare, he clattered away until another dusty bundle caught his eye.

'Well, old woman! You look fierce enough to frighten a whole army! And with a chopper in your hand! Come, give it to me. It's no more use to you. There now, it's mine. Thank you kindly, ma'am. I'll mention you in my will.'

He tucked the chopper into the rope round his waist and shuffled off.

'Now here's a pretty sight!'

He stopped before a cottage that was twinkling all over with fairy lights of fire. They winked round the gaping doorway, they danced along the bony roof, and glimmered festively within. A dead boy stared out of a dead window, as if he was dreaming it all.

'Waiting for somebody, young man? They're not coming, I promise you. Not even if you wait till Doomsday. Ah! What's that you're holding? A fiddle? What an idea! Were you hoping to charm your murderers with music? Give it to me. It must be worth something. Why, I might even learn to play it myself! Come along! Don't hold on so tightly. Give it to me, I say. I want it!'

He wrestled with the fixed grip until he got the fiddle away. The boy, with a sigh of clothing, fell to the floor.

'Now, where is the bow? What have you done with it?'

Quite by chance, the dead boy's hand had fallen so that his curled fingers pointed to a table within the cottage. The violin bow lay beside it.

'Thank you kindly, young man! I'll mention you in my will.'

He clanked and clattered into the winking ruin, like a vulture into Christmas.

'Ah! Ah! What have we here? Valuables?'

Under the table was a rough wooden box. Eagerly the tramp dragged it out and peered inside. He grunted in surprise. Beneath a downy coverlet of ashes that had kept it warm, lay the baby. Even as he looked, a black hole opened in the baby's face, grew astonishingly, and blasted forth a howl like an airy cannonball. It was still alive!

The tramp drew back in some confusion and dismay. He pondered.

'Now if you were a fledgling or an abandoned fox-cub, I would put you out of your misery. If you were a day-old kitten or a puppy, I would do the same. If you were—'

'If! If! If!' raged the baby in its own mysterious tongue, being in no mood to distinguish between one large blurry face and another. What did it care! There were more important matters on its mind—or, rather, on its stomach, which was all the mind it had. 'Don't bother me with your mumblings! I can't understand a word you're saying! Pick me up and feed me. At once, I say! Now! Now!'

The tramp, thrusting out his lower lip until it formed half a saucer projecting from his beard, laid aside the fiddle and bow and cautiously advanced a finger, probably with the intention of putting a stop to the uproar.

At once it was seized, by hands scarcely bigger than a mouse's, and conveyed to the waiting mouth. The tramp cried out in alarm; until he realised that there were no teeth to bite him, and soft gums closed in the expectation of nourishment. However, after a moment, the finger was rejected with every demonstration of injury and annoyance.

'That is not at all what I am used to! It tasted quite disgusting! Feed me at once, I say. *Now!*'

'Wait a minute, wait a minute! Be quiet! Let me think. How can I think properly while you lie there screaming? Be quiet, you little savage! There, there!'

Hastily—he could not do it quickly enough—the tramp untied his bundle and, after fumbling among his tattered wardrobe, produced a bottle, half full of stale wine.

'Here, now! It is the best I can do! You can't expect more from somebody like me. Here, drink it. It's good for you! Put hairs on your chest! Here! Take it!'

'Are you out of your mind?' fumed the baby. 'What do you expect me to do with an enormous thing like that? I'm not used to it.'

'Drink up, drink up!' urged the tramp.

'Idiot, idiot!' returned the baby.

The bewildered tramp took the bottle away and scratched his

head. He searched his belongings again; and, finding a piece of rag not so filthy as the rest, soaked it with wine and inserted a corner into the howling mouth. The baby sucked, gave several exclamations of surprise, and went on sucking with tremendous concentration. Presently it became very drunk, hiccupped hugely, chuckled, and went to sleep.

For a few moments the tramp remained squatting by the cradle; then he leaned forward and stared hard at the sleeper within. There was a curious expression on his frowsy, battered face. It was an expression of pleasure and simple pride.

The baby stirred, opened a drunken eye and uttered a faint complaint. Anxiously the tramp reached out a hand and began to rock the cradle. At the same time a queer, cracked, rusty noise issued from the verminous tangle of his beard.

'Hush a-bye baby,' he croaked, 'on the tree-top,
When the wind blows, the cradle will rock . . . '

And the wind did blow. It moaned and whined and wailed and whispered through the murdered village, disturbing clothing and lifting hair, as if it was looking for something, or for somebody . . . One by one the glowing embers perished, like red eyes closing, and the ashes turned and sighed.

'When the bough breaks, the cradle will fall;
And down will come baby, cradle and all . . . '

Long into the night the hoarse lullaby continued, sometimes accompanied by a melodious twanging as the singer plucked at the remaining strings of the fiddle to swell his song. At last there was darkness and silence. The ashes, the wind, the woods on the hillside and the very stars in the sky seemed to have been lulled into sleep.

The tramp awoke. The sky was already grey with the threat of morning. The ruins were cold and the cradle was quiet. He sat up, half-hoping, half-fearing that the small business of the night was over. The baby looked too peaceful to be still alive. He poked it with his finger.

'Ahem, ahem!' remarked the baby; and then, 'Feed me! *Now*!'

'What a mouth you've got! It's enormous! It is very ugly. You look like a split orange.'

'Feed me! Don't just stare at me! Food! *Now*!'

9

'Be quiet, be quiet! You have the worst voice in the world! Every time you open your mouth I get a headache!'

'What do I care! Stop mumbling and feed me!'

'No more wine. Not at your age. You look liverish already. You must have milk. That's it. Milk. Tell you what: I'll take you as far as the next village. You'll have milk there. Only—only hold your tongue while I go and find something to carry you in. A cart or a wheelbarrow. Hold your tongue, I say, or I'll—I'll tie it up with string!'

He banged and jingled off, pursued relentlessly by the baby's howls. Bleak and wretched was the morning village; ashes everywhere, ashes to the ashen, scattered like blossoms over the dead. At last he found a hand-cart that wobbled frightfully at every turn of its wheels. He trundled it back and loaded it, first with his wordly goods, and then with the cradle and its occupant.

'Tell me,' he puffed, as he heaved it aboard, 'do you prefer to travel with your face or your back to the horse?'

He began to push; but after no more than a dozen yards it became apparent that the load was too great and that, at any moment, one or other of the wheels would come off. He halted, lifted down the cradle and laid it in the street. He scowled, thrust out his lower lip and scratched his head. There was no help for it. With enormous caution—as if it had been recently glued—he lifted the baby out of the cradle and placed it back in the cart.

'There now! Don't cry. You'll have another bed in time. A four-poster, maybe, with curtains and a coronet. Who knows?'

Once more he set off, at first pushing and then pulling the cart, while his kettle, saucepan and tankard banged and clattered every step of the way.

Soon the little cluster of blackened dwellings was left behind as the tramp, with the baby trundling after, trudged along a road that twisted and turned, passed through dark woods and between barren fields, and to which he could see no end.

The wind blew and dirty clouds kept palming the sun—now you see it, now you don't—and still the tramp toiled resolutely on. For the most part, his companion was blessedly quiet, as the jolting and rattling had a soothing effect; but whenever he stopped to rest, the baby flew into a rage and abused him roundly.

'You are a monster!' shouted the tramp, putting his hands to his ears to shut out the howling. 'I am not a young man any more! Perhaps I am not as old as I look, but that is no business of yours. I am certainly not twenty, and I cannot drag you, mile after mile, without any rest! Do you want to finish me off?'

'Words, stupid words! You make a better noise when you rattle!'

'Very well then. We'll go on. But I'm warning you, if I drop dead on the way, you'll be worse off than ever!'

So the journey was resumed; for in the battle between these two selfish souls, it was always the weaker who won. The stronger might go to the wall or to the devil; who cared, so long as he came back with something to eat! Presently they became as a speck in the distance; and presently they were seen no more.

The unseen watcher rested for a while; then, with clenched fists, continued the pursuit.

2

Another March, but as far away from the last in place as in time; as far away, in fact, as by a thousand miles and a round dozen of years. Another March, then, in London.

Evening coming on and the usual strong wind blowing hats, capes, skirts, newspapers, sparks from cigars and, in general, a darkly rushing multitude along Bishopsgate Street in a homeward direction. So close-packed and unending was the throng, with its snowstorm of white faces, that it seemed a hopeless case that it would ever sort itself out and find its way to the right houses, kiss the right children and eat the right dinners.

'Pa! Pa! For goodness sake, Pa, do come along!'

A pretty, smartly dressed girl, about twelve years old, jumped sideways out of the moving tide and tugged at a long grey scarf to which was attached, by several loops round his neck, a somewhat elderly, shabbily respectable gentleman. She gave a further tug, and, after the manner of an experienced angler, landed her gentleman in a shop doorway over which was inscribed: 'Dolly's Famous Pickled Herrings and Continental Delicacies'.

'We're late, Pa! You know how I hate being late!' she muttered, struggling to poke unneccessary yards of scarf inside her companion's coat. 'Oh, why do you wear this horrible old thing?'

'Because you made it for me, my love,' returned the gentleman, with a wry smile.

'I wish you wouldn't call me that! It sounds so common. And anyway, I made it for you ages ago, simply ages! It's high time you gave it away to the poor.'

'But we are poor, my—er—dear.'

'We're *not* poor! I hate being called poor!'

'Very well then, my—er—child. We are in reduced circumstances. Is that better?'

'Much better. Now, Pa—' finishing off her efforts to make her gentleman tidy— 'you may ring the bell.'

He did so; and while they waited, the girl glanced back at the hurrying crowds. Her eyes were troubled as if she feared a follower. Uneasily she clutched her companion's sleeve. He glanced at her curiously.

'What is it, Perdita?'

'Nothing, Pa. I was only straightening your sleeve.'

He nodded; and, after a moment, the girl resumed her previous critical manner.

'I do hope that horrible woman isn't going to be there again.'

'What horrible woman? Do we know any horrible women?'

'You know perfectly well who I mean. Mrs Fairhazel. She's the most horrible, creepy, pretending woman I've ever seen. But being a man, you wouldn't know about such things. But I do. Anyway, I hate her . . . and she hates me.'

'But—' began the gentleman, presumably with the intention of offering some excuse for Mrs Fairhazel's unfortunate character, when the shop door was opened.

Mr Dolly himself greeted them.

'So kind of you to come, Mr Walker!' he exclaimed. 'And you, too, princess!'

The princess, after a moment's hesitation in which she made it plain that she was as much put out by that form of address as by 'my love', submitted, with tolerable grace, to being kissed on the cheek.

'Come in! Come inside!'

They entered, ducking cautiously under a fringe of sausages that hung, somewhat menacingly, from the ceiling, like a grove of truncheons. It was a weird, dim, profoundly odorous establishment—almost suffocatingly so—and populated by a shadowy crowd of casks, barrels, sacks, cheeses in muslin winding-sheets, and huge jars of pickled onions that bulged and glared, like watchful eyes.

It might have been a robbers' cave; and the proprietor himself, the robber chief—but retired from the profession on the grounds of extreme affability. He was a short, stout, swarthy individual with very black whiskers and very white teeth among which there was a liberal sprinkling of gold, as if he had swallowed his watch and was still eating the chain.

'Such a dreadful windy evening!' went on Mr Dolly, shutting and bolting the door and waving his hands deprecatingly at the weather. 'I was sure you wouldn't come! I said as much to Mrs Dolly. I said, nobody will want to come out on a night like this! But here you are! It really is most kind—most kind!'

Mr Walker made a feeble effort to stem the flood of Mr Dolly's gratitude, but soon gave up. He glanced at his daughter; and was instantly rewarded by: 'Your hat, Pa! Do take off your hat! Why do I always have to remind you? Your hat, Pa!'

Mr Walker gave another wry smile, into which his features seemed to compose themselves naturally, and removed the offending article, which was already at a tipsy angle from collision with a low-lying sausage.

'We're sorry we're late, Mr Dolly,' said the girl, after satisfying herself that her father's exposed head was a respectable sight and then throwing back her blue velvet hood and displaying a glossy profusion of black curls that was a good deal more than respectable. 'But grandfather here was so slow in getting along! Hobbling, like an old tortoise!'

'Tortoise? Grandfather? Come, come! That is no way to talk of your father, princess!'

'But he's getting so old! And so grey! Look! He's nearly white! It's silly to keep calling him Pa.'

'Come now, Perdita! That's enough!' said Mr Walker, with a sudden sharpness that had the effect (but only temporarily) of startling the girl into mildness. 'We mustn't keep Mrs Dolly waiting.'

The girl nodded; and, with a quick, firm step, led her companion—as if by an invisible halter—to the back of the shop where they were presently heard mounting the stairs.

For a few moments Mr Dolly stared after the ill-assorted couple; then he shook his head and made his way back to the front of the shop, picking a path between barrels and absently rapping them, like Ali Baba testing for thieves. He gazed through the window at the crowds that still streamed along the darkening street. He shook his head.

'Like the Amalekites,' he sighed, 'fleeing before King David.'

A curious sentiment. But as Mr Dolly was of the Hebrew persuasion, such biblical comparisons came readily into his mind. However, they went out of it just as readily. Truth to tell, Mr Dolly had not the faintest idea who the Amalekites were, or why they were absconding. Truth to tell, Mr Dolly's religious persuasion was only one among many, and by no means the strongest. His wife persuaded him, and that was stronger; his friends persuaded him, and that was stronger; and any tale of misfortune persuaded him, and that was perhaps the strongest of all. He was an excellent, kindly man whose chief unhappiness was the unhappiness of others and whose chief pleasure was in helping people and inviting them to dinner on Friday nights.

'And such people!' his admirable wife, Mrs Dolly, complained, but in the privacy of their bed-chamber. 'Lame dogs, lame dogs every one! Can you never find anyone else to invite? With so many lame dogs you should have gone into the veterinary business!'

But she would not have had it otherwise. Although she felt it her duty to point out such things, she could not help being proud of a husband who was famous for his kindness, not only in Bishopsgate Street, but even in faraway Poland where Mr Dolly's father had come from, and where he still had an uncle and cousins. There, in the little town where the Dollys had originated, Mr Dolly of Bishopsgate Street in London was still talked of as being a lavish provider, a Joseph in Egypt, and his shop enlarged to the proportions of Pharaoh's palace.

'Go to London,' was the advice given to those not making a go of it at home. 'Look up Mr Dolly of Bishopsgate Street. He will set you on your feet.'

So they went; and hardly a month passed by without some thin, needy Pole breathing sad tales of home across Mr Dolly's counter.

'But one of these days, my dear,' Mrs Dolly felt it her duty to warn, 'you will regret it. One of these days you will help a thief, or a murderer, maybe, running away from the police. It will happen, I know it! One of these days you will invite a monster to dinner on Friday night. After all, my dear, what do you really know about any of them?'

She was right, of course. He knew next to nothing about his lame dogs, except that they were lame.

Mr Walker and the princess, for instance. They had appeared in the shop one Friday afternoon, about eight years ago, quite out of the blue. All that was certain was that Mr Walker had looked so thin and worn that one's heart almost broke to see him standing there, with the tiny girl fiercely clutching him by the hand.

'I—I was just passing,' Mr Walker had said, with a look of terror at the child, as if he hoped she couldn't hear him, 'when I noticed the name over the shop door and—and I wondered if—if you could be the same Mr Dolly who used to have relations living in Poland?'

He mentioned the name of the little town and went on to explain that he had actually been there on business, some time ago.

Naturally Mr Dolly had been delighted and said that his uncle, Mr Dolska, was still alive and well, and even went to business every day even though he was eighty. Mr Walker must have met him. He owned a furniture factory and even exported mahogany wardrobes to Russia. He would write and tell his uncle about Mr Walker—

But it turned out that Mr Walker had not met Mr Dolly's uncle. He had heard about Mr Dolly and Bishopsgate Street quite by chance. There was no point in troubling the old gentleman. He was quite insistent about that. He had only remembered about Mr Dolly when he had happened to see the name over the shop door—

'So you decided to look me up!' said Mr Dolly cheerfully. 'What could be more natural than that?'

And what could have been more natural than for Mr Dolly to

invite Mr Walker and the child to dinner and to inquire, as delicately as he could, if he could be of any assistance?

Vigorously Mr Walker had protested that he hadn't come for charity. He wasn't a beggar. Far from it, he was a man who took a great pride in being independent. Only—only lately, what with the child growing so fast and needing so many clothes, things had been a little difficult. This confession caused him the most intolerable anguish. In short, he wondered if Mr Dolly, being in touch with people from his family's country, knew of anyone who wanted lessons in English, as he himself spoke several languages, Polish among them.

Of course Mr Dolly knew of dozens; in consequence of which Mr Walker began to prosper. He filled out, bought better clothes and the little princess grew and grew and became as imperious and demanding as any princess of Mr Dolly's acquaintance. They continued to come to dinner on most Friday nights; but, just as Mrs Dolly had said, Mr Dolly never really knew more about them than what he had found out on the first Friday afternoon when they had appeared in the shop, long ago.

'For instance, what had he, an Englishman, been doing in your little Polish town?' Mrs Dolly had asked, in the privacy of the bedchamber. 'What business had he been in; and how had he come so far down in the world? And what, I ask you, has become of the child's mother?'

Even Mr Dolly had to admit that this last was a real mystery. The first time the mother had been mentioned—when the princess had been tiny and not yet a princess—Mr Walker had gone very pale. He had glanced at the child and slightly shaken his head; and the matter had been dropped. It had been mentioned again, some time later; and the same pallor had affected Mr Walker's face and the princess had looked at him sharply, almost accusingly, as if she suspected him of having wickedly spirited that lady away.

Almost certainly there had been some tragedy, painful to recollect; but exactly what it had been remained a mystery that Mr Dolly's natural delicacy forbade him to probe. He was content to take Mr Walker at face value; and, as time went by, he felt amply rewarded by that value increasing as Mr Walker rose in the world, became a respected teacher of languages, a gentlemanly widower and a credit to the community among which he lived.

In Mr Dolly's opinion, all that his good friend lacked in the world was a woman's hand; and in the hope of providing one he had persuaded Mrs Dolly, against her better judgement, to invite various widows and single ladies of her acquaintance to dinner on Friday nights. So far, his efforts had not been crowned with success.

The latest in this long line of hands that Mr Dolly had, figuratively speaking, extended to Mr Walker, was Mrs Fairhazel, the forlorn relict of a Polish tailor who had left her with a little house in Stepney and a name she could never spell. Soon after he had passed away—he had been run down by a cart in Holborn only a year after their marriage—she had returned to the use of her maiden name, but had wistfully retained the 'Mrs'.

She was, thought Mr Dolly, admirably suited to the position of Mrs Walker. Whichever way you looked at it, except one, she was right for him. The exception was, as usual, the princess.

The shop bell rang; and Mr Dolly, his thoughts with Mrs Fairhazel, went eagerly to the door. But the caller turned out to be only a Polish youth by the name of David Kozlowski. This young man, who was about eighteen, had not been long in London, but, thanks to the efforts of Mr Dolly, was already doing well in the despatch department of a silk importer's, near the Tower. It was his first Friday night (he had either been too shy or too busy to come before), and he had brought a bottle of wine. Mr Dolly reproached him for his extravagance. The youth smiled with clever eyes; and Mr Dolly sent him upstairs.

A few moments later Mrs Fairhazel arrived. She was despairingly apologetic for being the last.

'Please don't think anything of it, dear Mrs Fairhazel! It was kind of you to come out on such a windy night!'

Mrs Fairhazel, who had been blown into a state of wispy confusion, protested that she had hardly noticed the wind at all, that it really wasn't at all windy, and that, even if it had been, she wouldn't have minded a bit.

'Mr Walker has arrived,' said Mr Dolly, displaying every link of his watch-chain smile. 'And, of course, our little princess. Such a pretty girl nowadays, don't you think? And anybody can see, with half an eye, that she's quite taken to you, Mrs Fairhazel!'

Mrs Fairhazel, thinking perhaps that what is seen by half an eye

17

might not correspond with what is observed by a whole one, nevertheless agreed that the princess was quite delightful and that she had been looking forward to an evening in her company. Having delivered herself of this, she fluttered a hopeless hand in the direction of her faded red hair; then, with a feeble little smile and an imperceptible straightening of her shoulders, suggestive of a determination to keep smiling even if she should be eaten by lions, she went upstairs.

It was an innocent deception. She was a victim, and she knew it. What really frightened her was the thought that everybody else knew it. Mr Dolly bolted the shop door, turned down the gas, and followed the last of his guests upstairs to his Friday night.

3

The Dollys' dining-room, which was situated directly above the shop, was, on Friday nights, a scene of pagan magnificence. Everything overflowed. The long table overflowed with dishes, the high-backed chairs overflowed with family and guests, the gilt mirror above the sideboard overflowed with their reflections, and the long-stemmed glasses overflowed with Mr Dolly's liberal wine—in consequence of which saucers had to be slipped under the cloth from where they rose like extinct volcanoes.

Mr Dolly himself, seated at the head of the table, also over-flowed—with pleasure and pride as he contemplated the abundance before him: the smiling china, the winking silver, the roasted fowl, the dumpling soup and the great stuffed carp that seemed to recline upon its dish with a gasp of delight, as if the prospect of being dined upon was every bit as delicious as the prospect of dining.

Always twelve at table: six guests and six Dollys . . . although to Mr Dolly it always seemed like half a dozen of the one and five of the other, as he invariably forgot to count himself. But what a family they were! Jonathan, his son, a sturdy sixteen and handsome as a lord; the duchesses, his two elder daughters; Miriam the youngest, who was fifteen and like a queen; and, at the far end of the table, seen hazily through a blaze of candles and sometimes waved to, calm, upright, resplendent Mrs Dolly—the empress. Like Burke's, there was a Dolly's *Peerage*. He loved to ennoble everybody, even if it was only to an aristocracy of the heart.

Friday nights were the happiest times of Mr Dolly's life, and it would have been churlish to spoil them for him. He was absolutely convinced that it was only necessary to throw people together, add food and wine in enormous quantities, and pop the mixture into his dining-room as if it was an oven, for the result to be something in the nature of a harmonious pie. So confident was he of this, that the sournesses, disagreements and even open quarrels that sometimes exploded right under his nose, passed him by completely; and when he was told about them later, he received the news with incredulous surprise.

'Couldn't you see that they *hated* each other?' Mrs Dolly would marvel, in the privacy of their bed-chamber.

'Who? What do you mean? Oh, them! Nonsense, my dear! They were getting along famously!'

'My God! Do they have to cut each other's throats and bleed all over the tablecloth before you notice anything?'

To which he would respond with the aforementioned incredulous surprise. He was hopeless. He would never learn. If he lived to be a hundred, please God, he would always be the same.

Even now, at this very moment, when they had only just finished the soup, and poor Mrs Fairhazel was already almost in tears on account of certain wounding and highly audible remarks passed by the princess, and the unfortunate Mr Walker, having failed to silence the one and not daring to comfort the other for fear of making matters worse, was looking as if he longed for the floor to open and swallow him up, Mr Dolly just went on overfilling the glasses and chattering away like a schoolboy without a thought or a care in the world.

And what was it all about? What was so important that it should take his mind off everything? Such an extraordinary thing! He had to tell everybody about it. He had been summoned for jury service. Imagine that! He, Herbert Joseph Dolly, had been called upon to perform the most important of civic duties. What an honour! He was as proud as a peacock and nothing less than the ceiling coming down would have silenced him. And even then, Mrs Dolly could see the whole house in ruins and her husband still going on about some person by the name of Magnus Carter that nobody cared two pins about. And waving his arms.

He knocked over a glass. Mrs Dolly rang the bell for a saucer. There was a tremendous crash, like a bomb exploding, from the direction of the kitchen; and a tousled female appeared as if she had just been disastrously hatched. The Dollys' maid.

Here it must be said that, although the Dollys were seen to observe the Sabbath inasmuch as there were lighted candles on the table and Mr Dolly, his wife, his children and the strangers within his gates did no work, they were seen to break it inasmuch as the maidservant within their gates, an Irish female known unaccountably as Brandyella, toiled exceedingly. She fetched and carried, fetched and carried, and, when out of sight, exploded with crockery as if repeatedly struck by lightning. She was a red-faced, home-loving young woman who rarely strayed further afield than the public house next door, where she sometimes sang.

' 'Twas nothin', ma'am, nothin' at all,' she said with a reassuring wave towards the kitchen. ' 'Twas only a teaspoon droppin' into the sink.'

Mrs Dolly compressed her lips. She pointed to the little lake of wine by Mr Dolly, which was beginning to remind her of blood.

'Please bring a saucer, Brandyella.'

Brandyella curtsied extensively and dispersed. Moments later there was another explosion, followed this time by sounds of an avalanche that terminated in a muffled oath. Brandyella returned with a saucer.

''Twas nothin', ma'am, nothin' at all. 'Twas only me rosary fallin' on the floor. A wonderful noise, considerin'.'

Mrs Dolly, not feeling equal to calling into account the girl's religious observances, expressed disbelief to her fork, while the saucer was slipped under the cloth to make another volcano. Brandyella departed. No further explosions followed; and Mrs Dolly wondered how things were going with Mrs Fairhazel now? Badly . . . badly . . .

Mrs Dolly liked Mrs Fairhazel, who was her friend, and very much wanted to see her settled with Mr Walker. It seemed such a suitable match. They were both so quiet and retiring that it seemed unlikely that either would find a more convenient partner than the other. Only—only Mrs Dolly wished that her friend would make more of herself. Perhaps she ought to dye her hair to bring out its natural colour? And why didn't she sparkle a little instead of just sitting there, twisting up her napkin and smiling foolishly at her plate?

She blamed Mr Dolly. He really ought to be bringing Mrs Fairhazel out. He ought, for instance, to ask her about her little house in Stepney. It would do no harm to remind Mr Walker that Mrs Fairhazel had some property. Everybody needed a push. But no! Not Mr Dolly! The jury system if you please!

'So there it is!' said Mr Dolly, leaning back and waving his arms again. 'On Monday I shall be sitting in judgement on a fellow human being! What do you think of that?'

'I think,' said Mr Walker, smiling good-humouredly, 'that whoever is in the dock will be a very fortunate person indeed, Mr Dolly.'

'How so? What do you mean, Mr Walker?'

'I mean that you are much too kind to find anybody guilty of anything, Mr Dolly. Everybody will be acquitted!'

Everyone laughed and agreed—excepting Mr Dolly who was a little put out by this reflection on his capacity for impartial judgement. But it served him right, Mrs Dolly thought.

'It is good of you to say so, Mr Walker, and I appreciate that it was kindly meant. But you must not suppose that I will not do my duty. I will listen to the evidence and, if the prisoner is guilty—beyond all reasonable doubt, that is—I shall have to say so.'

'I—I'm sure Mr Dolly will always do the right thing,' put in Mrs Fairhazel, plucking up her courage till it almost came up by the roots in her anxiety to come to the support of her host. Then, fatally recollecting that it had been Mr Walker who had expressed doubts and fearing that his daughter would be angrier with her than ever, miserably tried to undo the damage. 'But—but I do agree with Mr Walker, that—that Mr Dolly would find it hard to condemn anybody . . . unless—unless it was a monster that none of us would want to save.'

'Can you really imagine such a monster, Mrs Fairhazel?' asked Mr Walker.

'Oh—oh! I don't really know. A—a brutal murderer, perhaps,

or—or—' with a sudden flash of cunning that Mrs Dolly noted and approved—'or someone who was cruel to a child! I think that to be cruel to a child is a terrible thing.'

'Yes . . . yes. Cruelty to a child is certainly terrible,' said Mr Walker with feeling. He laid his hand unconsciously on Perdita's, from where it was instantly shaken off. He sighed. 'But—but if we make it more difficult and imagine a murder—a brutal one, if you like—committed by someone in a moment of horrible fear or passion. What then?'

Mrs Fairhazel, knowing the daughter's eye to be upon her, blushed and shook her head as if disclaiming all knowledge of passion.

Mrs Dolly thought it was very foolish of her to do so in the circumstances. Although, she had to admit, she found it hard to imagine Mrs Fairhazel and Mr Walker engaged in a passionate embrace, she felt that Mrs Fairhazel ought to be imagining it; and, what was more, she ought to be trying to persuade Mr Walker into imagining it. Faint heart, as they say, never won fair gentleman!

But it was too late. The moment had passed and everyone, suddenly intrigued by the idea of proposing crimes for Mr Dolly to pass judgement upon, began eagerly putting forward suggestions.

At first they were horrific, as nobody seemed able to think of anything less than murder—and murder most dark and bloody. Murder by axe, murder by knife, murder by poison, murder by iron bar with spikes, murder by wholesale, murder by retail . . . the whole table seemed to redden under such a gruesome burden and the candles blenched and shuddered at their wicks. It was uncanny to hear of such frightful deeds from such innocently laughing lips, for it was all in the best of spirits and the chief purpose was to make kindly fun of Mr Dolly's coming importance.

He took it well, holding up his hands at each and every suggestion and crying out, 'The evidence! Let me hear the evidence!'

Then matters took a lighter turn and Mr Dolly's two elder daughters, who sat next to two young men who were their declared admirers and consequently the butts of their wit, demanded to know what should be done with faithless lovers and people who forgot birthdays? If found guilty should they be hung in chains? The two young men, stung into replying, asked for heavy damages to be awarded against young women who made false accusations—didn't Mr Dolly agree?—while Miriam Dolly shrilly demanded the full rigour of the law to be visited upon sisters who borrowed money and never paid it back.

'Kozlowski! David Kozlowski!' cried Jonathan. 'You haven't given us a crime! Come along! This is Friday night at the Dollys! You're not allowed to sit as quiet as a mouse.'

It was true that the newcomer had hardly opened his mouth, except to put food into it. Although plainly anxious to please, he seemed a very shy young man; and now, when Jonathan demanded a crime from him, he looked as if he did not know what to do.

'A crime from you, David Kozlowski! Surely you can think of one? Please! Another murder if you like! Oh, for goodness sake, we're not asking you to commit one, you know,' protested Jonathan, as the young man's eyes suddenly widened and he went pale.

The cheerful talk died away and a sympathetic quietness fell upon the table as everyone could see that the young stranger was in difficulties.

'I—I do not understand English enough,' he muttered. 'I have not been here very long. I—I am sorry.'

Jonathan felt exceedingly uncomfortable as he realised he had distressed a guest. Kozlowski must have misunderstood him. God knows what he'd thought! Jonathan appealed to Mr Walker to translate what he'd said into Polish and put matters right. Mr Walker nodded and did so. The young man listened carefully. At length, his clever eyes gleamed.

'You speak Polish well, sir. You have a good accent.'

Mr Walker acknowledged the compliment and returned it by praising the young man's English, which he said was excellent, considering that he had only recently arrived.

'Oh, I studied hard in Poland, sir. It was always my hope to come to London. I have no family in Poland. They were all killed by soldiers when I was little. Good people brought me up; but they were strangers. It was not really my home.'

He looked round and smiled shyly, as if to say, 'That is all there is to me. You know everything. All I want now is to be happy with you all. Surely it is not too much to ask?'

Mr Dolly, deeply touched, assured the young man that London

23

would soon become his home, that it was a wonderful city and that he had known many, many people who had come, poor and lonely, and had found warmth and company and had risen in the world.

'Even our Mr Walker and the princess,' expanded Mr Dolly, eager to reassure the young man, 'were once strangers and lonely and not at all in good circumstances. But look at them now! Wonderful people! Yet you would hardly believe how sad they were at first!' And he went on to relate as much of Mr Walker's history as he knew.

He had no idea that he was embarrassing Mr Walker and enraging the princess, who had no wish to have her past poverty paraded and who glared at Mr Dolly as if all the crimes that had previously been proposed were mere misdemeanours compared with what Mr Dolly himself was doing; he wanted only to comfort the young man and inspire him by the best example.

Certainly it had an effect. The young man seemed keenly interested in Mr Walker. His shyness evaporated and when he learned that Mr Walker had actually been in the little town in Poland where he had been brought up, he asked quickly how long ago it had been? Mr Walker frowned hesitatingly.

'It must have been twelve years,' said Mr Dolly, obligingly. 'Yes, I should say twelve years . . . when our princess was only a baby.'

'Then—then perhaps I actually saw Mr Walker there!' said Kozlowski, with considerable animation.

'Possibly,' said Mr Walker, falling to massaging his fingers and studying the effect. 'But you would have been a child. I doubt if you would have remembered.'

'Children sometimes remember strange things, sir.'

'Come, come! Am I a strange thing, young man?'

'Oh, I did not mean anything wrong, sir! My English is so bad. I should have said it differently. I meant that it is children who are strange in the way they remember.'

He continued to stare at Mr Walker, who continued to massage his fingers, and at Perdita as if trying to justify himself by remembering them. But he gave up and turned away . . .

'You've forgotten your crime, Mr Kozlowski!' said Perdita sharply.

24

She did not care in the least what he might propose. She only wanted to embarrass him by repeating Jonathan's request as he plainly hadn't wanted to answer it. She disliked him intensely. She did not think he was at all shy, and did not feel sorry for him. She thought that he was a smooth, odious youth who only wanted to ingratiate himself with the Dollys and worm his way into the family. She had good reasons for thinking this. When he had stared so hard at her father, he had looked, not in Mr Walker's face, but at his frayed cuffs, his shiny elbows and his mended linen; and when he had looked at her he had seen, not her beauty, her good dress or her new brooch, but only that she was a poor man's daughter and so not worth bothering with.

'Your crime, your crime!' she insisted; and Jonathan joined her.

'No excuses, Kozlowski! Give us your crime!'

'You must sing for your supper, Mr Kozlowski!' demanded Perdita; and was satisfied to see the young man shrink and look miserable.

He stammered that he could think of nothing suitable, and begged to be let off, as if, thought Perdita, he was much too good to be able to imagine anything wicked.

'Your crime, your crime!'

The young man's eyes pleaded, but the princess was relentless.

'Your crime—your—'

She got no further. The young man was spared. A frightful, thunderous crash came from the general direction of the kitchen. The whole room seemed to shake, and the candles jumped. Brandyella again! She appeared, a picture of innocence and anxiety, her mouth open and her conscience shut.

'Please,' said Mrs Dolly fretfully, 'please don't tell me it was nothing at all! Please don't tell me that!'

Shocked, Brandyella surveyed the twelve at table as if they were a jury. She was amazed, she was outraged, she was—

The uproar broke out again. She was not guilty.

'There, ma'am! It's taken the words right out of me mouth! 'Twas not in the kitchen at all. 'Tis in the shop. It's murderers maybe, or them ruffians from the public house next door—which comes to the same thing!'

Thunder again, which could now be heard as being caused by a furious onslaught upon the shop door. Imaginary violence had become real, as if all the talk of it had conjured it up, had summoned it out of the night. Shakily Mr Dolly rose to his feet.

'You will be killed, you will be killed!' cried Mrs Dolly, forgetful of her imperial calm. 'You mustn't go! Let them steal everything! You mustn't go!'

'Nonsense, my dear!' said Mr Dolly courageously; but was not sorry to see himself joined by the two young men, one of whom picked up a poker from the fireplace and the other, after a moment's indecision, a pair of tongs.

'Come along, Kozlowski!' cried Jonathan, joining the others. 'You don't need any English for this! It's the same in any language!'

Even Mr Walker had risen to his feet; but was dragged down by Perdita.

'How dare you, Pa! You—you are too old! You are much too old to go!'

'She's right!' cried Mrs Fairhazel, plucking nervously at Mr Walker's other arm. 'She is quite right ... I mean that—that she is right that you mustn't go ... not that you are too old, of course!'

He sat; and the onslaught downstairs was renewed. The men left the room and went down into the shop. Mrs Dolly stared at the winestain by Mr Dolly's place. She saw it as her son's and husband's blood. She looked miserably at Mrs Fairhazel, who had at least succeeded in holding Mr Walker back. *She* would be all right. At least Mr Walker would be saved!

4

A woman. Nothing worse than that. A woman; black-haired, strikingly pale. Gown torn violently at the shoulder; and scratches, like nail-marks, on her skin, as if a hand had reached savagely to detain her.

Glaring in at the window, then rushing to bang, kick and shriek at the door till it shuddered on its hinges. But no one with her. No lurking gang of murderers ready to break in on her heels. The street was empty. She was alone, and wild with fear, as if, at any moment, pursuit was about to overwhelm her.

Mr Dolly began to unbolt the door.

'But—but it is dangerous!' cried out Kozlowski, as if still caught up in his mysterious terror of crime; then, recollecting himself, went on more calmly, 'She—she will do much damage! Surely some soldiers or police will come by soon. Would it not be better to—'

'Don't be ridiculous, Kozlowski!' exclaimed Jonathan. 'We are five men against her. What do you suppose she can do?'

The door was opened and a rush of wind caused the deep fringe of sausages to swing wildly and cast dreadful shadows; then, like a great tattered leaf, the woman seemed to be blown inside.

'Drunk as a duchess!' diagnosed Brandyella, from a safe distance. 'From the public house next door. Drunk as a duchess!'

But it was not of spirits that the woman smelled as she stood, swaying and staring about her; it was of a heavy, sweetish perfume strong enough almost to overpower the mingled odours of the shop.

'You are safe now, my dear!' said Mr Dolly, shutting the door and bolting it reassuringly. 'Where have you come from? What has happened to you?'

She backed away and, coming against a barrel, whirled round as if attacked.

'What is the matter, my dear? Let us help you,' pursued Mr Dolly, advancing towards her and holding out his hands.

She glared at him; and then at the faces that had gathered to surround her. For a moment there was, in her eyes, a look of desperate inquiry, as if she was hoping, improbably, for someone who might be familiar to her. Then a dreadful bleakness, as if wondering if she had fled from some unimaginable frying-pan into a still more unimaginable fire. At last, discovering that no harm was meant to her, that the faces smiled and the voices were kindly, she spoke. But it was in a language no one understood.

'I think,' said Mr Dolly knowledgeably, 'that it is Turkish. Or Greek, or something like that. Brandyella! Ask Mr Walker if he will come down to us. I believe he speaks a little Greek.'

'It—it is Russian!' said David Kozlowski suddenly. 'I think it is Russian. There were some Russian soldiers in my town not long ago. They sounded very like that. Yes . . . I am almost sure it is Russian . . . so there is no use in—in—'

'Maybe Mr Walker speaks a little Russian, too? He speaks many languages. Ask him to come, Brandyella.'

Brandyella departed and presently returned with Mr Walker who was accompanied by his daughter who would, under no circumstances, let him escape from her protection. Uneasily the woman spoke to him; and he confirmed that her language was indeed Russian. Everyone congratulated Kozlowski on his perspicacity, which embarrassed him.

'What is she saying, Mr Walker?' asked Mr Dolly after the woman had spoken in an urgent undertone, with many expressive gestures.

'My Russian is not very fluent,' said Mr Walker, 'but it seems that she has run away from somewhere . . . I think it might have been a ship. She is very distressed. She says she has been dreadfully ill-treated—nearly killed. She is frightened that she has been followed here.'

Mr Dolly, deeply stirred, clasped his hands together.

'Poor woman, poor woman! Thank God we heard her! To think that she might have been murdered at this very door!'

'I'll go outside and see if anyone is there,' offered Jonathan, with a valiant look at the street and a glance at Perdita, who responded with a shrug as if it was nothing to her if the heir to Pickled Herrings went to the devil. There was a light-hearted fiction that a romantic attachment subsisted between them: a fiction to which Jonathan subscribed humorously and Perdita not at all.

But there were to be no heroics. Once more Kozlowski made a shrewd suggestion. If Jonathan went outside then he would betray where the woman had taken refuge. So Jonathan stayed and Kozlowski's stock rose even higher.

The woman, bewildered by the talk, confided again in Mr Walker. Everyone bent forward, and she cowered back against the counter.

'What is she saying now?'

'She begs to be allowed to stay here for a little while. She asks you not to turn her out. She says she cannot pay you any money, but will do whatever work you like.'

Mr Dolly was shocked, outraged by such an idea. Of course she must stay! Under no circumstances must she go outside! What an idea! She must come upstairs and lie down and recover. Mrs Dolly would look after her.

Mr Walker translated and the woman responded with almost violent gratitude; while Brandyella, who was still convinced that it was a drunken duchess they had to deal with, heard the offer of work rejected and was driven to reflect bitterly on her own reception when she returned, mildly under the influence, from the public house next door. She muttered obscurely, and went to prepare her mistress. There was a commotion of assistance, and the woman was half led, half carried up the stairs by a bundle of gentlemen and taken into the parlour.

The Dollys' parlour was a stately room, furnished with low tables, a low, stately couch and several low chairs in petticoats in respectful attendance on it. It would have been a serious room, but for the fire that chuckled in the grate and the gas jets that popped and hiccupped like children after a party. It might have been said that the lights represented Mr Dolly, and the stately couch, the empress, his wife. Hence, when Mrs Dolly came in, she could not help feeling a certain pressure on her bosom when she saw, after all her previous alarms, a strange woman extended upon her furniture, and the gentlemen gathered eagerly about her.

'My dear!' she cried, observing at once how things were and taking note of them. 'Your gown—your gown is all torn! What has happened to you?'

'No use, no use!' returned Mr Dolly, triumphantly. 'She cannot understand a word! She is Russian, my dear. She speaks only Russian. She is helpless!'

Mrs Dolly recoiled, fell back a little on her daughters and Mrs Fairhazel. 'Oh! Oh, I am so sorry, my dear! I didn't know. Please, can someone tell her that I am so sorry?'

While Mr Walker conveyed Mrs Dolly's sympathy, Mr Dolly explained eagerly about the woman's terrible predicament.

'What a wicked world we live in!' sighed Mrs Dolly, when she had heard everything. 'It is a wicked world, my dear! Oh! Oh, please can somebody tell her that it is a wicked world?'

Again Mr Walker conveyed Mrs Dolly's sentiments; which were rewarded by a radiant smile from the couch. Mrs Dolly begged everyone to be seated as surely such crowding round could do the stranger no good.

'Mrs Fairhazel, do sit down—'

'But her gown, Mrs Dolly! It is so badly torn. It is almost falling off. I have some pins here, in my purse. I was just going to—'

'Oh, yes. How sensible of you to think of it. You are always such a sensible person, Mrs Fairhazel. A real treasure, don't you think, Mr Walker? But everyone else . . . do, please, sit down! Mr Kozlowski, there is no need to be shy. You must sit with us. And you, too . . . Good heavens! What is that you are holding? Surely they are from the dining-room?'

She spoke to the two young men who were still grasping their weapons. They blushed, as if they felt themselves suspected of having intended a murderous assault, with poker and tongs, on a lady in distress and discreetly put them back.

'She must have some brandy,' decided Mrs Dolly. 'It is the best thing for a fright. My dear, you must have had a terrible fright. Oh, oh! I keep forgetting! Please, can someone tell her that she has had a terrible fright? It is so awkward not being able to speak to her. It makes everything so mysterious.'

She looked round and was answered by a general frowning and nodding of heads. Everything was mysterious. The woman's dramatic arrival, her wild manner and her strange story could not have failed to create mystery.

What kind of a woman was she? As it was impossible to fix her station in life from her speech, a discreet but careful study of her person was undertaken by the ladies on the assumption that, though clothes might make the man, they were much more likely to unmake the woman.

Her gown was observed to be of a good quality red velvet, but clumsily let down at the hem; and, although there was expensive lace at her sleeves and bodice, it was none too clean. Likewise her gloves failed to find favour; and, in spite of the pretty, star-shaped brooch at her neck that glittered with real diamonds, her shoes did her no credit and she wore too much scent.

In her favour, however, was the fact that she would hardly touch the liberal allowance of brandy that Mr Dolly pressed upon her, and she was probably nearer forty than thirty. She was, thought Mrs Fairhazel, at least two years older than herself. All in all, it was hard to say, even after discovering that her name was Katerina Kropotka, whether she was a countess fallen upon evil times or a street-walker tumbled suddenly into a good one.

But what could not be denied was her striking, almost mesmeric beauty, produced chiefly by her pale complexion and her black, drowning eyes. Mrs Fairhazel regarded her mournfully and contrasted herself with her; and came off decidedly the worse. Mrs Fairhazel felt that were she to burst into song, to dance upon the table, to discard her clothing, she would not detract one atom of attention from the haunting Miss Kropotka.

Yes: *Miss* Kropotka. Her single state had been revealed when she had taken of her gloves and neither a wedding ring nor the mark of one was to be seen. Mrs Fairhazel, when she had got over her surprise that so beautiful a woman should be unmarried, could not help wondering if, perhaps, there was some fatal flaw in her nature. And wondered if Mr Walker was wondering the same; but decided that he was too good and generous a man to harbour such thoughts. Anyway, such a flaw, in a woman like that, would only draw attention to the possibility of perfection.

She lay on the couch, flowing in velvet, like a great red flower with her drowsy perfume drawing all towards her. Mr Walker, leaning forward in his chair, attended her like a physician. What was that she was saying? Mr Walker nodded, smiled and explained. Mrs Fairhazel felt that he had only just restrained himself from patting the woman's hand.

'Miss Kropotka says that she will never forget your kindness for as long as she lives. She does not know how she can ever repay you. She never thought that people could be so good.'

A warm sentiment which, Mrs Fairhazel thought, had probably been improved by translation. Then she chastised herself inwardly for thinking such a thing when she saw how everyone seemed deeply affected.

'Repayment? But we have done nothing!' cried Mr Dolly, beginning to walk about the room and wave his arms. 'Nothing at all! A sip of brandy! That's all. Will she have some dinner? There's soup, and fish and roast chicken . . . ask her if she would like to eat something.'

Mr Walker put the offer. The woman shook her head. She murmured something. Mr Walker rendered it.

'She thinks she will be safe now. She says she has troubled you enough.'

She made as if to rise from the couch; but with no great determination. Indeed, thought Mrs Fairhazel, you might have knocked her back with a feather. Again she reproached herself for such an unworthy thought. Miss Kropotka had been savagely attacked; the marks on her shoulder proved that. She was in danger of her life. Mrs Fairhazel would recommend herself to nobody by thinking the way she did.

'Oh, but she mustn't go!' she cried. 'Or at least, not yet. Should we not send for the police to protect her?'

But no; that was not a good idea. It had been decided downstairs that it would be best not to betray where Miss Kropotka was. So . . . ?

Mrs Dolly compressed her lips. She looked at Mr Dolly, who, as usual, saw nothing; she looked at Mrs Fairhazel; she looked at the ceiling.

'I suppose,' she said, 'that we could make up a bed downstairs. Miriam, will you tell Brandyella to—'

'No, no! She can stay with me!' interrupted Mrs Fairhazel impulsively. Well, not quite impulsively, as she wanted, with all her heart, to make up for her uncharitable thoughts, and she could see that Mr Walker and his daughter were as concerned as anybody, so that anything she could do in the way of assistance would be well thought of. 'I have my own little house, you know, in Stepney, and Miss Kropotka would be quite welcome. And safe, too; as there are two gentlemen lodgers upstairs. They are quite old, of course, but very respectable.'

'That's exactly like you!' said Mrs Dolly warmly. 'To think of something so sensible and kind!'

Mrs Fairhazel received the tribute with a blush, feeling it to be undeserved. She knew that her suggestion had proceeded from a scheme of absolutely Machiavellian cunning. She did not, of course, realise that Mrs Dolly had seen through her as if she had been a pane of glass. Like most good people, Mrs Fairhazel was deeply ashamed of her inner thoughts and believed them to be unique in their horribleness.

'I'm sure,' said Mrs Dolly, 'that Miss Kropotka will be in good hands.'

She said this to assist her friend's scheme, although she did not think it would come to anything.

'So I'm not to tell Brandyella anything, Ma?' said Miriam, who had shown no great inclination to leave the room anyway.

Having nothing better to do, she had been exerting herself in the exercise of her wiles upon David Kozlowski. She had drawn him into a corner and was fascinating him with her flashing eyes, her rounded arms and her numerous accomplishments. Quite overcome by the attentions of a daughter of the house, the young man stayed by her side. To Miriam's satisfaction, she saw that the good-looking youth had no eyes for that Russian woman. She might not have existed for all he cared.

'No, Miriam. The lady will stay with Mrs Fairhazel. Please, Mr Walker, would you explain that to her? Tell her that she will be quite safe.'

'You will do no such thing, Pa!'

It was Perdita who spoke. She had been crouching on the floor beside her father, dividing her looks between him and the Russian woman. The woman's beauty had fascinated her, and her scent had intoxicated her. She had been intensely proud that her father had been the only one who had been able to converse with her; and for once was able to overlook his many imperfections, such as his mended shoes and badly fitting waistcoat. It was odd that she never noticed Miss Kropotka's imperfections—a slight hardness of the mouth, a slight sineviness of the neck—at all; but possibly this was because she looked at the stranger through her own eyes and not, as she so often did with her father, through what she feared were the eyes of others. Miss Kropotka gave her father and herself an air of peculiar importance, and she was determined not to let her go.

'She can come back with us,' said Perdita. 'It is much nearer and we can manage quite well. She can have my room and I can sleep on the couch. It is settled, Pa. Please explain to her that she is to come home with us.'

Mr Walker was plainly taken aback; yet Mrs Fairhazel could not help fancying a glint of pleasure in his astonishment. She did not know what to say. She wanted to urge her own house again, but was frightened to do so. She did not want Mr Walker to think that she was trying to stop him enjoying the company of a beautiful woman.

Mrs Dolly, however, who guessed Mrs Fairhazel's predicament, said it was a foolish idea and that, if Miss Kropotka was not to stay with Mrs Fairhazel, then she must stay with the Dollys.

'Miriam! Tell Brandyella to—'

'Pa! Explain to her that she is coming to stay with us!'

'But, Perdita—'

'Please, Pa! I want her to!'

A strange situation. An argument over who should help a stranger. On the face of it, a dispute over goodness, a clash of kindnesses. But underneath, something rather different. There was an uneasiness, almost a fear that pervaded the room. Mr Dolly alone seemed unaware of it. It was extraordinary, thought Mrs Dolly, that he saw neither Mrs Fairhazel's unhappiness, nor Mr Walker's painful indecision, nor the disagreeable fact that the childish passion that Perdita had conceived for the Russian woman was getting out of hand. The woman herself must have been aware of it. It was distressingly obvious. Yet she did nothing; which was as good as encouraging it. Mrs Dolly could expect no help from her family. Her two elder daughters thought it amusing and were slyly imitating the Russian woman's speech to each other; and Jonathan was no better than his father. It was only to be hoped that Mr Walker would come to his senses in time.

He was talking to the woman. Her eyes widened. She stared about her; fixed her gaze on Perdita . . . and shook her head. Mr Walker spoke again; and she answered volubly. Mr Walker nodded.

'What did she say, Pa? What did she say?'

'She said that you are very kind, Perdita. Does that satisfy you?'

'What else?'

'That you are very pretty. Does that satisfy you?'

'What else, what else?'

'That—that if it is really not too much trouble,' murmured Mr Walker, studiously avoiding everyone's eyes, 'she will come back with us for the night. Does that satisfy you, Perdita?'

Perdita nodded vigorously, and Mr Walker went on to explain that, although Miss Kropotka was deeply grateful for Mrs Fairhazel's and Mrs Dolly's offers, she felt that she would be less trouble with someone who spoke her own language.

It was, when you thought about it, a sensible suggestion; but it produced in Mrs Dolly a feeling of deep dismay. Nevertheless, now it had been decided upon, she was mindful of Mr Walker's difficulties and made arrangements for some extra bed linen for Mr Walker to take with him. In addition, the two young men offered to accompany the Walkers back to their home in case Miss Kropotka's pursuer should still be in the neighbourhood. It would be no trouble as they were going the same way. It was suggested that Kozlowski should join them, but it turned out that his lodgings lay in the opposite direction. He remained behind for a few minutes after the others had gone.

'I think,' he murmured, gazing at the vacated couch, 'that Mr Walker did not do a wise thing.'

Then he thanked the Dollys courteously and, with handshakes all round and a longer one for Miriam, he took his departure.

Jonathan and his father put up the shutters, locked and bolted the shop door, and another Friday night was over.

'Did you notice,' said Mrs Dolly, in the privacy of the bedchamber, after the Russian woman had been talked threadbare, 'how they hated each other?'

'Who, dear? Who do you mean?'

'Good heavens! Didn't you see it?'

'See what, my dear?'

'That young man, Kozlowski, and that child!'

'What about them?'

'They hated each other! When you were all talking about crimes. I really thought it would come to blows.'

'Nonsense, my dear! They were getting along famously.'

'My God!'

'I thought . . . for a moment,' said Mr Dolly slowly, 'that you meant—'

'Meant what?'

'I thought you meant Kozlowski and the Russian woman.'

'What about them?'

'Didn't *you* notice, my dear?'

'What was there to notice?'

'That—that there were times when he seemed almost frightened of her.'

5

The Walkers lived in Shoreditch. They rented three rooms on a top floor in a short, blind brute of a street that by day was a fruit and vegetable market and, by night, a graveyard of the same. Cabbage leaves, like tattered bats, flapped in the wind, old dead apples gasped underfoot, and broken boxes, like burgled coffins, littered the way. The air smelled of decay.

Although it was a great improvement on the part of White-chapel where they had lived before in a squalid basement where the light was meanly handed in through bars, it was by no means a neighbourhood of which Perdita could feel proud. She kept apologising for it angrily, as if it had suffered a sharp decline in her absence and she was as shocked as anybody to see the state into which it had fallen.

As usual, Mr Walker bore the brunt of her discontent and, as usual, put up with it with a wry smile. Her complaining reached its climax when they came to the front door, which was kicked and scratched and lacking in paint in a manner most disgraceful. She held the Russian woman firmly by the hand, as if she feared that Miss Kropotka would run off in disgust, and somehow felt supported in her criticisms when the pressure of her fingers was repeatedly returned.

The two young men—their staunch protectors—who had carried pillows, blankets and sheets, offered to come inside; but Perdita dismissed them and Mr Walker was loaded like a mountain, with a fringe of snow showing under his toppling hat.

The house, thank God, was in darkness; it was dreadfully shabby inside and, in addition, Perdita had, in her youth, written her name several times on the wall. They went upstairs. 'Another floor—it's endless, endless! It's shameful, Pa, how we have to live like pigeons, under the roof!'

Candles were lighted. 'If gas rises, Pa, why hasn't it got any higher than the first floor?' A fire was kindled and a bed made up on the couch. This couch, like everything else the Walkers possessed, had seen better days and had resolutely put them out of its mind. It was a crippled article of worn black leather with an arched neck, rather like a dead horse. Needless to say, it was not Perdita who was to sleep on it, but Mr Walker himself.

Although Perdita was a strong and healthy young girl, and her father was getting on in life and had seen hard times, he always maintained a charmingly tender gallantry towards her, as if she was a fragile blossom to be protected from all but the gentlest of breezes.

Miss Kropotka, when she learned of the arrangement, showed not the slightest surprise. Plainly she considered it to be absolutely right for a gentleman to give up his comfort to a lady, even if that lady was only twelve years old. In an odd way she gave the impression that it was not because she regarded Perdita as being older than she actually was, but that she regarded Mr Walker as being younger. There was no doubt that he felt flattered by it; and, when the time came, gave up his own room to her with a cheerful smile and a courtly bow. Then, in high good humour, he went in to kiss Perdita goodnight.

Like a fond and partial gardener, Mr Walker had tended with particular care that portion of his shabby wilderness that was Perdita's. There were flowers on her walls, flowers on her coverlet, flowers on the little carpet by her bed; and there would have been flowers—real flowers—in the glazed pots on her window-sill if she had ever remembered to water them. She was sitting thoughtfully on her bed.

'Katerina is very beautiful, isn't she, Pa?'

'Yes. I suppose she is.'

'Suppose, Pa? Only *suppose*?'

'Very well. Beautiful without any supposing.'

'More beautiful, would you say, than me?'

'Let me look at you.' An obliging turn of the head; a careful scrutiny. 'No . . . no . . . I don't think I would go so far as to say that.'

'She is, you know, Pa. Her face isn't as round as mine.'

'Nor so soft, nor so bright, nor half so lovely, Perdita, my child.'

'Not true. She's at least three-quarters as lovely!'

'Five eighths and it's a bargain!'

'Oh, arithmetic! How I hate it! What will become of her, Pa?'

Mr Walker frowned. 'I don't know.'

'You must teach her English. Then I'll be able to talk to her and it will be company for me and I won't always be bored and worrying you.'

'But she is only staying here for the night.'

'You can't turn her out into the street, Pa!'

Mr Walker's frown deepened, and he thrust out his lower lip. 'We'll talk about that in the morning. It's late now. Goodnight, my dear.'

He bent to kiss her. She turned away.

'Pa!' she said, pointing imperiously to a place on the bed beside her. 'Sit down and talk to me now!'

'But we have talked . . . and she will—'

'No, she won't, Pa! And even if she does, she won't be able to understand. Please sit down and talk. Please! Just as you always do.'

Her voice took on a pleading tone that Mr Walker found impossible to resist. He sighed and seated himself, with elaborate precision, exactly where he had been bidden.

'Very well. But only for a little while, Perdita.'

'Perdita, Perdita! What a silly name it is! Why did you call me that?'

'Because it means 'lost girl', and you were lost, and I found you. That's why I called you Perdita.'

He spoke softly and dreamily, as he began upon what was plainly a nightly ritual, a kind of lullaby, in which he would repeat the same words, in the same order, and in the same tone of voice. Nothing was to be altered, nothing departed from, as any deviation would be pounced upon. Little by little, Perdita rested her head against his shoulder and fell to examining certain interesting activities of her toes, having got as far as removing her shoes and stockings in her rambling progress towards bed.

'So I was lost and you found me, Pa. Now tell me how you found me. Tell me exactly, like you always do.'

'I bought you—'

'For how much?'

'Three silver coins.'

38

'I thought it was four. Surely it was four?'

'No. Three silver coins. I remember it well.'

'How do you remember?'

'I remember saying, one for her eyes, one for her nose, and one for her mouth.'

'My toes! I'm sure you told me that there was one for my toes as well!'

'I never saw your toes. You were all wrapped up so I had to take your toes on trust. I bought you, my Perdita, at *face* value!'

'All right, then. Three silver coins. Not very much for a baby like me. Quite a bargain, I'd say. Tell me who you bought me from. And—and hold my hand tightly when you tell me! Who was it?'

He held her hand and gripped it.

'A broken-down man with a dreadful face and a ragged beard. A broken-down man with a kettle, a tankard and a saucepan hanging from a rope around his waist. A tramp pushing a cart along a street, a cart with a baby inside it.'

'Me?'

'You.'

'And where did that broken-down man find me?'

'He never said, he never said.'

'Did he steal me, then?'

'I expect he did.'

'From a rich house, a palace, would you think?'

'More than likely.'

'And there was nothing on my clothing? No little embroidered coronet, or motto in Latin or French?'

'Nothing at all. You were a mystery, a wailing, hungry mystery.'

'I hate that man! I hate him!'

'But he was so poor, and so—'

'But he stole me!'

'But I bought you.'

She considered the matter, weighing up the advantages and the disadvantages of the transaction; and plainly coming to no conclusion.

'How big was I?' she demanded, as if that extra trifle of knowledge would determine which way the scales swung.

'Oh, as big as your doll.'

She nodded and reached across her pillow to lift up the other occupant of her bed, a doll that regarded the world in a perpetual state of glazed astonishment, as if it couldn't get over the magnificence of the surroundings in which it found itself.

'Tell me,' said Perdita, idly nursing the doll, 'tell me how you looked after me. Tell me how you fed me.'

'With milk and honey and all things sweet.'

'There, my love, there!' To the doll, 'You would have liked that, wouldn't you! Now tell me what it was like when we came to London.'

'We were poor, very poor; so poor, in fact, that church mice were millionaires beside us. We lived in a damp and dirty cellar in Whitechapel. There was an old cat who used to visit, and a dog who barked and barked. I would go out during the day with a barrow and grindstone to sharpen knives. I would sing out, "Knives to sharpen! Scissors and knives!"' He imitated the old street cry as if it was the sweetest of songs. 'And you would be lying in a basket beside me.'

'Tell me what it was like when I first started to walk!'

'I could hardly believe it! One moment you were a helpless baby who might have been anything; and then, when I turned round, there you were, standing up in the basket like a full-grown woman!'

'And then—?'

'And then I knew I would have to work harder and harder, in order to be a credit to my full-grown woman!'

'And so you did, and here we are! And, Pa, you must not buy me so much, for you need a new coat and a new shirt and new shoes. Promise me, Pa, that you'll buy a new coat and throw away that old scarf, and I promise I'll make you another.'

Mr Walker smiled, kissed Perdita on the forehead, and rose to his feet.

'Pa!'

'Yes, Perdita?'

'Will you tell her—Katerina—about us?'

'Why do you ask?'

'I don't know. But will you tell her?'

'I thought it was always to be our secret.'

Perdita nodded.

'Goodnight, then.'

'Pa!'

'What is it now?'

'Come here! You must take this pillow. I don't need two. And you are much too old to be uncomfortable.'

'Am I really too old?'

'No, no, of course not! You know I only tease you because I want you to live for ever!'

With this last sentiment, Mr Walker agreed heartily and retired to the couch, encouraged and refreshed, as he always was, by the nightly talk. Not for worlds would he have forgone it; not for worlds would he have deprived himself of watching the dreamy smile on Perdita's face when she listened to her romantic history and contemplated the possible nobility of her origins. Whatever the chill of the room and the wretched discomfort of the couch, they were more than made up for by his sensation of inner security and warmth. The child he had created filled him with pride and joy.

'Oh! Oh, I thought you would be asleep!'

Perdita, having left her room and crept across the little landing, had cautiously opened the door of her father's room which the Russian woman was occupying for the night. Intense curiosity had prompted her intrusion, and a nagging fear that the events of the night had been a dream . . . not, of course, that she doubted that there was a visitor, but that the visitor was really rather plain and ordinary and by no means as strikingly beautiful as Perdita imagined. She meant only to look—

The woman was not asleep. She was not even in bed. She was standing by the window, still in her red velvet gown. Moonlight was streaming upon her and, as she turned to the door, her face was swallowed up in shadow.

'I—I wanted to get something,' muttered Perdita, attempting to excuse herself.

The woman murmured something in her own language, and held out her hand. The gesture was unmistakable. Perdita hesitated for a moment, then crossed the room and took the offered hand. She looked up. The woman was tall, almost as tall as her father.

'You are very beautiful,' whispered Perdita.

The woman smiled; and her looks and her heavy, drowsy scent exerted a powerful influence over the child. It was partly admiration and partly a jealous fear that Katerina would go elsewhere and someone else would possess her.

'You must stay with us. You must stay here.'

Katerina's grip on Perdita's hand tightened. Perdita's heart beat quickly.

'You—you must learn English. My father will teach you.'

Katerina raised a warning finger to her lips.

'Oh, he's fast asleep! I looked in to make sure. Do you—do you like him?'

A puzzled frown.

'You don't know what I'm talking about, do you? I'm glad. That means I can talk to you as I'd never talk to anyone else. Shall I tell you a secret? He's not my father at all. He bought me from a broken-down tramp, somewhere in Poland. Nobody really knows who I am. Almost certainly I'm a countess, or something like that. Isn't that wonderful and romantic? There now! You know everything, so you must stay!' chattered Perdita, confiding in Katerina with almost the same freedom with which she confided in her doll.

Katerina shook her head in smiling bewilderment; and Perdita rambled happily on: 'I know it's all double-Dutch to you. If it wasn't, I'd never have told you. The only people who really know are me, my pa, and that tramp who stole me . . . and he's probably dead by now! Do you think he's dead? He ought to be, for what he did! I must go back to my room now, in case Pa wakes up. Will you give me some of your scent? Never mind! I'll ask Pa to explain in the morning! Goodnight, Katerina. Will you let me kiss you goodnight?'

A look and a pursing of the lips made her request unmistakable. Katerina bent and offered her mouth. Somewhat awkwardly Perdita avoided it and brushed a kiss on Katerina's cold cheek; and, with a last, 'Goodnight!' returned to her own room.

The glazed doll, propped against the pillow, regarded her with astonishment and expectation. What had she been doing? Confide, confide! But it was not to be. The waxen beauty in tattered linen and chewed lace had been passed over in favour of another beauty in velvet as red as blood.

Perdita climbed into bed and put out her candle. Moonlight rushed in through the window, bringing with it a jostling train of shadows. They lay on the ceiling and crowded up the flowered walls. They made strange shapes, that bore no resemblance at all to their possible origins. A chimney-pot became a coffin, and the projecting corner of a gabled roof a witch in mid-flight. Perdita shut her eyes and prayed that it would be bright morning before she opened them again. Then, unable to stop herself, she opened first one eye, then the other.

'He's not there! He's not there!' she whispered in desperate relief. Then, 'No! No! Go away! Go away from me!' as she saw the one shadow that she dreaded most.

God knows what it was made of, but it was grim and threatening and loomed darkly over her. It was the shadow of a wicked tramp, with kettle, saucepan and tankard hanging from a rope round his waist.

Even as she stared at it in miserable terror, she fancied she could hear the faint clanking of tin as he crept nearer and nearer towards her.

She buried her head under the covers; and deep in the darkness she shook and cried with fear. It was a fear that she confided to no one, not even to her glazed companion of the night; yet it was a fear that haunted her both by day and in the awful shadowy dark. It was a fear that, one day, when she was happy and all was set fair, and when she least expected it to happen, the wicked tramp would find her and steal her away again, as he had done twelve years ago.

6

The house in which the Walkers lived, quarrelled, made up, hid home truths and told home lies in their three rooms on the top floor, was owned by a musical couple by the name of Streamer. There was a brass plate to that effect on the front door; and it was much admired by the fruit and vegetable market who felt it conferred a distinction on the street, like having a doctor.

Mr Streamer, who was rarely at home, played the violin in one of the London theatres; while Mrs Streamer taught the piano to small, discontented girls of the neighbourhood who had been persuaded that an ability to play that tormenting instrument would lead infallibly to a brilliant match. Thus from eight o'clock in the morning until eight o'clock at night the Streamers' house, like Prospero's isle, was full of strange noises, in the shape of an anguished stumbling over the keys of Mrs Streamer's piano, quaintly suggestive of brides on crutches.

It was always easy to tell when Mrs Streamer herself was playing, as, apart from there being a greater proficiency, there was an extra dimension of melancholy in the depression of every note. One might have supposed that her instrument had been equipped not with wires but with heart-strings; and the hammers hurt. On this present Saturday morning, the sounds she produced were more desolate than ever.

Mrs Streamer, a fat, cushionlike person with fat, cushionlike hands, was a woman on whom life left scars. Although she had a great capacity for forgiving, she had, like the amiable elephant, none at all for forgetting. Although she never bore grudges, she sighed under burdens; and although injuries never rankled, they most certainly ached.

Unhappily the chief inflicter of these injuries was the very one to whom she might have looked most for protection. It was Mr Streamer; carefree, thoughtless Mr Streamer, whose first name (derived from a remote Italian ancestor), was Giovanni. His employment in the orchestra pit, combined with those heating drops of Latin blood that still circulated in his veins, rendered him acutely susceptible to the charms of a succession of dancers, singers and actresses. He worshipped at their feet, he mooned over them and wrote them passionate love songs that Mrs Streamer was always finding in his pockets and in his fiddle case. Of course she forgave him, as it was in her nature to do so; but equally it was in her nature never to forget.

'There, there, my poor Giovanni!' she would say to the contrite, damp-eyed fiddler. 'We'll say no more about it. I promise that not a word of reproach will pass my lips. But it will leave a scar, you know. I can't help it, but as long as I live and breathe it will leave a scar.'

The cause of her present unhappiness was a strong whiff of scent and a glimpse she had caught on the stairs, earlier that morning, of a beautiful woman in red velvet. Knowing nothing of what had taken place during the night, she had at once connected the seductive apparition with her husband. She had convinced herself that here was some enchantress from the stage, some truant Cleopatra, smuggled into the house by Mr Streamer and concealed God knew where.

Now Mrs Streamer did not, as might another wife, storm through the house with poker or frying-pan in search of the wretched interloper; nor did she, as might another wife, pack up her absent husband's belongings and throw them out into the street. Mrs Streamer, fat, plain, and with a geometric fringe, retired to her piano and, arranging her portly fingers over the keys, particularly the black ones, began to play a nocturne of funereal gloom. She continued in this depressing vein until she was interrupted by a knock on the music-room door.

It was the child from upstairs: Perdita Walker. She was already several minutes late for her lesson; but Mrs Streamer gladly forgave her.

She taught Perdita the piano at a greatly reduced rate; partly because she was sorry for Mr Walker, and partly because Perdita was such a very pretty child and Mrs Streamer's artistic soul venerated beauty. During the years that the Walkers had lived upstairs there had grown up an odd friendship between Mrs Streamer and Perdita, as they were, apart from the elderly woman and her elderly daughter who came in to clean, the only females in the house. Mrs Streamer advised and assisted Perdita in her progress towards womanhood, while Perdita, in return, dispensed her beauty together with slices of cake and cups of tea at the little monthly concerts at which Mrs Streamer's most promising pupils were obliged to perform. It was Mrs Streamer's ambition that one day Perdita herself would grace the piano and amaze the company.

'I cannot have my lesson today, Mrs Streamer!' cried Perdita, flushed with excitement. 'I really can't! It's impossible!'

'Why is that, my darling? Are you unwell? You cannot be! Is it a fever? Let me feel your head!'

'No, no, I'm quite all right! It's just that we have a visitor.'

'But I didn't hear anybody—'

'She came back with us last night,' interposed Perdita, and went on to relate, at great speed, the events that had led to the Russian woman's presence upstairs.

As Mrs Streamer listened, she felt ashamed of herself for having so basely suspected Mr Streamer. It was in consequence of this that she responded with more warmth and concern than she might have done otherwise.

'You should have awakened me, my dear! I would have made up a bed—'

'Oh, it was all right, Mrs Streamer! She slept in Pa's room and Pa slept on the couch.'

'Your poor father!'

'He's not poor at all, Mrs Streamer!'

'Of course he isn't, my angel. All I meant was, that at his age—'

'And he's not old, either! People can go grey quite young.'

'True, true. I went grey soon after I married Mr Streamer. I only meant that your father, being such a tall, well-made man, must have been uncomfortable on the couch. But, as it was only for one night—'

At this point, Mrs Streamer, who had been sitting placidly, with her hands arranged upon her skirts, thinking, it must be admitted, more of Mr Streamer than of the Walkers, was astonished to discover that she was a mortal enemy, a vile tyrant, an unfeeling creature—a crocodile was proposed and subsequently rejected in favour of hyena—and, in short, as bad as the rest of them.

'But my precious—my sweet one—'

Furthermore, continued the sweet one, swinging the parlour door back and forth, as if to gain sufficient momentum for a really shattering slam, furthermore, she hoped that—that—

Here Perdita's eloquence was terminated by such a salty rush of feeling to her eyes, and such a gulping sensation in her throat that she was forced to pitch herself, head foremost, into Mrs Streamer's lap, and remain there, with shaking shoulders and ridiculous fists, while Mrs Streamer patted her back, smoothed her hair and exchanged bewildered looks with a plaster bust of Chopin that stood on the piano. She was entirely at a loss to know in which way she had sinned.

At last it came out, damply, from the folds of Mrs Streamer's gown. It was because she had said that the visitor was only going to stay for that one night, which was last night, so she was going to go today. It had been a horrible thing to say; particularly when Perdita had absolutely counted on Mrs Streamer's being on her side.

'But, my dearest, your father—'

He was useless, he was only a man, sobbed the dearest. How could you expect a man to understand that a woman like Katerina needed to be *begged* to stay? How could you expect him to understand a woman's pride? Only another woman could understand that. Only another woman could understand that a woman like Katerina would sooner be murdered in the street, than humble herself. Only another woman . . .

'My poor angel!' murmured Mrs Streamer, touched on her tenderest spot. To be appealed to as a woman moved her inexpressibly.

'Then you'll tell her to stay!' cried the angel, seizing her advantage with a rapidity that bespoke a natural aptitude and long practice.

'But, my darling, it's not really my place to—'

'But it is—it is! It's your house, Mrs Streamer! You can do anything you like! And I'm sure Mr Streamer won't mind.'

Mrs Streamer, thinking of Mr Streamer and a beautiful woman in the same house, absently fingered a melancholy little waltz on Perdita's trembling back.

'No, my dear,' she whispered. 'I don't think Mr Streamer would mind.'

'*Darling* Mrs Streamer! I knew you would understand! I knew you would be on my side! I *love* you, Mrs Streamer! You must come at once and tell them what we've decided, before it's too late.'

Helplessly Mrs Streamer found herself dragged, pushed and bundled up the stairs, thrust into the Walkers' parlour, and heard, to her bewilderment, that she absolutely *insisted* that the striking, almost dreadfully beautiful woman who was there should stay in her house, apparently for ever.

Events seemed to have moved so rapidly that Mrs Streamer felt she had lost all grasp of them. She felt that Mr Walker was not entirely easy in his mind; but Perdita's joy and enthusiasm were irresistible. As for the woman herself—Miss Kropotka—she was a complete enigma. She could only talk in Russian to Mr Walker; and whenever she seemed to say anything that went against Perdita's wishes, the child shouted her down. But she always ended up by smiling at Perdita. Was she just humouring her; or was there really an attachment between them?

Mrs Streamer gave up. She heard someone knocking on the door downstairs. Her second pupil of the day. She had to go, she really had to go. Yes, yes, of course it was all right for Miss Kropotka to stay. But—but it was not right for her to stay with the Walkers. There was a little room on the first floor landing. Miss Kropotka was welcome to that. No, no, she would not hear of Mr Walker's paying anything! It was, after all, her house and she could do with it as she pleased. She would be grateful if Mr Walker would stop insisting. If he really felt that he had to do something, then he could buy something for Perdita . . . a new pair of shoes, perhaps. Please now, she must go or she would lose a pupil!

She extricated herself from the room and hastened down the stairs. She knew she had done a foolish thing; but then she was a foolish woman. She was an artist—and artists always acted foolishly, impulsively.

The little room on the landing. It was the room where Mr Streamer practised the violin. It was his sanctum; it was where he wrote his passionate love-songs. Well, well, he would have to make a sacrifice too—and sit with *her* of an evening, and talk to *her*, and maybe even play sonatas with her, as he used to, long ago.

She opened the front door to her pupil.

'Well, my dear! Let us go and practise something cheerful, like a march!'

7
═══

Katerina had gone; and Perdita was in the blackest gloom. She refused to believe that the woman had only gone to fetch her belongings. Her father was hiding something from her. He had lied to her about what Katerina had really said. If she was meaning to come back again, why hadn't Mr Walker gone with her and helped her to carry things? He could easily have cancelled his morning lesson. Besides, it was dangerous. She would be going back to the very place she'd run away from. She would be murdered!

In vain Mr Walker protested that he had hidden nothing, that Miss Kropotka was not a child, that she knew what she was doing, that it was broad daylight, people were about, and she would be in no danger. It was in vain also that he suggested that the lady might have desired some privacy.

To Perdita, privacy was only another name for secrecy . . . the very sound of which deeply frightened her. Why had he said such a thing? If nothing was being hidden from her, why had he said that Katerina wanted to be secret? Mr Walker sighed, and Perdita went to stare miserably out of the window. She knew all about secrets. She would never see Katerina again.

However strong her desire for privacy—or secrecy—might have been, Katerina Kropotka was not exactly formed for it; or at least, not outwardly. Had anyone set out with the idea of following her, there would not have been the smallest difficulty. Her tall figure and striking appearance caused heads in their dozens to turn and bend after her, like stalks in a wind; so that as she made her way through the idling, bargaining Saturday crowds, the swathe of her passing was readily apparent.

From time to time, when she turned a corner or crossed a street and broke free of the crowds, she lengthened her pace when it could be seen that, like many tall people, there was the suggestion of a limp in her stride, an awkwardness, as if her shoes pinched. But like everything else about her it was distinctive and drew attention. Most people might be admired in spite of their faults; it seemed to be Katerina Kropotka's fate to be admired because of them.

It was only when she reached Whitechapel that a follower might have experienced any difficulty. It was somewhere between a public house and a street of old clothes that she paused, looked about her as if temporarily lost. At this point, a follower might well have taken refuge for fear of being seen. It would have been a fatal error. With an abrupt flurry of red velvet, she seemed to vanish into thin air . . . or, rather, into the thickly crowded air. Further pursuit would have been hopeless.

A few minutes later, exactly as if she had stepped inside an invisible glove and then stepped out of a hole in one of its fingers, she reappeared, walking rapidly down a small, mean street in the neighbourhood of the Tower. As she passed, certain children of perishable aspect, who had been hopping from chalked square to chalked square, like mathematically-minded sparrows, paused on single legs and eyed her warily, as if here was a fine velvet cat, wanted on several counts of murder, but at present otherwise engaged.

She stopped, looked back as if to reassure herself yet again that she had not been followed, and went into one of the houses. Inside it was dark and dingy in the extreme; and seemed to become darker as she mounted the stairs, as if somehow the cellar was situated under the roof. She entered her room. It was small and foul, with a window that would have fallen in pieces but for the dirt. Everything bespoke a kind of contemptuous neglect. A chair lay on its side; a shabby table was strewn with articles of clothing; and the bed, broken-backed, was unmade, stale and stained. The air reeked of scent.

She shut the door and dragged a trunk from a corner. She opened it and, after some tempestuous fumbling, produced another dress, also red, but darker and more purplish. Hastily she changed, crying out involuntarily as Mrs Fairhazel's pins pricked and scratched her; then she began to pace to and fro—three steps brought her to either wall—to shake out the creases from this second gown. There was fur around the hem, and, as she walked, it pounced and twitched as if small, sharp-toothed animals were snapping at her heels.

Presently she stopped and, returning to the trunk, took out a large bottle of scent and applied it liberally to her person; after which she began to push and bundle her possessions into a capacious carpet bag. This done, she crossed to the window, wiped away a spy hole, and peered through it down into the street. Apparently satisfied, she picked up the bag and went quietly to the door. She paused. There was a step upon the stair followed by a gentle double knock. She did not answer. The door handle began to turn. She watched it without alarm. It was as if she knew quite well who had called. The door opened.

'Well, what do you want with me now?'

Her visitor came into the room as discreetly as a ghost; and almost as pale. It was David Kozlowski. She had addressed him, not in her incomprehensible Russian, but in his own native Polish.

'You ask me that?' he muttered, passing his hand across his forehead in a gesture of bewilderment. 'You ask me that when I have been half out of my mind with worry and misery? I've been waiting all morning. I didn't go to work. I had to know. What happened? For God's sake, tell me what happened! When I saw you at that window last night, I nearly fainted! I could hardly breathe! I didn't know what to do!'

He leaned back against the door as if the memory was overcoming him. Only incidentally, did it seem, that he pushed the door firmly shut. Katerina, observing this and, perhaps, drawing certain conclusions, slightly shrugged her shoulders and put down the carpet bag she had been holding. The young man stared from the bag to the open trunk, then round the wretched little room, as if it was a place that held many dear memories for him.

'You can have no idea how I felt!' he said piteously.

'Oh, but I did know. That was why I spoke Russian. I knew it would be better for you that way. You see, even then, even at that moment, I thought only of you and your feelings.'

'But why—why did you come there?' demanded the young man, ignoring the confession of tenderness.

'Because I knew you would be there . . . and—and there was nowhere else I could run to. I was nearly caught, you know—'

'Your dress . . . all torn like that! And those scratches! You had been caught stealing again! That was it, wasn't it?'

'If you choose to think that of me, then think it,' returned Katerina, indifferently.

'But what else am I to think? For God's sake, tell me what else am I to think?'

'I cannot answer for your thoughts, my David,' said Katerina, shaking her head. 'They have always been your own affair.'

'Liar, liar!' cried the young man violently, but not neglecting to keep his voice low. 'My thoughts are yours! You know that!

Everything—everything I have is yours! My heart, my soul, my life!'

'Even last night?' murmured Katerina, with a slight smile which had the effect of reducing the young man's passion somewhat.

'What do you mean?'

'I thought, my darling, that you had found someone else ... someone more suitable ... that girl Miriam—'

'Never, never, never!'

'Don't be angry, my David. You know that there is nothing that would make me happier than for you to fall in love—really in love and not your present wild feelings!—with someone who would make you happy. Nothing would please me better, my child, than for you to get a good wife and security. It will make no difference to us. We will always be friends.'

'For God's sake don't talk like that! You make everything sound horrible! You—you speak Polish so badly! You speak everything badly!'

'Is it so important, my child, for you and me always to choose right words?'

'Don't call me a child!'

'Why not, my David? Have I not the right? Am I not old enough to be your mother? Am I not twenty years older than—'

'It is only eighteen years!' interrupted the young man furiously; then he reddened as he realised that his correction had only made matters worse. He made a gesture to seize her in his arms; but quickly let them fall to his sides as if he knew, all too well, that such a course of action would prove hopeless.

'Try not to be so miserable, my darling. You must know that, whatever happens, you will always be in my heart.'

'Your heart?' cried he bitterly. 'It is a prison—an iron prison! You feel nothing!'

'Why do you try to hurt me?'

'Can anything really hurt you, Katerina?'

Although everything about him, his face, his actions, expressed the deepest anguish, there was in it all an element of play-acting. It was as if he was expressing what he felt was expected of him rather than what he actually felt; and it was possible that his companion guessed this. Impulsively—that is, if she ever did anything impulsively—she reached forward and touched his cheek with her hand, almost as if she was wiping away tears. He drew back, startled, and stared at her hand.

'Oh, Katerina, forgive me!'

'What is there to forgive, my darling, between us?'

They stood, staring at each other; and the sounds of children's shrieks and children's laughter came faintly into the room. The young man looked down at the carpet bag.

'You are leaving here?'

'I am going to the Walkers.'

'But—but I thought it was only for last night!'

'I have a room there now. It will be better than—than this.'

She gestured around her. The young man looked uneasy.

'It will be all right,' went on Katerina. 'You will be able to visit me there, I promise.'

'No, no! It will be too dangerous!'

She looked at him sharply, but did not disagree.

'Then we will find places to meet.'

'Yes, yes, of course.'

'Besides, I will be able to work for you.'

'How do you mean?'

'I have found out something.'

'What?'

'The girl—she is not his daughter. She came into my room last night and told me about it. Of course, she thought I couldn't understand. She just wanted to confide her secret and be safe at the same time. It was very amusing. She told me that he bought her—actually *bought* her!—from some old tramp in Poland, when she was a baby. Now she thinks that she's somebody important—a countess, would you believe! But we know better, don't we, my darling? A baby and a tramp! Does that not remind you of something?'

'Remind me of something? What do you mean?' said the young man, who had apparently fallen into a reverie and had not been listening.

'A baby and a tramp. How strange you are, my love. I can remember a time—and not so long ago—when you would have been wild to know more. Your head was full of nothing else, my David.'

'It is full of you, now.'

'The old man with his tin kettle and pot and saucepan hanging from his middle,' pursued Katerina, ignoring the interpolation, 'and the stolen violin. Nothing, nothing mattered to you so much! The violin—'

'Please, let's stop talking about such things!'

'But what if they are the ones?'

'Why should they be? At a time like that, such things must have been common. Maybe there were hundreds of old men with babies. The ones—the ones I saw most likely died in a ditch.'

'Why do you want to think so?' asked Katerina, watching him closely. 'Is it because they are poor, my darling one?'

'If you choose to think that of me, then think it,' said Kozlowski, repeating Katerina's own words and imitating the air of indifference with which she had uttered them—only not quite so successfully, as he was unable to conceal a look of shame and almost panic in his eyes.

'I don't want to think anything about them,' he said, 'because I know it to be impossible. Besides, as I told you, all that is in the past; and the past is—is dead.'

'Is it?'

'You know what I mean. There's nothing now for me but you, Katerina.'

'Of course there isn't, my darling!' murmured Katerina, picking up her bag. 'And there's nothing now for me but you, my David!'

They stood for a moment, gazing into each other's eyes with the tenderest love; behind which, however, there lay the deepest dread and even hatred. Then David opened the door and they went downstairs together. They parted at the corner of the street.

'You'll leave it, then?' he asked anxiously. 'I know they are not the ones!'

'Of course they are not, my darling.'

'Then you'll do nothing?'

'My poor David! Don't you know that all I want is for you to be happy?'

She returned to Shoreditch, stopping only in the market to buy some fruit. Perdita was overjoyed to see her and she was dragged to inspect the little room on the landing that had been made ready for her. She was absolutely delighted with it, and quite overcome by everybody's kindness. She broke out in floods of Russian that even Mr Walker could only guess at; and put the fruit on the table. Then wine was drunk to celebrate Miss Kropotka's moving in; and the Streamers' house acquired an all-pervading aroma of scent.

8

All change must, to some degree, be both for the better and for the worse: for the better because change must vary monotony, and for the worse because, even it if sweeps away injustice and oppression, it disposes also of those small items that have brought, into a prevailing gloom, disproportionate joy.

When the even tenor, or, as it was more often, the shrill soprano of the Walkers' life underwent a change in consequence of Katerina, it meant courtesy and restraint for a little while on the part of Perdita, and buttons sewn on Mr Walker's coat. It meant no more bad dinners in the greasy chop-house in Shoreditch High Street, but a table laid at home, with cooked meats, pies and what could only be described as Russian *in*delicacies generously bought by Katerina from a shop in Houndsditch. It meant Katerina's learning English and Perdita's learning a Russian song; which so pleased her and gave rise to so much good temper and cheerfulness when she warbled it, that Mr Walker could not help feeling that three was now company, when before it had sometimes seemed that two was a crowd.

All this was for the better; for the worse, however, was the feeling of constraint that was laid upon the nightly ritual between father and child. Voices were kept low and the recital curtailed. There was no doubt that Perdita felt an awkwardness about her aspirations and Mr Walker felt an awkwardness about encouraging them. The stranger's presence seemed to pervade everything, like her scent.

Sadly Mr Walker noted the loss of the small nightly pleasure; but not for worlds would he have told Perdita of it. Pride prevented him; and he reflected that the change was due, more than anything, to Perdita's growing up.

Jonathan Dolly thought so too. Unlike Mr Walker, he had nothing to regret, and he regarded Perdita's improved temper and manners with unfeigned satisfaction. He called quite often at the Streamers' house with jars of pickled herrings and chopped liver, sent by his father who wanted to help Mr Walker in the responsibility he had undertaken. Mr Dolly would have brought them himself but he was fully taken up with his jury service, so he entrusted the delicate task to his son.

It was a delicate task because Mr Dolly did not want his friend, Mr Walker, to feel that the presents were a charity. He knew it would have wounded him. He had talked the matter over with Mrs Dolly and she had brought him to understand—although it was something far removed from his own nature—that with some people kindness can be harder to bear than the trials of poverty. It was as if they had a raw place and a helping hand always fell upon it.

'Nonsense, my dear!' said Mr Dolly; but nevertheless took care to impress on his son that, under no circumstances, was he to allow Mr Walker to imagine that the gifts of food were anything to do with him.

They were carefully wrapped and addressed to 'Miss Kropotka' or 'For the attention of Miss Kropotka'; and Jonathan, to whom delicacy was second nature, but not, alas, first, would deliver them as furtively as if he was going to blow up Parliament.

However, whatever he might have lacked in discretion, he more than made up for in gallantry. He would often bring a bag of sugared almonds for Perdita—the vastly improved Perdita—which he bought at a confectioner's on the way.

Perdita took them from him, because she was fond of sugared almonds, but she could never bring herself to thank him directly as it would have encouraged him, so she always pretended that they were from Mr Dolly.

Jonathan accepted the evasion humorously; but at the same time he could not help feeling a faint distress as he was too much the born businessman not to worry that he might be throwing good money after bad. Often he wondered how he might outmanoeuvre her.

One morning, about a week after Mr Dolly had begun upon his jury service, his son and heir came briskly along Shoreditch with a parcel under his arm, sugared almonds in his pocket, and Spring, together with a certain element of calculation, in his heart.

It was one of those mornings when April was in the air, although not yet on the calendar; and the sun was shining brightly. Jonathan observed with interest that there was an old woman selling daffodils at the corner of the Streamers' street.

She was enthroned in them, she was ensconced in them, she inhabited them like a wrinkled old beetle in a golden retirement. She exclaimed aloud as Jonathan approached that she had never, in all her born days, laid eyes on such a handsome, well-dressed youth, and called the world as witness to the fact. Was he courting? Ah, a blush! And it became him like the red on an apple!

'Daffies, sir, for your lady-love! Daffies for regard, as they say! Three bunches for the price of two!'

She held out her arms, crowded with gold. Jonathan pondered; he smiled.

'I'll take them!' he said; and then, discovering, as one often does, that three bunches were on the skinny side, entered into a brisk bout of bargaining and ended up with six bunches for the price of three.

Flushed with this successful stroke of business, he made his way through the fruit and vegetable market, bosomed high in daffodils, and bombarded with shrill inquiries as to where the funeral was, as, in the experience of the fruit and vegetable market, floral tributes came at the end of an association rather than at the beginning.

He knocked on the Streamers' door. Sounds of music came faintly from within as Mrs Streamer coaxed a pupil through a song.

'Early one morning, just as the sun was rising,
I heard a maid sing in the valley below.'

The shrill voice faltered, and Mrs Streamer's rich contralto took up the refrain:

'Oh, don't deceive me, oh, never leave me!
How could you use a poor maiden so!'

She sang it with feeling; she sang like one on whom life had left scars. A moment later the door was opened by Mr Streamer himself. There was a guilty look on his face as if the song's significance had not escaped him.

Mr Streamer was a stout, middle-sized man with more heart, more soul, more tender regrets and more whiskers than were strictly good for him. He had a gentle face and soft, appealing, blue eyes; but with his great bush of brown whisker, and his hair parted in the middle and arranged in two curly horns, he bore an uncanny resemblance to a ram peering forth apprehensively from a thicket.

There was something on his mind. He looked at Jonathan as if not seeing him.

'Parcel for Miss Kropotka,' murmured Jonathan. 'I'll take it up to her.'

Mr Streamer stared at him thoughtfully; and then at the daffodils. Jonathan declined to reveal their intended destination.

'Oh, gay is the garland, and fresh are the roses,
I've culled from the garden to bind on thy brow,'

sang the infant nightingale from the music-room.

'Oh, don't deceive me, oh, never leave me!'

improved Mrs Streamer.

'How could you,' they sang together, 'use a poor maiden so!'

Mr Streamer looked distinctly uncomfortable. He stood aside and Jonathan came in and began to mount the stairs. Mr Streamer followed him.

'She's having a lesson,' he said. 'Mr Walker is with her. He's giving her her English lesson.'

They had reached the first floor landing, where the aroma of Katerina's scent was peculiarly strong. Mr Streamer frowned at the door of the little room that had once been his sanctum, and from which he was now excluded. A sound of voices came from within: first Mr Walker's, then Miss Kropotka's, low and fluctuating. Mr Streamer listened.

'What was that she said? A pound of pomegranates? She cannot have said that! It must have been something in Russian. Or else her pronunciation is really diabolical. I wonder what it was she meant to say?' muttered Mr Streamer, with a touch of anxiety and a deepening frown.

It was pretty plain that he did not approve of Miss Kropotka; which, considering her beauty and his susceptible nature, was rather surprising. It could only be supposed that either he resented having to give up his sanctum more than might have been supposed or that he had made an early assault on the Russian woman and had been repulsed with heavy losses.

Jonathan, who hoped to see Perdita alone in order to present the daffodils, continued up the stairs, leaving Mr Streamer still eavesdropping on the lesson. Downstairs, the singing broke out again.

'Remember the vows that you made to your Mary.
Remember the bower where you vowed to be true.'

Mr Streamer remembered—either the vows, the bower, or something else altogether. He hastened after Jonathan.

'Oh, don't deceive me, oh, never leave me!
How could you use a poor maiden so!'

Mr Streamer looked quite panic-stricken at the thought. He pushed past Jonathan and reached the door of the Walkers' parlour first. He knocked rapidly and smiled nervously at Jonathan, who was plainly annoyed.

'Only for a moment,' he said. 'I only wanted to ask for something.'

Perdita opened the door. Everything about her proclaimed that she was wearing new shoes. She scarcely looked at anything else. Mr Streamer skipped inside, followed by Jonathan, bearing daffodils. Perdita eyed them suspiciously. Some final fragments of song drifted up:

'Thus sang the poor maiden, her sorrows bewailing.
Thus sang the poor maid in the valley below.'

Then Mr Streamer shut the door and stifled the gentle complainant in the valley below.

'I was wondering, Perdita,' murmured Mr Streamer hurriedly, 'if I could beg a favour of you?'

Perdita shrugged her shoulders, glanced again at the daffodils, then back at her shoes.

'I have had a little accident, my dear. My instrument. I didn't want to worry Mrs Streamer. She is so sensitive, you know. But it is damaged . . . not exactly beyond repair, but very near it. Such an extraordinary thing! One of those dancers, you know. Her foot right through it! Temperament, of course; but we are all artists! Naturally, it is being repaired, but it will take time . . . yes, it will take time.'

'How can we help you then, Mr Streamer?'

'I remembered that, when you first came, your father had an old violin. I think he put it in the loft. I was wondering, if he still has it, if I might borrow it? I will be very careful, of course.'

'I suppose it will be all right, Mr Streamer.'

'Thank you, thank you, Perdita! I would have asked your father, but he is busy; and I didn't want to upset Mrs Streamer, you understand!'

He hurried out, erected the loft-ladder—which hung from a stout hook in the wall—and climbed up. His feet twinkled in the air. There came a thumping and a bumping on the parlour ceiling; then he came down again, replaced the ladder and presented himself, flushed and dusty and clutching the violin under his coat.

'It's a fine instrument!' he panted. 'It only needs re-stringing. I will take the greatest care. Thank you, thank you . . . there is no need to mention it to Mrs Streamer. I—I will tell her myself!'

As he departed, the old song's refrain came up from the valley below.

> 'Oh, don't deceive me, oh, never leave me!
> How could you use a poor maiden so!'

Jonathan smiled at Perdita. There had been something faintly comic about Mr Streamer. Perdita, however, felt bound not to see it.

'If I was poor Mrs Streamer,' she said, 'I would have broken that fiddle over his head!'

Jonathan thought he ought to defend his sex; but reflected that Mr Streamer was not a particularly outstanding example of it.

Besides, he wanted to give the daffodils to Perdita while they were still alone. First he put the parcel for Miss Kropotka on the table; than he gave Perdita her sugared almonds. 'Please thank your father,' she said calmly. 'It was very kind of him to think of me.' He retained the daffodils. Perdita watched them expectantly. Then, perhaps as much to her annoyance as to his, Mr Walker and Miss Kropotka came into the room.

'Goot morrnink!' cried Katerina, filling the room with red velvet and scent. 'Iss right?' she inquired proudly of the daffodil bearer.

He assented and observed, from amid the daffodils, that it was a very fine day indeed for the time of year. Baffled, Miss Kropotka applied to her teacher, and some words in Russian passed between them. She laughed, and Jonathan felt himself go red. He wished he had not bought quite so many daffodils. He did not in the least know what to do with them. Everybody was looking at them: Mr Walker with admiration, and Miss Kropotka and Perdita with something else. For whom had he brought them? For a beautiful woman much older than himself, or for a vain and greedy girl of twelve? Either way he was struck by the incongruity of the daffodils, and began to harbour some very unpleasant thoughts about the old woman who had sold them to him.

'Jonathan,' said Perdita quietly, 'has brought a parcel for Katerina from his father, and—'

She paused and stared at the flowers. Katerina also regarded them with interest.

'Daffodils,' began Jonathan courageously, when there came a knock on the door.

The visitor was Mrs Fairhazel. She came into the room in a little storm of wisps, with a hat like a schooner going down in them.

'Oh, Mr Walker!' she cried, overcome by the number of people in the little room. 'I—I was just passing . . . well, not passing really, but I was nearby so I thought I would call to see how you all were! I wondered if there was anything I could do for Miss Kropotka—Why, what beautiful flowers, Jonathan!'

She smiled nervously at them, as if the yawning trumpets were open mouths, ready to bite her. She looked at Katerina, and then at Perdita, and then at the daffodils again. She said no more about the flowers, feeling herself to be on dangerous ground. She hoped they were for Perdita but would rather have died than embarrassed anyone by saying the wrong thing.

'I really came,' she said, addressing Mr Walker, 'to ask you if you would come to my house to dinner on Friday night. You see,' she went on anxiously, 'I thought, as it will be the Jewish Passover, and Mr and Mrs Dolly and the family will be celebrating it with Mrs Dolly's brother, as they always do, that I would like to give a little dinner myself. It won't be very much, I'm afraid. Nothing like Mr Dolly's. My house is rather small, you know, and the dining-room table only pulls out for one more leaf! But the two gentlemen from upstairs will be coming and I would be so pleased if you and Perdita would come, and—and Miss Kropotka, of course . . . but I won't be in the least offended if she has something else to do! It will only be a roast, you know . . .'

She stopped, as if suddenly feeling that she had said rather more than was necessary. Mr Walker smiled.

'Thank you, Mrs Fairhazel. It will be a very great pleasure. We will be honoured to come.'

Mrs Fairhazel sighed with relief. She looked at the daffodils again. Jonathan stretched his lips in a smile. He wondered if he might not come to an arrangement with the flower-seller on the principle of sale or return. Miss Kropotka said something in Russian to Mr Walker. Everyone looked at Mr Walker expectantly. He explained: 'Miss Kropotka says what beautiful flowers you have brought, Jonathan.'

'They are for Perdita!' said Jonathan in an accidental shout that arose from that sudden courage that sometimes turns the course of battles. 'I got them in the market. They are in season, you know,' he went on, feeling a need to throw up some defences. 'They were amazingly cheap—'

'How wonderful of you!' cried Mrs Fairhazel rapidly, as if she feared that if she didn't rush in, the young man would change his mind. 'To have flowers brought for you, Perdita, is a great tribute. And daffodils! They are for regard, you know. They are quite romantic. You should put them in water, dear—'

'I will put them,' said Perdita, relieving Jonathan of his golden burden, 'where I please!'

She went to the window, opened it, and flung the flowers out into the street.

The action was so unexpected that, for a moment, the only sounds in the room came from the market outside. Mr Walker strode to the window and shut it.

'For God's sake, child! Are you out of your mind?' he demanded, with an anger that was startling in a man so mild. His face had gone quite red.

'No, I'm not out of my mind!' shouted Perdita, as much frightened as angry. 'They were mine, weren't they? He gave them to me. So I can do what I like with them! I hate flowers! And I hate him giving them to me! Why should it always be you who won't take things from people? Why should it only be all right for you? I'm as good as you are, aren't I? I hate charity! I won't have it—I won't!'

Following this, she did the only thing that was possible in the circumstances. She burst into tears and rushed to take refuge with her favourite of the moment, Katerina. She clung to her, buried her face in Katerina's scented skirts, heard Mrs Fairhazel making stupid excuses for her, heard Jonathan declare that it didn't matter at all and that it was foolish of him to have brought her flowers; and felt Katerina's hand stroking her hair. She looked up; and Katerina smiled faintly down. She felt that she had an ally . . .

Whose fault had it all been? Mrs Fairhazel's, of course. It had been because she'd suggested that there was something between herself and Mister Pickled Herrings! That was why she'd thrown the flowers out of the window! And good riddance to them. And to him! Was he going?

'Goodbye, Mr Walker . . .'

And her pa! It was all his fault, too. He shouldn't have shouted at her.

'Goodbye, Mrs Fairhazel . . .'

Was he going to dare to say goodbye to her?

'Goodbye, Miss Kropotka . . .'

She heard the door open and the squeaky brat downstairs still singing:

> 'Oh, don't deceive me, oh, never leave me!'

But he did.

'Pa?'

'What is it, Perdita?'

'I forgot to tell you something,' she said meekly; and detached herself from Katerina.

She wanted to apologise, but could think of no other way of making amends than by changing the subject and pretending that nothing had happened.

'Mr Streamer came up.'

'Indeed?'

'He wanted to ask you for something but you were busy with Katerina; so he asked me. Was that all right?'

'I expect so.'

'He'd had an accident. He'd broken his violin. Someone had trodden on it. He was very upset.'

'I expect he was. It is his living.'

'He didn't want to worry Mrs Streamer.'

At last she succeeded in her intention. Her father showed a sudden interest and her previous behaviour was forgotten. She continued. 'I told him that I thought it would be all right. Did I do the right thing, Pa?'

At this point Katerina asked Mr Walker something in Russian. He looked at her as if he hadn't understood. He shook his head; and returned to Perdita.

'You—you gave it to him?'

'He got it for himself, Pa. Out of the loft.'

'Then you didn't go up there?'

'No, Pa,' said Perdita, observing with satisfaction that the old look of worry and concern had come over her father's face—the look that meant she could do anything she liked because he loved her. 'I would never go up that ladder and into all that darkness and dirt! Was I right, Pa?'

'Yes . . . yes. I was only frightened that—that you might have fallen and—and hurt yourself,' he muttered. 'Badly.'

Everyone smiled over the father's concern: Mrs Fairhazel with pleasure, Katerina with interest, and Perdita with relief. Downstairs the lesson was ending and the two nightingales sang together:

'Oh, don't deceive me, oh, never leave me!
How could you use a poor maiden so!'

9

Jonathan Dolly was not angry. Any reddening of his face, and deep breathing, convulsive clenching of his fists, was due, almost certainly, to the exertion of walking downstairs. He observed, in passing, Perdita's inscriptions, dating from her youth, on the wall. He stopped. He took out a pencil and made certain improvements. They read now:

> PERDITA WALKER LOVES
> PERDITA WALKER
> LOVES
> PERDITA WALKER.

He went outside; and the fruit and vegetable market, having previously taken note of the daffodils going in to the Streamers' house in a bunch, and having seen them coming out in a shower, drew its conclusions and offered its condolences. It was suggested that he gather up the fallen flowers and take them home to his mother, all other women being a snare and a delusion. It was noticeable that this advice came chiefly from the female stall-holders and was evidence that women, on the grounds of superior experience, tend to hold their own sex in low esteem.

He went back to Bishopsgate Street and retired to the stony, watery room in the basement where the mysteries of pickling were performed. There he occupied himself with chopping up cooked chicken livers and tearing the guts out of herrings in a manner that could only be described as personal.

Soon after five o'clock Mr Dolly, the juryman, came home. His family assembled to greet him. They did this because they felt he needed their support after his solemn labours of the day. He was all in black. He was wearing the clothes he kept for the Day of Atonement, and, as he stood in his cave-like shop, he resembled, not so much a robber chief who had retired, but an undertaker who had not. He dressed like this to show his great respect for the court; but the effect on a defendant must have been dispiriting in the extreme.

'How did it go today, my dear?' asked Mrs Dolly.

'It's a terrible business, a terrible business,' said the juryman.

He took off his hat and gave it to Miriam, who bore it away like a memorial; he took off his coat and gave it to Jonathan, who carried it off as if he was going to bury it.

'You can have no idea,' said Mr Dolly, passing his hand over his hair, 'how tiring it is, sitting there and listening to every single word. Sometimes it can be most unpleasant.'

He sighed, and Mrs Dolly thought he was looking thinner. Jury service was not agreeing with him. But it was not to be wondered at when you considered that Mr Dolly, who had never in his life passed judgement on anyone, had never doubted, never suspected, but had always responded straight from his heart, was now called upon to doubt everything, suspect everything, and to pass judgement without ever referring to his heart at all. His watch-chain smile was now only on his waistcoat, across which it glinted mirthlessly.

'I don't know why it has to go on for so long,' said Mrs Dolly, with a touch of bitterness in her voice. 'Surely it's not necessary?'

'One has to get at the truth,' responded the juryman, frowning a little as if he felt that the dignity of the court was being impugned. 'It's not like buying a pound of liver, you know.'

'I don't see why not,' said one of his daughters who had brought his slippers and was waiting for him to remove his outdoor shoes. 'If something is rotten you can smell it at once!'

'Don't be foolish!' said Mr Dolly irritably. 'Don't talk about matters you don't understand!'

It exasperated him to hear the processes of the law being called into question, when he himself was part of them. The solemnity of the court awed him immensely; and the importance of the case he was trying absorbed him to the exclusion of everything else.

It involved the landed gentry and touched more closely on Burke's *Peerage* than on Mr Dolly's. It was down on the list as 'Standfast v. Standfast'; and if you opened up Mr Dolly, you would find it on his heart, too.

The title (a baronetcy) and the estate (in Gloucestershire), were in dispute; and very grievous it was. A claimant had turned up from Australia declaring that he was the rightful heir who had disappeared some thirty years ago and whose death had, wrongfully, been presumed. He claimed that he was Robert Standfast, uncle to the present baronet who, consequently, ought not to be a baronet at all.

Naturally the present baronet, Sir Charles Standfast, who had only enjoyed the estate and title for about a year, was outraged, and declared the claimant to be an impostor and a scoundrel, and, furthermore, he would have his groom horsewhip him if ever he dared set foot on his land. And naturally the claimant, who hadn't enjoyed anything very much for the past thirty years, declared that he was not an impostor and that the land, the groom and very possibly the horsewhip were his anyway.

The claimant's story—repeated many times, turned upside-down, inside-out, dredged, sifted and generally dismembered for the edification of the jury—was that, far from having died thirty years ago, he had been knocked on the head when leaving a tavern in Wapping and had awoken to find himself stripped of all his possessions and on board a vessel bound for Australia.

So severe had been his injury that he had lost all memory of his past life. A scar was offered in evidence but unfortunately it was overgrown with hair; and, delicacy on the part of the jury preventing deep investigation, the claimant's head was withdrawn and returned to its rightful place in the court.

He had settled in the town of Bendigo—a map of Australia was produced and Bendigo identified—where he would have been content to end his days—'A pity he didn't!' shouted Sir Charles Standfast; and was ordered to keep quiet—when he had happened to read, in a Melbourne newspaper, an account of his brother's death. At once everything had come back to him; and he had written immediately to the only surviving member of the family who would have remembered him—his aunt, Miss Augusta Standfast, whose name had appeared in the article. Letter and newspaper were produced, handed to the jury, passed along, dropped, picked up again and handed back to the usher with a sheepish smile. A favourable reply to the letter being received, the claimant had returned at once to occupy his rightful place. 'In gaol!' shouted Sir Charles, and was told that he would be removed from the court if he interrupted again.

In support of the claimant's identity was an old servant—'I sent him packing six months ago for laming a horse!' shouted Sir Charles, and was removed from the court for a quarter of an hour—a porter at the claimant's college, and the old aunt. 'She's as mad as a hatter!' shouted Sir Charles; and had to pay for it with another quarter of an hour.

The old lady was absolutely unshakeable in her conviction that the claimant was her nephew Robert, and sat throughout the proceedings fiercely clutching him by the arm. But for her the claim would almost certainly have foundered; so all the energy of the family's legal advisers was directed towards undermining her. It was not a very elevating matter, and Mr Dolly grieved deeply to see an old lady bullied unmercifully by a counsel young enough to be her grandson, and forced to admit that she was little better than a senile old fool.

But it was the law, and one had to get at the truth. It was no good shutting one's eyes to it; so day after day Mr Dolly sat in the jury box, kept his eyes open and his heart in Chancery, and came back home a sadder, but—he stoutly believed—a wiser man.

He took off his shoes and his daughter bore them away like little black coffins.

'Do you think it will be finished before Passover?' asked Mrs Dolly.

'There's still a great deal of evidence to come,' said Mr Dolly, putting on his slippers. 'Nothing can be decided until everything is heard. It's not like buying a string of onions, you know. These matters—'

He stopped as he became aware that there was a customer in the shop.

'Don't mind me,' said the customer. 'I'm not in a 'urry. You serve the ladies first, sir.'

'They are my family,' said Mr Dolly.

'Reely?' said the customer. 'Many congratulations, sir.'

He elevated a hard round hat at the ladies, to underline his admiration, and fitted it back neatly into the groove it had left round his head. He was a spry but rather shrunken little man with a grey muffler, a rusty black coat, and an air, as he peered about him, of having a tail and looking for something to nibble in the cheesy line.

'To begin with, I'll take 'alf a dozen of the Famous,' he said, producing a string bag from his pocket and laying it on the counter. 'Pickled 'errings, of course, if you'd be so kind, ma'am.' He turned to Mr Dolly. 'Please carry on with your conversation, sir. I'll be all right. I just fancy a browse.'

Mr Dolly excused himself and said that he had just been about to go upstairs. The customer tipped his hat; then looked at Mr Dolly rather quizzically.

''aven't I 'ad the pleasure,' he said, 'of seein' you before, sir? Westminster 'all, was it? Standfast vee Standfast? Member of the jury? Third from the left in the back row? Not mistaken, am I, sir? I never forget a face.'

Mr Dolly confessed, and the customer, apparently satisfied, began to skip about the shop, lost in wonderment at the amazing variety of Mr Dolly's stock. Pickled herrings weren't the half of it! Sausages! A king's ransom of them! And cheeses! More than the mind could contain! He was absolutely floored by it all! What was that? Chopped liver? Might he try a snippet to go with the herrings? And that? Polish salami? Another snippet, if you'd be so kind! Why, a man might spend a fortune in such an establishment; particularly if he was, like the customer, a mere infant in the gastronomical line!

'But carry on, sir, please carry on and don't mind me. I'll just browse. You were talkin', wasn't you, about Standfast vee Standfast? I was in court myself for an hour or so this mornin'. That's when I saw you, sir. It's quite a coincidence, ain't it?'

Mr Dolly agreed that it was; but did not accept the invitation to carry on talking about the case. The customer tapped a jar of pickled onions.

'Dare I risk 'em? Or will they—if you'll forgive the expression, ladies—repeat on me? I'll risk a couple, ma'am, if you'll be so kind! As we was sayin', sir, about Standfast vee Standfast. What's your opinion on it?'

'I'm afraid I cannot talk about it, Mr—Mr—'

'Mr Clarky, sir. Clarky by name and clerky by nature, so to say. I'm Mr Leviticus's clerk. Mr Leviticus of Gray's Inn, of course. Might I inquire what's in 'ere?'

'Pickled cucumbers.'

'Amazin', the variety! A real Aladdin's cave, sir! I'll try a small one, if you'd be so kind, ma'am. As we was sayin', sir, about Standfast vee Standfast . . . never fear, sir! I won't inquire as to your opinion. Bein' a solicitor's clerk, I understand your feelin's in the matter. Member of the jury and all that. Absolutely right, sir. Letter of the law. And if I should say anythin' out of place, you must stop me and strike it from your mind. It's not my place to influence you, sir. Besides, you must 'ave it all for yourself. That Australian fellow's lyin' 'is 'ead off. You've only got to watch 'is 'ands to know it. Keeps washin' them together every time 'e's in the box.'

'Please, Mr Clarky, this is very wrong of you!' said Mr Dolly, becoming rather agitated.

'So it is, so it is, sir! And you must strike it from your mind! That sausage there, sir, the one at the end . . . might I ask what manner of creature it is?'

'Hungarian.'

'Amazin', absolutely amazin'! I'll try a snippet, if you'd be so kind, ma'am! As we was sayin', sir—and please strike it from your mind if I should say anythin' to offend—it's all a pack of lies. The old lady's past it. She don't know whether she's comin' or goin'; and that lawyer of 'is 'as a name in the trade that you wouldn't give to a dog! It's criminal, the money it's costin' the family! Robert Standfast must be turnin'—'

He stopped as the shop door opened. He tapped the side of his nose.

'I'll go on browsin',' he murmured as he skipped away, 'while you serve the gentleman.'

It was Mr Walker. He seemed pleased with himself and greeted the family warmly.

'Jonathan,' he said, 'I have a letter for you.' He smiled rather conspiritorially. 'From Perdita.'

He handed over a large sealed missive such as might have passed between sovereign states after the conclusion of a war. Jonathan took it, broke the seals and read. The contents were not extensive. In fact they consisted of only one word. 'SORRY.' He beamed.

'What's that?' asked Mr Dolly, unconsciously reaching out his hand as if the letter was yet another affidavit or sworn statement for his inspection.

70

'Nothing, Father,' said Jonathan, not giving it up. He felt that any explanation would be embarrassing.

Mr Dolly, suddenly realising that he had trespassed on a private matter, attempted to make light of it. He spoke to Mr Walker.

'It's a sad day, Mr Walker, when there are secrets between father and child!'

He smiled ruefully.

'Beg pardon,' said Mr Clarky, coming out of his browse and appearing to sidle round a sausage, 'but 'aven't I 'ad the pleasure of seein' you before, sir?'

He addressed Mr Walker, and stared at him intently.

'No, no. I do not think so.' He looked away.

'Are you sure, sir? In court, maybe?'

'I have never been in a court. And I hope never to go into one.'

'Very wise, sir. Could it 'ave been in our office, per'aps? Mr Leviticus, of Gray's Inn?'

'I don't know any Mr Leviticus,' said Mr Walker quickly.

'That's queer, sir. I could 'ave sworn I'd seen you before. And I never forget a face. But no matter. Strike it from your mind, sir. If anythin' comes back to me, I'll let you know, sir. It's Mr Walker, ain't it?'

'Yes.'

'That's not the name I'd 'ave put to the face, sir . . . so it just shows I'm beginnin' to fail in my mind. Well, well, it 'appens to all of us,' he said; and, making no further mention of Standfast v. Standfast, as if it had quite slipped his mind, he paid for his purchases and, with a final elevation of his hat, skipped out of the shop, cheerfully swinging his laden bag.

After he had gone there was a moment's silence in the shop, during which Mr Dolly, the juryman, tried to strike from his mind everything that Mr Clarky had said. But he couldn't quite manage it. He kept remembering what the spry little man had said about the claimant washing and washing his hands. Perhaps this was because he noticed, with a slight pang, that his friend Mr Walker was doing the same thing. He was staring at the closed door and, as if unaware of it, was washing and washing *his* hands.

10

Standfast v. Standfast continued to drag its twisted length through Westminster Hall, and, when the court rose, back to Bishopsgate Street where it became, mysteriously, Dolly v. Dolly. So much did the juryman take his duty to heart that Standfast v. Standfast supplanted everything else in his life.

When he rose in the morning, the claimant and the old lady waited at his right hand, and Sir Charles, his mother and his younger brother waited at his left; and when he laid him down at night, they all sat on his chest. They haunted him in the shop where the very sausages became so many swords of Damocles suspended over his head, threatening him with disaster if he should come to a wrong decision; and they accompanied him even through the windy Friday night when he and his family went to Bethnal Green to celebrate Passover Eve in his brother-in-law's house.

Mr Dolly's brother-in-law, Mr Brill, was a large, imposing man who strongly resembled his sister, Mrs Dolly, both in features and in deportment. He was listed, in Dolly's *Peerage*, as the baron. He was cantor at the local synagogue and had a fine tenor voice with a singularly sweet falsetto that was much admired. He had once been an opera singer but had given it up when he had married Mrs Brill, who was a deeply religious lady, not listed in the *Peerage*. But old habits die hard, and he liked to wander off, in the midst of orthodox chants, into fragments of Italian opera, when he thought Mrs Brill was not listening.

But on this night Mr Dolly felt that he sang only of Standfast v. Standfast; and when Miriam, who was the youngest at table, asked the Four Questions, Mr Dolly felt that she wasn't demanding the prescribed explanation of the ritual, but was directing yet another inquiry into Standfast v. Standfast.

The visit of Mr Clarky to the shop had only made matters worse. Whereas before he had been inclining, ever so slightly, towards the family, now, because of the sly attempt to influence him, he was inclining towards the claimant. Then, when Mr Brill, humming something from *The Barber of Seville*, ceremonially washed his hands in a silver-plated basin, Mr Dolly thought helplessly of the claimant, washing *his* hands; and when he tried to strike it from his mind, the claimant was replaced by his friend, Mr Walker, who was also washing his hands.

So the evening wore on, and the Lord duly delivered the Children of Israel from the house of bondage; and Mr Dolly wondered when his lordship in Westminster Hall would deliver Standfast from Standfast; and Mrs Dolly, who watched her husband with troubled eyes, wondered when *he* would be delivered from all of them.

In Stepney, where Mrs Fairhazel's modest little house stood by itself at the end of a row, as if, like Mrs Fairhazel herself, it was discreetly widowed; and, rather like Mrs Fairhazel herself, was full of unexpected treasures in the way of pretty china, charming little articles of furniture and delicate water-colours, Mr Walker sat in the dining-room as silent and preoccupied as was Mr Dolly in Bethnal Green.

He, too, was thinking of Mr Clarky, whose visit to Mr Dolly's shop had made matters worse. He, too, was troubled over decisions; although, in his case, they concerned himself—and his child. He looked at Perdita who seemed to fit in so well with the pretty china and well-chosen furnishings. She wore a new dress to go with her new shoes, and her hair winked and gleamed like a cluster of blackberries ... such as one catches sight of, just out of reach among brambles.

The recollection made him smile, and he glanced down at his hands as if remembering the scratches he had once got ... Then he drifted back through darkness, pain and degradation, and so to an earlier time. Then back to the present and Mrs Fairhazel's dinner, and the consciousness that he was not being a good guest after all the trouble his hostess had taken.

She smiled at him, divining that his thoughts were elsewhere. She asked him gently how Miss Kropotka, who had not come, was progressing with her English? He stared, collected his thoughts, and answered, 'Slowly, slowly. But she will learn.'

73

Mrs Fairhazel looked so pleased that one might have supposed it was because Miss Kropotka's studies were close to her heart, instead of, she was ashamed to admit to herself, because it was apparent that Mr Walker had not been thinking about the beautiful Russian woman at all.

He had been thinking of Mr Streamer and the borrowed violin; and of how nearly he had come to disaster. Mrs Fairhazel had been right; nothing had been further from his thoughts than the scented Katerina . . .

Mr Streamer, however, whose Latin blood lent soul to his fiddle, passion to his heart and a certain helpless shiftiness to his dealings, *was* thinking of Miss Kropotka.

He had retired early and Mrs Streamer was already fast asleep, when he had heard the front door open and shut and, shortly after, the sigh and rustle of Miss Kropotka's velvet on the stairs. *He* had sighed and rustled, as he lay beside Mrs Streamer, who was snoring in three-four time in the conjugal bed. He wondered if Miss Kropotka snored; and reflected bitterly that he was not likely to find out.

His Latin blood simmered dangerously in his veins. The woman was in his sanctum, his private place. Therefore she was, in a sense, his. Was he not master in his own house, and did not a master— like a lord of old—have certain rights?

Mrs Streamer moaned softly in her sleep, broke briefly into an agitated six-eight, then went back to snoring in waltz-time. Mr Streamer sniffed the air; and smelled Miss Kropotka's scent. His Latin blood began to boil. With infinite caution he removed himself from the conjugal bed.

'Giovanni . . . ' moaned Mrs Streamer in her sleep.

He froze; he waited . . . until the snoring was resumed. Then, with gleaming eyes, predatory crouch and feather-light feet, he left the room. It was not for nothing that he was known, in musical circles, as Don Giovanni Streamer.

There was a light upstairs, right at the top of the house. That was odd; the Walkers were still out. Mr Streamer listened. He could hear curious noises. They reminded him of those orchestral passages marked *coll legno*, when one strikes the fiddle strings with the wood of the bow, thereby producing a quaint scrabbling noise, rather like inquisitive pigeons' feet.

He began to mount the stairs *pianissimo*. He saw that Miss Kropotka's door was open. Wave upon wave of her scent came out and engulfed him; but she was not inside. He gazed at her bed that was tumbled from her interesting person; and wondered if he should wait for her? Then he thought better of it, and continued up the stairs.

The light was still there, flickering uncannily; shadows loomed and embraced, and the pigeons' feet still scrabbled inquisitively. He reached the top landing.

The ladder to the loft had been put in place and the trap door was open. The light was wandering about, somewhere under the roof. Even as he watched, it was suddenly obscured. A naked foot appeared followed by what seemed to be a little crowd of weasels or rats. Then another foot, a flowing down of red velvet, a candle, and, bending over it, Katerina's weirdly lighted face. She was smiling triumphantly.

She was half-way down the ladder before she saw the night-gowned, night-capped, profusely whiskered Mr Streamer looking up. She cried out in alarm.

'What the devil are you doing up there?' demanded the master of the house, temporarily forgetting that the lovely explorer could not speak his language.

She completed her descent, gave Mr Streamer the candle and explained, by means of dumb-show, that she had been stowing away some unwanted baggage.

'Iss all right?'

She stood very close to him, and her eyes, absolutely enormous in the candlelight, watched him anxiously. She was amazingly beautiful and smelled like the Arabian Nights. Mr Streamer, his mind running very much on those lines, nodded. He found it hard to believe her but, after all, there was nothing of value in the loft beyond some tattered scraps of carpet and the Walkers' battered old trunk.

He helped her to close the trap-door and to put the ladder back on its hook. She rewarded him with a grateful smile. Mr Streamer did not think it was enough. He led the way downstairs and halted outside Katerina's room. She made to take the candle from him. He drew it back, thereby illuminating his own face, which shone like the burning bush.

'Katerina!' he mouthed ardently.

'Meestair Streamer!' she returned, reproachfully.

'Ssh!'

He pointed towards the conjugal room, then up to the loft, then to Katerina, and lastly to himself. Nothing could have been plainer: he would keep quiet about her if she would keep quiet about him. He smiled affectionately and blew Katerina a kiss across the candle. She blew one back so passionately as to extinguish the candle and leave them both in pitch darkness.

'Katerina, oh, Katerina!' breathed the deeply smitten Mr Streamer, with every drop of his Latin blood on fire.

'Anuzzer time!' whispered Katerina, slipping into her room and shutting and locking the door. 'Anuzzer time, my poor darling boy!'

Mr Streamer, unable to believe, for a moment, that the darkness in front of him was empty, stretched out his arms. Then discovering that it was, and expressing a very unfavourable opinion of Miss Kropotka, he returned to the conjugal bed.

'Giovanni!' moaned Mrs Streamer, presumably in her sleep. 'Giovanni . . . Giovanni . . . '

Mr Streamer took no notice. He was thinking of 'anuzzer time'.

Mrs Streamer opened an eye, and observed a smile lurking in her husband's whiskers. She sighed and got out of bed.

'Where are you going?' demanded Mr Streamer apprehensively. 'My dear.'

'Only to play the piano, my love.'

'At this time of night?'

'I will play very quietly. And I will only play until the Walkers come back.'

She wondered whether it would be better to speak to Mr Walker when he came in, or to wait until the morning to ask him to tell Miss Kropotka that she must leave.

'We must be going home, Mrs Fairhazel,' said Mr Walker, emerging from a reverie to discover the lateness of the hour. 'Perdita must be tired.'

'You may speak for yourself, Pa!' said Perdita. 'I am not in the least tired!'

She had enjoyed the evening a good deal more than she had expected to; and did not want it to come to an end. She had been seated between Mrs Fairhazel's two gentleman lodgers who had been flattering her in the most shameless way.

They were a pair of elderly bachelor brothers by the name of Wilkinson; one had been a sailor and the other a sergeant of Marines. Now, in their retirement, having found a comfortable berth in Mrs Fairhazel's house, they occupied themselves with a little carving, a little model boat building, and a great deal of keeping an eye on things. In particular, they liked to keep an eye on their fair landlady, whom they revered and cherished as if she was made of glass.

They had divined, from careful observations taken of Mrs Fairhazel's anxious preparation of her person, that she was, as they put it, sweet on the gentleman who had come to dinner—Mrs Fairhazel would have perished instantly of shame had she heard them—so naturally they were concerned to study, examine and approve him

To be honest, they were a little disappointed at first. He was a shade older than they'd hoped. But, on the other hand, he was clean, neat and gentlemanly, and not at all likely to drink too much and treat Mrs Fairhazel badly when in his cups. He was a well-educated man who knew his way about the world and spoke many languages and earned his living by teaching them; which was a good thing as a man without a trade was like a ship without a mast, a drifter and a danger to navigation.

But then again, he was the devil of a dreamer and hardly opened his mouth; which would have been hard on their fair landlady who was the best and the only listener they knew. But his little girl was a real charmer, you had to admit that, and the brothers vied with each other in paying her court.

Again Mr Walker drew attention to the lateness of the hour and again Perdita protested her total wide-awakeness.

'Early to bed and early to rise,' said one of the brothers sagaciously, 'makes a young lady healthy, wealthy and wise.'

'But what's the use,' cried Perdita, 'of being healthy, wealthy and wise if you have to sleep through everything?'

The brothers laughed delightedly and said that Perdita was as bright as paint, and asked good-humouredly, 'Where did you manage to find such a little charmer, Mr Walker?'

Mr Walker looked up in some confusion.

'I—I—' he began, when Perdita cried, 'Under a gooseberry bush, of course!'

The brothers glanced approvingly at one another at this evidence of the delicacy of Perdita's upbringing and scored a mark in Mr Walker's favour. They put down his quietness and abstraction to shyness and modesty in the presence of the fair sex. A right and proper attitude. They had always been so themselves, which, quite possibly, was why they had never married.

When the Walkers had taken their leave with warm handshakes for the father and a tiny crocodile carved out of ivory for his daughter, the brothers expressed moderate approval of Mr Walker, and unstinted praise for the child. Mrs Fairhazel was grateful although, to her shame, she herself would have reversed that order.

Similarly Perdita, as she and her father walked back through the black and blowy night, expressed pleased admiration for the brothers Wilkinson, and only a grudging tolerance of Mrs Fairhazel, who had provided them; while it was possible that Mr Walker would have reversed that order. He had been aware that the brothers had scrutinized him closely and he had been uneasy.

'You were very quiet, Pa,' said Perdita, clutching his arm. 'You should have been at our end of the table. We were talking about battles and islands and natives and witch-doctors. Did you know that witch-doctors can destroy somebody just by looking at them? Is it true, Pa?'

Mr Walker, whose thoughts had reverted to Mr Clarky, muttered, 'I would hope not, my dear.'

He quickened his pace. Perdita protested that she was wearing new shoes and could not walk so fast.

'Then I'll carry you!' he declared.

She offered no objection and he picked her up as easily as if she had been a baby again. In spite of his years, he was still a powerful man, and his inner anxiety lent him an added strength. Suddenly he had become frightened that he would lose everything; and he almost ran, with the child in his arms, back to the obscure house in the obscure street where they lived.

'Even if he remembers,' he thought, 'he will never find me here!'

Then he opened the dark door and he and the child vanished inside the dark house.

Not very far from Shoreditch, in Bishopsgate Street, another door opened, and a figure came anxiously out into the night. It was Brandyella, emerging from the public house next door. She was faced with a terrible journey. Not only was she buffeted by the wind and threatened with all manner of fearful shadows, but, in addition, she had to put up with the misery of a tilting street, a receding shop and a keyhole that kept sliding away from the key.

The friend who had accompanied her to the public house (she never went alone as it was not lady-like) had long since departed, at the request of the management in consequence of breakage and Irish song; so Brandyella was alone and in difficulties.

'Allow me! Allow me to 'elp you, miss!' said three or four gentlemen outside the shop.

'We're shut!' said Brandyella thickly. 'Come back in the mornin' . . . whichever one of ye wants to get in!'

'That's a 'ard thing to say to an old customer!' said the three or four gentlemen, raising three or four hard, round hats. 'Could you not oblige me with a 'alf dozen of the Famous and a snippet of cheese? Allow me, miss! Let me 'old the key'ole steady while you slips in the key!'

'I can't sell you nothin',' said Brandyella, graciously submitting to assistance. 'I'm only the bleedin' maid.'

'Never!' said the three or four gentlemen, mysteriously shrinking into one. 'I took you for a daughter of the 'ouse!'

'Bleedin' duchesses!' said Brandyella sourly.

'Amazin'! Why, when I was in 'ere the other day, for my 'alf dozen of the Famous, and that gentleman, Mr Walker, came in . . . You know the one I mean?'

'I know the one.'

'Agreeable gentleman, I'd say.'

'Better than his daughter.'

'Married man, is 'e?'

'Was.'

'Widower?'

'So that's the way of ye!' exclaimed Brandyella, having at last solved the enigma of which way the key turned.

'Live nearby?' inquired the gentleman, now offering assistance with the door-handle.

'In here.'

'No, no. I meant that Mr Walker, miss.'

'Down Shoreditch. Just off the High Street. Fruit and vegetable market. Plate up. Name of Streamer. Piano. Keep off! Keep off!' cried Brandyella, entering the shop and colliding with the hanging sausages.

'I'm much obliged to you, miss,' said the gentleman, lifting and replacing his hat again, precisely in the groove it had left round his head. 'Allow me to give you your key and 'elp you with shuttin' the door.'

When the Dollys returned from Bethnal Green, Brandyella, having failed to discover the whereabouts of her bed, was fast asleep on a sack in a corner; but fortunately the Dollys themselves were too mellow from Passover wine to notice her. They were cheerful and laughing, and even Mr Dolly was joining in a repetition of the last song of the night: *Only one kid*.

It was a children's song that stretched through all creation, as kid, cat, dog, stick, fire, water, ox, slaughterer, Angel of Death, and God himself came, one after another, to conquer and destroy what had gone before. Then Mr Dolly's voice faltered and his brow darkened, as if he felt that, even after God, there came another to swallow everything up: Standfast v. Standfast, in Westminster Hall.

I I

'There was a gentleman to see you, Mr Walker,' said Mrs Streamer, as her esteemed tenant came down the stairs in the morning. 'He called last night, after you had gone out.'

Mr Walker, who had been dressed for the street, responded in an extraordinary manner. He started, almost missed his footing, and stared at Mrs Streamer as if she had accused him of a murder.

'A—a gentleman . . . to see me?'

'Why, yes. He—'

'What did he want?' interrupted Mr Walker, quite fiercely. 'Did he say anything?'

'I was just going to tell you, Mr Walker,' returned Mrs Streamer, considerably taken aback. 'He wanted to change his lesson from this morning to Monday. He hoped it would not inconvenience you, and that, if he didn't hear from you, he would expect you on Monday morning. His name was Mr Gooch.'

Once again, Mr Walker's response was remarkable. A look of overwhelming relief came over his face.

'Mr Gooch! Oh, yes, Mr Gooch! Of course, of course!' he cried. 'Monday, did he say? Monday will be admirable! It will suit me admirably! Thank you, thank you, Mrs Streamer!'

Then, as if aware that his manner must have puzzled Mrs Streamer exceedingly, he explained, rather anxiously, that he had only been frightened in case the gentleman had turned out to be someone who had come for a lesson he had arranged and forgotten about; which would have cost him a pupil . . . and, in these hard times—

His explaining was cut short by a loud knocking on the front door. Mrs Streamer went to answer it. It was her first pupil of the morning—a small prodigy who proceeded, with a heavy scowl and a perspiring shilling, through the hall and into the music-room without uttering a word. The alluring prospect of making a brilliant match did not, as yet, appear to entrance her. Mrs Streamer turned back to her esteemed tenant on the stairs. He had gone. She sighed.

She had been lying in wait, so to speak, for Mr Walker, meaning to kill two birds with one stone: both to give him his message—which she had done—and to speak to him about Miss Kropotka—which she had not. She had decided against mentioning that delicate matter last night as she had remembered Perdita's attachment to Miss Kropotka; and had thought it would be better to catch Mr Walker on his own. But she had missed her chance. She shook her head and went in to her pupil.

Upstairs, Mr Walker divested himself of his coat and explained to Perdita that his lesson had been postponed. He was remarkably cheerful; it was as if he really had had a narrow escape. Of course it was ridiculous of him to worry and jump a foot in the air every time there was a knock on the door! It was a whole week since the unlucky meeting and nothing more had happened. That man had obviously decided that he had been mistaken. He smiled and settled down to read while Perdita went on singing her Russian song and accompanying herself with a spoon on the table. She thumped away like anything; so loudly, in fact, that not only did she drown the shouts of the fruit and vegetable market but also the sound of a second knocking on the front door, so that Mr Walker was happily spared that sudden clutching at his heart and wild start of alarm that had plagued him for the past week.

Having no assistance on a Saturday morning, and Mr Streamer needing his beauty-sleep, Mrs Streamer left her pupil to revolve upon the piano stool which resembled an enormous thumb-screw and went to the door.

'Good mornin', ma'am,' said the caller, a spry, rather shrunken little gentleman who courteously raised his hard, round hat. 'Might I 'ave the pleasure of a word with—' he consulted the brass plate—'Madame-Adeline-Streamer-Piannerforty?'

'I am Mrs Streamer, sir. What can I do for you?'

The gentleman, overcome with confusion at finding himself to be addressing the brass plate herself, raised his hat several times.

'Lessons, ma'am, lessons, if you would be so kind. On the forty.'

'Ah! You have a daughter, perhaps, who wishes to learn the pianoforte, sir? Please step inside.'

The gentleman skipped across the threshold and Mrs Streamer shut the door.

'How old is the child, sir? Has she had any training? One likes to begin very young, you know. The fingers are more supple . . .'

The gentleman looked downcast.

'No children, ma'am, not so much as a twinkle in the eye . . . there bein' no Mrs Clarky up to the present date . . . from which you will gather that the name is Clarky, and employed by Mr Leviticus of Gray's Inn. It's for meself, ma'am. I 'ope you don't consider me too far gone in the way of poor fingers.' He held them up. 'I just 'ad a fancy, ma'am, that I'd like to learn the forty. Nothin' in the public concertizin' line, of course; but just a simple chune. Can it be done, ma'am?' he inquired hopefully.

'Indeed it can, Mr Clarky!' said Mrs Streamer energetically. 'When would you like to begin?'

'I was rather 'opin', ma'am, that we might make a start this mornin'. Weekdays is out, as Mr Leviticus keeps me 'ard at it from Monday to Friday.'

'I have a lesson at the moment, Mr Clarky, a talented child—'

'Might I wait, ma'am?'

Mrs Streamer thought for a second, saw no objection, and conducted Mr Clarky into the music-room where he sat in a corner, attentive and admiring, while the talented child demonstrated the suppleness of her fingers by putting her thumb to her nose and waggling them defiantly at Mrs Streamer's back whenever it was turned.

At length the lesson came to an end and the talented one slid thankfully from the stool. Mr Clarky rose.

'I always,' he said, producing a small bag of sweets from his pocket, 'like to keep somethin' about me for the little ones. You are a very clever little girl, my dear,' he said, bestowing the sweets. 'And if ever I was to meet your mother, I would tell 'er so.'

With a highly suspicious look, the talented one fled.

Mr Clarky approached the piano, remarked in an admiring tone on the number of keys, wondered if he could ever become familiar with them, and inquired if the bust of Chopin was, by any chance, a likeness of Mr Streamer?

Mrs Streamer said it was not, and invited Mr Clarky to adjust the piano stool to a comfortable height. He did so, commenting on the ingenuity of the mechanism. Then he sat and pushed back his cuffs.

'I don't, of course,' he said with becoming humility, ''ope for anythin' as remarkable as what we 'ave just 'eard, ma'am. It wasn't in me mind to go into the art as deeply as that.'

Mrs Streamer admitted that the talented one was exceptional; but she had, after all, been studying for some time; and Mr Clarky was not to despair . . .

'No, ma'am, no. I know me limits. Just a chune on the forty 'ere, to play when I'm with me friends. That's all I ask. Somethin' like *Sally in our Alley*, or *There's a Tavern in the Town* . . . or there's a particular favourite by name of *The Fine Old English Gentleman*. Are you familiar with that one, ma'am?'

'I believe I have the music somewhere here,' said Mrs Streamer, beginning to search for it.

'I can 'ardly credit, ma'am,' said Mr Clarky, eyeing the keyboard and flexing his fingers by way of taking several quick fistfuls of air, 'that I'm sittin' 'ere, waitin' to be instructed in the art. Now don't trouble yourself, ma'am, if it's not to 'and. It goes like this!'

And he began to sing, in a loud, rasping roar:

'I'll sing you a good old song,
Made by a good old pate,
Of a fine old English gentleman
''Oo 'ad an old estate!'

Whatever he might have lacked in musicality, he more than made up for in enthusiasm. The whole house rang with his voice.

'Please, Mr Clarky—I do know the piece. There's no need to—'

'Beg pardon, ma'am! I forgot meself. I must 'ave disturbed the other people in the 'ouse. There are other people, I take it?'

'There's only Mr Walker and his daughter upstairs, and I'm sure that—'

'Mr Walker, did you say! Now I know a gentleman of that name. Is 'e—?'

But before Mr Clarky could pursue his inquiries, the music-room door opened and Mr Streamer's anxious head appeared. Mr Clarky looked vaguely disconcerted. Mr Streamer came into the room. He was wearing a violet-coloured quilted dressing-gown that Mrs Streamer had bought him, and was, inexplicably, clutching his violin-case. He peered uncertainly at Mr Clarky. Mrs Streamer explained that Mr Clarky was a new pupil. Mr Streamer looked relieved and Mr Clarky apologised for having disturbed him. Then observing the violin case, took the opportunity to remark upon the fact that it was an instrument to which he could never aspire.

'It needs soul,' said Mr Streamer. 'And passion, sir. Without passion, never approach the violin.'

Mr Clarky expressed admiration, and begged to see the instrument out of its case. He had never beheld one, he said, closer than from the gallery. He seemed to have transferred his interest from the piano to the violin in much the same way as he had, in Mr Dolly's shop, flitted from sausage to cheese to pickled cucumber. Somewhat reluctantly, Mr Streamer opened the case.

'Surely, my dear,' said Mrs Streamer, 'that is not your instrument?'

'Borrowed, my dear, borrowed. My own is—is being repaired at the moment. An—an accident . . . '

'A beautiful object,' said Mr Clarky, delicately lifting it out of the case. 'A Straddle Various, per'aps?'

'No, no!' said Mr Streamer hurriedly. 'It is not a—a Stradivarius. It is a Polish instrument. I—I borrowed it from Mr Walker, my dear—'

'Mr Walker again!' exclaimed Mr Clarky, keenly interested. ''e's cropped up again! A musical gentleman, is 'e?'

'No. He teaches languages, Mr Clarky.'

'Indeed, ma'am! A scholarly 'ouse'old, if I might say so. 'As 'e, might I be so bold as to ask, been with you long?'

'About eight years.'

'A single gentleman?'

'A widower, I understand.'

'Of course, of course! You mentioned a daughter. But forgive me, ma'am. You must think me very inquisitive. It was just that you said 'e teaches languages . . . and I've always 'ad an inclination that way meself. Do you think, ma'am, 'e'd take me on? Nothin' deep, of course, but just a snippet of French, say, and a slice of German?'

Mrs Streamer, recollecting Mr Walker's distress over the imagined loss of a pupil, thought it very likely that he would be glad of Mr Clarky.

'Then shall we strike while the iron's 'ot, ma'am?' cried Mr Clarky.

'But your lesson—'

Mr Clarky elevated his hat; then took two shillings from his pocket and laid them on the piano.

'I've travelled far enough in the art for one mornin', ma'am. Let me digest it. Just sittin' 'ere, with a forty on one side and a Various on the other,' he said, apparently under the impression that Various was a generic term covering all stringed instruments, 'I feel that I've made a beginnin'. After all, ma'am, I am but an infant in the musical line.'

'I will call him!' offered Mr Streamer eagerly.

He was anxious to escape before his wife resumed her inquiries into the fate of his violin, a wedding gift from Mrs Streamer herself, as he dreaded the infliction of further scars. Hastily he departed, in a rush of quilted violet, like a king pursued.

Mrs Streamer said, 'While we are waiting, Mr Clarky, we will begin with a simple scale.'

Mr Clarky, who had hoped to go upstairs, revolved upon the piano stool in a thoroughly lowering direction and faced the keyboard.

'Mr Walker!' came Mr Streamer's voice.

'What is it, Mr Streamer?'

'There's a gentleman to see you . . . about some lessons.'

'Thank you. I will be down directly.'

'You must set your mind to it, Mr Clarky,' said Mrs Streamer severely. 'I cannot teach you if you do not attend.'

'Apologies, ma'am. The art is very demandin'.'

There came footsteps, descending the stairs.

'Continue, Mr Clarky, continue. I will go and see if it is Mr Walker.'

Mrs Streamer, virtuous, conscientious, thoroughly good—and hoping to catch Mr Walker on his own for a moment and mention Miss Kropotka—firmly revolved her pupil back towards the keyboard and left the room.

'It is Mr Gooch back again, I suppose?' said Mr Walker, half-way down the stairs.

'No, Mr Walker. It is a Mr Clarky. But I wanted—'

Before she could initiate the delicate matter, Mr Clarky had played truant from the piano and popped out beside her.

'What a surprise!' he exclaimed, beholding his quarry, petrified upon the stairs. 'You'll 'ardly believe it, ma'am, but this is the very Mr Walker I was mentionin'! This is the very gentleman I 'ad in mind!'

12

Whatever doubts Mr Clarky might still have been harbouring, they were instantly dispelled by the ghastly look of shock on Mr

Walker's face. For a moment Mr Clarky feared for him; but the gentleman began to recover, thank God, a little. In a second or two he would be all right. Well, now for it!

'This is a real pleasure, sir, a real pleasure!' he declared; and then, to Mrs Streamer, 'I once 'ad the honour, ma'am, of knowin' Mr Walker, in earlier days!'

Mrs Streamer, seeing no present way of catching her esteemed tenant, sighed and withdrew. He turned back to Mr Walker, who was sensibly clutching the bannister rail for support.

'When I 'appened to see you the other day, sir, you could 'ave knocked me down,' he said, 'with a feather.'

Mr Walker, still speechless, stared at the spry little gentleman as if he wished that such a feather, or something more substantial, might come to hand.

'Who is it, Pa?'

A young girl appeared behind Mr Walker on the stairs; a very pretty young girl with a clear voice and a proud manner.

'It—it is an—an old acquaintance of mine, Perdita.'

Was it fancy, or did the gentleman extend an arm slightly, as if to keep the girl from coming nearer? Now why did he do that? Mr Clarky elevated his hat.

''ave I the pleasure, sir, of be'oldin' your daughter?'

'Yes, yes. This is my daughter . . . Perdita.'

Mr Clarky fumbled in his pocket.

'With your permission, sir, but I always like to keep somethin' about me for the little ones.'

He produced a bag of sweets and offered them to the girl. She looked at him coldly, every inch the lady.

'I am not,' she said, 'a little one. I am nearly thirteen.'

'Beg pardon, beg pardon!' cried Mr Clarky, lifting his hat to emphasise the apology. 'It's the poor light, miss, and I couldn't see you clear! So let me see what else I 'ave.' He fumbled again. 'I like to keep somethin' about me suitable for all ages!'

He produced a small tortoiseshell comb which he offered in place of the scorned sweets. The girl descended, a picture of elegance, and graciously accepted the comb.

'And when,' inquired Mr Clarky courteously, 'is the 'appy day, miss—the birthday, I mean?'

'February the fourteenth!' said father and daughter together.

They glanced at each other and smiled; as people do when they find themselves saying the same thing at once. Mr Clarky, having no cause to suspect that the date might be a fictitious one, thought nothing of it.

It had been invented, of course—almost drawn out of a hat—both to give father and daughter an actual day to celebrate on, and, more importantly, to fill in the gap that was the real beginning of Perdita's life. It had become, through the years, peculiarly precious to them; and any possibility of its loss filled Perdita with a placeless dread.

'Ah, St Valentine's Day!' said Mr Clarky, gallantly. 'I shouldn't be surprised, miss, if you wasn't born to be the Valentine of the 'ighest in the land!'

That pleased her and she came down another step, but not, Mr Clarky was surprised to see, the gentleman himself. He frowned and once more seemed to wish the girl away. Mr Clarky, respecting this, brought up the matter of lessons and wondered if Mr Walker might care to accompany him to the end of the street, during which pleasant stroll they might settle matters to their mutual convenience?

'I'll fetch your hat and coat, Pa!' said the girl, going back up the stairs.

A fondness there, very pleasing to observe.

'You can't go outside looking like that!'

And pride—oh, yes! And pride!

Mr Clarky waited until Mr Walker was suitably attired, and was interested to notice that the gentleman seemed almost humble compared with his daughter; but then you could never really tell what was inside. He would have to be careful . . .

The morning was bright and the fruit and vegetable market was in full and uproarious swing. Paper bags and apples flew, cabbages rolled, and, round the backs of stalls and barrows darted gangs of villainous little children, ready to steal anything and everything that was not actually nailed down.

Even as Mr Clarky strolled, with half an eye on Mr Walker beside him, a tiny criminal with bankrupt eyes extinguished one of them in a knowing wink, and thieved a pineapple off a stall, right under his very nose. Mr Clarky watched him vanish; then he tapped the stall-holder on the shoulder.

''ow much,' he inquired, 'is your fruit?'

'A shillin' to you, sir.'

Mr Clarky tendered the coin, but declined the pineapple that was offered in exchange.

'I've already 'ad it,' he said, nodding in the direction the diminutive felon had taken; 'in a manner of speakin'.'

He looked to see how his companion had taken the incident; and was pleased to see that Mr Walker was looking quite gentle.

'You are a very law-abiding man, Mr Clarky.'

'It's my livin', sir. One 'as to safeguard one's livin'.'

They strolled on; and Mr Clarky wondered how he might come to the point without antagonising the gentleman, for he suspected that, in spite of Mr Walker's quiet manner, there was a devil of a temper within. Mr Clarky was not unacquainted with Mr Walker's breed, and had had experiences that had left him humbled and shaken.

'Well, Mr Clarky,' muttered Mr Walker, not looking at his companion, 'I believe you wanted to discuss some—some lessons with me.'

Mr Clarky sighed. The gentleman was making it plain that he was unwilling even to meet Mr Clarky half way. Now why was that? What had he to lose? What had happened to him in all the years that he should be content to go about like this, to live like this, and to—to raise his hat like this to an ordinary street-trader who wished him good morning? The girl felt differently, that was plain!

'I 'ave no wish, Mr Walker, sir, to intrude upon your privacy,' he began cautiously. 'I respect your right of Personal Liberty, which you will find in Stephen's *Laws of England*, edition of forty-four, as 'avin' reference to your power of locomotion, of changin' your situation, of movin' your person to whatsoever place your own inclination may direct, unless by due course of law.'

They had come to the end of the little street where it spilled out upon the main thoroughfare. Mr Clarky noticed that the daffodil-seller, deep in her golden nest, had, at the mention of 'law', turned all her yellow trumpets, like hearing instruments, upon them. Mr Clarky proposed extending the stroll a little way towards Holborn. Mr Walker shrugged his shoulders, and agreed. They

89

sauntered on, until Mr Walker paused to gaze into the window of a jeweller's.

'If,' he muttered, and Mr Clarky was relieved to hear him begin the conversation, 'you have such respect for my personal liberty, why have you come to me here?'

'Believe me, sir, if it wasn't necessary, I wouldn't be 'ere, standin' next to you in the open street, when I might be takin' the air in 'yde Park,' said Mr Clarky, allowing a note of reproach to creep into his voice.

Mr Walker smiled faintly, which, in Mr Clarky's experience, was a good sign, and encouraged him to proceed: 'You must come forward, sir! You really must!'

Mr Walker's smile vanished and was replaced by a frown that rapidly deepened into a scowl. It was a scowl that Mr Clarky recognised . . . although perhaps no one else who knew Mr Walker would have recognised it in him. Mr Clarky held off while Mr Walker fixed his gaze on a gold locket and chain that would have set off his daughter's young neck and bosom most handsomely.

'There is no *must* about it, Mr Clarky.'

'I beg pardon, sir, but it just slipped out. I spoke from the 'eart, if you will pardon the expression.'

The scowl passed, and in its place came a look of earnest inquiry as Mr Walker attempted to decipher the price on the locket and chain.

'Three pound, sir,' said Mr Clarky, obligingly; and was moved to see Mr Walker's attention being transferred to a silver bracelet that was a matter of ten shillings. A strange man . . .

A small individual of tender years—or they would have been tender had not the city streets toughened them to the consistency of iron—was loitering near the jeweller's open door. Mr Clarky watched him shrewdly. The individual sidled effortlessly closer to the threshold. He seemed to have little eyes all round his head.

''ave a bag of sweets!' said Mr Clarky, suddenly producing one and thrusting it under the individual's startled nose.

The child gave a shriek of fright, snatched the bag and fled in guilty confusion.

'It is the duty of a citizen,' said Mr Clarky, 'to prevent a crime bein' committed by any means that comes to 'and. Which brings me, in a roundabout way, sir, back to why I'm 'ere. To prevent a crime, sir.'

'What crime?'

'Why, Standfast vee Standfast, of course, sir!'

Mr Walker looked astonished, genuinely astonished. Every feature expressed total incomprehension. Was it possible that the affair that was shaking a large part of Gloucestershire and had resounded, day after day, in Westminster Hall, that was the talk of Gray's Inn and Chancery Lane and the nightmare of Mr Leviticus, who represented the family, was entirely unknown to him? Or was he so indifferent to everything that the price of a trinket now mattered more to him than the fate of a great estate?

'I know nothing—nothing at all about any—any Standfast v. Standfast!'

'But your friend, sir, Mr Dolly of Bishopsgate Street. 'e's on the jury. 'asn't 'e spoke of it?'

'No, no. I have hardly seen him since he began his duty. He said nothing. He—he is very conscientious, you know. He would not talk about the case with me. What is it? What is this crime, then? What is Standfast v. Standfast, Mr Clarky? Please tell me.'

'There's a claimant, sir, a claimant 'oo's put 'imself forward as bein' Sir Robert Standfast—'

'Good God!'

The man was shaken, no doubt about that, thought Mr Clarky. The man was startled, could hardly believe his ears! The man, in a manner of speaking, looked as if he didn't know whether he was on his head or his heels. Which was hardly surprising as it wasn't every day that a man hears that someone has come forward claiming to be *himself*!

With great agitation Mr Walker protested that the claim must fail, that it was impossible that it should succeed. Mr Clarky shook his head, explained all the circumstances and confided that Mr Leviticus himself had had the gravest doubts about the outcome. Angrily Mr Walker brushed everything aside. The claim must fail!

'And if it don't, sir?'

'That—that is no concern of mine!'

'With respect, sir, it is.'

'Then what of my right of personal liberty, Mr Clarky?'

'Which you 'old only by due course of law, sir. Now, by

knowin' what you do know, and still 'oldin' back, you will be aidin' and abettin' a perjury, sir. In a manner of speakin', you will be compoundin' a felony. And Mr Leviticus and me would be accessories to the fact. No, sir, you must come forward.'

'You cannot make me.'

'With respect, sir—and with the deepest respect!—we would 'ave no choice but to issue a writ of subpoena. Better by far, sir, for a gentleman like yourself to come forward of your own accord. After all, what can you 'ave to lose by it? And—again with respect, sir—God knows that you and your daughter would 'ave a great deal to gain!'

'What can you know of such things?' cried Mr Walker, almost in a shout.

The man had flown into the most alarming passion. Perhaps he was a little off his head? His father, recollected Mr Clarky, had sometimes been strange. But he calmed down . . .

'Let us wait, then. Perhaps the jury will throw out the case after all.'

'And if they don't, and you come forward? What then? Why, the gentleman from Australia gets sent for trial for perjury and goes to prison for it. Not right, sir. As we agreed before, it is the duty of a citizen to prevent a crime. Your way, sir, wouldn't be so much boltin' the stable door after the 'orse 'ad gone, it would be more like shootin' the 'orse and the groom! And speakin' of prevention, sir, I think it would be advisable to make some little purchase out of the window to avoid any unpleasantness.'

The jeweller, having grown uneasy about the two men loitering outside his shop, had despatched his apprentice for a constable, who was now approaching. Mr Walker went into the shop and purchased the silver bracelet. He had been meaning to do so anyway. When he came out Mr Clarky nodded shrewdly.

'Very pretty, sir, very pretty indeed. But, with respect, I fancy the young lady would 'ave liked the gold object better. I'll leave you with that thought, sir—with the deepest respect, of course—and the others we talked of. Everythin' to gain, sir, and nothin' to lose. Don't put us to the trouble of a subpoena, sir!'

13

After Mr Clarky had left him, he stood outside the jeweller's shop, with his hand in his pocket, clutching the bracelet he had bought for Perdita. The street was crowded and passers-by kept jostling him; but they might have been flies. A woman with a bloated basket and a bloated child angrily demanded to know who he thought he was, standing in her way like a lump of wood?

'Mr Walker ... I am Mr Walker,' he responded helplessly.

'Then why don't you *walk*?'

He nodded, and moved on. The meeting with Mr Clarky had shaken him severely; he had been dealt quite a blow. He was still feeling stunned, and in no condition to go straight back home. He had to collect his thoughts. Thoughts! Whose thoughts? Walker's ... Walker's ...

He stopped again and stared at a reflection in a shop window. Who looked back? Mr Walker, gentle, respected Mr Walker, moderately successful teacher of languages ... Mr Walker ...

A man and a woman, arguing bitterly over a bottle, knocked into him and asked him if he thought he was a lamp-post?

'I am Mr Walker,' he responded unhesitatingly.

He had been Mr Walker for a good many years; in fact he had been Mr Walker for more years than he had been anything else. He had chosen that name for himself with great care. He could still remember the solemnity of his feelings when he had taken it in place of—Standfast. He had, at that time, meant it to symbolise so much in the way of determination and hope. Walker. Well, it had been a long, long walk; but he had arrived in the end. 'It is Mr Walker, my dear!' 'Dear Mr Walker, how pleasant to see you!' 'Come in, Mr Walker!' He was, he felt, in the deepest sense, a self-made man, and everything about him bore witness to the fact that he had come by the materials honestly. So why, why should he be disturbed to find out that what he had long ago discarded was now being claimed by another man? Why should he feel so frightened and angry?

'Oh, for God's sake, let him have it!' he exclaimed.

'You mind yer bloody business!' said the woman, believing him to be arbitrating between herself and her companion in their dispute over the bottle.

He walked away quickly as the woman was drunk and likely to attack him. He reached the market, and stopped to gaze at the massed yellow trumpets of the daffodils. He wanted to buy them all for Perdita. Then he remembered he had already bought her the silver bracelet. Surely that was enough. He really ought not to spoil her. Parting with ten shillings had been absurdly spendthrift of him. He had been meaning to buy himself a new pair of shoes. God knew, he needed them! But, as always, everything turned out to be for the child, as if he was everlastingly in her debt. Everything, everything . . . and yet, in the end, nothing. But that was not true—

He went into the house, eagerly clutching the bracelet in his pocket. Mrs Streamer had been waiting for him. She came out of the music-room in a rush, waving her fat white hands at him as if he was a piano of an unusual design that she was anxious to play.

'Mr Walker—oh, Mr Walker! Might I speak with you for a moment?'

He paused, nodded, smiled . . . and was every inch Mr Walker.

'Mr Walker, you must tell her to go! I cannot have it any longer! The room, the house, everything smells of her scent! People are beginning to talk! And—and Mr Streamer's room . . . he needs it. Mr Streamer is—is—She must go! And—and I do not think it is good for your dear Perdita to be so attached to a woman like that. And she neglects her music. There is my concert on Tuesday and she has hardly practised. She must go! I would tell her myself but she would not understand me. I leave it to you, Mr Walker. As soon as possible!'

Mrs Streamer talked at a tremendous rate and got very breathless. It had all been stored up inside her and now it came out. Like most kind people when they are at last brought to the pitch of complaining, she rather overdid it, and then was ashamed.

'Please don't think,' she said, worrying her fringe, 'that I don't like her. I'm sure she is a very fine person—in her own country. And, of course, she is very lovely. No one could deny that. It is

94

just that she is not—not *suitable*, Mr Walker. But I leave it to you. You must do as you think best. As long as she goes, Mr Walker, I don't really mind. There is no need, by the way,' she added as an afterthought, 'to mention anything to Mr Streamer. I don't want to worry him. He is such a sensitive man.'

With a troubled smile and a final despairing wave, she went back into the music-room and began to play something that required a good deal of crossing of the hands.

Mr Walker went slowly up the stairs. He paused outside Katerina's door, where her scent absolutely stifled the air; then he heard her voice above. She was with Perdita.

Mrs Streamer's demands would have to wait. He felt angry with her. He suspected that her chief reason for wanting Katerina out of the house was on account of that worthless husband of hers. Most likely she'd caught him with Katerina. She was a fool. She ought to have thrown *him* out. The man was incorrigible. Now she came tearfully to him with her, 'Mr Walker—oh, Mr Walker!' My God! What a dismal tune she was playing!

He was still standing outside Katerina's room, expending his fretful anger on Mrs Steamer who was pouring out her soul in music, when he heard Perdita and Katerina begin singing the Russian song Perdita had learned. Ordinarily it would not have displeased him, but at the present moment it seemed intolerable.

Mrs Steamer had been right, of course, about the woman's influence on Perdita. She had only been voicing, in her ridiculous way, an uneasiness he himself had felt but had been too cowardly to express or even to hint at. He had always been the soul of courtesy to Katerina, never failing to admire her, to be delighted to welcome her upstairs, and to be grateful for the bad Russian food she kept bringing back from Houndsditch.

Her supply of money seemed as inexhaustible as her scent. Perhaps she was selling off some of the pieces of jewellery with which she adorned herself? He supposed that she had managed to bring them with her from Russia. She had left there following some tragic incident about which she was disinclined to talk; and then she had had a bad time when she had come to London, and she did not want to be reminded of that either.

Naturally Mr Walker had respected her desire for privacy, even though he knew that, under the circumstances, it was a stupid thing to do. But what else could be expected of a man like Mr Walker, a man of courteous trust, of unfailing patience and humility? In this, in his trust of people, he had modelled himself on his friend, Mr Dolly; but the humility was something entirely of his own. Whenever he thought about it, he felt he was approaching nearer and nearer to some imaginary self.

There was laughter from upstairs, followed by a cry of delight from Perdita. How the devil were they communicating with each other? Was it, perhaps, something instinctive with them? He loathed and despised such an idea. It suggested that there were seeds in Perdita of which he knew nothing, and that they were responding to Katerina as if there was a kinship between the woman and his child. He could not bear the thought that Perdita might be closer to such a woman than she was to him.

The door upstairs opened, and Perdita called down: 'Is that you, Pa?'

'Yes, my dear.'

'Then come up quickly, Pa. Katerina is here!'

The girl's voice calling him, and the touch of imperiousness about it, gave him pleasure. He held the bracelet in his pocket, and suddenly felt how unimportant everything was when, at this very moment, he had it in his power to delight his child. He ran up the remaining stairs as eagerly as a young man.

Perdita greeted him in high excitement. She held out her hand.

'Look, Pa, look what dearest, darling, lovely Katerina has just given me!'

She was holding a gold locket and chain. They were a good deal more handsome than the ones in the jeweller's shop that he had been unable to afford. His fingers tightened helplessly on the ten-shilling article in his pocket. He felt it bend out of shape. Thank God he hadn't come into the room with it in his hand! The look of disparagement that would have come into Perdita's eyes would have been unbearable. He remembered Mr Clarky's words: 'The young lady would have liked the gold object better.' Of course she would! Only a fool would have chosen silver instead of gold.

'Look, look at it, Pa!'

'It—it is very pretty,' he said, 'my child.'

'It was my mother's,' said Katerina to him, in Russian.

She smiled at him, her usual gleaming, knowing smile. The

96

room stank and reeked of her scent. He did not want to take his hand out of his pocket, in case the paltry bracelet had caught on his sleeve. He felt humiliated and wretched. It was not the humility he had made for himself, but another, that fitted him like a suit of nails.

'You—you should not have given it. You must keep it. It—it is too valuable for a child.'

Particularly when it so outshone the gift her father had bought her.

'But I love to give. It will suit her. She has nothing of gold. Only silver. Let her have gold!'

Let her have gold! Yes indeed, let her have gold.

'What is she saying, Pa?'

'That—that the chain was her mother's.'

'It is beautiful! And what did you say?'

'I said that—that she ought to keep it.'

'No, no! She gave it to me! I didn't ask, I promise! And—and anyway it's broken! Look! On the catch. It's been pulled and the links have come apart. But we can get it mended, can't we, Pa? It won't cost much!'

No. It wouldn't cost much. Even a Mr Walker might be able to afford it. Perhaps he could sell the wretched trinket in his pocket to cover the jeweller's charge? Even as he thought it, he knew that it was a contemptible, self-pitying thought. The repair would cost no more than a shilling. Again he remembered Mr Clarky. 'Nothing to lose and everything to gain.'

He took his hand out of his pocket; the bracelet remained safely behind. Was it possible that he had contemplated, for an instant, changing his way of life for the sake of a trinket, when all the urgings and pleadings and threats to which he had been subjected earlier had failed to move him?

'Mrs Streamer says you have been neglecting your music,' he said to Perdita, with an effort to restore himself to everyday concerns. 'She says you have not practised for her concert on Tuesday. I was looking forward, Perdita, to hearing you perform best of all.'

'Very well, Pa,' said Perdita, still in high good humour over her present, and anxious to show it to everybody. 'I'll go downstairs right away and ask her if she can give me a lesson now.'

She ran from the room. He waited until he heard her go in to Mrs Streamer, then he turned to Katerina. She was sitting on the couch, engaged in playing with her gown. She was twitching the skirt so that the fur round the hem danced and jumped round her ankles. She was utterly absorbed in herself.

'I am sorry to have to tell you,' he began abruptly, 'but you must understand that—that the room is needed. I am afraid that you must find somewhere else.'

He realised that he had sounded harsh, and regretted it. He would much preferred to have been gentle. After all, the woman had done him no harm. But somehow he felt that any gentleness on his part would have put him at a disadvantage.

She left off playing with her gown and looked up at him incredulously. He realised that he had spoken in English and so was forced to go through the same painful procedure in Russian. Her look of incredulity deepened.

'What has happened?' she asked. 'Why do you say this to me?'

'Nothing has happened. The room. I told you. That is all.'

'That is all?'

'Yes. The room. It is better that you leave as soon as possible.'

'Ah! I see it! It is because I gave the child gold! That is it. You are angry, even a little jealous, perhaps? Very well, I take the present back.'

'No. It has nothing to do with that.'

'Then what? Ah! Of course! The woman downstairs! She hates me. She knows her husband looks at me and would like to come to my room. She is stupid. And he is an old goat.'

'It has nothing to do with Mrs Streamer,' he said, unwilling to appear merely as Mrs Streamer's emissary.

'Then I do not understand. Perhaps it is you—you, Mr Walker? Why? Did you not bring me here? Have we not been friends? Have I not brought food into the house, good food? Why have you changed?'

These were questions he made no attempt to answer; instead he confined himself to repeating that her room was needed and that she must go. It was true that he relented sufficiently to offer whatever assistance he could, but nothing would deflect him from his purpose. Katerina, who had risen from the couch, was pacing the room in evident agitation. God knew what she was thinking of him! That he was a monster of cruelty most likely!

Suddenly she halted and stared at him. For a moment there was still anger in her eyes; then she smiled, her gleaming, knowing smile.

'I understand. You are frightened of me. That is it. It is you who want to come to my room, and you are frightened. Yes, I understand. It is not easy for you. You are frightened I will say no. Poor Mr Walker! But you should not be so—so timid.'

Her smile broadened. Her extraordinary beauty gave her a complacency and self-assurance that amounted almost to stupidity. It was plainly inconceivable to her that she could fail to arouse desire, although whether she could satisfy it was another matter.

Mr Walker grew red with anger. It was not that Katerina's looks had failed to impress him, it was her suggestion that he should creep downstairs while Perdita was asleep that had repelled him. There was nothing she could have said that would have offended him more or made him even more determined that she should leave the house.

It was possible that she guessed at something of the kind. She took a pace back, stared at him uncertainly, then said, 'You are frightened of the child. Yes, that's it! You are frightened of the child.'

'Get out!'

'You are a fool, Mr Walker, and you will pay for it . . . you and your rubbish up there!' She gestured towards the ceiling and the loft above it, where the old trunk was, and the old things in it. 'She was not alone. There was another one, you know. And it is the other one you will have to pay!'

Before he could speak, before he could seize her and shake out of her whatever it was she knew, she had rushed from the room; and he could hear Perdita already coming back upstairs. He leaned against the wall and hoped with all his heart that his face, which had endured so much of wind and weather, so much of bitterness and pain, so much of harsh deprivation and aching solitude, would not now betray the fear and anguish that raged within.

14

If wild, destructive wishes had been slates, holes in the road, brewers' carts, omnibuses or careering cabs, Katerina Kropotka would have been mangled a million times before she had gone half a mile through the town. But wishes, however impassioned, remain wishes and the woman survived.

She had left the house in a violent hurry, delaying only to put on a furious hat, snatch something from a drawer, and renew her fading scent. She rushed through the streets thinking only of revenge. Again, if wishes had been diseases, sicknesses or insects in the brain, Mr Walker would have been in a bad way; but wishes were only wishes and needed action to bring them to fruition. She hated the man, not just because he had told her to get out, but because he had refused her; she was as disastrous as a bad fairy.

Presently she reached a looming neighbourhood, close to the river, of tall brick walls, ropes, hoists, and hangman's doorways, twenty feet in the air. They were warehouses, although, as the bad fairy approached, they might better have been called *be*warehouses.

Anxiously she scanned the signboards until she found the premises she sought. She muttered with satisfaction and went in through a side door.

Saturday morning and not much doing. A youth in green baize sleeves and brown apron sat behind the counter, picking his nose with the safe end of a pen. His eyes, on the small side, widened to almost normal proportions when he saw what a beauty the wind had blown in.

'Your servant, ma'am! And what can the 'ouse do for you in the 'olesale line?'

'I vant to see Meestair Kozlowski!'

Katerina's English was as bad as her Polish, which was as bad as her Russian. She seemed to have more a loan of languages than a gift for them.

The youth examined the end of his pen.

'Business or—ah—pleasure, ma'am?'

'Vy you ask? I vant to speak vith him.'

'Business is business, ma'am. Pleasure in this 'ouse ain't allowed.' He spoke feelingly.

'It is business. Private business.'

The youth brooded. Katerina touched his sleeve impatiently. The youth yielded.

'Seein' as 'ow it's Saturday mornin' and the cat's away,' he jerked his head in the direction, it might be supposed, of his employer's sanctum, 'I don't see 'ow it can do any 'arm for the mice to 'ave a game. If you'd care to take me arm, ma'am, I'll show you the way.'

He lifted the counter and gallantly conducted the beauty down lanes and passages and corridors of nailed-up packing cases, until they reached a small office, which was really no more than another packing-case, with a glass door. The youth tapped on it importantly with his pen, and opened it without waiting for a reply.

'Visitor for you, Kozlowski. Against the rules but I made an exception.'

Kozlowski, who had been writing in a ledger, looked up. His face went as white as the page in front of him.

'What are you doing here?'

He spoke in Polish. The youth departed, baffled; doubtless regretting that he had not made the use of plain, eavesdroppable English a prior condition of the favour. The shock on the one hand and the eager smile on the other had looked promising.

Katerina did not answer. Instead she moved, as much as was possible, round the tiny office, as if to imbue every cranny of it with her scent.

'I thought we agreed that—'

'How important you are, my David!' she exclaimed admiringly. 'How distinguished, with your own room and your desk!'

She seated herself on it, crossed her knees and began playing with her gown, making the fur round her ankles dance.

'You should not be here!'

'Are you ashamed of me? Have I grown ugly? I do not think so. You no longer love me. That is it. My darling has forgotten me.'

She sighed and looked sad.

'Of course I have not forgotten!' muttered David, with an anxious look at the glass door.

'And the love?'

'You know that I love you!' he said; and then, as if fearing that she might be misled by the look on his face, added, 'I will always love you!'

She nodded with satisfaction. He was still her darling little David. He was still her abject slave.

'Have you no wine to offer me, or a little brandy, even?'

'No, no! We do not keep anything here.'

Again she looked sad.

'Ah! There was a time when you would have gone through fire to fetch me a glass of wine, my David! I have lost you. I know it.'

'Katerina, please! Don't make fun of me!'

He spoke with real anguish, partly because he was frightened they would be overheard, and partly because her presence always excited him. He wanted more than anything to have done with her and, at the same time, he wanted more than anything to make love to her again; even though he knew, in his heart of hearts, that neither would happen. They were bound to each other irrevocably.

'I do not make fun of you. I swear it!' She reached forward and gripped his wrist.

He was amazed. She hardly ever touched him. Something extraordinary must have happened to make her do such a thing. He put his other hand over hers. Her skin was like ice.

'What is it, Katerina?'

'They are the ones! The old man and the child! I have found out. I have found the things . . . everything. Even the violin! You must go to them! He is frightened. I don't know why. He must have done something. I can tell. There is something he is hiding. Perhaps it was then, in the village. Perhaps he killed somebody. It must be something. He is so frightened.'

She spoke urgently. Her eyes were glittering with excitement. She really believed that some monstrous crime was being concealed. She could imagine no other reason for the man's fear. It was quite beyond her to understand that a man might be frightened of something else, might be frightened only of a lie being found out; a lie that, having been sustained for a lifetime, had gathered so much substance—like a huge snowball—that it had come to loom far larger than life.

'You must go to him. And to her. You will be like a—a bomb!' said Katerina, pleasurably.

He took his hand away from hers. He was confused and deeply afraid. He did not know what to say.

'You will come today! You will come back with me!'

'No, no! We—we cannot be together!'

'Then I will go first. You come later. I want to see it.'

'No . . . no. Today is—is impossible!'

'Why impossible? Is this not more important? Is not this something you have always dreamed of?'

'It—it was a long time ago.'

'She is still the same! She is still your sister!'

David felt the sweat run down his face. His wrist hurt under Katerina's ferocious grip. Her words had thrown him into a wild, unreasoning dread. He knew the cause of it, but even now could not bring himself to tell her. He too had his snowball . . . and it was freezing him.

'I—I must think about it.'

'What is there to think? I want you to come. Like a bomb!'

'You want me to destroy them, don't you? I see it now!' muttered David, trying to find in anger a means of escape. 'You just want me to be your instrument. Again!'

She loosened her grip on his wrist and began, gently, to massage the deep indentations her nails had made. It was necessary to placate him a little. But that was easy . . .

'But is that not what you have always wanted, my darling?' she murmured. 'To be my—my *instrument*?'

She observed, from the sudden look he gave her, that her power over him had not diminished. She was pleased.

'Yes, I have always wanted to be—*that*! But you always refused.'

'Always? Have you forgotten that time?'

'No. I will never forget that.'

'Was it not exciting?'

He nodded. He recollected perfectly the excitement she referred to; and he recollected a certain dreadful event that had preceded it. With him, the memories were always separate; with her, he sensed that they were together. He was terrified of her.

'Then you will do as I ask?'

'I—I—'

'I will come to your room. I promise.'

'No, no! You will be seen!'

'Then you must come to me.'

'But the danger?'

'All the better! A little excitement, eh? But no. You are afraid.'

'Yes! I am afraid!'

'You come at night. Very late. They will be asleep. You know the house?'

'Yes, yes!'

'My room is on the first floor. There is a window at the back. There are curtains . . . grey, like a graveyard! I will leave it unlatched. And—and I will leave a ladder. It is settled. You will come tonight?'

'No . . . I cannot come tonight.'

She frowned. Had she perhaps misjudged him? She leaned towards him, bringing her face so close that he could see the spots of dried perfume on her neck. Momentarily he closed his eyes. Katerina's scent did not so much cover a multitude of sins as suggest them, strongly.

'You will come tomorrow, then?'

'No. I—I must be somewhere else. I will come on Monday night.'

'My darling! Then afterwards . . . in the morning, you will come back and do as I ask?'

'Yes.'

She nodded. 'You see? I trust you. And look! I have brought a little present for my darling lover!'

She fumbled in her purse and drew out a gold watch on a torn velvet ribbon.

'Is it not pretty? You must wear it all day on Monday. It will tell you when it is right to come to your lady's window.'

She held it out. He shook his head.

'You stole it!'

'If you wish to think such things of me, my David, you must think them. Your thoughts are always your own. But, come! It was my—my father's. Yes. It belonged to my father! He gave it to me as he was dying. He said: "Here is my gold watch, my beautiful Katerina. Take it and give it to whoever wins your heart." There now. Take it with my heart!'

He hesitated for an instant; then he took the watch.

Long after his visitor had gone, David Kozlowski sat at his desk with his head clasped in his hands. The watch, unwound, lay beside the ledger, telling a silent lie. From time to time the young man lifted his head and stared at it; then returned to the comfort of his hands. He knew himself to be both doomed and damned; but there was nothing he could do. Fear and desire tortured him equally and he did not know which way to turn. Perhaps had wishes been knives, knotted scarves or suffocating pillows, Katerina Kropotka would have been a subject for judicial inquiry. But wishes were not enough; and a little more was needed than the tears that trickled through his fingers and blotted the ledger in front of him. He was crying like a child.

15

The Dollys had visitors: the baron, Mrs Brill and Mrs Fairhazel. As it was the afternoon of the Sabbath, and Passover to boot, Mrs Brill looked upon Mrs Fairhazel as if she was an intrusive insect. Mrs Brill, being Jewish and a cantor's wife, felt herself to be twice chosen: once by Mr Brill and once by God. She was a short, stout, owlish lady for whom nothing was holy enough. Had she come to the gates of Heaven and not seen a *mezuzah* on the doorpost, she would not have gone in. She went about with her nose in the air, she sat with her nose in the air, and only lowered it over Mr Dolly's chopped liver, which, after receiving sworn assurances that it was properly *kosher*, she gobbled like a vulture. She embarrassed Mr Brill dreadfully, and he longed to catch her out.

'All this,' said the good lady to Mrs Fairhazel, 'must seem very strange to you, my dear.'

She was referring to the unleavened bread and the Dollys'

Passover crockery; and she smiled a tight little smile as if to say, 'Unfortunate Gentile! But if God has not chosen you, pray do not expect anything other than the barest civilities from me.'

Gently Mr Brill suggested that Passover customs were probably not strange to Mrs Fairhazel, whose husband had been Jewish. He reminded Mrs Brill that he himself had conducted the funeral service.

It was to no avail. Mrs Brill merely said, 'God rest his soul,' ate some more chopped liver and smiled her tight little smile as if to say, 'He would be sitting here among us now, if he hadn't married a *shicksa*.'

Mr Brill, sensing the derogatory term in his wife's expression, retaliated by humming a melody from a mass by Josef Haydn, and hoped he would be asked what it was.

They were in the parlour. The Dollys' elder daughters were out, walking with their admirers, and had reluctantly taken Miriam with them. Jonathan was downstairs, patiently awaiting the demise of the Sabbath in order to open the shop for a couple of hours.

Mrs Dolly wished he would come upstairs and help with the entertaining as Mr Dolly just sat in a corner with a face as long as one of his own sausages and hardly opened his mouth. It was that case, of course—Mrs Dolly could not bring herself to utter the name of it even inside her own head. It was horrible how other people's quarrels could make such a misery of a good man!

Courteously she helped her sister-in-law to some more chopped liver and glanced ruefully at her friend, Mrs Fairhazel. She was dying to know how Mrs Fairhazel's dinner had gone, and if Mr Walker had shown any more definite inclinations when he had had the opportunity of seeing the extent of Mrs Fairhazel's domain. She wanted to know what Mrs Fairhazel had worn, how she had done her hair, and if Mr Walker had noticed either. She wanted to know who else had been present—particularly if the Russian woman had come—and if, by any chance, Mr Walker had brought flowers. But Mrs Fairhazel had only managed to get out something about the brothers Wilkinson before Mrs Brill looked up from her plate and inquired, 'Are they Jewish?' in a tone of voice that suggested that, if they were not, they had no business to be mentioned on the Sabbath.

Mr Brill hummed an air by Mozart; and Mrs Dolly wondered how her brother could have married such a woman.

'And did Miss Kropotka come?' she asked, determined to satisfy at least a part of her curiosity.

'Kropotka? Kropotka? Is that a Jewish name?' inquired the holy one, with a laden piece of *matzoh* raised, like a tablet of the law.

Mr Brill broke openly into a melody from the opera *Norma*; but the holy one ignored it. Her plate was empty and she felt obliged to extend the glumness that had come over her to the company.

'A terrible thing about your uncle,' she said, not so much to Mr Dolly as to the table beside him, on which there was another dish of chopped liver. 'That such a thing should happen to a Jewish family! But God will punish those responsible!'

Mr Dolly frowned. The terrible thing referred to had been the death of his uncle, old Mr Dolska. It had taken place some months before, but he had only heard about it in the last few days, when it had seemed like a mere drop compared with the monstrous ocean of Standfast v. Standfast that daily drowned him.

'He was getting on, you know. He must have been more than eighty . . .'

'He was a *Jew*!' said Mrs Brill reproachfully.

'*O Isis und Osiris!*' burst out Mr Brill, and began to walk up and down the room.

'Yes, he was a Jew,' admitted Mr Dolly with no great enthusiasm. Of course it was sad about the old gentleman; but it wasn't as if he had been cut off in his prime. It was true that there had been unpleasant goings-on at the time; but who could say that he wouldn't have passed away anyway? After all, at eighty—

It seemed that there had been trouble in a camp of Russian soldiers just outside the town. Someone had been killed and soldiers had gone into the town looking for Jews to blame. They'd done some damage to Mr Dolska's furniture factory and broken his windows. Of course it was a nasty business; but to say that it had broken the old gentleman's heart and finished him off was ridiculous. And what was even more ridiculous was that attitude of the son, Mr Dolly's cousin. Because he hadn't got any compensation for the damage he had decided to shake the dust of Poland from his feet and come and settle in London.

This did not please Mr Dolly. He liked to help people, yes; but his cousin, judging by his letters, already spoke good English and was very comfortably off. There was nothing Mr Dolly could do for him. And what was more, he would come and find out that Dolly the Provider, Dolly the Joseph in Egypt, Dolly the Great, was nothing more than a humble shopkeeper, and Pharaoh's palace was a humble, rather smelly shop.

Ordinarily such thoughts would not have occurred to Mr Dolly; but Standfast v. Standfast had made him cautious, suspicious and inclined to turn over every stone for the unworthy motive that might lie beneath it.

'What a pretty gown that is that you are wearing,' said Mrs Dolly to her friend. 'Did you wear it for the dinner?'

She glanced apprehensively at her sister-in-law; but that good lady had been helped to more chopped liver so she contented herself with looking contemptuous.

Mrs Fairhazel was about to embark eagerly on a detailed exposition of what she had worn, what she had served for the main course, what time the Walkers had arrived and what time they had left, when Jonathan came up from the shop with the extraordinary news that Mr Walker himself was downstairs.

Mrs Fairhazel felt her heart beat rapidly and her cheeks grow warm. At once she was horribly ashamed. She was behaving like a foolish schoolgirl who had just fallen wildly in love for the first time. She was old enough, alas, to know better. She hoped desperately that nobody would notice; but at the same time she couldn't help hoping that *he* would have an inkling when he came upstairs . . .

But he wasn't coming upstairs. He only wanted to speak to Mr Dolly. Perhaps it was as well. Had he come, she knew she ought to have helped things along; but the effort would have been beyond her . . .

'You must *insist* that he comes upstairs!' Mrs Dolly was saying to her husband. 'You must tell him that we will all be very hurt if he does not come to see us.'

Mr Dolly agreed that he would do his best, and followed his son downstairs. Mrs Fairhazel tried to avoid catching her friend's eye.

Mrs Brill finished a mouthful and asked if the gentleman was Jewish. On being told that he was not, she looked meaningly at Mr

Brill: 'Do you see now what kind of family your sister has married into? No better than *goyim*! No wonder the uncle died!'

Mrs Fairhazel fidgeted. There were voices in the shop, chiefly Mr Dolly's. It was raised, as if in incredulity. Then the shop door slammed shut. He had gone away! But surely that was his voice again, talking with Mr Dolly? They were coming upstairs!

'Come in, Mr Walker! Come inside!'

Good heavens! He was looking so pale and anxious! And Mr Dolly was looking so angry. Had they quarrelled about something?

Mr Dolly, apparently speechless, paced the room. Mr Walker just stood in the doorway, looking as if he wished very much that he was somewhere else. 'Mr Walker,' cried Mrs Dolly, 'come and sit with us!'

He looked at her, saw Mrs Fairhazel, smiled with a sudden warmth; was about to say something, when Mr Dolly stopped pacing, clapped his hands to his head and cried: 'AMERICA!' in outraged capitals.

General amazement. What was the meaning of it? Mr Dolly pointed a finger at Mr Walker as if he was a criminal.

'America! What do you think of it! Our friend, our old friend wants to take himself off to America! London is not good enough! His friends are not good enough! He wants to pack up, in the middle of the night, and go to America!'

'Oh, no!' cried Mrs Fairhazel involuntarily. 'You—you cannot be wanting to go!'

Mr Walker looked at her. Again the sudden warmth; but behind it there was a great deal of distress that she could not understand. She felt how remote she was from him.

'You are not really thinking of leaving us?' said Mrs Dolly.

'He is, I tell you he is!' insisted Mr Dolly, in tones of the deepest outrage. 'He came here only to ask if there was anybody we knew there—'

'There is my cousin—' began Mrs Dolly; when Mr Dolly shouted, 'Don't tell him anything! Don't help him! Let him go and live among the savages in a—a tent, if he wants to! *Then* he will be sorry he left us!'

Mr Walker's news, which had been confided hurriedly, nervously, even desperately, had had an alarming effect on Mr Dolly.

He would always have been distressed by the idea of parting with a friend; but now, when everything oppressed him, when everything aggravated him, it was too much for him to bear. He really felt that he was being deserted.

'I—that is, we would be very sorry if you were to leave us, Mr Walker,' said Mrs Fairhazel. 'Is it—is it truly necessary?'

'Yes . . . yes. I have thought . . . and—and I can see no other way—' He spoke disjointedly. 'I—am thinking of Perdita . . . a change . . . it would help her . . . '

'That's right! Blame the child!' put in Mr Dolly. 'Would you believe it, he wouldn't even come upstairs to say goodbye because of the child!'

'I—I did not want to leave her alone. There—there is no one in the house . . . '

'Anyway, I put paid to that!' said Mr Dolly. 'I sent Jonathan to sit with her. And there's another thing. He won't find any Jonathans in America!'

Suddenly he calmed down, as if he realised he had made everyone feel awkward. For a moment he seemed to be almost his old self; and a link or two of watch-chain appeared in his smile.

'Come now, my friend! Have a little chopped liver and let's talk it over! Why America? Are things so bad here?'

'No . . . no. Not at all, Mr Dolly.'

'Perhaps you need more room? It's understandable. Our princess is growing. I'll look around for you. I'll find something. As soon as my jury service is over, I'll have time. It cannot go on much longer—'

'Are you sure of that?' put in Mr Walker quickly.

'Of course I am. I know dozens of places that might suit you! There, you see? No more talk of America!'

'No, no, I meant your jury service. The case. It is nearly finished then?'

'Yes. I think we have heard everything. Soon we will have to decide.'

A solemnity had fallen upon Mr Dolly, and a haunted look, as if the parties of Standfast v. Standfast had suddenly grasped him by either arm and were pulling him apart. His friend and his family seemed to recede from him and dwindle. He sighed.

'We will have to decide.'

'Then you have not made up your mind?'

Mr Dolly looked at Mr Walker as if from a long way away.

'I am afraid I cannot talk about that with you. It would not be right.'

'But I know a little about the case,' said Mr Walker, rushing in, it seemed to Mrs Dolly, where even fools would have better sense than to tread. 'This false claimant—'

'This *claimant*, Mr Walker,' said Mr Dolly severely. 'Whether he is false or not is for us, the jury, to decide.'

'Yes—yes! I understand that! But I wanted to point out—'

'I do not want to hear anything about it. I will not be influenced by anybody. Even by you, Mr Walker!'

Mr Walker bit his lip and began to look angry.

'If you will only listen—'

'Please, Mr Walker!' said the juryman, raising a judicial hand. 'I appreciate that you mean well. But you really cannot know anything about it. You can only have read about it. I have been there. I have seen these people, day after day. They are not just names, you know. They are real people that one can understand. I have heard all the witnesses, I have listened to the lawyers . . . wise, informed people, Mr Walker. Not fools, I assure you. Does it not stand to reason that I must know more about it than you do, Mr Walker?' He paused, and looked round at the rest of the company. 'Believe me,' he said, rather more amiably, 'these people, the Interested Parties, you know, are not at all what we are used to. They are titled people. It is a matter of a very important family. There is a great estate in Gloucestershire. It is not at all like Shoreditch or Bishopsgate Street, my friends. You can have no idea—'

'I cannot see,' interrupted Mr Walker impatiently, 'that it makes any difference whether they come from Gloucestershire or Timbuktu!'

'You are talking of something you do not understand!'

'What is there to understand? A liar comes and tells you he is somebody; and a mad old woman supports him! What is there to understand in that?'

'I will not hear another word!'

'You are going to make a terrible mistake!'

Mr Dolly went very red. He knew he was behaving in a most unnatural manner, even unforgivably, and he dreaded to think of what Mrs Dolly would say to him in the privacy of their bed-chamber; but Mr Walker seemed to have gone out of his way to goad him. He wanted to make amends; but he could see no way of doing so without betraying the solemn duty he had sworn to perform and which was steadily eating away at his soul.

'I tell you again, Mr Dolly, that you will make a terrible mistake,' repeated Mr Walker.

Mr Dolly turned away, and Mr Brill, assuming the privileges of a brother-in-law, clapped Mr Dolly on the shoulder and suggested that all differences of opinion might be drowned in a glass of wine. Mr Dolly nodded, and Mrs Dolly's heart bled for him. She resolved that, under no circumstances, would she bring the matter up again that night. If she had her way, she would have drowned Standfast v. Standfast, and everybody connected with it, in the largest, deepest barrel of brine.

Mrs Fairhazel's heart also bled—for the Dollys, for Mr Walker, who had looked so frightened and distressed, and for herself, because there was nothing she could do to help.

Mr Walker left; he seemed too upset even to say goodbye. It had been a wretched, wretched time. Mrs Brill alone was able to derive any moral satisfaction from it.

'What can you expect,' she asked, looking up from the last of the chopped liver, 'when a Jew mixes himself up in the business of Gentiles?'

'A crucifixion,' said Mr Brill, under his breath.

16

The arrogance, the pig-headed arrogance of the man! To refuse even to listen! 'You know nothing about it, et cetera . . . et cetera . . .' 'You do not understand, et cetera . . . et cetera . . .' The insolence of the man, the unbelievable insolence!

Mr Walker rushed along Bishopsgate Street, absolutely bewildered with rage. He scowled, he muttered to himself, he elbowed people out of his way, returned glare for glare, threat for threat; he cursed the vehicles that delayed his crossing the street, he cursed a chance burst of laughter because he thought it was directed at him, he cursed the wind that blew in his face, and even a button that came off his coat as he savagely tried to fasten it. Where was his humility now? Trifles, stupid trifles—but once the pot was boiling anything served to keep the fire ablaze!

The sky darkened, lighted windows glared; faces became lurid, ugly; streets stank and drunkards heaved.

'Spare a shillin', yer—'

A beggar had stepped out of nowhere, waving a tin. The angry man knocked into him and sent him flying. He stopped and guiltily helped him to his feet.

'Are you blind?' he muttered.

'As a stone, yer honour!'

A face like a half-eaten apple was presented for his inspection. Blind, stone blind. He felt sick with shame as he stared at the battered old wreck, got up in the rags of a bygone fashion, with a stick for tapping and a tin for the receipt of consideration.

'Spare a shillin', yer honour?'

He gave the beggar a shilling and hurried on. For minutes afterwards he could hear the coin being rattled in the tin. The sound seemed to follow him, and it brought eerily to mind the sound of a battered kettle, tankard and saucepan, knocking and clanking against one another.

He reached a covered passage between buildings, with a lamp hanging from its arched roof and illuminating iron gates beyond. It was the entrance to Gray's Inn. He looked uncertain, as if wondering if this was really his destination.

He approached the gates, but they were locked. Lamps glimmered within and trees rustled, like troubled documents. He rang on the bell and a door-keeper came, a weary man with a weary eye.

'I—I want to see Mr Leviticus.'

He was answered by a prolonged stare at his battered hat and his cracked boots. His face received no attention.

'Out.'

This was a blow. He hadn't counted on this happening. He'd imagined everything being done in a rush.

'Where has he gone? Where can I find him?'

Another stare, this time at his missing button. It was followed by the news that the door-keeper was not in Mr Leviticus's confidence as to where he went for the week-end.

'Mr Clarky, then?'

Also out. It was, after all, Saturday night.

'Do you know where he lives?'

Not in Mr Clarky's confidence either. In fact, not in anybody's. This was revealed with an air of deep melancholy. Mr Walker produced a coin; and intimations of confidence twinkled.

'Come back on Monday. Half-past six in the evening, as Mr Leviticus will be in court all day. Who shall I say?'

'Walker. Tell him Mr Walker will call. Half-past six exactly.'

He went back into High Holborn, half expecting to come across the beggar again. He still felt guilty about knocking him down; and also the ragged fellow had stirred such a poignant memory of a time when he had been—the idea struck him forcibly—between selves. But the man was nowhere to be seen.

He took a cab back to Shoreditch. This was a great extravagance, but he had been absent for longer than he'd intended and he was agitated by the possibility that Jonathan would have gone and Perdita would be left alone.

Katerina had been out when he'd rushed round to the Dollys with his sudden idea of packing up and escaping to America, but God knew when she'd be coming back.

As he sat in the jolting, leathery darkness of the cab, he gnawed his fingernails and cursed his stupidity over the trunk. It had been madness to keep it. He should have got rid of it years ago. Already it had given him some bad times. In Whitechapel, where there'd been nowhere to hide it, the child had wanted to rummage in it for possible toys and he'd had to take her out—almost dragging her—to buy her something to distract her. When they'd moved to the Streamers', the loft had been a godsend. Even so, he should have got rid of the things. They were only inanimate articles such as any sane man would have thrown away. Did he really suppose that he would ever need them again?

The cab was slower than walking. It was intolerable! When *he* had been walking, every vehicle had got in his way, most likely delaying him until Mr Leviticus had gone out, and so forcing him to wait for two whole days; now, by some bitter irony, the cab seemed to be making way for every wretched creature on foot.

Shout at them, hurry on! What could it matter to them to wait for a minute and let him go first? They were only idling by, with no sign of urgency, when his was a matter of huge importance. God help them if he should arrive too late! The woman must have come back by now!

He caught his breath as he saw a child almost knocked down by a cart. People were killed every day, every hour, in the streets: good, innocent people! Why not *her*?

She had told him of *another* who had been there. Had she meant in that desolate place? He struggled to recall it in every detail: the blackened cottages, the still shapes . . . He tried to look out of the corner of his mind's eye for a sign of movement that, at the time, he had missed. Nothing. Yet she had been telling the truth. He was sure of that. She had warned him that he would have to pay that other one. Very well, he would pay, and pay, and pay . . . to the end of his life if it proved necessary. Mr Leviticus would see to that. On Monday, at half-past six.

Jonathan Dolly had kept faith. It had not been hard for him. He had known Perdita for so long that it was hard to imagine a world without her. To say that he regarded her as a sister would not have been true. He had very little time for his sisters and he had a great deal for Perdita.

Of course her rudeness and conceit irritated him, as what had been comical in a child was by no means endearing in a girl fast becoming a young woman; but he supposed it would pass. It hadn't passed with his sisters, but that was another matter. He thought highly of the princess. He, too, had his *Peerage*, though it was rather more selective than his father's. Probably Perdita was the only one mentioned in it.

Naturally there were times when he felt like pickling Perdita, or suspending her from the ceiling with the sausages until she promised to improve. But mostly he thought of her with warmth, and, for a youth of sixteen, with tenderness.

It was not to be supposed that he was so prudent as to realise that, in three or four years, Perdita would become a very beautiful young woman who would be a great asset in the pickled herring shop if he should marry her and take her into the business. Jonathan Dolly was no more prudent than his father. Habitually he thought no further than the end of his nose; and at the end of that handsome feature was Perdita Walker, twelve years and two months old; rude, conceited, sorely in need of a lesson—and as much at home in his heart as the blood that kept it warm.

'I don't know why you were so grateful to him, Pa,' said Perdita, after Jonathan had gone. 'It was only Jonathan, after all. And he likes being here. He thinks it quite a favour.'

The evening passed with the usual quarrels and makings-up, and with a game of chess that Perdita terminated, again as usual, with scattering the pieces over the floor. Then the nightly talk, much the same as ever; except, perhaps, a little more about buying the baby, and a little more about that baby's enchantingly aristocratic ways . . .

'You've left out the horrible man! You've left out the broken-down tramp!'

'I forgot—'

'How could you forget him?'

'He's not important. It is the baby that—'

'He *is* important! He's the only one who ever knew about the house he stole me from. If he's not important, *I'm* not important! Tell me about him . . . but first, hold on to my hand.'

Katerina did not come back until after they were asleep. Early on the Sunday morning, before there was any sign of the woman stirring, Mr Walker proposed that he and Perdita should take a trip down the river, to Greenwich, as the day looked fine. Perdita reproached him for extravagance and advised him to buy a new pair of shoes instead.

'Are you ashamed of me, then?'

'Of course I am, Pa! I hate to see you looking shabby!'

'Never mind, my love—'

'Don't call me that!'

'Never mind, I will make it up to you!'

He would make it up a thousandfold! On Monday, at half-past six.

The morning continued fine; the sun shone and, at last, the daughter smiled. She felt that there was something odd in her father's mood; not unpleasant, but a little melancholy. When he talked—usually about the past—she felt that there were other things he wanted to say; but for some reason or other could not come out with them. She understood him, perhaps, more deeply than he understood her. She was exceptionally good-tempered; she linked her arm with her father's when they walked, and kissed him quite spontaneously when they sat to admire the sunlight on the river.

'Why did you do that, my love?'

'Do I have to give a reason, like—like geometry,' said she, graciously submitting to the vulgar endearment, 'for giving you such a sparrow-peck, Pa?'

He laughed, and she slipped her arm through his and buried her hand in his coat pocket.

'What's this, Pa? A secret?'

She took out the ruined silver bracelet. She examined it. He grew very red.

'It's beautiful, Pa! Could we have it mended?'

'You—you like it, then?'

'I said it was beautiful, Pa. I can't say more than that. How did it get so bent?'

He didn't answer; and Perdita, after a searching look, did not press him.

He wondered if she had guessed? But that was impossible. She was only a child. She could never have guessed such a thing. How could she be expected to understand his feelings? And yet the look she'd given him had been so strange for her; it had been almost compassionate.

They sat on the tumbledown terrace of a tumbledown public house that backed on to the river and afforded a wide view of sunshine and shipping. From time to time a fair-haired child, in a long, unequal yellow dress, white stockings and unnaturally large black boots, would emerge from the bar parlour to gather dirty glasses with the gay insouciance generally associated with the acquisition of rose-buds.

'Can I brung yer sumfink?' courteously inquired this child, her small fists enormous with glasses, as if she had grown them, like crystals. 'Brannyunlemmun?'

Mr Walker nodded, and asked Perdita what she would like?

'Oh, I don't know. What do I like, Pa?'

'If I remember—' he sighed—'you like wine, sweet wine.'

'Very well, Pa, as long as it doesn't go to my head. I should not like to be drunk.'

Their drinks arrived and they sat sipping them until it was time to go. When they climbed into the waterman's boat, Mr Walker offered his daughter her choice of seats.

'Tell me,' he asked with a sudden smile, 'do you prefer to travel facing, or with your back to the horse?'

'You mustn't mind my pa,' explained Perdita to the affronted waterman. 'He's been in the oddest mood all day.'

Katerina had come back; noises could be heard in her room and her scent was very much in evidence, but she did not appear. Perdita was certainly curious, but she showed no particular anxiety. Her passionate attachment, like others she had had, was beginning to wane.

Mrs Streamer took it into her head to have another word with her esteemed tenant. Her previous outburst had so weighed on her conscience that she had become quite miserable about it. She hoped that Mr Walker had not upset Miss Kropotka as she, Mrs Streamer, was the last person in the world to want to make anyone unhappy. In fact, if Mr Walker hadn't yet spoken to the lady —

'But I have, Mrs Streamer.'

'Oh dear! I didn't really mean you to — to —' She trailed off into dismayed noises and worried at her fringe.

Mr Walker turned away to hide his indignation. He knew it was pointless to blame Mrs Streamer for everything; but it was exceedingly hard not to. He went upstairs. He could hear Katerina moving about in her room and singing. She sounded as if she was happy. He wondered for a moment if her threats had only come out because of a senseless fury, and that she had really meant nothing by them?

He continued to the top landing. He looked about him and frowned. Something was different. Suddenly he realised what it was. He hurried downstairs again.

'Mrs Streamer! Where is the ladder to the loft?'

'Oh, Mr Walker, I was going to tell you about it. Miss Kropotka — such a fine person really! — took it as she wants to clean her window from the outside. So thoughtful! We really have misjudged her!'

He went back without a word. Katerina's action in deliberately cutting him off from the loft, and so getting rid of the articles in the trunk, dismayed him. The threats had been real. Somehow, somewhere there was—another. In his heart of hearts he dreaded that this other would have a prior claim. Furiously he renewed his resolve that he would pay and pay and pay! He had created the child; she was his! Even if he had to destroy himself utterly to keep her, he would do so. Tomorrow evening at half-past six, it would be settled. This determination afforded him a certain satisfaction; and, for a time, overcame his deeper fears.

Next morning he remembered he had a lesson to give to Mr Gooch; and he was scrupulous in fulfilling his obligation. He took Perdita with him as she was still on holiday from her school. Mr Gooch was a wine importer in Old Street. He was learning French and German in order to improve his business connections on the Continent. He was a man who was very careful with his money, and he saw no reason why his wife and numerous children should not receive some benefit from the lessons he was paying for. He liked to have them all in the room with him when Mr Walker came, and would often get Mr Walker to repeat something if he thought one of the family had missed it. If anyone had suggested that he was swindling Mr Walker, he would have been indignant and most likely pointed out that, if he sold a bottle of wine, it made no difference to him if one person or a dozen drank it.

He was a businessman, and value for money was an article of faith with him; that is to say, he would have thought himself a fool if he didn't get it, and an even bigger one if he gave it. He had put off the lesson from Saturday to Monday as Mrs Gooch had taken two of the children off into the country for the week-end and they would have missed what he was paying for.

Mr Gooch received the arrival of Perdita doubtfully. He was a large, colourless-looking man whose clothes seemed rather too full of him.

'I hope,' he said, ushering Mr Walker into the crowded room in which the lesson was to take place, 'that your daughter will not—um—distract you? Would it not be better if—um—she was to wait in the—um—kitchen?'

'She will not distract me in the least, Mr Gooch. In fact, I hope she will take the opportunity of learning something.'

'In that case,' said Mr Gooch, with a knowing glance round at his family, 'do you not think it would be fair to make a reduction? After all,' (with a clever laugh) 'you can hardly expect me to pay for your daughter's tuition as well!'

Mr Walker thought for a moment.

'Very well, Mr Gooch. If I teach you for half the money, will that suit you?'

'Yes . . . yes,' said Mr Gooch, with another glance at the family, as if to say, 'See what a shrewd stroke of business your father has made! Aren't you proud of him?' 'I think that would be quite fair, Mr Walker. I think that would be a just and reasonable arrangement.'

When they left the clever businessman's house after the lesson, Perdita looked at her father.

'Pa! I hardly knew you! I've never seen you so—so cold and polite. Poor Mrs Gooch! She looked as if she was going to crawl under the table with embarrassment. When you said you'd let him off half the money, you sounded so contemptuous! It served him right!'

Mr Walker said nothing. It had not been his intention to be contemptuous. He had really wanted—and quite desperately—to restore the humble teacher of languages it so pleased him to be. His failure distressed him deeply.

At a quarter to six, he left Perdita in the care of Mrs Streamer, to practise hard for the concert tomorrow. He felt it was necessary for every little concern of their daily lives to be preserved. He kissed Perdita before he went out.

'Why did you do that, Pa? You're not going to be out for long?'

'Must I give reasons,' he returned, with an anxious smile, 'like geometry, for giving you a sparrow-peck like that?'

Perdita laughed delightedly. It pleased her inordinately that her father had remembered so perfectly what she had said.

17

Gray's Inn, twenty-five minutes past six. Everything shadowy, (not to say shady): gates, griffins, trees, quiet lawns, muttering paths, houses like tall black deed-boxes with contents listed inside the lids (three judges and five Misters, one nearly new). Pairs of lawyers, also shadowy, strolling, murmuring, chuckling judiciously over costs; and yellow eyes winking out of chambers. An enclosed place, as far removed from the world as might be got by five hundred years of rigmarole . . .

Raymond's Buildings. Number Six. H. Leviticus, second pair. Mr Walker, hat brushed, button sewn back on coat, nervous, a little light-headed, had a sudden desire to take out a pencil and add 'Numbers and Deuteronomy'.

A little brandy taken to stiffen his resolve had rather weakened his legs. He paused on the stone stairs, (upstairs and downstairs and in my lawyer's chamber) and held on to the iron banister. Footsteps tapped rapidly down.

'So 'appy to see you, sir! Really 'appy!'

Mr Clarky: shrunken, spry, eager—an old friend . . . Suddenly solicitous.

'A glass of water, sir—or somethin' a little stronger, per'aps?'

'No, no. It is quite all right. It is only the stairs. So many . . . '

'Understood, sir, perfectly understood.'

Hand discreetly under Mr Walker's elbow, to help him up the rest of the flight.

'I am quite all right, I tell you.'

'Understood, sir, perfectly understood.'

Hand removed, but left hovering.

'I—I am a little early, I fear.'

'Early sow, early mow, as they say, sir.'

'I—I do not want you to think I am coming cap in hand, Mr Clarky,' muttered Mr Walker, who had been trying to stop himself wondering childishly if the money he needed (to pay and pay and pay), would be in the lawyer's office, as if thirty years' wages had been saved for him. 'I would not have you think that of me.'

'Understood, sir, perfectly understood.'

'It was you who came to me.'

'Goes without sayin', sir, goes without sayin'.'

'*With* saying, please!'

'Shall be done, sir, shall be done!'

Mr Clarky's habit of repeating himself made Mr Walker feel

quite dizzy, as if *he* was being repeated, upstairs and downstairs and in his lawyer's chamber.

'Mr Leviticus is in 'ere, sir. Allow me, sir—' hand under the elbow for an instant—'the carpet's a bit worn. Mr Leviticus—this is the gentleman. As you will see, sir, this *is* the gentleman.'

Mr Leviticus, a huge old man behind a huge old desk, rose like a mountain and stared at him. Then he extended a hand that seemed to turn itself into a chair.

'Sit down . . . sit down.'

Hand under elbow again.

He sat down. Mr Leviticus continued to stare at him; then he cast a knowing look at Mr Clarky, and Mr Clarky cast a knowing look back; and Mr Walker, who was in the middle of these knowing looks, felt knowledge passing clean through him, like light through a ghost. He had a sudden, horrible feeling that the lawyer did not recognise him, that Mr Clarky had made a frightful mistake, and that he really *was* some nondescript Mr Walker who was a humble teacher of languages living in poor circumstances in Shoreditch, hounded by calamity, and nothing more than that.

Then Mr Leviticus smiled, and it was like great clouds rolling; and he chuckled, and it was like the sun coming out.

'Yes, yes, oh, yes! You are a sharp fellow, Clarky! Heartiest congratulations! Heartiest congratulations to all concerned!'

'Your 'at, sir!' murmured Mr Clarky, coming deftly to relieve Mr Walker of that article clutched on his knees. 'The gentleman,' explained Mr Clarky, bearing the hat away, as if he had only been waiting on his employer's approval before extending the courtesy, 'was particularly anxious about is 'at. The gentleman did not want us to suppose that 'e 'as come, cap in 'and, Mr Leviticus. The favour, if I might make so bold, is to be regarded as from 'im to us.'

'So,' said Mr Leviticus, 'the gentleman has his pride. But not, I fancy,' he smiled faintly at Mr Walker's worn attire, 'very much else.'

Mr Walker, sitting under this pitying scrutiny, felt tears come into his eyes. He wanted to stand up and cry out that he was a teacher of languages, and was much respected, that he had many friends, that he had a lovely daughter, that he had a good home and was not in want; and that he would leave now—he was not a beggar!

'I—I have managed . . .' he began, and was overcome by a shameful desire to weep as he had not wept since he had been a child, in front of the huge old man in his airless room, that was crawling all over with books, like leathery worms, ' . . . well enough . . . well enough, Mr Leviticus.'

Mr Clarky coughed; and Mr Leviticus, whose neat crown of black hair was still as black as the day he'd bought it, frowned at his fingers. Suddenly, he did an extraordinary thing. He put his hands to his hair and, with a deft jerk, turned it back to front.

For a moment Mr Walker had the dazed notion that he was looking at the back of Mr Leviticus's head that was bulbous and wrinkled, like an accidental face. Then the mountainous old gentleman jerked again; and there was Mr Leviticus, heaving away like an avalanche so that the various villages on his slopes, in the shape of medallions on his watch-chain, trembled in alarm.

'You remember? You remember that? It always made you jump!' he guffawed, plainly delighted that he had succeeded in making Mr Walker jump again.

'It always does make 'em jump,' confirmed Mr Clarky; and memories came nudging back to Mr Walker, like sticks under a bridge.

'You used to call me "Uncle Herbert"!' said Mr Leviticus, rubbing his hands with pleasure.

'They all call him that!' murmured Mr Clarky, proudly confirming the scale of his employer's uncledom.

'So . . . so, here you are at last, sitting in front of me! Heartiest congratulations again, Clarky! I understand—Clarky tells me—that you have a daughter? Clarky says she's a lovely child. Well, we must get Mrs Leviticus to paint her picture!'

He gestured round the room, and Mr Walker saw, wherever there was a space between books, framed watercolour paintings of pretty children fondling lambs or playing with kittens. One might have supposed that they were eminent members of the legal profession still in a state of innocence; but they were actually Mr Leviticus's grandchildren, done by Mrs Leviticus, who was said to have talent. The scheme was even carried to the medallions that the old gentleman wore on his watch-chain, on which Mrs Leviticus had tried her hand at the delicate art of the miniature.

Surely, thought Mr Walker, a man who so loves children must be kind. He wondered, and he could not stop himself, if his money was in the desk?

'Come now, my young friend.' He started to hear himself addressed thus. 'Where have you been all these years? But before you tell us, we must celebrate! Clarky! The prodigal has returned! Kill the fatted calf!'

The fatted calf, represented by a decanter, was duly slain, and its blood poured into glasses, where it winked and blinked and trembled.

'First, the little ones!'

'We always,' murmured Mr Clarky, 'put the little ones first.' And Mr Walker thought for a moment that he was going to produce a bag of sweets and offer it to him.

'To the lovely daughter!'

They drank. Excellent people, excellent people, thought Mr Walker, enormously relieved that the worst was over.

'To the prodigal's return!'

'That's to you, sir,' murmured Mr Clarky.

They drank again. Then Mr Leviticus settled himself in his chair and presented a picture of mountainous affability.

'And now you have a tale to tell. Tell us why you made off. Was it on account of some young lady? From what I remember of you, I wouldn't be surprised. Or a gambling debt? Again, I wouldn't be surprised. Come now, you may speak freely. (Clarky! A little more port wine!) Out with it, out with it! It was a girl, wasn't it, you young scamp!'

'No . . . no. It—it was nothing like that,' said Mr Walker, looking at the beaming lawyer incredulously. Could the man really have thought, have imagined that?

'Then what was it? Not a murder, I hope!' chuckled Mr Leviticus. 'That wouldn't do at all, would it, Clarky!'

''e don't mean it!' murmured Mr Clarky, as if he perceived in the gentleman a strong impulse to go off into a rage.

'Nor that,' muttered Mr Walker. Why was the man trying to belittle him? 'I left because—because I could no longer stay.'

'That was obvious,' said the lawyer dryly. 'But what we are

trying to discover is why a young man with everything in the world to look forward to—title, wealth, position—suddenly abandoned it all and chose to vanish as if from the face of the earth.'

'If I told you, you would not believe me,' said Mr Walker, remote and aloof. It was the truth. The old lawyer would never have believed him . . .

'Try me,' said Mr Leviticus. 'I am listening.'

'Very well. I left because of those very things you say I ought to have stayed for. They disgusted me. Can you believe that?'

'Try me,' said the lawyer. 'I am still listening.'

'Pay no attention,' murmured Mr Clarky anxiously, 'to 'is manner, sir. 'e's always like that. 'abit of court. But 'e's believin' you. I can tell 'e's believin' you, sir. Just give 'im a chance.'

'My way of life,' said Mr Walker, trusting in Mr Clarky's judgement and being aware of how much he depended on the lawyer, 'and the way of life that stretched before me, had become unbearable.'

'In what way? Had there been a quarrel? I heard of none.'

'Nothing like that. Shall we say that I had a sudden desire, a sudden need to go out into the world and live among ordinary people? Shall we say that I had become sickened with being little better than a rich parasite? Shall we say that I wanted to make something of myself, by myself?'

'If you insist, we shall say it,' said Mr Leviticus.

'Shall we say,' continued Mr Walker, with a faint smile, as if he realised how young and foolish everything sounded, 'that I wanted to do some good in the world? Can you believe that?'

'That is a great deal to expect a lawyer to believe,' murmured Mr Leviticus, making a church of his fingers and looking inside. 'But as I said before, try me; I am still listening.'

The children peered down from the walls and peeped from the old mountain's watch-chain. They would have understood . . .

'That is all. There is no more.'

'When did this—this revelation come to you? A vision, perhaps . . . or a blow on the head?'

''e don't meant it, sir!' confided Mr Clarky. 'It's just 'is way. 'e's with you, sir. I can tell.'

'It is not easy to talk about it now, so very long afterwards, Mr

Leviticus. It is harder even to think about it,' said Mr Walker, struggling with a desire to impress the lawyer and, at the same time, to maintain a certain concealment. 'When we are young, everything seems clear, easy and straightforward; and we act. When we are old, everything is difficult, foolish and pointless; and we do nothing. When we are young, we think with our hearts; when we are old, we think with—with our joints.'

'And never, I suppose,' murmured the old gentleman, examining the medallions on his watch-chain, 'with our heads?'

''e's as soft as butter, sir,' put in Mr Clarky. 'When 'e looks at the little ones, I can tell.'

'When I was at university,' went on Mr Walker, speaking now with a certain eagerness, 'I used to read a great deal. There were several of us—all wild young men, you would say—and we used to talk and argue into the early hours. We talked, as young people do, wildly, earnestly, very cleverly of what was wrong with the world. And of course we knew exactly how to put it right! We talked politics, we talked philosophy, and I've no doubt we talked a great deal of nonsense!' It had not been nonsense, of course, but it was impossible to explain the fiery enthusiasm and high nobility that had filled him at the time. And because it was impossible, he felt the need to belittle it, to deprecate his own ideals.

'And you gave up everything, you ran off for—that?'

'I was wild and foolish enough to—to—'

'To make the world a better place?'

'If you put it like that.'

'It was the way you put it; not I.'

'I warned you that you would not believe me.'

'And how did your—your great crusade prosper?'

'Badly, I'm afraid. Badly, as you might have expected. When my money ran out—and it did, very quickly!—I made the interesting discovery that ideals and poverty make bad bedfellows. I drifted . . . and downwards. As the poem says, I visited the bottom of the monstrous world.'

'Did you never think of coming back?'

'I believe I would sooner have put a bullet through my head!'

'Certainly it was empty enough,' said the lawyer coolly.

'It's 'is way, sir, it's only 'is way!'

'It was empty. Quite empty.'

Mr Walker knew that he had failed, failed dismally in his attempt to present the young man he had been and to convey the high hopes and passionate determination that had once driven him; but, at the same time, he felt a sly satisfaction in having concealed from the lawyer the man he really was. He felt he was like a skilled card cheat, who had cunningly substituted one card for another.

'And yet,' said Mr Leviticus, gazing at the man before him with a certain puzzlement, 'here you are, a respectable teacher of languages, with a pretty daughter. A far cry from the bottom of the monstrous world, my friend. Are we to suppose that the regeneration—the resurrection—was brought about by something as simple as—as the love of a good woman?'

Mr Walker flushed but did not answer, and the lawyer was driven to reflect that, in spite of his grey hairs and beaten countenance, the shabby teacher of languages was still something of a child. Mr Leviticus, being in his way quite a collector of children, estimated his age at about twelve. He took out his watch, examined it, and frowned.

'Clarky!'

'Mr Leviticus?'

'Your opinion, Clarky. If what we have heard was to come out in court, do you suppose that a jury would accept the gentleman's reasons for leaving a rich home as being likely?'

'But they are true!' cried Mr Walker angrily.

'Clarky?'

'I own,' said Mr Clarky, 'that I would like a little more, Mr Leviticus. No reflection, sir'—to Mr Walker—'the legal side of it.'

'There is no more! I have told you the truth!'

'I will not be so cynical,' said the lawyer, 'as to say that the truth is not important. But I would be a poor lawyer if I was to promise that it was everything. Come now, my young friend! Was there no more pressing reason for your decamping? Was there nothing that a jury might get its teeth into?'

'Nothing.'

'No theft, perhaps? Always a good reason. Was there no breaking open of your father's bureau, and no stealing of sixty-seven pounds and some trifle of shillings?'

This was a shock. He'd forgotten about that shameful incident.

'It 'ad to come out, sir, it 'ad to come out!'

'So you knew about that?'

The lawyer shrugged his shoulders.

'But I needed that money!' muttered Mr Walker. 'I—I had nothing. I took it only to get away. I left a note so that no one else should be blamed. I intended it to be the last thing I would ever have. Surely—surely I was entitled to—'

'To nothing! You were entitled to nothing. It was theft. You committed a felony. And *that* was why you ran away. Because you were a thief!'

'I know it's 'ard, sir; but believe me, it's nothin' to what 'e is sometimes! You're gettin' off light, sir!'

'Clarky! Is that better? Would you consider theft to be a more likely reason?'

'I own,' said Mr Clarky gravely, 'that I would prefer it, Mr Leviticus.' Then to Mr Walker, 'No reflection, sir. It's only the legal side.'

'For God's sake!' cried Mr Walker, glaring from lawyer to clerk with a mixture of terror and rage. 'You know I've told you the truth! The money had nothing to do with it, nothing! You can't mean that people, ordinary, decent people would sooner believe a—a crime than an ideal?'

'Ideals are not evidence, my friend. Sixty-seven pounds is.'

'Then I'll have nothing to do with it!'

Did he mean that, did he really mean it?

'Sit down, sit down, my friend,' urged the lawyer, rising to his feet and dwarfing, with his great bulk, the shabby teacher who had jumped out of his chair as if to rush from the room. 'If you flinch from trifles like this, you would make a poor showing in court.'

'I—I will not allow you to—to destroy me like this!' muttered Mr Walker; but nevertheless resumed his seat.

'No one is trying to destroy you. Believe me, we have only your best interests at heart.'

''e gave you a bad time, but it's only 'is way. Soft as butter, really.'

'Yours and the child's best interests.'

('What did I tell you? 'e'd never 'arm a little one!')

Mr Walker bowed his head, and Mr Leviticus went on to explain how strong was the false claimant's case; that it was an exceedingly impudent fellow they were having to deal with; and that it was going to take a great deal to bring him down.

'But surely,' interposed Mr Walker, 'he will not stand up in front of me?'

'It will be in front of a jury, my friend. And that is another matter.'

'But he is a liar!'

'He is being believed. That is what matters.'

'But there must be people who can still remember me?'

'Thirty years is a long time. People forget a debt in a week; how can you expect them to remember a face for half a life-time?'

'Have I no family left? Are they all dead? What of my aunt?'

'She is over ninety—'

'Is she blind, then?'

'No. She is in full possession of her faculties,' murmured Mr Leviticus; and went on to infer, as delicately as he could, that those faculties, even in their prime, had never been notable. In fact, it was Miss Augusta Standfast herself who chiefly supported the claimant. It was she who had corresponded with him and doubtless provided him unwittingly with the intimate information he needed, and sent him the money to come to England.

'But why? She never had any great feelings for me?'

'She had quarrelled with your brother and detested his wife and children. The chance of your return to dispossess her enemies was something she always dreamed of. And when the chance came—'

'But she must have known the man was a liar!'

'Possibly she once had her doubts; but no longer. She is fully persuaded. Have no doubt about that. So many reminiscences have already been exchanged that he is indeed her nephew . . . not perhaps of fifty-odd years, but of one at the very least. Such things can happen. I mean that a lie, if sustained for long enough, can quite supplant the truth. Particularly when there is an advantage to be gained.'

Mr Clarky coughed. Mr Leviticus glanced at him. Mr Clarky took out his watch meaningly. Mr Leviticus nodded.

'I have taken the liberty,' he said to Mr Walker, 'of asking the Interested Parties to come here tonight. I have done this in the real hope that we may bring matters to an end. It is possible that we might persuade the Interested Parties to withdraw from the case. It would be better so.'

'Yes ... yes. It would be better,' whispered Mr Walker, shrinking from the idea of standing up in court. 'Thank you, Mr Leviticus.'

'Do not thank me, my friend. I have taken this course not for your sake, but for the sake of the law. I do not wish to stand by and see it abused. I too have ideals, my friend—even though I was not fortunate enough to have a family to distress in order to satisfy them.'

('It's only 'is way, sir, it's only 'is way!')

'I believe in the law. I hold it to be a remarkable achievement. I think it a great wonder that the state, in all its majesty, can, on occasion, rise up in wrath to defend the poorest of the poor. I will not have it mocked. Clarky!'

'Mr Leviticus?'

'A little more of the fatted calf before our friend here has to face the world!'

18

The world! Standfast v. Standfast—important people, not at all like Bishopsgate Street or Shoreditch—you can have no idea! Heard on the gravel path, like a regiment; heard coming up the stone stairs; heard in the outer room; an uproar of feet and angry mutterings ...

Standfast v. Standfast! Darkly flashing faces, shrugging furs, black gowns, check trousers, watch-chains, highly polished boots; and a mingled aroma of brandy, camphor, smelling-salts and horses.

Spry Mr Clarky darting hither and thither with chairs. Standfast seated on one side, and Standfast seated on the other, with *versus* somewhere in the middle—possibly with Mr Walker.

Standfast on the one side consisting of two long-faced, heavily built young men, and their long-faced, heavily built mother in furs; Standfast on the other side consisting of a dapper attorney, a rather fleshy, bronzed gentleman, and a kind of black fog containing an ancient female who looked as if she has been shot through both cheeks. Very gaunt, ghastly and haggard was this female; and immensely dignified and disagreeable as she settled herself with a dry rattle, as if, somewhere in the black fog, there were bones.

The Interested Parties. The children who frolicked on the walls looked somewhat taken aback, as if, by Parties, they had expected something more in the way of strawberries, cakes and balloons.

The dapper attorney—Mr Johns of Chichester Rents—nodded to Mr Leviticus, as one learned friend to another. (Colleagues, sir. Nonsensical affair, of course. But one has to live. Lord, what fools these clients be! Might take a bite of dinner afterwards and put a little business in each other's way?)

A glance at Mr Walker. Mouth lowered; eyebrows raised. (Oho! What have we here? Another witness? Oh, you old fox! But I'm up to the game. Well, as one learned friend to another, all's grist that comes to the mill. And it puts up the costs!)

Mr Johns exchanged a knowing smile with his learned friend; which is to say he parted with one, and never got it back. Accordingly he transferred a similar investment to the fleshy gentleman and the ancient female.

Standfast on the other side also glanced at Mr Walker, much as if he was something left over from a previous case. They put their heads together, like horses; and muttered, like people. The two young men looked irritated and ill at ease, as if they found the room too small for them; their mother merely looked as if she considered herself to be too big for the room. Important people . . .

'Well, Leviticus!' demanded one of the young men, who had his mother's face and his father's eyes and could think of nothing better to do with them than to scowl. 'Why have you brought us here?'

'You will hear in good time, Charles.'

The young man's scowl deepened; and dapper Mr Johns looked amused. (You are in for a shock, young man. Unless I'm very much mistaken—ha-ha!—my learned friend is about to make an offer out of court. Best thing. Bite of supper afterwards . . .)

'Clarky!'

131

'Mr Leviticus?

'Sir Robert Standfast's glass is empty. Will you offer him some more port wine?'

Sudden movement on the part of fleshy gentleman. Rapid looks from side to side—and a glance to the floor by the leg of his chair. Affable smile at Mr Clarky, and plainly about to mention something—an oversight. Then a sudden loss of all expression as Mr Clarky, decanter in hand, approached the shabby teacher of languages, the humble inhabitant of Shoreditch, the left-over article who hadn't so much as opened his mouth, and filled his glass to the brim.

'What—what the devil's this? What's going on here?' inquired the fleshy one, furiously bewildered.

'Just leave this to me, sir,' advised Mr Johns. 'My learned friend is only trying to unsettle you. An old trick. I would have expected something a little sharper from my learned friend.' (Too old! Past it. Ought to make way for a younger, astuter man. Might offer him a junior partnership and take over the chambers? Always rather fancied Gray's Inn. Bite of something afterwards. Sandwich, maybe . . .) 'Leave matters in my hands, Sir Robert.'

Sir Robert? Ah, the claimant! Of course! The man from Australia! How odd not to have thought about him before! As if for the first time Mr Walker became aware of his counterfeit.

The fellow looked nothing like him at all! A man with a large, smooth face and disappointing eyes; and with a fringe of pepper-and-salt whisker running round his countenance so that he looked as if he was becoming unravelled. A man with fiercely shining boots, a tie-pin and a ring; and a high, nagging, claimant's voice.

Mr Walker, feeling distinctly light-headed, lifted his glass to his weirdly improbable self. The claimant answered with a baronet's scowl. Mr Walker made a sudden outrageous grimace, as if to catch out his other self in an imaginary mirror. The claimant looked affronted. Every inch the rightful owner of an estate in Gloucestershire; every inch the beloved nephew of the ancient lady by his side. Mr Walker would have taunted and tantalised him more, but for the claimant's being distracted by certain grunts and gasps and tremblings by his side.

'Entie! Ent Augusta!' he cried. 'She's having a fit, Mr Johns! Loosen her somewhere! She's having a fit!'

The old lady's face was white—no more than a pallid stain in all her black; and her eyes were wide. They were fixed upon the worn and shabby man who had turned full towards her; and they were frantic with recognition!

'*Robert! Robert! It is Robert!*'

She made as if to fly towards him; but she was not going to get off so lightly. The claimant, sensing a serious defection from his cause, seized her by a scarf or veil or some other trailing item in which she had wrapped herself. Instantly he became entangled. Fought. Was obscured by veil upon veil of black like an angry cancellation. Cursed; asked assistance of his attorney. None forthcoming. An unseemly contest. Panted affectionately:

'Entie! Ent Augusta, come back!'

'Robert! It is Robert!'

'I'm your Robert! For Christ's sake, Mr Johns—ah! You stewpid owl besom! Come back!'

But the lady had escaped him. With wild enthusiasm, and trailing storm clouds of gossamer, she flung herself upon Mr Walker and beat him repeatedly on the chest with her dry old fist.

'Robert! It is my darling Robert!'

'Yes . . . yes. It is Robert,' he whispered, almost secretly.

How strange it was! She had never cared much for him in the past; had never shown him any affection; had never in her life before embraced him. But now he was the most precious object in the world!

She was crying. Tears sparkled, burst, then ran everywhere as if her face was a dried-up river bed; and Mr Walker, finding himself so overwhelmed by ancient draperies and ancient recollections, wept too . . . perhaps as Odysseus might have wept when his old dog came out to greet him—and died.

He supported her as best he could, and was deeply moved by how frail she was—he remembered her as being upright and stern—and deeply distressed by how she gasped and panted for breath—he remembered her as hardly seeming to breathe at all—and was saddened by how she peered up so anxiously into his face, as if he was a saviour who had come back to restore her, to fill out her cheeks and put the flowers back—he remembered her in a garden.

Standfast v. Standfast faltered in one of its parts. There was a

133

falling out between claimant and attorney. The claimant was all for staying; the attorney was all for going. The claimant was all for fighting to the last ditch; there was no case; without Miss Standfast, there was no money; therefore, without Miss Standfast, there was no attorney.

Mr Johns, calm, professional, able to dissociate himself from the sordid affairs of clients, approached learned friend—much as Mahomet might have approached the mountain—with a slightly rueful, slightly deprecating smile. Shocking affair. Entirely mis-led. Acted in good faith. Clients never to be trusted, as learned friend must well know. Who better, ha-ha! But learned friends must stick together. Know of an agreeable place not far from here. Understand beef excellent. Dinner, perhaps, afterwards?

No response. (These damned, arrogant old men from Gray's Inn! He would dine extravagantly. Alone.)

Mr Johns departing, bowing coldly from the waist. Mr Leviticus looking up, rumbling. Has not Mr Johns left something behind? Mr Johns pauses. His hat, perhaps? No. His client.

The claimant, with stuff-of-pioneering-stock determination, still arguing the toss. Impossible not to admire the fellow's impudence. He would probably have made a first-rate nephew. He was a man after any old lady's heart; always provided that it was situated in the vicinity of property.

But his case was hopeless. Poor devil! Under a threat of prosecution for perjury he was persuaded to go. Even then his impudence did not desert him. He wanted, for old time's sake, to kiss Miss Standfast's aged cheek; and when this was denied he offered to shake hands all round. The last seen of him was a portly, reproachful countenance that looked, more than ever, as if it was becoming unravelled.

Standfast v. Standfast was demolished. Its coils and complications would soon slide away from Bishopsgate Street and wither in Westminster Hall. All that remained of it was to count up the costs. A small matter beside the happy scene of a family re-united.

The fire chuckled, glasses clinked and the children round the walls seemed to brighten visibly, as if at last there was a prospect of strawberries, cakes and balloons. The very books of leathery law seemed to soften and expand, as if they contained nothing worse than fairy tales. And a kind of fairy tale it was! What would Perdita say to it all?

Two chairs were removed and the third put next to Mr Walker's; and Mr Clarky's murmur: 'Sit down, ma'am, sit down. Sir Robert won't be goin' away!'

Mr Leviticus was nodding and smiling, the young men were nodding and smiling, and Lady Standfast was nodding, too. She was a formidable woman, with half a dozen dead foxes round her shoulders, looking as if they had perished in an impious attempt.

'You have done well, dear Mr Leviticus. We are all grateful to you. I speak for the family, Mr Leviticus. You have served us well.'

Mr Leviticus acknowledged the tribute with a cautious inclination of his head.

'We will not trouble you much longer, Mr Leviticus,' continued Lady Standfast graciously, 'but before we leave, I would like to assure you, on behalf of the family and particularly of Sir Charles, that anything we can do, in the way of assistance—such as clothing, a little game perhaps, and vegetables from the estate— for this person,' she nodded towards the shabby man who sat beside the mad old lady, 'who you have provided, will be forthcoming. We are not ungrateful, my good man,' said Lady Standfast to her brother-in-law. 'We understand that you must have put yourself out.'

Lady Standfast was a person of breeding. She understood that the poor have feelings, like anyone else. She fumbled in her reticule for a sovereign.

She had not, of course, ever seen her brother-in-law. When she had married into the family, he had been no more than a name. She was absolutely convinced that it had been by means of some ingenious legal trickery, the precise nature of which she made no attempt to fathom, that Mr Leviticus had put the forces of wickedness to flight.

'Come now, Aunt Augusta,' she said, rising and advancing upon the old lady with an outstretched hand. 'We must be—ah!'

She stepped back with a startled cry. Even her foxes looked amazed. The old woman had gone for her! Had actually snapped at her! Had darted her head as if to bite!

'Did you see that? Did you see what she did to me?'

'And what has she done to me? What have they all done to me? They hate me, they hate me!' screeched the old woman, turning to her nephew and renewing her hammering on his chest. 'Throw them out, Robert! Throw them into the street! Robert, Robert, my darling! Throw them out! Into the street, into the street!'

The old woman raged on, screaming for vengeance on her oppressors; and her oppressors suggested variously that she ought to be put away (Lady Standfast), put out to pasture (one young man), and put down (the other young man); while the humble man whose very existence seemed to have provoked it all, sat in shame and bewilderment.

Grimly he became aware that, so far as they were concerned, he was no better than the false claimant. In fact, given a choice, they would have taken the man from Australia. At least his boots were not cracked.

The shouting and screaming oppressed him dreadfully. Why didn't Mr Leviticus do anything to stop it? Why was he sitting there, like a stone? It was getting worse. It was grotesque!

'She's out of her mind! Any fool can see that!'

'They hate me! Into the street with them, Robert!'

'Robert, Robert, Robert! How many more of them is she going to find? How many more vagrants and tramps is she going to swear to?'

'Horse-whipping, that's what they'll get! I'll take an oath—'

'An oath! An oath!' screeched the old woman. 'He'll take an oath and I'll take an oath! I swear on my father's grave that this is Robert! Look, look! On my father's grave!'

She dragged out of her multitudinous garments a worn leather bag, and shook it violently.

'On my father's grave!'

The bag did indeed contain some dried lumps of earth. She carried it everywhere, like a bible. Poor, mad, forgotten old woman! The leather bag with its grimly ridiculous contents was her most treasured possession. It greatly comforted her. It was as if it reassured her that she had once had a father who had loved her. How or when she had come by the earth—or whether, even, it was earth from a grave at all—were matters not to be discovered. It had become invested with so great a wealth of memory and love

136

that once the old woman had sworn upon it nothing thereafter would shake her.

Lady Standfast and her sons regarded the bag with hatred. It was plain that if they could have snatched the bag and emptied its contents out of the window they would have done so.

'For pity's sake, Mr Leviticus, can you not put a stop to this?' pleaded Mr Walker.

Mr Leviticus nodded. He rose to his feet.

'Lady Standfast! Charles! William! Have you lost your senses? Do you suppose that I brought you here to indulge in some foolish masquerade? Do you suppose that I would use one falsehood to expose another? Do you sink me to the same level as Mr Johns? Whether you like it or not, you must accept the fact that the gentleman who is sitting here *is* Robert Standfast.'

'Really, Mr Leviticus!' exclaimed Lady Standfast, shocked. 'What a thing to say! I do believe that the demented old woman has persuaded you! I am surprised at you, Mr Leviticus! I would have thought a lawyer would have known better!'

'I repeat, ma'am, whether you like it or not, this gentleman is Robert Standfast. Or, rather, Sir Robert Standfast.'

'Horse-whipping, that's what he'll get!' promised the existing baronet.

'Hold your tongue, young man! Lady Standfast, I am quite satisfied who this gentleman is. I myself will take an oath as to his identity.'

'That is extremely unkind of you, Mr Leviticus. We have always regarded you almost as a family friend. And now you turn against us. It is quite shocking,' said Lady Standfast with an air of dignified reproof.

It was hard not to feel any pity for the woman, who was quite unable to take in the fact that her life and hopes were suddenly overthrown—and by a stranger. There was nothing admirable in her obstinacy, as there had been in the claimant's impudence; there was only a dull stupidity, such as was all too common among people of her class. Even so, it was hard not to feel pity as she began to falter and at last to give way before the moral and physical bulk of the lawyer.

She sat down, and drew her sons beside her.

'If,' she said uncertainly, 'this really is Robert—which I find hard to believe—then what is to be done about it, Mr Leviticus? Please will you oblige us by explaining what is to be done?'

'Into the street!' advised the old lady instantly. 'Into the street with them, Robert!' And she went on to pour out all the wrongs that had been visited upon her—her room taken, her friends denied, her dog destroyed and her rose garden uprooted. But now that Robert was back, all would be changed! 'Into the street with them, into the street!'

'I ask again, Mr Leviticus,' repeated Lady Standfast, when the old woman had worn herself out, 'what is to be done?'

Mr Leviticus began to explain that, as the gentleman was now the lawful owner of the estate—

'I'll horse-whip him if he so much as sets a foot on it!' shouted the about-to-be-dispossessed one.

'You will do no such thing, young man!' said the lawyer curtly. 'If you attempt anything of the kind, you will go to prison.'

The young man went very red. He approached the lawyer's desk.

'Clarky! I think you had better fetch a police constable!'

The young man retreated. He sat down beside his mother. He was confused. He could not understand what was happening. Things were being done behind his back. He disliked Mr Leviticus. He had always disliked him. He thought he was probably Jewish. Mr Leviticus and his mad great-aunt had done something fearfully underhanded. He should never have come to London. He always hated it. He could never understand why the Queen kept a house there. He wanted only to be back in Gloucestershire with his guns, his dogs and his horses. Above all, with his horses. He blinked.

'Will you not shake hands with me, Charles?'

The dispossessor extended his hand to the dispossessed. A magnanimous moment, inexplicably lessened by the young man's mother urging: 'Shake hands with your Uncle Robert, Charles.'

The young man obeyed. His grip was not of the firmest; his look was not of the straightest; his heart was neither in one nor the other. Yet he too was to be pitied—though God knew why! Nevertheless, it was the thing to shake hands. It was a gentlemanly thing to do. First Charles, then William (firmer of grip, but weaker of eye), then a most cordial embrace with the half-dozen dead foxes, reeking of camphor.

'Brother-in-law!'

'Sister-in-law!'

Was that a tear, or a loose sequin?

'Mr Leviticus tells me,' said Lady Standfast, who had been arming herself with information from that source in order to make up for lost ground, 'that you have a daughter, Robert.'

'Yes. I have a daughter. Her name is Perdita.'

'Mr Leviticus tells me that she is very beautiful.'

How shrewd of Lady Standfast to seize upon it!

'She is indeed.'

'I would have expected no less, Robert. The mother—your wife—I understand, has passed away? I am deeply sorry, Robert. I would like to have met her. I am sure we would have been friends.'

'She—she died soon after the child was born.'

'In childbirth, then? So sad, so sad. Would it not be possible for—for her to be laid to rest in our own church? Would you not be happier to have her resting with the family, Robert?'

Mr Walker fell into a sudden bleak gloom, that seemed to be at the very heart of his being. He felt chilled by an old wind, and lonely. There was a vision in his mind's eye of a blackened little village, with a scattering of dusty dead. Slaughter and horrible indignity. A woman lying by a table, her skirts tumbled in an unseemly fashion, and her face dissolved in blood. Had she been the one?

'She is buried,' he muttered, thinking of ashes and time, 'with her own family . . . abroad.'

Lady Standfast talked on, effortlessly taking command as her natural sense of authority reasserted itself. Of course it had been a blow; there was no denying that. But it might have been worse. The man was soft enough, and quite gentlemanly, in a mild way. One came across them like that sometimes—gardeners who turned out to be dukes, and that sort of thing. He would probably be satisfied with one of the guest rooms. There need be no upheaval, and the sooner the old woman got that into her head, the better!

Really, when one thought about it, it might be quite pleasant to have him in the house. A pity she had given away her dead husband's clothes. They would have fitted Robert quite well. Briefly she wondered how it would have been had she married

Robert instead? Why, they would all have been in Gloucestershire now, and none of this need have happened! But never mind. One cannot alter the past. Anyway, they *would* all be in Gloucestershire; so if you looked at it that way, it made no difference.

But there was the daughter. How old? Not yet thirteen? He must have married late. But one does hear of such things. Thirteen? If we give her four years, then she can marry Charles. Must mention it to him. And William. Once and for all William must be made to understand that he was the younger brother. The child must be for Charles!

'Charles, my dear, you must teach your cousin Perdita to ride. We must all take little Perdita under our wing.'

The mention of Perdita's name produced, as always, a strong effect upon her father. He stared, smiled, as her name came into his bleak and lonely mood as she herself had done. He remembered the awful darkness in which he had been wandering when he had found that spark of light. He remembered how he had blown upon it with his foul breath, and shielded it with his foul hands until at last it had glowed and warmed him so that the darkness had dispersed. The recollection gave him a fierce inner joy; and, for an instant, he was enormously happy . . .

'Why did you ever leave us, Robert?' inquired Lady Standfast curiously.

Her thoughts had reverted to how well the man would have looked in his dead brother's clothes. Life was so unfair!

'I left because—because,' he began, and faltered. How was it possible to explain to these people? He stared at them—these frayed-out ends of what had once, perhaps, been a sturdy line. How was it possible to make them understand?

'Because of a youthful indiscretion,' completed Mr Leviticus. 'An indiscretion. Nothing more remarkable than that.'

'I left,' repeated Mr Walker steadily, 'because I had stolen some money. I ran away because I had broken open my father's bureau and taken sixty-seven pounds.'

The family stared; the family looked at one another; the family considered the matter; the family smiled.

'Haw—haw—haw!' guffawed the young men. 'Naughty old Uncle Robert!'

The family understood.

19

Handshakes again, and embracings. 'We look forward so much, et cetera . . .' 'Put them in the street, et cetera . . .' 'Our love to Perdita, et cetera . . .' and then at last out into the night air. Ah, thank God! But nothing settled, nothing really settled. No money—

Mr Clarky coming after. With the money, perhaps?

'Accompany you to the gate, sir?'

'Thank you, Mr Clarky. A fine night.'

'Very fine for the time of year, sir. And if I might make so bold as to observe, sir, so were you. Very fine, I mean. 'e gave you a 'ard time, but that's 'is way. And you came through it, sir. Never wavered an inch. Mr Leviticus concurs, sir. 'eartiest congratulations, Sir Robert!'

Mr Walker acknowledged the tribute with a faint smile. He was tired. They reached the gate.

'Allow me to fetch you a cab, Sir Robert.'

'No, no. The walk will do me good. I need the air, Mr Clarky.'

'Understood, sir, perfectly understood. But we don't want you knocked on the 'ead.'

Mr Clarky peered through the archway towards High Holborn, very much as if it was Low Holborn, and every passer-by was a likely knocker on the head.

'Why should anyone want to rob a shabby fellow like me, Mr Clarky?'

'If I might take the liberty, you are a gentleman of means, Sir Robert.'

'Does it show?'

'It was always there, Sir Robert. It only needed bringin' out.'

'And now it's out! But you speak with the benefit of hindsight, Mr Clarky.'

'Very true, sir, very true. And—er—speakin' of benefits . . .'

Here Mr Clarky looked a little uncomfortable. He elevated his hat and wiped the groove it left with the back of his hand. 'Speakin' of benefits, and always bearin' in mind that you never came to us cap in 'and, Mr Leviticus 'as instructed me to mention that if there is any present embarrassment in the way of funds, you 'ave only to nod your 'ead, Sir Robert, and all will be attended to.'

The money! He was being offered the money!

'You 'ave only to nod, sir.'

The man who needed money so badly, inexplicably found himself unable to nod. There seemed to be a ramrod in his neck.

'Or raise your 'and?' suggested Mr Clarky courteously.

Hand inexplicably made of lead.

'Or wink?' Very deferentially.

Eye inexplicably marble.

'Or if there is any little inconvenience,' went on Mr Clarky, racking his brains to find an approach that might be acceptable, 'or awkwardness that might 'ave come up, Mr Leviticus 'as instructed me to say that we will be 'appy to act on your be'alf. In a word, Sir Robert, you should regard your affairs as bein' in our 'ands.'

'Thank you,' he murmured; when he might have said: 'Yes, there is a little inconvenience in the shape of a woman who wants to destroy me; and there is an awkwardness in the shape of someone—*another*—whose existence is a threat to my child.' But, 'Thank you', seemed to be the limit of his speech.

'On a footin', sir, on a footin',' said Mr Clarky, elevating his hat and proceeding as if a sound businesslike relationship had been established. 'Valued client and attorney. Mr Leviticus 'as instructed me to call upon you in the course of the next day or two to receive your instructions, Sir Robert. Would you care to name a day and a time? Shall we say tomorrow at eleven in the mornin', sir?' concluded Mr Clarky, naming them himself.

Mr Walker agreed; and the spry little man accompanied him through the glimmering archway into High Holborn itself, where he wished him, with respect, a very good night.

He began to walk eastward towards Shoreditch, when someone stepped awkwardly into his path. He started and recoiled. It was the blind beggar he had knocked over on the Saturday.

'Spare a shillin', yer honour?'

He tried to walk on, but the old wreck thrust his tin at him with the information that he was without roof, bed or friends, that he had taken no nourishment for a week, and that if his honour could see his way clear to alleviating his unhappy condition by means of the coin previously referred to, he would receive divine recognition of an altogether exceptional order.

'How can you tell that I'm not as poor as you?' he asked the blind one.

'Nobody's as poor as me, yer honour. And don't I know yer voice? Why, you're the one what knocked me over!'

'And gave you a shilling.'

'Lost it, yer honour. Give us another. A shillin' to me is a 'ouseful of money!'

A coin was dropped into the tin.

'I'll drink yer 'ealth, yer honour!'

'Shall I help you to a public house? There's one nearby.'

'What name, yer honour?'

'The Red Lion.'

'No good. They'll turn me out.'

'Turn out a blind man?'

'I'm not savoury, yer honour. I'm ill spoken of.'

'What have you done?'

'Murdered, yer honour. A dozen or more times. For another shillin' I'll tell yer of 'em—'

'No—no!'

'Or if I can be of service in any way, yer honour . . . I'm still 'andy!'

He fled from the man. No doubt the beggar had only meant to offer his services in some menial way; but it had been impossible for him not to think that the blind murderer had meant something else; and it had been impossible for him not to hear himself saying, 'Yes . . . yes. There is a woman, and someone else . . .'

He was sure that he could hear the evil beggar tapping after him, and rattling the coin in his tin. He walked faster; and at last was forced to take a cab.

Perdita was angry with him. He was dreadfully late. She had been worried sick. In fact, she had *been* sick. If he didn't believe her he might ask Mrs Streamer who had given her a glass of water and put a wet towel round her head. See, her hair was still damp! She had had a wretched time!

'Forgive me, my love—'

'And don't call me that!'

Mr Walker smiled. Perdita's very sharpness eased and pleased him. He loved his home, with the Streamers downstairs and the market outside, and the Dollys nearby. It seemed wonderfully warm and real. Then some lingering drift of Katerina's perfume reached him. Had she been upstairs? No, no. She had been out all the while. There had been nothing for Perdita to do but thump on Mrs Streamer's piano in readiness for the concert. It had been wicked of her father to leave her for so long! Where had he been?

'In Gray's Inn, Perdita.'

'I hate Gray's Inn!'

'But you have never been there.'

'Of course not! I don't go into places I hate. What were you doing in Gray's Inn?'

'I went to see a lawyer.'

'What for? What have you done wrong? Tell me! You're not going to—to prison, or anything like that?' cried Perdita, suddenly alarmed. She could conceive of no other reason for visiting a lawyer than trouble.

'No. I am not going to prison.'

'Then we're going to lose everything, aren't we!'

He thought; then answered; 'Why must it be bad news, Perdita?'

'Then it must be good news! Tell me, tell me!'

Of course, he would have to tell her; but not now. He wanted to savour to the full this last night when Perdita and Mr Walker would be together. Inevitably it would be different afterwards . . .

She continued to plague him, and he continued to resist. The lawyer and his news accompanied them to the chop-house where they dined; returned with them and even invaded the nightly ceremony, coming grotesquely between the baby and her purchaser, entering into the Whitechapel cellar, and interrupting the very day on which Perdita first stood up.

But he would not tell her the news. At the very most he was prepared to concede that, viewed in a certain light, the news might, quite possibly, be considered good. He kissed her goodnight, and went himself to bed.

He lay for hours, it seemed, in blackness, meditating on the journey of his life. He heard Katerina come in and go to her room. He heard her moving about and singing softly to herself. He thought he heard her open her window. A clock struck the half hour. But which hour was it? He thought of rising to consult his watch. The singing had stopped and the house was quiet. From far off, outside, he could hear the sound of shuffling feet, as if some reveller was lurching for home. Then he fancied he could hear a stick tapping, and a coin rattling in a tin.

He grew cold as ice and thought of going quietly to the loft and ridding himself, once and for all, of his secret. But the ladder to the loft had not yet been replaced. He remembered that. The woman had not relented. He should have told Perdita the news. It would have been better to have done so.

It would indeed have been better. Across the little landing, separated from him by two doors and a stretch of scented darkness, Perdita lay in utter terror. She, like her companion in wakefulness, had heard the sounds of shuffling feet. But to her it was no reveller. It was her terrible familiar, the wicked tramp, with kettle, saucepan and tankard, looking for her. She fancied—and was it fancy alone?—that she could actually hear the clink-clink-clink as he came nearer and nearer.

These terrible fears of hers were a thousand times worse than ever before. She was convinced that, before the good news came, she would be snatched away by that hideous tramp who had stolen her so long ago.

Clink-clink-clink! He was coming! Clink-clink-clink! He was climbing up to the window! Clink-clink-clink!

20

Clink-clink-clink!

'Spare a shillin', yer honour!'

No reply.

Rot your guts! thought the blind beggar, I know you're there!

The shilling he had got earlier had gone on gin. Now, a little recovered, he was on the rampage again, with a button in his tin to make a noise.

It was night, but in his darkness, it made no odds. He had tried to follow the soft touch who'd knocked him over and paid twice for it, but had lost him. Now he wandered in foreign parts with a stink of rotting vegetables in his nostrils. A sound.

'Spare a shillin', yer honour!'

Still nothing. Queer, that. Most likely some creeping first-timer out to kill. Drown in shit, then!

Clink-clink-clink!

'No roof over me 'ead—nothin' to eat or drink for a week past. Spare a shillin' for the poor and needy, yer honour!'

A sound of breathing, coming fast. A smell of sweat. Clink-clink-clink!

'Only a shillin', yer honour, and I'll tell yer horrors!'

A scrape of feet. The blind one shot out his tin like a weapon; and accompanied it with reproof. Was not his unseen listener ashamed not to behave like a Christian for the sake of a shilling? Behold a poor sinner! Once a dreadful murderer—now a soul haunted.

Clink-clink-clink!

'Ought to be famous and in a waxworks as an educational object. Listen! The first time I did it—the first one I did in was a girl—Tell you how for a shillin'!'

A sharp intake of breath—then a fumbling noise and a great weight dropping into the tin. What's that? A stone, you dirty pig in the dark?

'Oh, God forgive me for thinkin' ill of yer honour!'

A watch! Silver, or gold?

'Tell me, yer honour, tell me before you go! Silver or gold? I got to know else I'll be cheated! Silver, or gold?'

God curse this blackness! Silver, or gold?

The blackness, even if it had been as total as the blind man's, could never have been sufficient for the other. For him, every dark street was as white as paper, along which he moved as plain as ink. Every shadow, except his own, avoided him and left him defenceless; while *that* shadow, glimpsed out of the corner of his eye, caused him continual terror as it crept and darted, now behind him, now by his side. Every window watched, every doorway remembered; and a public house, suddenly sending forth a roar of light, threw him up in every stark particular.

The first-timer, out to do it. To do what? Why? Why, *it*, of course. A recollection of wild eyes, open mouth and gasping breath filled him with unbearable excitement. Not quite a first-timer, then? By no means. He had done *it* before. So why was it always *it*? Why not give *it* a name? *It* had one. Look, there's no one about! Say *its* name!

Again the frantic recollection. That was *it*. The other—he stopped as his shadow dropped into a basement where it *must* have been seen!—the other had just drifted into his brain, like a piece of grit. The other had been impossible. Just to prove it, he had purposely brought nothing with him for *it*.

Why, he had only a penknife with a blade that was hardly two inches long! He had measured it when he had sharpened it. He had tried the edge on a piece of paper that he had afterwards burned. One couldn't do *it* with a penknife! Again, why say it, instead of the word?

So he went on through the moonless, starless night, always in a broad daylight of fear . . . trying to hide his very thoughts from himself. He was both inflamed and tormented by recollections that lay one upon another. Murder and its passionate reward changed and changed about, as *it* became first one, then the other: the killing and the embrace.

How had such an idea ever come into his mind? What terror or hatred had given it birth? Was it because his future was threatened, or his past? He tried to think it was because of his future, because of the hopes he entertained, because of the prospects that were opening up; but he could not convince himself. The future only caused him apprehension; the past caused him pain. So that was it! At last he knew! Thank God he'd understood in time! To do *it* for such a reason would be madness!

There was a narrow passage beyond which were little gardens and the backs of houses. He could see windows, all quiet and dark, save one that glimmered round its edges. Below it there was a ladder, placed against the wall. It would be madness . . .

*

147

Clink-clink-clink!

The stink of rotten vegetables and fruit was all round the blind one. He must be in a market. He got down on his hands and knees to feel among the cobbles for an apple, maybe, left behind. He found an onion, bit into it, and had the oddest sensation inside his head. Having nothing left to cry with, he tingled and tingled till his nose wept buckets. He squatted back on his heels. Suddenly he heard the strangest noise.

'*Hoo—oo—ooh*'

It was followed almost instantly by a rattle of wood and glass. Then nothing. It had been like an owl . . . or something else that the blind one remembered. He wiped his weeping nose and stood up. Yes. It had been like that something else. Anxiously he began to shuffle away. Clink-clink-clink! What a racket he was making! He took the watch out of his tin. Oh, God curse this blackness! Is it silver, or gold?

21

Tuesday morning and the Streamers' house in an uproar. The elderly cleaning woman and her elderly daughter—gaunt souls in cloth caps as inevitable as matted sandy hair—were making fierce onslaughts on the stairs and landings; Mrs Streamer was in the music-room, shuffling chairs; and Mr Streamer had retired back to bed. It was the day of the concert.

As the bells of Shoreditch (ever sanguine of prosperity), boomed eleven, Mr Clarky boomed on the front door. Anything less would have gone unheard. The door was opened, Mr Clarky whisked within, and the door slammed shut before rubbish from the market could blow into the hall.

'Good heavens!' cried Mrs Streamer, coming out of the music-room with a wild look in her eyes and a vase of flowers in her grasp. 'Mr Clarky! What are you doing here? You are not to come before Saturday! I cannot possibly take you now. It is the day of my concert.'

'I called, ma'am,' began Mr Clarky; when Mrs Streamer shouted up the stairs, 'Has she come out yet?'

'No, ma'am.'

'Miss Kropotka! Miss Kropotka! Oh, such a selfish person! She must know that we always use that room for coats! Please, Mr Clarky! Saturday!'

'Understood, ma'am, perfectly understood. Saturday it is. I look forward to *A Tavern in the Town*. I still pursue the art, ma'am. But I called to—'

'So good of you to understand, Mr Clarky! But now, as you see, everything is happening at once! The readiness is all, Mr Clarky, as the poet says; and we must make ready. My concert . . . for my gifted pupils. Some day, perhaps, you will be performing, Mr Clarky? I am sure you are very gifted. You have a good touch. But not now, Mr Clarky. We must walk before we can run. Miss Kropotka! Miss Kropotka! I don't know what to do! We must clean her room. Oh, Mr Clarky, if only you knew what I suffer on these occasions!'

'Understood, ma'am, perfectly understood. But I called to 'ave a word with Mr Walker.'

'He is upstairs. But do not upset the child. She is to perform, you know. A real little artist in the way she gets distracted. Miss Kropotka! Please, we must clean your room!'

Mr Clarky, braving brush, broom, and menacing cloth caps, went upstairs. The smell of scent on the first floor landing was peculiarly heavy and stale. Mr Clarky reckoned that the room from which it emanated would take a deal of cleaning.

Mr Walker was expecting him. He was standing by the window in the little parlour. The room was full of grubby sunshine and golden dust that seemed to have come up from the rest of the house as if in search of repose.

'Perdita,' he said, after greeting his visitor, 'this is Mr Clarky. He has come from Mr Leviticus of Gray's Inn.'

Perdita, brushed, beribboned and generally decorated for her forthcoming performance, acknowledged Mr Clarky with a solemn curiosity, behind which there lurked a night's anxiety, a night's wild wondering, and a night's nameless fears. What was the news?

He had still said nothing. He had extended expectation to its very limits—perhaps even beyond them. He had driven the child frantic with hints, denials and teasing contradictions. He had, in short, behaved like a child himself. Partly this was because he wanted to remain as Mr Walker until the last possible moment, and partly because he knew that Perdita would fly downstairs to tell Katerina at once. Of course, the woman would have to find out; but let it be later . . .

('Miss Kropotka! Please! We need to clean the room!')

'Mr Clarky has some news for you . . . my love,' he said, mischievously emphasising the endearment that she always found so degrading. Very soon she would discover that it was not degrading at all when it came from the lips of the personage he really was!

'Then I take it,' inquired Mr Clarky, 'that the young lady 'as no idea?'

'Oh, she has ideas, Mr Clarky! Thousands of them! But nothing, shall we say, in particular.'

'This is all nonsense, Mr Clarky!' said Perdita, with supernatural dignity. 'Pa is being silly! Please tell me what it is about. I'm not a child, you know. Is it good news, or bad news? It makes no difference to me.'

Mr Clarky raised his eyebrows and glanced at Mr Walker, who nodded and withdrew slightly, as might one who has just lighted a firework. Mr Clarky beamed. He fumbled unconsciously in his pocket; he might have been about to produce a very large bag of sweets.

'Your father 'as dropped no 'int, miss, say, of 'orses?' he murmured, with the ghost of a respectful wink at the baronet.

'What's this? Oh, Pa! You haven't gone and bought a horse? Not when we need so much else! How could you, Pa! Mr Clarky! He's not to have it! You may take it straight back!'

'Understood, miss, perfectly understood. But did your father drop no 'int of, say, 'ounds?'

'Not a dog! Pa! You must be mad! How can we feed it? Where can we keep it?'

'And a little river, miss, with fishes in it?' pursued Mr Clarky, with intense enjoyment.

'Fishes?'

'And a large 'ouse, and a family to go inside it, and property, and livestock—'

'Livestock?'

'And orchards, and trees and green'ouses and carridges,' went on Mr Clarky, wracking his brains to enumerate the full extent of the gentleman's possessions, before crowning them with the grandest of all. 'And a title, miss? Did 'e drop no 'int, say, of a baronetcy, miss?'

Throughout this catalogue, Perdita's expression had been growing more and more incredulous as she looked from Mr Clarky to her father, to her shoes, to the ceiling, to a length of hair-ribbon that she had pulled undone, and back to her father again.

'What is this all about? I don't understand! Please, please tell me, Pa!'

'You may tell her, Mr Clarky.'

'It is my 'appy duty, miss,' said Mr Clarky, approaching his final revelation in a measured kind of way, 'to inform you that your father 'as come into considerable property in Gloucester-shire—'

'And?'

'And a title, miss. It is my 'appy duty to inform you that your father 'as come into a baronetcy, miss; in consequence of which 'e is now Sir Robert Standfast,' concluded Mr Clarky, with a bow to Sir Robert and a flourish of his hard round hat. 'I 'ope and trust that the news is good news, miss? For, if you will pardon the liberty, you are now a rich gentleman's daughter, miss!'

The rich gentleman's daughter did not reply. The rich gentleman's daughter stared down at her shoes with a weighty frown, as if she suspected an invisible hand of making an attempt on one of them with a view to pulling the attached leg; and that, if she caught it, she would stamp on it. Then she peered most searchingly at Mr Clarky, and most searchingly at her father, as if to detect in either gentleman a joker of the most reprehensible kind; then back to her shoes again which seemed, in a topsy-turvy world, the only articles on which she could place any reliance.

Then she asked for it to be told to her all over again; for she had not lived in the world for twelve years without having acquired a worldly caution and suspicion of her fellow creatures. Mr Clarky obliged; while the countenance of the rich gentleman's daughter underwent severe changes of expression that were suggestive of a violent altercation taking place in her breast—an altercation between amazement and doubt, between wild longing and flat disbelief, between a powerful impulse to sing and shout and dance, and an equally powerful impulse to rush away and cry. At length she drew near to her father with an air of unnatural timidity.

'Then—then it is true? It is all true?'

The baronet confirmed it, smiled Mr Walker's smile, and held out Sir Robert Standfast's arms. He awaited the explosion of happiness that surely must come. What else was the value of good fortune but to bring delighted astonishment to a child? What else was there in life, but to enchant a child? What other way was there of dissolving the dross and refining the gold?

'It is all true, Perdita!'

She shook her head.

'Oh, Pa!' she whispered. 'What will the Dollys say?'

The baronet experienced an inward jolt, as if he had mounted to a step that was not there. Was this all? Was, *What will the Dollys say?* the sum total of wonderment? He could hardly credit it. He felt cheated and angry that the fullness of joy must wait upon the Dollys! For a moment, he despised them.

Downstairs he could hear the house being thumped and banged and buffeted into splendour by Mrs Streamer and her cohorts. How ridiculous it was that everything should be going on as usual! How ridiculous it was that he should feel such an emptiness within him because a child had not shouted for joy!

('Miss Kropotka! Why do you not answer us? Miss Kropotka!')

And how ridiculous it was that he should feel such a stab of dread, and such a sense of everything collapsing, like a house of cards, at the mere mention of that woman's name!

But Perdita was smiling now. A great beam was spreading, helplessly, across her face. He'd seen it before, even when she had been angry with him, and she'd caught sight of a present that he'd brought her. At last she believed in her good fortune! She had only been bewildered before. It had come as such a shock. Naturally she hadn't been able to take it in. Now—now would come that wild delight he so longed for.

'Mr Walker—Mr Walker!'

Mrs Streamer, her face flushed and her geometric fringe in ruins, coming in like a piece of upholstery! For God's sake, what did the woman want?

'Oh, Mr Walker! Would you ask Miss Kropotka if we might clean her room? She doesn't answer. Please will you speak to her in her own language. Such a selfish person! But we must have the room. For the coats, you know. It is my concert, Mr Walker!'

'Later, later, Mrs Streamer. We—we are engaged at the moment.'

'Really, Mr Walker! Only for a moment—Oh, Perdita, child! You look so feverish! You are not unwell, I hope? I count upon you, my angel! Mr Clarky! Have you upset her? Such a delicate child! And the performance! Perdita! You must go and lie down for a while!'

She would come out with it. She would tell the woman. She was bursting with it. And the moment would be lost . . . would be flung away on fat Mrs Streamer who cared about nothing beyond her wretched little concert!

'I am not at all upset, Mrs Streamer.'

She kept it in! She understood! Mr Clarky was watching her with admiration. And so he should! Mrs Streamer went away, complaining of everyone's selfishness and of how no one understood how she suffered.

'The family, Pa. Tell me about them. How many are there?'

He told her.

'Are there any other children?'

'No . . . no. You will be the only one.'

Ah, that pleased her!

'And will I have a horse of my own, Pa?'

'Yes—yes! You will have a horse and new clothes and everything you want.'

('Mr Streamer! Mr Streamer!')

What was the woman shouting about now?

('Mr Streamer! No one helps me! Miss Kropotka's room! Have you another key? We must get in to clean it!')

'And will I be Perdita Standfast, Pa?'

'Yes, of course you will be! Do you not like the name?'

'I expect I will get used to it, Pa.'

Why was she suddenly so strange? Why were there shadows behind her eyes? Why did she seem to shrink within herself? And, worse—why did she seem to shrink from him?

'Mr Leviticus 'as instructed me,' said Mr Clarky, drawing a bulky package from his coat, 'to make available—'

('Miss Kropotka! We are coming inside! Miss Kropotka—')

'—to make available, Sir Robert, these funds for—'

'*Mrs Streamer! Mrs Streamer!*'

What now? What was happening down there? They were screaming—they were all screaming! Mr Clarky stared. Perdita went as white as death. Footsteps rushing up the stairs. Mrs Streamer—frantic!

'Mr Walker! Please come! Miss Kropotka! Please come! Not the child! For God's sake, not the child! Mr Walker—'

'Please, miss, stay up 'ere with me. Your father would want you to. Please, miss . . .'

Mr Walker followed Mrs Streamer downstairs to the first floor landing. The smell of stale scent was unbearable. Katerina's door was open and the cleaning woman and her daughter stood outside. They were shaking with terror.

He went into the room. It was in wild confusion. Possessions scattered everywhere, as if a madman had been at work. A chair had been knocked over and the bed was a calamity of wrenched blankets and torn sheets. A pillow, flung despairingly aside, lay propped against the wall. There was a deep imprint still upon it, marked out in rouge and eyeblack, like the miraculous image of a saint.

The room's occupant, heedless of the dreadful disorder, heedless of the staring onlookers, heedless of everything, was stark naked. She was kneeling by the window as if in prayer. Her head was outside. She had not fallen to the floor because the window frame secured her. It must have come down on the back of her neck like an executioner's axe. Katerina's death was as grotesque as her life. She had been murdered.

'You—you must send for the police,' muttered Mr Walker, staring with horror upon the scene. 'At once—at once!'

He went back upstairs.

'There—there has been an—accident. Katerina . . . she is dead.'

He looked at Mr Clarky, not daring to look at Perdita. Mr Clarky nodded imperceptibly.

'An accident . . . an accident . . .'

'It's all right, miss—it's all right—'

But it was far from all right. Perdita did not scream, or burst into a storm of tears. Instead she shrank into the furthest corner of the room, as if she would lose herself in the walls. Her eyes were huge.

'He killed her! It was him! It was the tramp! I heard him in the night. I heard him banging and clinking. He was coming for me! He was coming back for me!'

The father stared at her in bewilderment. She was almost mad with fear. He did not know what to do. The rod that he had made for his own back belaboured him mercilessly.

A dreadful silence seemed to have fallen on the house, and the very shouts from the market outside served only to deepen it. It was very like the quietness he remembered in the slaughtered village. But that silence had been broken; nothing, it seemed, could break this one. It was within himself. Dully he tried to understand what it was that he really feared, and what lay at the heart of his gnawing uncertainty and shadowy unhappiness. It was the silence, the awful silence . . .

Shortly before the police came, he asked Mr Clarky if he would do whatever he could to bring the murderer to justice. He felt that his daughter would never be easy in her mind until her nightmarish fears were shown to be groundless. He was aware that such a task lay beyond Mr Clarky's province, but he had great faith in him. If necessary he would speak to Mr Leviticus so that suitable arrangements might be made. Mr Clarky was obliged; but pointed out that the gentlemen of the police force were a good deal more able than he.

'Nevertheless, Mr Clarky, I would be grateful for your efforts. You see, I—I feel a certain responsibility . . .'

'Understood, Sir Robert. Perfectly understood.'

22

Murder lends a distinction to everything. The house in which it has been committed becomes—just such a house; so that, even without the curious crowd outside and the police constable at the door, one would know it from a thousand houses all alike. The fatal room, even without its waxen occupant, becomes—just such a room; and one would know it from all other rooms in the house. And the victim, even without the hapless attitude and horribly shocked countenance, becomes inseparable from the crime; so that, if one glances at a likeness, taken perhaps years before, one seems to know, as if with a deep instinct, that the matter is—murder. Even those who have been acquainted with the victim in life are apt to search their brains for some recollection of a sign, a look, that they feel must have been there; as if, before the mark of Cain, there must have been a mark of Abel.

'The body of the deceased,' wrote the surgeon, who had been summoned to the house in Shoreditch, 'was that of a well-nourished female between thirty and forty years of age. There was extensive bruising to the shoulders and upper arms, and abrasions round the mouth. Death was brought about by a violent blow to the back of the neck, executed with considerable strength. The fatal weapon was a sash window . . .'

At this point the surgeon saw fit to interpose a short condemnation of sash windows in general; and suggested that, had the window been of the casement variety, the unfortunate woman might still be alive. Although this was the first time he had come across such a window being the instrument of murder, he was not surprised and referred to several cases, from his own experience, of such windows being the cause of injury; and he gave it, as his stern opinion, that they were a hazard to health. This was a mania of his, and, sooner or later, he hoped to make his name by it. Most likely he would; as the more idiotic the crusade, the more certain it is to attract attention, particularly when its madness is lent respectability by a degree in medicine.

He read over what he had written; and frowned. Certainly the body was that of a well-nourished woman. No doubt about that. Yet he had a curious feeling that he ought to have described it otherwise. The expression, 'the body was in an advanced stage of decomposition', came into his mind. Now why should he have thought that? He puzzled for a moment and then decided that it was probably because of the strong smell in the room. At first it had seemed merely like stale perfume; but now it reminded him unpleasantly of the disagreeable odour that emanated from bodies that had been floating in the river for several days. He wondered if there could have been some internal disorder—a suppurating abscess, perhaps?

The artist who, later, had been required to draw the woman's likeness, such as she might have appeared in life, also produced an oddity, as if he, too, sensed an inward sickness. However much he softened the staring eyes, closed the shouting lips and dispensed with the disfiguring stains, caused by blood lying stagnant in the vessels on the cheeks and at the end of the nose, he still made of it something unwholesome. One had only to glance at the likeness to know, as if with a deep instinct, that the matter was—murder.

The likeness had been ordered by the police inspector, who hoped that it would be recognised and that someone would come forward. As it was, the dead woman's brief history, obtained by repeated questioning of the other occupants of the house, had merely tantalised him; and the most rigorous search of her room had resulted only in further frustration.

Although, on the face of it, the crime had been committed by some chance thief who, observing the ladder left so carelessly outside, had effected an entry, had been surprised and had killed the woman, almost by accident, in the panic of his flight, the inspector was by no means convinced that such had been the case. There were certain circumstances that suggested something different.

Possibly had not Mr Clarky—the spry little lawyer's clerk from Gray's Inn—been on hand, the inspector might well have been content to accept the most obvious explanation; but the little fellow's presence undoubtedly spurred him on to display his more recondite skills.

Inspector Groom was a tall, close-buttoned individual of Scottish extraction and London refinement: a hybrid, a mongrel, so to speak, and, as is so often the case, rather more acute than the pure-bred article. Ordinarily he was not an easy man, he was not a forthcoming man, he was not a man readily to admit another into his deliberations; but on the present occasion it amused him to open his mind.

He and the lawyer's clerk, being in the same line of business—although at opposite ends of it—had a nodding acquaintance with one another, which the inspector always felt to be rather patronising on the part of the clerk. Indeed he felt that the denizens of Gray's Inn and Chancery Lane in general tended to look down upon him as being a mere artisan in the trade; so he was particularly anxious to take the present opportunity of impressing with the complexity and ingenuity of his craft.

'I take it,' said Mr Clarky, who had gone into the little room on the landing in pursuance of Sir Robert's wishes and, it must be admitted, of his own curiosity, 'that there is no real 'ope of layin' the villain by the 'eels, Mr Groom?'

'Not an expression we use nowadays,' returned the inspector with a quiet smile. 'Clapping a hand on the shoulder is more to the point, Mr Clarky.'

Mr Clarky acknowledged his error. To his relief, the murdered woman had been laid upon the bed and covered with a sheet. There was no doubt that his stomach had been turned, and even now he averted his gaze from the bulky, still shape, whose features showed through like a stain.

'For my part,' said Mr Clarky, gazing out of the window on to the yard, 'I wouldn't know 'ow to begin, Mr Groom. Footprints, might one suppose . . . and whatever is missin' from the room? Is that 'ow you would go about it?'

'But we do not know what is missing, Mr Clarky. We can only conjecture. All we know for certain is what remains. But . . . but something is missing, or I'm a Dutchman, Mr Clarky,' said the inspector, opening his mind by a fraction and allowing a beam to shoot forth and dazzle the clerk.

Mr Clarky looked suitably dazzled.

'Would you care,' went on the inspector, with a deceptive air of encouragement, 'to hazard an opinion as to what might be missing, Mr Clarky?'

'To be honest, Mr Groom, I would not care to. Bein', so to speak, a mere infant in the art, I would only expose myself to ridicule.'

'Then I will tell you. A trunk, Mr Clarky, or a bag. There are many articles here. They must have been carried in something. The lady of the house believes that the unfort'nate woman had a carpet bag. But there is no sign of it; and no one else is able to shed any light upon its whereabouts.'

'You are a sharp man, Mr Groom,' admitted Mr Clarky, with honest admiration. 'I would never 'ave thought of a bag bein' missin'.'

'You would be surprised, Mr Clarky, if you knew of half the sharpness that goes into a case before either you or Mr Leviticus gets so much as a sniff at it.'

Mr Clarky expressed a suitable degree of surprise; and offered, as a humble supposition, that the murderer had taken the bag with whatever articles had come readily to hand. The inspector frowned and pointed out that several items of value—pieces of jewellery—had been left behind. Mr Clarky boldly suggested haste as being the reason. The inspector demurred. There were aspects of the case, perhaps not apparent to the untrained eye, that suggested something different; or, added the inspector, he was a Dutchman.

'It is a 'ole art!' murmured Mr Clarky. 'Such as I never would 'ave believed.'

'Nor your colleagues, neither,' said the inspector, with a touch of bitterness.

Mr Clarky bowed his head; then ventured to inquire what in particular had escaped the untrained eye. The inspector smiled and stroked the back of his head, as if his intellect was protruding.

'We will observe, Mr Clarky, that the unfort'nate woman was stark naked.' He made to draw back the sheet, but Mr Clarky assured him that he recollected the circumstance sufficiently. The inspector sighed. He was prepared to respect Mr Clarky's delicate stomach. After all, a lawyer's clerk was not used to such sights.

'Setting aside the unfort'nate, then,' went on the inspector, 'we will observe that there is a night-gown on the floor by the bed.' He held up the grubby article. 'We will observe that it is not torn, such as would have been the case had it been forcibly removed. Therefore we must assume that, either she had not yet put it on, or that she herself had removed it for—' here the inspector discreetly lowered his voice—'for an intimate purpose.'

'Washin' 'erself?' proposed the untrained Mr Clarky.

'Come, come, Mr Clarky! There are no ladies present. We are two gentlemen together. The intimate purpose to which I refer, is an amorous encounter. We must consider these matters, Mr Clarky. They are part of the human drama.'

'Shakespearian, Mr Groom, truly Shakespearian!'

The inspector smoothed down his swelling intellect again, with a hand to the back of his head. He opened his mind by a good inch or two more.

'We will observe the pillow, Mr Clarky; and we will take note of the deep imprint it still bears. We will observe that the door was locked upon the inside. We will observe the window, and the ladder left so carelessly outside it. We will take note of the fact that the lady of the house has informed us that the unfort'nate herself placed the ladder there in order to clean the window.'

Throughout this recital, the inspector had paced about the room, pointing to each item as he mentioned it. He paused.

'Now, bearing all this in mind, Mr Clarky, would you care to hazard an opinion as to what probably took place? You have, at your disposal, as much knowledge as I have myself.'

'But not the art, Mr Groom. Not the art.'

'Try, Mr Clarky. Hazard an opinion.'

'I would be ashamed, Mr Groom, in front of such a man as you!'

The inspector smoothed his head, and nodded indulgently.

'As you wish, Mr Clarky. Now, having observed all these matters with the untrained eye, we will now look at them with the trained eye. We will observe the unfort'nate's discarded clothing and note that it is none too clean. We will observe the state of the unfort'nate's room—setting aside the disorder of the crime—and observe that it, too, is none too clean. We will observe the unfort'nate's feet—' he lifted a corner of the sheet, and the naked feet seemed to spring up, venomously—'and we will note that they, too, are none too clean. In short, we will observe a carelessness, a slovenliness, a sluttishness wherever we look. We will observe the abode of a woman who concerned herself with nothing that she could cover up and hide; and whose whole capital was in her face. We will observe, Mr Clarky, the person, the linen and the abode of a woman who would never have thought of cleaning her window in a month of Sundays. So what are we left with now? We are left with a ladder placed outside for quite another purpose. For an assignation, Mr Clarky! The caller in the night was expected. The caller in the night was known to the unfort'nate, Mr Clarky. This was no

160

crime committed by a chance thief. This was murder committed by a lover, Mr Clarky; or I'm a Dutchman!'

'To say that I would never 'ave thought of that,' breathed Mr Clarky, 'would be to do you no justice, Mr Groom. The sharpness—the sharpness of it all!'

The inspector, highly gratified, proceeded now to open his mind to its full extent. He invited Mr Clarky to behold the lover cautiously mounting the ladder that has been left for him. Perhaps the window has been left open for him; or perhaps he taps upon the glass. The woman opens it; and, while he climbs inside, she makes herself ready, dropping her nightgown on the floor in her careless excitement. Whether or not a fatal purpose was in his mind from the outset—from the very moment he set out into the night—can only be conjectured. The absence of a serviceable weapon would suggest that there was no such purpose; on the other hand, he might have intended to achieve his object with his bare hands. At all events, he cannot but be inflamed by the sights displayed to him upon the bed. He approaches, and, casting caution to the winds, flings himself upon her in a˙ ecstasy of passion, to which the state of the bed bears ample witness. Then, when it is over, he reaches for the pillow that the fierceness of the encounter has displaced. She, thinking nothing, expecting nothing, watches with a smile. It is her last; for in an instant, he has forced the pillow down upon her face! She struggles desperately; but it is hopeless. The abrasions round her mouth and the bruising of her shoulders testify to the violent strength employed. At length, her struggles cease. The lover rises. Goes quietly to the window. Begins to descend; when, horror of horrors, the woman rises from the bed and comes staggering towards him! She does not cry out because she still cannot believe what he has done to her. She reaches the window. He is already on the ladder. She leans out. Now—now she is about to cry: 'Murderer!' Too late. He seizes the window frame and brings it down with a dreadful force upon the back of her neck. This time he has made no mistake. The woman is dead.

Thus Inspector Groom, with considerable theatrical force, reconstructed the crime in the little room; while she alone who could vouch for the truth of it lay under the sheet as if quietly listening. Mr Clarky felt himself to be perspiring; and the inspector, conscious of the effect he had made, looked down upon the spry little lawyer's clerk with a mixture of indulgence and affable contempt.

'I can only be thankful,' murmured Mr Clarky with utter sincerity, 'that I 'appened to be on 'and to gain such an insight into the art.'

'And might I inquire, Mr Clarky, if you are on hand in a professional or a private capacity?'

Mr Clarky, shrewdly judging the inquiry to be professional, did not dissemble. Partly this was because it was his duty to assist the inspector, and partly because the demonstration he had just had of Mr Groom's powers did not encourage him to suppose he could conceal anything from him. He related the entire circumstance that had led up to his being in the Streamers' house, and modestly indicated his own part in restoring Sir Robert Standfast to his family and his estate. Although the inspector privately considered it to be a piddling affair, he was courteous enough to express admiration for Mr Clarky's perspicuity.

'I imagine that Sir Robert and his daughter will be leaving here soon, Mr Clarky? It is, after all, hardly the neighbourhood for a baronet.'

Mr Clarky nodded. In view of what had happened, Sir Robert and his daughter would be leaving for Gloucestershire as soon as possible. The child was distraught and terrified of spending so much as another night in the house.

'Then I trust,' said the inspector, 'that I will be informed as to the gentleman's whereabouts? He was, as I understand it, the only one who was able to speak the unfort'nate's language?'

'That is so, Mr Groom. Sir Robert, in his day, has been a great traveller.'

'He seems a pleasant enough gentleman.'

'But—but a little unsettled, Mr Groom.'

'Hardly surprising, in the circumstances.'

'I fancy it is a little more than that, Mr Groom,' said Mr Clarky, rather led on by the inspector's admiration for his own astuteness, and unwisely anxious to make a good showing. 'He is, in some ways, a curious gentleman.'

'Curious enough for—' murmured the inspector, with a meaning glance at the quiet sheet.

'Good 'eavens, no, Mr Groom! Not like that at all!'

'Nevertheless, perhaps I ought to have another word?'

'I would be obliged, Mr Groom, if you could 'old off . . . at least until the young lady is 'erself again. I would be greatly obliged; and so, I am sure, would Mr Leviticus.'

'I will respect your feelings, Mr Clarky. I know that it is not in you to mislead me. You have quite a name among us in the Force for probity, Mr Clarky. And very unusual, if I may say so, in your line.'

'And you too, Mr Groom, 'ave a 'igh reputation in Gray's Inn and Chancery Lane. You are 'eld in esteem, Mr Groom, in the profession; which, as you must know, is not always the case in your line either. There 'ave been instances—'

'And there have been instances, Mr Clarky. We both bear the burden of the unworthy.'

'Understood, Mr Groom, perfectly understood.'

Thus the two gentlemen came to some sort of an understanding as they waited, murmuring discreetly in the dingy little room, until two men, with a handcart and a rough coffin, came to take Katerina Kropotka away. They were well pleased with themselves, were Inspector Groom and Mr Clarky; and each felt that he had got the better of the other: the inspector because he had asserted himself, and Mr Clarky because he had subjected the unwitting inspector to a most skilful cross-examination in the course of which he had obtained, for his own advantage, everything that the inspector knew.

Not that either gentleman thought any the less of the other on that account; as it does not do to belittle those we feel we have outwitted. Inspector Groom thought that Mr Clarky was quite a bright little fellow, so long as he confined himself to piddling law suits; while Mr Clarky thought the inspector to be quite a gifted individual, provided he remained within his artisan status. He admired exceedingly the inspector's reconstruction of the crime. He believed that, in most respects, it was accurate. One thing alone puzzled him. There had been no further mention of the missing bag.

In this, both gentlemen, shrewd as they were, had been twice misled: once by Sir Robert Standfast who had said nothing about the bag as he dreaded that any search of the loft would betray him; and once by that arch-deceiver, Mr Streamer, who trembled that any admission of his knowledge of the bag's whereabouts would mean that his own midnight encounter with Miss Kropotka would come out and would leave scars on the heart of his beloved wife.

23

Sir Robert Standfast and his daughter were to leave London on the Thursday morning. It was arranged that they should travel from Paddington Station to Gloucester, where they would be met and driven to Standfast House, which was some five miles away. The two intervening nights were to be passed at an inn off Gray's Inn Road, highly recommended by Mr Leviticus, as another night in the Streamers' house, where every door, stair landing and window (especially every window!) shrieked *murder*, was unthinkable.

The delay in leaving London turned out to be a mixed blessing, the worst of it falling upon Sir Robert himself. It exposed him to the terror of the *other one* that the murdered woman had threatened him with. As this *other one* was unknown to him, every footstep, every chance look, every half-smile from a stranger, caused him to sweat and shake. It was useless for him to tell himself that his fears were probably groundless; they kept rising from the depths of his soul, as if from an inexhaustible well of dread. There were times, indeed, when he did not really know what he was frightened of; perhaps it was fear itself.

For Perdita, however, the delay operated more kindly. It provided a resting-place, a stepping-stone, so to speak, between one life and another. The inn, being patronised by small gentry and respectable litigants from out of town, and looked after by clean chambermaids and sober waiters, seemed like a preparation for the grander existence to come; and the change went a long way towards relieving her grief and subduing her own morbid fears. She took to the new surroundings with an energy and enthusiasm that left the brain reeling.

In no time at all, it seemed, she was intimately acquainted with every detail of the establishment. While her father still blundered, lost himself in strange corridors, found himself on unknown landings, she was familiar with everything. She knew the location of all the public rooms, the destination of every passage and stairway, the habitations of the principal guests, the lurking-places of the servants. She knew which of them was Joe, which was Harry, who kept a sad little canary, which was Betty and which was Susan. Her father, on the other hand, was still apt to forget who he was himself, and often looked bewildered when addressed as 'Sir Robert'.

Of course she was a great favourite, as a pretty girl must always be, until one has got used to her looks. The small gentry smiled at her, the respectable litigants openly admired her, and the servants disloyally confided to her the personal failings of all the guests: this one was as deaf as a post, that one was as blind as a bat, and the old gentleman who always sat in the corner as if he was asleep, when nobody was looking drank like a fish.

It was, for Perdita, a golden time; brief in duration but long remembered. In the strange perspective of memory, it grew larger as it receded: the passage outside her room, where pairs of polished boots stood to attention outside the doors like magical sentries just failed in total invisibility, and where Betty, the chambermaid, winked in passing, becoming, somehow, as long and durable as the Avenue of the Sphinxes.

On the Wednesday they made their farewells. But before that, the excellent Mr Clarky, like a spry, shrunken Mercury in a hard round hat, had sped ahead of them, 'preparing the case', as he put it; so that when the father and daughter called, they were spared the awkwardness of having to explain their changed circumstances, and could devote the time to the melancholy pleasure of saying goodbye.

The Streamers were inconsolable. Crushed as they were by the horror of the little room on the landing, and oppressed by the sweet, heavy scent that lingered no matter how long the windows were left open, they received the news of the departure of their upstairs tenants with the deepest distress. They all took tea in the music parlour where the silent piano and the pallid bust of Chopin seemed to be paraphrasing the poet by suggesting that, though their heard songs had been melancholy, those as at present unheard were tomb-deep in gloom. Mrs Streamer, her fringe wildly ungeometrical, wept copiously and even Mr Streamer gave way to a Latin tear and hoped that Mr Walker,—er—Sir Robert, would not mind if he kept the borrowed fiddle for a little longer as his own instrument was not yet repaired.

Sir Robert did what he could to comfort the couple who had been so kind to Perdita and himself for so long. He promised them that nothing had really changed and that, if Mrs Streamer was agreeable, he would like to retain his tenancy as he and Perdita could not imagine staying anywhere else when they visited London. He spoke in all sincerity. He was sufficiently overcome by the emotion of leaving old friends as to believe that a baronet from Gloucestershire would actually lodge in three dingy rooms in a dingy house in a Shoreditch street market. But then parting is apt to make simpletons of us all. Nevertheless, he meant what he said to the extent of leaving certain of his old belongings in the Streamers' loft.

Next they went to Stepney and to Mrs Fairhazel's neat little house. Here, however, the farewells were different. There was a restraint about them that suggested that the parties chiefly concerned were particularly anxious not to deceive either each other or themselves. Mrs Fairhazel's two lodgers, the brothers Wilkinson, remained in attendance—'Aboard', they would have put it; as if their fair landlady was their flagship, suddenly endangered and therefore to be protected at all costs.

'I wish you well, Sir Robert,' said Mrs Fairhazel, emphasising the title with quiet courtesy. 'And Perdita too. It is a wonderful thing that has happened for you.'

'We—we will be back soon,' said Sir Robert. 'And I hope you will come to visit us in Gloucestershire.'

'I will look forward to that,' said Mrs Fairhazel, with a faint smile.

Although she knew, as well as anyone, that beggar maids had married kings, and that goose-girls had captivated princes, she had little faith in the chances of a widow with a modest property in Stepney making substantial inroads in the affections of a baronet with a rich estate in Gloucestershire. Nor, to be honest, was she, at that moment, desirous of doing so.

Mild as was her nature, she could not help being angry with the man. She felt he had deceived her. The quietness and modesty that she had once so admired in him, she saw now as condescension. His very presence in her house seemed to humiliate her. She wished he had not come. For the first time in her life she did not feel ashamed of her own thoughts; consequently there was a dignity about her that caused Sir Robert to flush unaccountably, and Perdita to remain subdued.

The brothers Wilkinson, satisfied that their flagship had remained inviolate, that her colours had not been struck, accompanied the callers to their cab, which had been kept waiting, and bowed rather stiffly as they drove away.

In the cab, Sir Robert remained sunk in thought. Mrs Fairhazel had displayed no curiosity about his change of circumstance. She had not asked him how or why it had come about. It was as if she had been indifferent to it. He wondered how Mr Clarky had explained matters to her; and found himself wishing, with all his heart, that, on this one occasion, he had done so himself.

They went to Bishopsgate Street, where Dolly's Famous Pickled Herrings and Continental Delicacies was looking discouragingly bare. Being near to the end of Passover, and the Passover stock diminishing, the shelves showed more wall than goods, and the rich sausage grove seemed to have fallen into a bleak winter of barren strings and empty hooks. It was as if the Angel of Death, missing the sign on the doorpost, had entered and touched the shop with an icy hand.

But Mr Dolly was as welcoming as ever, and it would have needed a very keen eye indeed to have detected, under his warm manner, any sense of bewilderment and hurt.

'Sir Robert! Sir Robert Standfast! So good of you to come! And you must have so much to do! Mrs Dolly said you would never find the time! But here you are! And—and Perdita, too!'

It was noticeable that Perdita was no longer the princess. It was as if an eligibility to be mentioned in Burke's *Peerage* precluded a place in Dolly's.

'My dear old friend! So you are going to Gloucestershire! A long way, but not the end of the world! Not so bad as America, eh? You will come back, of course, for one of our Friday nights? Mrs Dolly thinks it will be too far for you; but I am sure you will remember us! Sir Robert Standfast! Who would have thought such a thing? Now I understand why you were so angry over the

lawsuit! How foolish you must have thought me! Mrs Dolly always said that I took it too much to heart! But it's all finished now, and you're off to Gloucestershire! I only wish it were Friday now and you were coming to dinner! But another time, another time! I would ask you for tonight, but we are all upside down! My cousin—the one from Poland, you remember—is expected at any minute and we are getting ready for him! Otherwise we would ask you. So . . . so it is tomorrow that you go? Please—you must take some chopped liver! Let me pack some up for the journey! And some cheese and *matzohs*. There would be more, but it is still Passover. Jonathan—Jonathan! Bring in a basket for our friends!'
Thus Mr Dolly, with expansive gestures and watch-chain smile, skipping about his ransacked cave of a shop, where all the mingled odours still lingered, like the rich ghosts of yesterday.

The visitors did not go upstairs. Brandyella appeared briefly, to gape in awe at the brand-new baronet and store up every detail of him for future use in the public house next door. The Dolly daughters came down and wished Sir Robert and his daughter a safe journey; and Jonathan came back with a basket that Mr Dolly eagerly filled. Gravely the heir to Pickled Herrings shook hands with the baronet's daughter.

'I don't suppose that we will meet again.'

'Of course they will be coming back!' cried Mr Dolly, before Sir Robert could answer for himself. 'And very soon—very soon! Gloucestershire is not the end of the world! They will be back before you know it! Mrs Dolly thought you wouldn't—that you would be too busy. But no one can be too busy to come and see old friends. So I wish you both a safe journey and a quick return! I know that Bishopsgate Street is not Gloucestershire; but it is somewhere where you will always be welcome. God bless you, my friends!'

So Mr Dolly did his best to make the farewell easy; and it would have taken an exceedingly sharp ear to have detected, under the warmth and affability of his voice, any trembling, or hesitation, or note of strain that might have suggested an injured heart.

Mrs Dolly did not appear. She was fully occupied with preparations for the cousin; and it would have taken a very tormented mind indeed to have supposed that she had not come down because she could not bring herself to face the friend whose long pretence had so toppled her husband in his own esteem; and that, at that very moment, it was she and not the household that had been turned upside-down, and that she had retreated to the privacy of her bed-chamber to weep for foolish, trusting Mr Dolly whose absurd pride in the dignity of being a juryman had taken such a fall. It distressed her immeasurably to see him sinking deeper and deeper into that darkness of the spirit that comes with the going down of faith.

The train was to leave for Gloucester at a quarter to ten, and they were in their places a full fifteen minutes beforehand; which made their farewell to Mr Clarky, who stood patiently on the platform, uncomfortably protracted.

Necessary purchases had been made: a black fur muff—no sooner seen in a shop window than discovered to be absolutely indispensable for a young lady travelling—for Perdita; and a hat, shoes and gloves for the gentleman. He still wore his shabby outer garments as there had been no time to replace them so that he presented an oddly inconclusive air, rather like some worn article of furniture that one might see lying outside in a yard, that is either in the process of being restored, or of falling further into ruin —there being no immediate means of knowing which way the change is going.

At last the great clock stood at a quarter to ten, and the huge tumultuous station gathered its energies for a gigantic effort. There was a violent slamming of doors, a shriek of whistles, a gnashing of pistons and a loud billowing forth of sulphurous smoke and steam. In a moment, Mr Clarky was a wraith, waving; and beyond him, dimly in the smoke, a full ten thousand top hats, it seemed, like a tempest of black chimneypots, were waving too, as one half of the world shouted its goodbyes to the other half, and seemed to go backwards while the other half went thunderously, uproariously West.

24

The train rushed on, whooping and screeching like an iron child out of an iron school and mad to get at the countryside. It dashed among the patchwork counties, but nothing would do—nothing would do! A sheep-dappled hillside, a smooth-running river, and—

Leave it behind—leave it behind, there's better to come!

Gipsy caravans, fringed and smoking, like painted old women; a gate hung all over with waving children, as if they'd been put out to dry; and—

Leave 'em behind—leave 'em behind!

A drowsy village, a sleeping pond with a man under a green umbrella, fishing for his supper; and a—

Leave it behind—leave it behind!

A landscape as wide and lumpy as Mrs Streamer's bedspread with a huge Mrs Streamer under it, stitched up with hedgerows and prickled all over with churches; and—

But nothing would do—nothing would do! and the scenes, whirled away in flying smoke, became recollections almost as soon as they appeared.

Perdita stared at them with a tumultuous excitement that she could only contain by a supernatural effort of self-control that would have amazed those who knew her. Even so, she could not restrain herself from making ceaseless demands upon her father to look at this—to look at that—and to grow angry with him when he looked too late and there was nothing to be seen any more but smoke.

She had fallen into that strangely double state of mind in which she wanted to be both observer and observed; to be both the marvellously travelling girl and someone envying and admiring the fortunate one. She wanted to be lowly and exalted at the same time; to give up nothing; to be both what she was and what she was becoming; as if she dreaded that joy and success, like the scenes that whirled past the carriage windows, would also pass from prospect to retrospect in the twinkling of an eye.

At Reading they were joined by a refined couple who sat in a terrible silence, as if they had quarrelled with the world and one another. The gentleman hid himself behind his newspaper, while the lady stared out of the window. From time to time, when the passing landscape was not to her taste, she glanced at the shabby individual and the young girl sitting opposite; and it was plain, from the slight tightening of her lips, that she was wondering what the railways were coming to, that she suspected the shabby one of travelling without a first-class ticket, and that it was only good breeding that prevented her coming right out with it. She tried hard not to observe the young girl, with her flashy eyes and smart new muff, as the girl was insolently observing *her*, and she did not want to become involved in a skirmish of looks. She spoke to the newspaper.

'Is the Queen still in Scotland?'

The newspaper rustled, and returned: 'I see that she is still in Balmoral.'

A deep sigh, and: 'London must seem empty without her.'

Silence, then: 'Is there any more news of Lady Diana's engagement?'

'No. Nothing at all,' replied the newspaper.

'Surely there must be something. How else is one expected to know what is going on in the world?'

'I see it says,' offered the newspaper, 'that the Duke of Somerset is going to the South of France.'

'Is he taking all the family?'

'It doesn't mention them.'

'Perhaps there will be something in tomorrow's newspaper.'

Silence again; and Perdita wished with all her heart that their baggage—two new trunks, prominently labelled 'Sir Robert Standfast' and 'Miss Perdita Standfast'—had been kept in the carriage with them. As it was, she concentrated fiercely on devising some means whereby her importance might be conveyed in a thoroughly natural manner.

'Pa!' She had contemplated, in one of her more far-fetched schemes, addressing him as Sir Robert, but had regretfully abandoned it.

'Yes, Perdita?'

'Who do you think will be meeting us at Gloucester?'

'A servant, I expect.'

That was good. But it was a pity he hadn't said, '*One* of the servants.'

'Pa!'

'What is it now, Perdita?'

'Do you think my aunt—Lady Standfast—will be at the station?'

Brilliant! And it had the desired effect. The lady's expression, after a moment of bewildered indecision, softened. She smiled, almost timidly, and nudged the newspaper.

'My dear,' said she to Perdita. 'What a pretty muff you are carrying.'

Perdita returned the smile, with warmth. The lady nudged the newspaper again. It descended, by degrees, revealing, in a cautious sequence, a furrowed brow, inquiring eyes, a full-bottomed nose, conspicuously veined, imperial whiskers and a sharply diminishing chin.

'It is so pleasant to travel on the railways nowadays,' said the lady, addressing herself to the pretty girl's father. 'It is such a convenience, don't you think? And such a comfort. When one travels—as one must—first-class, one knows that one will meet only with first-class companions. One knows that there are some people—foreigners, one supposes—who pretend to disapprove of all such distinctions; but one notices that such people are always rather low. One never finds that first-class people, really worthwhile people, our aristocracy for example, disapprove of such things. And surely they ought to know! Not that one has anything against working people, or the poor, or even foreigners; but where would one be if they all wanted to live in respectable neighbourhoods and travel in first-class carriages? One must keep a sense of proportion in such things!'

Before any reply could be made, the gentleman took over from his wife.

'Standfast? Lady Standfast? Did we not hear the young lady mention Lady Standfast?' he inquired. His wife verified the fact. 'And was it not Gloucester that she mentioned?' Again his wife confirmed it. 'Then they must be the Standfasts we have read about, in the newspaper.' He gazed at Sir Robert, and his little blue eyes grew quite moist. 'Forgive me, sir, but are we right? Are you and the young lady indeed connected with the family we have read about?'

'My father,' cried Perdita delightedly, 'is Sir Robert Standfast! We are on our way home!'

The couple expressed the keenest pleasure. It was not often that one had the good fortune to find oneself travelling in the same carriage as people in the newspaper. Surely if any proof was needed of the advantages of first-class arrangements, then here it was! And to think that one would never have known had it not been for that lucky mention of Lady Standfast! It was an extraordinary coincidence and one would not easily get over it.

'We read, sir,' enthused the gentleman, 'that the estate is very extensive and that Standfast House goes back to the seventeenth century.'

'In parts,' corrected his wife. 'There were additions in King William's time; and, I believe, new stables were added only last year.'

'We understand, sir,' continued the gentleman, after having acknowledged his wife's correction, 'that your aunt, Miss Augusta Standfast, is ninety-two. Remarkable. A tribute to fine breeding!'

'And dear Lady Standfast—she was a Westley, I believe— with her two sons. So brave to be widowed with two sons! Charles and William, are they not? One remembers when they were christened. It seems so short a time ago. It was in the newspaper. There were several lines about it. Such a blessing, the newspaper, don't you think? It enables one to keep in touch. It makes one feel quite a family. However lonely one might be feeling in one's own residence, one knows what is going on; and one can send cards.'

'And one is able, sir, to converse,' said the gentleman. 'For instance, we have read that Charles and William have done a great deal to improve THE HORSE.'

Sir Robert nodded; and refrained from remarking that the time and effort might have been better spent in improving themselves. Although the couple were not particularly to his liking, he could see that Perdita was childishly pleased to have made their acquaintance.

They 'conversed', as the gentleman would have it, all the way to Swindon, where they were to leave the train: one so admired Charles and William for their generous encouragement of THE HORSE, which, after all, was the glory of England . . . one looked forward to reading, in the newspaper, that the Queen had conferred honours . . .

'Ah! Swindon already! Might we, sir,' inquired the gentleman, fumbling in his waistcoat pocket, 'have the honour of leaving our card?'

Sir Robert inclined his head, and the card passed into his possession. The lady nudged her husband and glanced meaningly at the newspaper. He comprehended instantly.

'And the newspaper, sir! Perhaps you would care to peruse it? There are one or two items of interest about the Royal Family—'

'Although,' interposed the lady, 'one must feel saddened to see that the newspapers nowadays feel obliged to print so much that cannot be of interest to people like oneself. Sometimes one finds that the Court Circular and the Society News are quite squeezed up into a corner! But even so, one would not be without it, as it helps to keep one in touch.'

When they had gone, Sir Robert looked at the card. Floridly engraved, it read: 'H. H. Bloggs of Reading, Purveyor of Elegant Commodes for the Nobility and Gentry.'

He would have thrown it out of the window, but Perdita insisted upon keeping it. He shrugged his shoulders and handed it to her. She put it away in her purse with evident satisfaction. He frowned. The warmth and charm she had displayed towards the manufacturers of Elegant Commodes—a warmth and charm conspicuously lacking in her treatment of people *he* valued—had exasperated him. He had been really distressed by her obvious enjoyment of the worthless, almost degrading interest the couple had displayed in them. He himself had felt a mounting anger; and something of those feelings of disgust that had helped to drive him from his home rose up once more in his heart. Then he remembered that Perdita, after all, was little more than a child; and he wondered if, perhaps, he was being unjust to her. Was it not possible that he, too, at her age, had taken an innocent pleasure in the effusive deference of lesser mortals? He tried to remember, but it was too long ago; his childhood, with all its pleasures and pains, remained an uneasy blank.

Thoughts of home invaded him; and he tried to rebuild the house in his mind. But rooms kept sliding about, staircases doubled back on themselves, the great hall vanished and he received no more than an impression of remoteness and size. There was nothing he could recall with any distinctness or particular affection, saved a scarred corner of a kitchen table and an ivy-covered walk that led from—from he could not remember where, towards an expanse of water. But he would find it again, and he and Perdita would walk there; and, in time, it would become Perdita's Walk.

This thought pleased him, and, for the first time, he felt a genuine warmth at the prospect of his home-coming. After all, he was returning as the master. Whatever it was that had first driven him away might now be swept aside. He was no Prodigal Son, but rather an Odysseus who was coming home to cleanse his house of abuses.

An admirable sentiment; but one, he reflected wryly, that placed him on rather too superhuman a plane. He had lost too much in the years; and had scarcely energy enough for the cleansing, so to speak, of his own fingernails.

He became aware that Perdita had taken Mr Bloggs's card out of her purse and was studying it with renewed satisfaction. He felt a sense of outrage that, while he had been struggling to recapture the ideals of his youth, she should have been contemplating, with greedy delight, those very things that his ideals had caused him to despise. How had it happened that he had created in her the very opposite of what he was himself?

'Pa!'

'What is it, *my love?*'

She laughed.

'You're trying to make me cross, aren't you!'

He did not reply.

'But not today, Pa. I refuse to be cross today!'

She flourished the card at him.

'Pa, we ought to write to them. We ought to tell them all about the house. It would please them so much to think that we remembered them. I think they must be very lonely. It was a shame you didn't talk much to Mr Bloggs. I'm sure you would have liked him if you'd got to know him. Couldn't we ask them to dinner, Pa? Then they could see everything for themselves!'

His anger gave way to guilt, and he reflected how cruelly he had misjudged the girl. The pleasure she had derived from the encounter, she was more than willing to return. She displayed more true generosity than he did. Hers was the finer nature . . .

Thus the father—forgetful, as is so often the case, of what he himself had done—was humbled by one of those instinctively warm gestures of which all children are capable. Perhaps it is the absence of calculation that endears; as if Hamlet might have said, 'There's nothing good but thinking makes it bad!'

He took up the newspaper that had been left for him, meaning, rather absurdly, to find those items about the Royal Family that Mr Bloggs had thought might interest him; as if, by doing so, he would be making amends. He turned the pages. Suddenly his attention was caught by a brief entry.

'The Recent Murder in Shoreditch. A vagrant, discovered to have been loitering in the neighbourhood on the night of the crime, has been taken up by the police. The individual, of bad reputation, is at present being held in custody pending inquiries by Inspector Groom. An early arrest is anticipated.'

At once the dark business of the murder rose up in every grim particular. The woman's scent was in his nostrils, the woman's threat was in his ears, and the little room in which she knelt, dead, was before his eyes. Fear—surely an unreasoning fear—clutched at his heart again. His thoughts became shadowed; everything, even the home-coming to which he had, only moments before, looked forward, was overcast; and he felt a kinship, not with the returning Odysseus, but with that other wanderer of antiquity—the Wandering Jew, who was doomed to journey for ever and never find rest.

They reached Gloucester at twenty minutes past one o'clock, and were met by a servant who conducted them, with evident enthusiasm, to the waiting family coach. It was only then, when he and Perdita were seated side by side in the comfortable leather gloom, and the affable hills of Gloucestershire began to roll by the jolting windows, that he awoke to the dignity of his position and the consequent absurdity of his fears, and was able to dismiss them from his mind.

Gloucestershire, as Mr Dolly had so shrewdly observed, was not Shoreditch or Bishopsgate Street; and when the tall iron gates of Standfast House were opened to admit the coach, and closed after it had passed through, the returning master felt a deep sense of security and relief. Ancient trees, sparkling and shining from the effects of a recent shower, nodded familiarly; and suddenly recollected lawns moved as if to enfold him. The past vanished like an evil dream, and it was almost with a shock of surprise that he felt a child's hand reach out and grasp his own.

At once he prayed fervently that the start he had given and the look of bewilderment that had momentarily crossed his face had not been noticed; that Perdita had been too lost in her own wondering thoughts to have sensed that, for an instant, she herself had been lost in his, that her whole brief existence had, in that instant, been blotted out, as if drowned under a green tide of memory.

Then the many-windowed mansion came into view, and with a barking of dogs, a fluttering of handkerchiefs and a bobbing of white caps and aprons, Lady Standfast, who had decided to put a good face on the calamity and had ousted her son from his room to make way for his uncle, came tolling down the stone steps in a black bell gown as if she were ringing out the old baronet and ringing in the new.

'Brother-in-law! Niece! My dears! When we heard . . . Overjoyed! My dears!'

Embraces, smiles, exclamations, servants beaming—some even with tears in their eyes; everyone, everything, shining with delight!

'Welcome, welcome home!'

The steps, the porch, the very smell of memory, and the Great Hall—heart and soul of the house.

'Do you remember it, Robert? Do you remember?'

Tall, gracious, smiling down upon the wanderer's return. All forgiven. Laughter in the rafters; chuckles behind the doors; and sunshine sliding down the bannisters, like the bright ghosts of children, and tumbling on the marble floor.

'Do you remember it all, Robert? Do you remember?'

Birds and beasts gazing down from the walls. Heads of antlered stags, sharp foxes, otters, badgers, stoats and rapacious eagles with glass eyes—a vast congregation of fur, feather and sightless bone; and over and above all, suspended on a wire from some mysterious height, there swayed a gigantic black swan with its wings extended in a mockery of full flight.

'Do you remember it, Robert? Do you remember?'

The huge bird brooded over the dead heads and the living ones, over the laughter and rejoicing and, as it had always done, over the whole house, like the Angel of Death.

'Do you remember, Robert? Do you remember?'

25

On Friday morning in Bishopsgate Street another wanderer was welcomed, and another family rejoiced. Mr Dolly's cousin—Clarry Dolska, head of the family—arrived from Poland, with two large trunks and an expensive-looking crocodile dressing-case, in a cab. Clarry Dolska, rich as Croesus, clever as Solomon, with a large sum of money already transferred to a London banking-house, in a coat with a sable collar and a hat like a beehive in mourning.

'*Shalom—shalom*! How do you do! Pleased to meet you! What a journey—what a journey! But thank God I am safe! So—so this is Bishopsgate Street! And this—this is my cousin, Herbert Dolly! *Mazeltov*! And this must be his wife and children! *Mazeltov* again! So this is the business—Famous Pickled Herrings! *Mazeltov*! But what's this? No branches? Only the one premises? Well, well, we will have to see what can be done about that! Just give me a few days to settle down, and we will see! Noo! My trunks! Please, do you mind? My God, what a journey! So—so here we are! At last Clarry Dolska comes to London! *Mazeltov*!'

Clarry Dolska, large, important; eyes twinkling behind gold-rimmed spectacles that also twinkled. Affability, generosity, benevolence personified. Was anything needed, was anything lacking, was anything not absolutely tip-top?

'Well, well, we shall have to see what can be done about that!'
Impossible not to have hopes raised!

'The girls! Is there anything doing there? Young men? Prospects?'

'Well, there is—'

'Don't tell me now! Just let me settle down for a few days. Give me a little time; and then we shall see what can be done!'

Clarry Dolska, more of a father than a cousin; and more of a father than the father himself. Mr Dolly, helplessly feeling like a mouse: small, penurious and mean. Unable to stop thinking that the cab had cost him a fortune; it must have come all the way from Warsaw!

Upstairs in the room lovingly prepared for the honoured guest.

'Noo? So this is it? But it will do, it will do! Very nice, my dear! And flowers! *Mazeltov*! But in a little while, when I've had time to settle down, we shall see what can be done, eh?'

Impossible not to entertain dreams of rebuilding on a lavish scale . . .

'Ah! My trunks! Just put them down there! No. Don't go. I have something to show you. It will interest all of you!'

Impossible not to think of rich gifts!

'Do you see now? Take a look at these shirts! Feel the quality; examine the workmanship! The best. They cost me, I suppose, as much as you would pay for a whole suit. But they will last a lifetime. It pays to buy the best. People will always respect you for it. Jonathan, my dear boy, take one!'

The dear boy, beaming with pleasure, overwhelmed with gratitude, thinking the world of the great man, took a shirt—

'Hold it up, my dear boy! Yes . . . yes, you are of a size. See! See how it makes him look a *mensch*! My goodness, a real *mensch*!'

Impossible not to agree.

'There now! That's enough. Don't crease it. Put it back again.'

The dear boy, confused, bewildered, embarrassed, hopes all at sea, surrendered the priceless garment. Clarry Dolska nodded.

'When I've had time to settle down, we shall have to see what can be done, eh? Now! Take a look at these, cousin! Such a pair of trousers! They cost me as much as—as you might have paid for your whole wardrobe. But just examine the stitching. Feel the cloth! Hold them to the light! Now, against yourself! Ah! What a difference! They make you look a real *mensch*, cousin! Like I said, it pays to buy the best! Just put them down there, cousin. But we shall see, eh? Just give me time, a few days, and we shall see what can be done! Noo! Now we come to the presents! Don't think that Clarry Dolska comes all the way from Poland empty-handed! Don't think that Clarry Dolska doesn't understand what is expected of him! There—there—there! For you, my dears!'

Gifts, from a wise man of the East. Glass beads for the Dolly females and a box of cheap Dutch cigars for the Dolly males. The Dolly family speechless, presumably at the magnificence. Clarry Dolska nodding indulgently; remarking on how well he had chosen; advising matching garments for the jewellery and matching wines for the cigars; and hoping that the gifts would be treasured for the lifetimes of the recipients. When he heard that there were to be guests for dinner, he strongly advised putting the cigars away as it would be a shame to fritter them on strangers.

'So . . . so . . . we are to have people to dinner! *Mazeltov*! Business people, eh? Always important. Good connections. Never neglect them. I look forward to meeting your valuable connections, cousin.'

Mr Dolly thought gloomily of his daughters' two impoverished admirers, of faded Mrs Fairhazel, of indigent David Kozlowski, and—and of no one else. What a dish to set before Clarry Dolska! If only Sir Robert and his daughter had waited! That would have been something, at least, to salvage the pride of Famous Pickled Herrings, and shore up the broken legend of Pharaoh's palace and Joseph in Egypt!

Valuable connections! For the first time in his life Mr Dolly understood that he did not have any. For the first time in his life he saw himself as he really was; and it was an unedifying spectacle. A poor little shopkeeper in a poor street, unable to find his daughters rich husbands, unable to provide his son with good shirts, unable to offer his wife a good enough home; and unable, even, to provide his cousin with dinner company he might respect.

He was a nothing, a nobody; and his whole life had been an absurd pretence. Pharaoh's palace, indeed! Joseph the Provider, indeed! His gleaming Friday nights, once so dear to his heart, had really been no more than a tableful of beggars who probably despised him as much as he despised himself.

It was no good for Mrs Dolly to tell him that he was worth a hundred Clarry Dolskas; he knew she was only doing it to try and lift the darkness from his spirit, as a good wife should.

The nothing, the nobody, caught sight of himself in a mirror; and nodded. How badly, how cheaply he was dressed! He went down into the shop, reflecting that he had not a single item of the best. There was nothing of him that would last . . . excepting his hopelessness, his bitterness and his shame.

Passover had ended; the robber cave reeked with good tidings and the sausage grove was in bloom again. But Mr Dolly, threadbare Mr Dolly, shivered in a winter that was eternal.

Ah! A customer! But, no. Not even that. It was the spry little man who had told him of Mr Walker's becoming Sir Robert Standfast. What was his name? Oh, yes. Mr Clarky.

Mr Clarky, discreet—not to say secretive—slipped inside the shop and came at Mr Dolly sideways, as if he was less visible that way. Like most people embarking for the first time on a criminal investigation, Mr Clarky had advanced notions on the need to be unobtrusive.

'A word, sir; only a word, if you would be so kind.'

Mr Dolly was kind; and Mr Clarky acknowledged the fact by raising his hat.

'An inquiry, sir. On be'alf of a mutual acquaintance. And, if you would be so good, 'alf a dozen of the Famous. But take your time.'

Mr Dolly took his time.

'The lady, sir. The unfortunate who was recently murdered.'

Mr Dolly frowned. The horrible affair was something he wished to forget. He pointed out that a certain Inspector Groom had already questioned him.

'Understood, sir, perfectly understood. But,' murmured Mr Clarky, dropping his voice to the merest whisper, as if the very barrel to which Mr Dolly had resorted for the Famous contained an eavesdropper, 'as the tragedy 'appened under the very roof where our mutual acquaintance was residin' at the time, it is only to be expected that 'e should take an interest. Preyin' on 'is mind. And on 'is daughter's.'

Mr Dolly sighed and began to fish for herrings.

'Fit for a king, sir, fit for a king!' said Mr Clarky, doing a little fishing on his own account. 'Now as I understand it, the unfortunate first made 'erself known on these very premises. Am I right, sir?'

Mr Clarky was right. Mr Dolly recollected the Friday night in question. But it all seemed so long ago.

'Not too long, I 'ope, for you to call to mind any circumstance that might throw a light?'

No light; as Mr Dolly had already told Inspector Groom. But surely someone had already been taken into custody? Had there not been something in the newspapers about an arrest?

'A vagrant, sir. Possibly a witness, if 'e wasn't blind. But never the criminal, sir, or,' said Mr Clarky, taking a leaf from the inspector's book, 'I'm a Dutchman!'

Plainly Mr Clarky was not a Dutchman.

'Now, as I understand it, there was some mention of the unfortunate 'avin' been followed? Was there, per'aps, anybody you 'appened to notice in the street outside?'

Nobody.

'And the other gentlemen? As I understand it, there were other persons present. Did none them see anything that might throw a light?'

The darkness was universal. Everbody had stayed inside the shop; as Inspector Groom had been informed. Even Mr Dolly's son, who had had some foolish idea of running outside, had, thank God, been prevented.

''oo prevented 'im, might I ask? Not the unfortunate 'erself, I take it, sir?'

No. She spoke only Russian. It had been a young man by the name of Kozlowski. A very sensible young man.

'Do you think 'e saw anybody, then? I fancy, maybe, I'll take another pair of the Famous while you're about it, sir.'

Mr Dolly fished again; and recalled that Kozlowski's reason for stopping Jonathan rushing out had been because he thought it foolish to give the poor woman's refuge away.

'Very sensible, sir. And far-sighted. Unusual in a young man nowadays.'

Mr Dolly agreed. David Kozlowski was a fine young man who was sure to do well in the world. Although he'd not long come over from Poland, he was already well-placed. But was there anything else Mr Dolly might do for the gentleman?

'Well, now! Per'aps I might 'ave 'alf a pound of the chopped liver, if you would be so good, sir? And anythin' else you might care to recommend for a single person like myself to make up a real supper for a Friday night?'

Although Mr Dolly had finished his fishing, Mr Clarky had not.

'As it happens, Mr Clarky,' said Mr Dolly, with sudden animation, 'the very people who were present on that occasion are coming here again tonight.'

'Are you suggestin', sir, that I intrude myself?' inquired Mr Clarky, beginning to reel in his line.

'It is quite possible,' went on Mr Dolly, with increased animation, 'that one of the others might remember something! So that, if you have nothing better to do—'

'On a Friday night, sir, I would 'esitate. As I understand it,' said Mr Clarky, anxious not to lose his catch by too hasty a heave, 'you are of the 'ebrew persuasion, and Friday night is an Occasion. Would I not be, as the French 'ave it, *dee tropp*?' he concluded, throwing in the item of education to make himself more acceptable.

'You would be very welcome, Mr Clarky, very welcome indeed!' exclaimed Mr Dolly, thinking very much of his cousin, whose loud voice he could hear, and thinking that, in default of the baronet himself, at least he would be able to offer the clerk of the baronet's lawyer.

'If you are sure, sir—'

'Mrs Dolly and I will be very disappointed if you do not join us for dinner, Mr Clarky! I insist!' cried Mr Dolly, to whom the lawyer's clerk from Gray's Inn suddenly appeared as a valuable connection.

'But the chopped liver, and the Famous, sir? Will they keep for another night?'

'Leave them for another time, Mr Clarky! We will see you for dinner tonight.'

'But again, to intrude myself—'

'Don't talk of intruding! And I'm sure somebody will remember something! It's possible, even, that young Kozlowski did see something. And you can stir his memory. Now I come to think of it, he did seem very alarmed. I said as much to Mrs Dolly, that night. Did you notice, I said, how frightened that young man

183

seemed to be? It all comes back to me now! We dine at seven, Mr Clarky.'

'I am much obliged, sir, and I look forward to the occasion. And, takin' advantage of your kind offer, I will leave the chopped liver and the Famous for another time.'

Mr Clarky raised his hat again, and departed from the shop with the suggestion of a skip and a scamper in his step. There was a smile on his face as he trotted straight back to Gray's Inn, where he confided to Mr Leviticus the extent of the progress he had made.

There was no doubt that the lawyer and his clerk had been troubled by Sir Robert's involvement—however slight—in the crime; and there was no doubt that they were even more perturbed by their noble client's interest in it. Although it could be easily explained, it could also be uneasily explained.

Though neither of them would ever have dreamed of confiding as much to each other, it was possible that they wondered, separately, whether Sir Robert's involvement might not be deeper than it appeared to be; and whether the baronet was not a more devious person than either of them had at first supposed. But nothing passed between them beyond a few pleasantries that it would be a fine thing to beat Inspector Groom at his own game.

26

David Kozlowski had been in a terrible quandary. Although it had been quite a simple matter, he had worried over it until he had driven himself into a state, almost, of nervous collapse. Should he or should he not go to the Dollys for dinner? He was expected; but, to be honest, he had been feeling so ill for the past few days that he had not felt equal to going anywhere.

He had been sleeping badly and even the landlady of the house where he lodged had remarked on how poorly he had been looking. This had worried him frightfully—it is always unnerving to be told that you are not looking well—and at the first opportunity he had examined himself carefully in a mirror. My God! He had looked ghastly! There had been black rings round his eyes that might have been drawn in ink.

He was feverish. He must have caught a chill . . . perhaps by being out late at night.

(Out late at night! Now that was a stupid thing to have come out with! Nothing like it was to be mentioned, even inside his own head; nothing that could be connected, even remotely, with *that thing*!)

He ought to take more care of himself. It would be madness to go out into the cold air on Friday night! As it was, his work was suffering. He could hardly make an entry in the ledger without making a mistake. Instead of 'bale', he had written 'pillow', and instead of 'invoice' he had put down 'window'; and so had had to tear out the page. Once and for all, he decided, he would not go out.

But supposing he did? What could he be expected to know?

(To know about what? Anything . . . affairs of the day, politics, gossip, subjects for conversation . . . but not, of course, *that thing*.)

He had bought newspapers, and read them thoroughly. There had been nothing on the Tuesday, which had considerably unnerved him. (Why?) But then, on the Wednesday, he'd got the most terrible shock. It was there, in plain black print—Murder in Shoreditch! Every detail had been reported. Horrible—horrible!

His shock had been absolutely genuine; for in some extraordinary way, he had been able to think of the newspaper account as being something entirely different from *that thing*.

All the same, he had burned the newspaper as he had noticed that, quite without thinking, he had underlined every single word. Again he had decided that his health was too poor to leave his room.

So he vacillated; and when the time actually came, he walked past the shop in Bishopsgate five or six times, on the other side of the road, before he finally made up his mind. He would go. The Dollys were important to him. They were the very sort of people who could help to establish him. It would be madness to neglect them.

This was the reason he gave himself; and it was a good one. The other was not a reason at all. It was something dark and unwholesome, that he did not permit even to be mentioned inside his head.

The young man was consumed with curiosity to know what would be said about *that thing*; and the idea of its being talked about in his absence filled him with unspeakable terror.

He entered the shop, greeted Mr Dolly and went upstairs in a state of enormous excitement. His brain was buzzing like a beehive as he planned for every eventuality, for every false step, for every danger that might befall him. He went into the parlour—and was struck down as if by a thunderbolt!

He was introduced to Mr Dolly's cousin, Mr Clarry Dolska who had just arrived from Poland. He felt himself go as white as paper, and could hardly stand up.

But Mr Dolska didn't know him. His name meant nothing. An important person like Mr Dolska could hardly be expected to know anything about an insignificant orphan like David Kozlowski. There was no reason for anybody to know.

The young man's pallor was remarked on; but he was able to explain that he was just getting over a chill.

To be honest, Clarry Dolska was a little disappointed. He hadn't expected the Queen of England; but at least *somebody* for a Friday night! It was a sad thing, but one had to admit that his cousin was no *mensch*. His friends! Noo! Look at them! One needed such friends like a hole in the head. Such friends one could get wholesale. Young men with no prospects. A widow with hardly a stick of property. Noo! A pretty face? Pretty faces were two a penny! And quiet, like a mouse. Who needed such a woman on a Friday night? The only one worth bothering with was the little lawyer—in a moment of foolhardy ambition, Mr Dolly had promoted Mr Clarky in his profession. A lawyer, at least, one could always do with. He took Mr Clarky by the arm and went in to dinner with him as if they were already old friends.

The Dollys' table, pride and joy of Mr Dolly's life, was in a state of highest magnificence. Their whole treasury had been ransacked, scrubbed, polished and put on display. Kings might have sat down and been humbled, and queens driven into envious despair. There was such a gleaming, such a shining and winking, such a wealth of visible good things, and such a promise, from the

186

aromatic steaming round the lids of tureens, of even better invisibles, that one might have supposed angels were coming to dinner. Even Brandyella, that toiling maiden, was resplendent in a new cap and apron of unimpeachable white, and resembled, being somewhat flushed from her exertions, a beaming lamp in a snowstorm of starched muslin.

A real Friday night! And yet—and yet, there was something oddly unreal about it. In spite of all the lavishness and endeavour, there was something shadowy about it—as sometimes happens when a happy occasion is sought to be repeated, and people come, and leave their hearts at home. It was as if the guests had failed, and sent their phantom eyes . . .

There was no doubt that the Walkers (they must always be known as that!) were missed; but it was not their ghosts that haunted the feast. It was, rather, the ghost of that other Friday night itself; so that, when there came the expected explosion of crockery from the kitchen, there was such a start, such a glancing towards the door, that when Brandyella appeared with her customary dismissal of the uproar as being nothing, nothing at all, ma'am, she was greeted almost with relief.

Inevitably the murder was talked about, and inevitably the Russian woman's first appearance, banging on the shop door in terror, was recollected. Jonathan Dolly thought it a great pity that he had not rushed out into the street when he had wanted to. He might well have caught Miss Kropotka's pursuer red-handed . . . or, as it had turned out, before his hands had had the chance to become that colour. Like everyone else he was sure that the pursuit was connected with the subsequent crime.

Mrs Dolly, earnestly supported by Mrs Fairhazel, thought it a good thing that he had not gone out, as he might have been killed too. She would always be grateful to David Kozlowski for having prevented any such foolhardiness.

David Kozlowski, exceedingly pale from the effects of his chill, drank some wine.

The two young men—the admirers of the elder Dolly girls—remembering that they had been armed with poker and tongs, sided with Jonathan. Surely the three of them might have caught the man? Although David Kozlowski's idea had seemed a good one at the time, now it made one wonder . . .

Jonathan nodded; and everyone, it seemed, looked at David Kozlowski. *But for you, she would still be alive*, he felt everyone was thinking. *But for you . . . but for you!*

He spilled his wine. A saucer was fetched and the purple puddle formed the image of a pillow stained with the imprint of a congested face. The young man tried to cover it with his hand.

Mr Clarky, to whom all this might have been deeply interesting, was unable to take advantage of it as he was in the clutches of Clarry Dolska. The conversation only reached him in snatches as Clarry Dolska was telling him about Fox and Hankey of Lombard Street, to whom he had transferred his money.

'I can't say as I've 'eard of them, sir, but I'm sure you've done the best thing.'

(That young man looks poorly. I wonder why?)

'The best! Exactly what I have said to my cousin, Mr Clarky! Always go for the best! It is cheaper in the long run!' said Clarry Dolska, and went off into a long rigmarole about his poor father —God rest his soul—even on his deathbed buying cloth to be made up into a suit and insisting on its being the best. Mr Clarky was a little confused until it turned out that Clarry Dolska was wearing the very suit and that it would last him a lifetime.

(Now why is that young man trying to move the saucer?)

'We have always been in the furniture business,' said Clarry Dolska. 'Perhaps you understand something about it?'

Mr Clarky confessed ignorance, so Clarry Dolska obliged with an account of the extensive scale of the Dolska enterprises, and his plans for opening premises in London. Mr Clarky was lost in admiration; and also, to some extent, in events at the other end of the table.

'Surely,' Mrs Dolly was saying, 'the man has been caught? Didn't I read in the newspapers that someone had been arrested?'

Although she hated the talk about the murder, and was deeply frightened by it, she felt obliged to take part. She would much have preferred to talk about the astonishing elevation of the Walkers, and perhaps express some dissatisfaction with the absent ones, but she felt it would have given her friend, Mrs Fairhazel, unnecessary pain. She could see, by the way Mrs Fairhazel's eyes kept going to the chairs the Walkers had occupied, that her thoughts were very much with them. Poor woman! There had been real hopes there!

Of course, Clarry Dolska was a bachelor, but—Mrs Dolly bit her lip to stop herself thinking such impossible and odious thoughts.

'An—an arrest? Did you say someone had been arrested?' demanded David Kozlowski. 'Who was it?'

His voice shook, as did his hands, which, however, he managed to conceal in his lap, even though it meant exposing the tell-tale stain on the tablecloth.

'It was in the newspaper. Did you not see it?'

'No. I didn't see that.'

He had not, in fact, opened any newspaper since that first terrible shock. He had been tempted, of course—agonizingly tempted!—but he had managed to stop himself. His feelings had been something like those feelings that made him refuse to give *that thing* any other name.

'Mr Dolly! Was it not in the newspaper that a man has been arrested?'

Mr Dolly, hearing his name, looked up gratefully. If there had been a ghost at the table, then it had been the ghost of Mr Dolly. His cousin, seated in the place of honour on Mr Dolly's right hand, had expanded until he sat, so to speak, on Mr Dolly entirely and obliterated him. Consequently Mr Dolly, in order to overcome any feelings of bitterness and to revive the glories of Friday night, had been drinking more wine than was perhaps good for him and was feeling dizzy.

He stared; saw Mrs Dolly through, as it were, a thousand candles, and past, as it were, a thousand faces, floating in bright mists at the end of the table. Smiled at her; waved; and explained that he had been reliably informed. Then, sensing that he had been somewhat incomplete, enlarged his statement. He had been reliably informed by his friend Mr Clarky that the newspaper article to which Mrs Dolly had referred was not to be depended upon, and that the actual murderer (to which he found it necessary to append more *ers* than are commonly employed) had not yet been caught. Or if he had, then Mr Clarky was a Dutchman.

The sudden consideration of Mr Clarky's being a native of the Low Countries afforded Mr Dolly some internal amusement, and he chuckled lengthily.

He observed that Mrs Dolly was looking at him anxiously. At

once he divined that she had spied some cause for concern at the table, and wished to draw his attention to it. He looked carefully about him for those signs of discord that, she always affirmed, escaped his notice. But she was mistaken. Her overzealous heart must have led her into error. Everyone was getting along famously. Everyone was smiling, some quite broadly. Miriam, even, was laughing outright. What a pretty girl she was! But Jonathan shouldn't be stopping her like that! She was doing no harm.

'Lerrerlaugh, Jonathan!' he advised; and, in order to make her feel comfortable, he did so himself.

Mrs Dolly's anxiety took a turn for the worse. She despatched dumplings, gravy-boats and tureens in Mr Dolly's direction, as if they were troops to the aid of a beleaguered fortress. Courteously Mr Dolly passed them on, and, for a few moments, there was a sensation of the dinner revolving, like planets.

Clarry Dolska compressed his lips and composed a letter inside his head to the family in Poland that would sink their precious Joseph the Provider once and for all. He wondered what the little lawyer must be thinking of it all?

Mr Clarky was thinking: Now why did that young man try to hide his hands? And why does he always look away when I try to catch his eye? Then Mr Clarky's meditations were again interrupted by Mr Dolly's cousin from Poland who wanted to know what Mr Clarky thought of his idea of importing furniture from the family factory and opening a showroom for it in London?

Suddenly Mr Dolly recollected that Mr Clarky had had no opportunity to confirm his statement about the newspaper report.

He tried to attract his attention; by smiling; by tapping on the side of his wineglass with his knife—'Leave it, dear! Leave it. Brandyella will clear away the pieces!'—and finally by leaning behind his cousin and tapping Mr Clarky on the shoulder. Clarry Dolska frowned.

'Please, cousin! Myself and the gentleman are talking. Business matters.'

Mr Dolly was overcome with remorse for his gross breach of manners. He did not dare to meet Mrs Dolly's eye. She was always telling him that he interrupted people. He apologised. Clarry Dolska (having mentally added one or two telling sentences to his letter to Poland) shrugged his shoulders and went on about importing furniture from the family's factory.

'But—but I thought it was burned—burned down!' said Mr Dolly, wanting to take a real interest in his cousin's concerns.

'A small fire among some wood-shavings, a few windows broken. Nothing more,' said Clarry Dolska dismissively.

'But that—that's terrible, Clarry!'

'Noo! You call it terrible? The terrible thing was not the damage, but that there was no compensation. That's what finished off my poor father, God rest his soul! You, as a lawyer, Mr Clarky, must understand. Do you not think I was entitled to compensation? Maybe I can still claim? What do you think?'

'I 'ardly know the circumstances, sir.'

'I will tell you what happened, and then you can judge for yourself. It all started in the Russian camp outside the town. Noo! Soldiers! One of them—an officer unfortunately—got his throat cut. Killed like an animal. So his wife, or his mistress—who knows with these Russian women?—did it. She had got herself mixed up with some man from the town, and the pair of them had done it together. Such a business! Well, they never found the man. Nobody had ever seen him. It might have been one of a dozen the woman knew. Believe me—and I don't like to say so in front of the girls—she was that sort of a woman. No wonder the man kept himself out of the way! Noo! To be seen with a woman like that! So they never found him; and she had run off with her husband's money. Maybe the man went with her? Who knows! So what happens next? Who do they blame? The Jews. So they come into the town like madmen, and start smashing up everything. Noo? Do I have a case? Am I not entitled to compensation?'

'Do you know what that reminds me of, Clarry?' exclaimed Mr Dolly. He had just seen a way of leading the conversation back to the newspaper report of the arrest, which somehow he felt impelled to do, in the most natural manner imaginable. 'Do you know what it reminds me of? Miss Kropotka! Our Russian woman! As soon as you mentioned a Russian woman, I thought of her! Didn't it make you all think of her? Such a beautiful woman, too! Exactly like the one you mentioned, Clarry! And murdered by somebody no one ever saw. It's exactly the same. Kozlowski! You remember her! Don't you think it is exactly the same?'

The young man stared at him in what seemed to be utter incredulity. He drew in his breath with a noise as if he was trying to cough. Then he slid sideways off his chair and fell to the floor.

I've killed him! thought Mr Dolly instantly. What have I said? What have I done? I've killed him—killed him! His face—like a stone! His eyes—like death! And that cry! As if his soul was being dragged out of him! I've killed him!

But the young man had only fainted.

A rush of gowns, a dancing down of curls and ringlets, a reaching of hands, and a calling out for smelling-salts and brandy!

'Loosen his collar—Let me lift his head!—No, no! You must keep the head down!—But the brandy—Only a sip, in case he chokes—The smelling-salts . . . Look, look! His eyes are opening! He's coming round! A cushion, quick! A cushion for his head! David—David Kozlowski! It's all right! You're all right! You only fainted . . . No—no! You mustn't get up yet! Lie still. . .'

The young man, excessively pale, sunken-looking and haunted about the eyes, as if he had passed through the valley of the shadow alone, and without God, murmured over and over again that it was his chill . . . he was so sorry . . . he ought never to have come out that night. It had happened so suddenly . . . A dreadful dizziness and a shouting in his ears . . . then falling.

In a little while he was helped into the parlour where he lay down on the couch for about an hour. Mr Clarky offered to see him back to his lodgings; but the young man absolutely refused any assistance and went home alone.

That night, in the privacy of their bed-chamber, after they had talked over the events of the dinner, Mr Dolly said to his wife— rather hopefully, she thought, 'Do you think it might have been due to the wine? It was very strong, I thought. At one time I was feeling a little dizzy myself. You—you didn't notice anything, did you?'

'No, my dear. I didn't notice anything at all. I thought you were getting along famously!'

27

'So it was a chill after all,' murmured Mr Clarky, as he returned to his lodgings near The Angel. 'It was all because of a—a chill.'

The night air was snappish, but not unpleasant if one walked briskly; which Mr Clarky found needful to do in order to clear the head and promote the circulation after a heavy dinner.

'Now I wonder what sort of a chill that young man 'ad? Was it a chill on the stomach? Was it a chill on the liver? Or was it a chill on the soul?'

The poetical nature of this last idea pleased him and he fairly skipped along up the City Road, humming a favourite air. Then he slowed down and sighed. It was not dissatisfaction with his own voice that depressed him; it was that the musical activity reminded him that he had engaged to present himself at Mrs Streamer's in the morning for another lesson on 'the forty'.

A deep reluctance overcame him. Though the art was one that might well afford him pleasure in his declining years, he did not feel himself sufficiently over the hill, as he put it, to contemplate them with anxiety. He did not feel at all elderly. His rather withered, shrunken appearance had come upon him quite early in life, and time had merely toughened it, like a nut.

His reluctance to go for his lesson increased. He knew he had been remiss. He had not practised. Mrs Streamer would be disappointed in him. Besides, his present inquiries could not, by any stretch of the imagination, be furthered in the Streamers' house. Inspector Groom would have picked the premises clean enough for vultures to despair.

Mr Clarky, like any schoolboy, considered the possibility of a bilious attack. Then he shook his head. It wouldn't do. He really ought to go. A task begun ought not to be so lightly abandoned. It showed a want of application. Anyway, by doing something that was irksome, he would be improving his character and laying up capital in heaven.

He stopped to give a night-child a bag of sweets, and warn it of the consequences of breaking into occupied property. Then, feeling his resolve to go for his lesson begin to falter again, he ate a sweet himself. He was enormously curious about David Kozlowski and would much rather have spent the morning in pursuit of that interestingly ill young man than of the art of music.

The fruit and vegetable market was crowded when Mr Clarky presented himself at Mrs Streamer's door. Since the murder, business in the street had been as brisk as lettuces. It had become a place of popular pilgrimage, and the fatal house was obligingly pointed out by way of a sideline to more orthodox trading. Remembrances of the murdered one were offered with bags of apples; and, although the fruit and vegetable market admitted that it might have been knocked over with a feather when the crime had become known, it had not been, by and large, and taking into account the murdered one's flaunting and provocative air, altogether surprised. In fact, nothing really surprised the fruit and vegetable market beyond the occasional discovery, in a box of pineapples, of a spider as big as a hat.

The latest item of interest, and freely offered to Mr Clarky as he waited, was, of course, the taking up of the blind vagrant, who was well known to all the street-traders as an evil omen and a ghastly sight. It was plain he'd done the crime; and chilling was the description of his mounting the ladder with dreadfully questing hands. Robbery had been his purpose; as had been proved by his having been caught trying to sell the murdered one's watch.

''er watch?'

Now why had Inspector Groom, who had so punctiliously made Mr Clarky acquainted with details of the arrest, kept this matter of the watch to himself? Was he, perhaps, meaning to dazzle Mr Clarky, unfairly, with a further blaze of his art? Was he letting Gray's Inn and Chancery Lane pursue chimeras and waste their substance on the desert air, while Scotland Yard confided professional amusement to the interior of its sleeve?

'Are you sure it was 'er watch?'

'Well, it wasn't his!' returned the informant, with the air of one who has drawn an inescapable conclusion.

Mr Clarky smiled. It was possible that the Inspector had not drawn the same conclusion; and had not thought that the watch, because it was not the vagrant's, was, therefore, of necessity, the murdered woman's. In which case, his omitting to mention it was understandable. Even so, Mr Clarky felt hurt.

The door opened and Mr Clarky was admitted into the house of the crime.

It was clean-swept and curiously empty-looking. The stairs looked uneasy, and the walls forlorn. Mr Streamer, in violet quilted dressing-gown and with his little ram's horns somewhat crumpled, let him in and shut the door quickly after him. He expressed relief in subdued tones that he was who he was, and not another person wanting to see where the murder had been committed. There had been dozens; and Mrs Streamer had been made so unhappy by them that she would no longer come to the door herself. Hence Mr Streamer felt it his duty to perform this little office for her.

'Scars, you know,' he murmured, as Mrs Streamer, black as a bunch of grapes, emerged from the music-room. 'Such things are bound to leave scars. It's only Mr Clarky, my dear!'

'Ah! Mr Clarky. Your lesson—'

'If it is not convenient, ma'am . . . '

'No—no. We must have the lesson! It helps to take one's mind off—off other matters.'

Mr Clarky supposed she was referring to the murder; but, in actual fact, it was to a transgression of Mr Streamer's, with a lady from the theatre, that had recently come to light. Mr Streamer had, of course, wept tears of contrition, knelt and pressed his pale brow against Mrs Streamer's knees (hence his crumpled horns); but he had not, as yet, received forgiveness, and was in that state of being anxious to oblige and to please his injured lady in any way that he could.

Eagerly he followed Mrs Streamer and Mr Clarky into the music-room, darted about dusting the chairs, offered to turn the pages, and even to accompany the lesson on his violin. Mrs Streamer did not seem to hear him; and recollected that Mr Clarky had expressed a desire to learn *There is a Tavern in the Town*.

Mr Clarky nodded. All things considered, it was his favourite tune. Only last night, while walking up the City Road, he had been singing it. He began to render it, as if to reassure himself that he and Mrs Streamer had the same tavern in mind.

'There is a tavern in the town, in the town,
And there my true love sits him down, sits him down . . . '

Mrs Streamer, seated at her instrument, sighed and continued:

'And drinks his wine 'mid laughter free,
And never, never thinks of me—ee—ee!'

The '*me*' trailed away like a silver thread, and the pallid bust of Chopin, on the piano, seemed to shiver slightly; as did Mr Streamer in his embroidered slippers, and he wished another piece had been chosen.

Mr Clarky, who, from long experience, was inclined to divide the world into plaintiffs and defendants, had, in the present instance, no difficulty in assigning the roles to their respective performers. However, as he was acting for neither, he expressed himself as being overcome by the art, and sang the chorus. The defendant joined him, in patches:

'Best of friends . . . Stay with you . . . Well with thee . . . ' Each of which utterances was accompanied by a most heart-rending look at the plaintiff, who worried her fringe and continued with another verse:

'He left me for a damsel dark, damsel dark . . . '

Mr Streamer thought helplessly of Miss Kropotka; wondered how Mrs Streamer had divined his intentions in that direction, and supposed her to be heaping coals of fire on his hapless head.

'Each Friday night they used to spark, used to spark . . .'

Mr Streamer wretchedly recollected that Friday night when he had singularly failed to spark; and the episode of Miss Kropotka's bag in the loft. He shuddered. That bag, in common with a multitude of things, weighed heavily on his conscience. It brooded in the loft like a bird of ill omen. If, by any chance, it should come out that he knew about it—and, in Mr Streamer's experience,

things had a habit of coming out in the most unexpected ways—
then he might well go to prison for withholding evidence.

> ' . . . Adieu, adieu, adieu.
> I can no longer stay with you . . . '

How dreadfully apt! If only the bag could be happened upon,
by accident. It would be infinitely more desirable to hand it over to
little Mr Clarky than to the grimly large Inspector Groom. The
Inspector had terrified him.

> 'I'll hang my fiddle on a weeping willow tree . . . '

'What was that, Giovanni? What were you singing just now?'

'Not singing, my dear! I was saying . . . to myself . . . that I—I
must put Mr Walker's—er—Sir Robert's old violin back in the
loft. Now that I have my own, you know. I must put it back. I will
do it directly, while I think of it!'

Before he could be exposed to any inquisition, he whisked out
of the room, flew up the stairs, and, after a brief battle with the
ladder, vanished into the loft with a flurry of quilts and embroidered slippers.

Moments later, as Mrs Streamer was mournfully requiring
somebody to dig her grave both wide and deep, wide and deep, Mr
Streamer returned to the music-room, absolutely astonished.

'Look at this! Look what I have found! Would you believe it?
Her bag! Her carpet bag! It was in the loft! I found it while I was
returning the violin! To think it was there all the time! Isn't it
amazing! I wonder when she put it there? I never saw her go to the
loft! Did you, my dear? Please, please, Mr Clarky, will you give it
to the inspector?'

The woman's bag! Inspector Groom had, as usual, been right.
There had been a bag. It was a shabby, patterned thing. But it was
empty. No name—nothing. Only a scrap of crumpled paper. Mr
Clarky examined it while Mr Streamer continued to express
amazement at his lucky find and to reiterate his bewilderment as to
when the bag might have been put in the loft.

'If you will excuse me, ma'am,' murmured Mr Clarky, 'but I
really ought to forgo this mornin's tussle with the forty. I must
take this 'ere article to Inspector Groom directly. 'e would expect
it of me, ma'am.'

He rose, and, after engaging to return on the following Saturday morning in order to pursue the art, he left the house clutching the bag to his bosom as if it was a baby.

Mr Clarky, though no one would have suspected it from the twinkle in his eye and the elasticity of his step, was in something of a quandary. Duty and desire were conflicting within his breast. It was his plain duty to take the bag to the inspector at once. It was his desire to do otherwise. Undoubtedly Inspector Groom would take it amiss if he delayed. After all, the gentleman had taken the trouble to call at Gray's Inn and inform Mr Clarky of the arrest. That had been honourable. On the other hand the inspector had, for reasons of his own, withheld the matter of the watch. That had not been so honourable. Therefore was not Mr Clarky justified in withholding, for a little while, the matter of the bag?

Mr Clarky, finding, as we all do, that there are occasions when two wrongs make a right, decided that he was. Accordingly he walked rapidly away from Shoreditch in the direction of Whitechapel. The crumpled paper in the bag had contained an address. It was the address of a silk-importer's warehouse in the vicinity of the Tower.

He had not the smallest idea of what he might find. Probably nothing at all. The address might have been scribbled down because the woman liked silks and had learned of a place where she might get them cheaply. He must keep an open mind.

But no mind, except an idiot's or a politician's, is open at both ends, and Mr Clarky could not help wondering what he would do if his present journey led him in an unlucky direction. Although the suspicions he had formed during the previous evening at Mr Dolly's had been encouraging, he still feared for Sir Robert's deeper involvement.

He reached the street; he found the warehouse. He hesitated, both because of an uneasy fear over what he might discover, and because Inspector Groom would undoubtedly regard his course of action a being a piece of unwarranted interference and a gross trespass on another's professional prerogative. But if it turned out, as was likely, that nothing would be gained from the visit, then nothing would come of it beyond the inspector's displeasure. He went inside.

The youth in the green baize apron sat behind the counter,

studiously picking his nose. He was unimpressed by the caller's appearance, and contemptuous of his possession of a shabby old carpet bag. He finished off one nostril and began upon the other. Mr Clarky coughed. The youth looked up. Affected surprise; affected courtesy.

'And what might we be doin' for you, sir? A dozen bales of our best satin, perhaps? Or a hundred yards of red taffeta? Or a mile of tabby? Or birdet? Or desoy? Or paduasoy? How can we serve you, sir? Say the word!'

Mr Clarky looked staggered. He'd had no idea of the complexities of the trade! It was a whole art, in which he was as a mere infant! But then one supposed that the ladies would be more at home in it.

The youth shrugged his shoulders and removed an invisible thread from his sleeve.

Mr Clarky could not help observing that such a well turned-out young gentleman as, at present, was before him, must, in the course of his business dealings, often have occasion to charm the ladies. Doubtless the proprietor had had that in mind when he had employed him?

The youth did not think it unlikely.

Mr Clarky opined that the youth must be on smiling terms with as many handsome women as he, Mr Clarky, had had hot dinners.

The youth did not deny it.

Mr Clarky put it that the youth, by the very nature of his employment, must be quite a man of the world.

The youth admitted it.

Mr Clarky, tipping his hard round hat till it was rakish, leaned a confidential elbow on the counter and suggested, between men of the world, that the youth knew what was what, and where to find it, eh?

The youth smiled dashingly; and called Mr Clarky an old goat.

Mr Clarky confessed that, in his heyday, he had been inclined to dalliance, but now that his way of life had fallen into the sere, he was but an empty bag. He illustrated the point by flapping open the carpet-bag and shutting it, like a pair of bellows, so that a ghostly emanation of stale scent was wafted into the air.

The youth sniffed and said, 'Ah! That reminds me.'

'Of what?'

'A lady of my acquaintance.'

Mr Clarky said, 'Go on!' in tones of awed incredulity.

'Straight up!' responded the youth.

'Never!'

'Saw her last Saturday. Red velvet and fur. Hair as black as soot, and eyes of the same colour. Whiff me again!'

Mr Clarky, divining that the youth desired to be refreshed with a further ghostly inhalation, flapped the bag again. The youth sniffed.

'Hat with a feather. Foreign accent. Good looker. Something doing there, I shouldn't wonder. Whiff me again!'

Mr Clarky, saying it was an art, a whole art, obliged.

'Came privately. To see a colleague. Gave me the glad eye, though; coming and going. About five foot nine inches in her shoes.'

Mr Clarky, without waiting to be asked, puffed the bag yet again.

'Gave him quite a turn.'

'Who?'

'Me colleague. Glass door, you know. Couldn't help noticing,' explained the youth. 'Not really up to it, these young 'uns. Case of a boy trying to do a man's work, if you ask me. Frightened of it, if you know what I mean. Whiff me!'

The bag gasped open, and the scent hovered forth like the phantom of the murdered woman herself.

'Had to give him something to bring him up to the mark. Fancy that! I nearly went in and told her, "You're wasting your time there, miss!"'

'What did she give?'

'A watch. A gold watch.'

'What's 'is name?'

'Kozlowski. David Kozlowski . . .'

28

Mr Clarky's spirit rushed, like Archimedes, naked through the streets crying, 'Eureka! Eureka!'; while Mr Clarky, confidential, knowing, man-of-the-world Mr Clarky, restrained himself from following suit. Instead, he tipped his hat a little further over his eyes—to conceal the glints in them—and continued conversing with the youth as if the name 'Kozlowski' had meant no more to him than Waterloo Bridge.

At last, sighing regretfully that the price of silk was beyond his means, he departed from the warehouse, sauntered to a corner, turned it; and suddenly seemed to be caught by the wind and whirled away.

He took a cab to Scotland Yard. The temptation of proceeding further on his own, and actually confronting Kozlowski, had not been great. There had been no telling how that overwrought young man might have behaved; and Mr Clarky, although spry and well-preserved, was not strong. He had, after all, been reared in the confines of Chancery Lane and Gray's Inn, where the sun, when it shone, seemed to appear more for the prosecution than for good health and defence.

Besides, there was always the possibility that he had drawn the wrong conclusions. After all, he was—as he had admitted to Inspector Groom—a mere infant in the art of detection; and the relationship between Kozlowski and the murdered woman might have admitted of a dozen different explanations, and all of them innocent. Therefore Mr Clarky decided it would be both wiser and more proper to lay the case before Inspector Groom and leave further action to his professional discretion. There was also another reason for Mr Clarky's retreat—for retreat it was—but he felt ashamed to mention it.

It turned out that Inspector Groom was not on duty, having worked until very late on the previous night. However, if it was a matter of the utmost urgency, he could be found at his home. Mr Clarky obtained the address and set off again.

Inspector Groom lived modestly, just off the Pentonville Road. There, behind a white-painted gate with a latch that clicked infallibly behind you when you went in, like handcuffs, he and Mrs Groom had in their custody two small Grooms, aged eight and nine. Presumably because Inspector Groom was haunted by a prospect of having to lay a hand upon the shoulder of his own flesh and blood, they were children of supernatural honesty, much given to bearing witness against each other in a worthy pursuit of righteousness. When Mr Clarky arrived, a simultaneous accusation was in progress over the authorship of a broken window, and Mrs Groom, a lively, pretty woman, was at her wit's end to decide which of them should be sent to the 'lock-up'. She desisted from her Solomonic labours for long enough to install Mr Clarky in the front parlour, where he was soon joined by the Inspector himself, looking remarkably fresh after his slumbers.

'An unexpected pleasure, Mr Clarky!'

Mr Clarky apologised for intruding himself on the inspector's domestic circumstances, but—

'A glass of sherry, Mr Clarky?'

Mr Clarky expressed agreement and the inspector, drawing a considerable bunch of keys from his pocket, selected one, unlocked a cabinet and withdrew a decanter and two glasses. Then, placing them on a table, he moved quietly to the door and opened it so unexpectedly that the two smaller Grooms (who had succeeded in baffling their mother's inquiry) tumbled inside the room.

The inspector did not seem in the least discomposed by having caught the eavesdroppers in the act. On the contrary, he seemed almost proud of the precocious zeal thus displayed in investigation; and, after having heard evidence against several neighbours, he presented Mr Clarky as being a distinguished representative of Chancery Lane and Gray's Inn. At once the two small Grooms regarded Mr Clarky with a marked dislike and plainly looked for something to accuse him of, until the inspector said that Mr Clarky was well thought of at the Yard. Then they became affable and Mr Clarky would have given them sweets had not the inspector returned them to the custody of their mother.

'Well now, Mr Clarky,' said the inspector, smoothing down the back of his head as if preparing that sleek place for a large eruption of intellect. 'I take it that you have made a discovery?'

He poured out some sherry and gestured Mr Clarky into a chair. He himself remained standing. His gaze fell upon the carpet bag that Mr Clarky clutched upon his knees. Mr Clarky felt uncomfortable, as if his possession of that item of evidence constituted a slur upon the inspector's abilities. Hastily he offered it with an account of the entirely fortuitous circumstances under which it had come to light. He was particularly careful to imply that nothing had been further from his mind than going behind the inspector's back with the idea of gaining an unfair advantage . . .

'You have, of course, already called at this address?' murmured the inspector, examining the scrap of paper that Mr Clarky had thoughtfully replaced. 'Come, come!' he went on encouragingly, as Mr Clarky showed some reluctance to answer. 'We are two gentlemen together. It would have been unnatural of you not to have taken, shall we say, a peep at the premises. So you peeped then?'

Mr Clarky, a little red in the face, confessed to a peep.

'And you found?'

'That a young man by the name of David Kozlowski is employed there.'

'Acquainted with the unfort'nate?'

'She called upon him last Saturday.'

'He admitted it?'

'A colleague of his told me. I did not think it my place to see 'im myself, Mr Groom.'

'This colleague's description reliable?'

'Remarkable.'

The inspector stroked the back of his head as if something massive was stirring.

'Well now, Mr Clarky, where is the cat?'

'The cat?'

'Come now! Let us not beat about the bush! You have brought me the bag. Now I want you to tell me where is the cat that has been let out of it. There *is* a cat, I take it? There *is* something else?'

Mr Clarky felt more than ever that he was a mere infant in the inspector's presence. Information that he had been eager to give, of his own accord, now seemed to be skilfully elicited from him. He related his observations of David Kozlowski at Mr Dolly's Friday night table. He described the young man's extreme agitation when the murder had been spoken of, and his extraordinary collapse when Mr Dolska had talked of the crime in Poland. Nor did he forget to mention Mr Dolly's description of the young man's fear when the Russian woman had first appeared in the shop. The youth in the silk warehouse had also spoken of the young man's seeming to be frightened of the woman when she had called and given him a gold watch . . .

Mr Clarky paused to sip his sherry. The inspector frowned majestically.

'So what do we have, Mr Clarky?' he inquired, renewing operations on the back of his head. 'In your opinion, what do we have?'

'I would 'esitate to venture in your presence, Mr Groom . . . bein' a mere infant in the art, so to speak . . .'

'Do we have,' pursued the inspector, 'a murderer who is struck to the heart at the mention of his crime? Or do we have a sensitive young man whose very soul shrinks from matters of violence? Do we have—bearing in mind the tale of the Polish gentleman—a young man who, in his native land, became the secret lover of a married woman, murdered her husband and fled with her to London; only to be confronted—dreadfully unexpectedly—with a reminder of that crime, and so faints at the horror of it? Or do we still have our sensitive young man who has foolishly gone out into the night air while still suffering from the effects of a bad chill? Do we have a damned soul, driven, for some reason unknown, to murder the cause of his damnation? Or do we have a timid, modest young man, shy with the ladies, who is visited in his place of employment by the unfort'nate for the innocent purpose of purchasing silk?'

'The art!' murmured Mr Clarky. 'Oh, the art of it!'

The inspector smiled.

'So what *do* we have, Mr Clarky? Will you venture an opinion?'

'I would not make so bold, Mr Groom.'

'Would you not say, Mr Clarky, that the notion of a double murderer is, perhaps, a trifle melodramatic?'

Mr Clarky hung his head in shame.

'Then why, Mr Clarky, would I consider it highly advisable to call upon that young man without delay?'

'You 'ave lost me, Mr Groom.'

'What small, unconsidered trifle have you let slip that suggests, to the trained mind, that all might not be above board with that young man?'

Mr Clarky, like the base Indian who inadvertently had thrown away a pearl richer than all his tribe, was absolutely floored to hear of it. Begged for enlightenment. The inspector shook his head; and Mr Clarky gave up.

He knew perfectly well that the unconsidered trifle had been the gold watch; but he did not want to embarrass the inspector by saying so. The inspector had, after all, omitted to mention that detail when he had confided the arrest of the blind vagrant, so for Mr Clarky to bring it up would force an admission. It would, in a sense, belittle Inspector Groom—and in his own house, with, quite possibly, his dreadfully virtuous children within earshot. Although Mr Clarky, like any of us, liked to shine, he felt that, under the present circumstances, it would be better to do so by reflected light (the inspector's), than to seek to emit a blaze on his own. He was content for the inspector to take credit for everything.

'Would you care to accompany me, Mr Clarky?' the inspector offered courteously, after he had taken leave of his family and, in the process, cut short a promising inquiry into a misdemeanour committed by Mrs Groom in the kitchen.

Mr Clarky declined. The inspector nodded sympathetically. He understood Mr Clarky. The spry little fellow from Gray's Inn, although undeniably astute, lacked a certain essential of the inspector's craft. He was not a born hunter. The inspector knew it; and Mr Clarky knew it.

Mr Clarky was no country gentleman. He was not of that school of bull-necked huntsmen, in their butchers' coats and hangmans' caps, that declares that the quarry enjoys the chase. What might have been natural for a pack of dogs was not natural for him. He shrank from confronting David Kozlowski, even as he had shrunk earlier, and retreated from it, because he was both frightened and sickened by the thought of that young man's naked terror, which would have outweighed a whole world of guilt.

He retired to his lodgings and comforted himself that he had only acted on behalf of Sir Robert Standfast; and that that gentleman would undoubtedly be well pleased with his efforts. Even so, he could not avoid seeing, in his mind's eye, a young man's face as white as a tablecloth, sightless and speechless with dread.

He was, as it happened, quite wrong. Far from being speechless, David Kozlowski was extraordinarily talkative and friendly. He had been summoned from his little office in the silk warehouse and asked if he would be good enough to accompany Inspector Groom to a certain police station in the vicinity of Shoreditch. His colleague—the youth in the green baize apron—was asked to come too, as his presence, the inspector humorously declared, would serve to kill two birds with one stone; but only figuratively speaking, as it was merely a matter of identifying stolen property.

Throughout the journey the two youths hazarded innumerable guesses; but the inspector refused either to confirm or deny them as he said that prior knowledge might influence their judgement.

They reached the police station on the best of terms with one another, and entered its precincts like old friends. They were conducted to a small, whitewashed room, furnished with a table, a desk and three chairs, where the two youths were invited to wait, while the inspector spoke with an officer outside.

The youths, temporarily deprived of their good-humoured conductor, lapsed into silence. Somewhere, either inside the police station or very near at hand, a baby began crying. It was a nagging noise, aggravating the air so that one marvelled that no one went to put a stop to it. Then the inspector returned and, almost at once, the crying ceased . . . for all the world as if the inspector had been absent for the purpose of examining the baby rather severely, and had given it up as a bad job.

However, he looked pleased enough; and when an officer poked his head round the door to inquire if he was ready, he nodded and addressed the two youths with massive jocularity: 'Ho—ho—ho! Now for it, eh? Now the cat comes out of the bag! What have we here?'

A distant tapping, as of a clock or some equally relentless object. A shuffling, a muttering, an urging forward . . .

Enter a blind man. Face half-eaten—hardly a face at all. Verminous, ragged, filthy beyond all washing. His very soul alive with rats! But blind—blind—blind!

'You, young man!' Not Kozlowski, but the youth in the green baize apron. 'Have you seen this article before?'

What article? A watch!

'Yes. I have. I saw it given to Kozlowski by a lady in his office, last week. I recognise it by the torn velvet ribbon. You never said you lost it, Kozlowski! You're lucky to get it back.'

'The lady who called. Was she like this?' A likeness was produced; not very like, but enough.

'Yes. That's her.'

'Now, my blind friend. Take this article in your hand. Feel it carefully. Now tell me, is it the article that was given you in the night?'

'That's it! That's it!' Tap—tap—tap! 'Is he here? Is his honour here?'

One must keep clear. One might catch something off such a person.

'Is he standing by?' Tap—tap—tap!

The breath of a person like that would be horrible . . .

'I can smell sweat!' Tap—tap—tap! 'Out of me way! Curse this table! Let me by!'

That face! It makes one sick! And that hand! God knows where it's been!

'Where are you, yer honour?' Tap—tap—tap! 'No need to be shy of me!'

Blind man's buff! Round and round one goes. Catch as catch can! Never catch me!

'Ah! Ah! Got you, yer honour! Now, for the love of God, tell me, yer honour, is it silver or is it gold?'

The damned baby was crying again. Hateful noise. Somebody ought to put a stop to it, once and for all. Sounded as lost and lonely as the end of the world! For God's sake, stop that wailing! It will drive one mad!

Silently Inspector Groom watched the young man who was crying his eyes out, like a child.

29

The arrest of David Kozlowski for the murder of Katerina Kropotka completed the destruction of Mr Dolly, both in his own estimation and, he felt, in the estimation of the world; in other words, of Mrs Dolly. The monster, the murderer she had always predicted he would invite to dinner, he had invited. The table he had set for her had been desecrated; the home he had provided had been stained. He was ashamed.

Mr Dolly was not a proud man, but he was, in a sense, a vain one. His greatest pleasure was to shine in the world's eyes; and his world was Mrs Dolly. He could no longer bear to meet her gaze; and a morose silence invaded the bed-chamber.

Inevitably the Polish business had come out: that Kozlowski and the woman had been the very ones who had committed the murder there, and that Kozlowski had been the one who had been searched for and on whose account so much damage had been done. And inevitably Clarry Dolska blamed Mr Dolly — 'Noo! A monster like that you have as a friend! Such friends!' — and wrote to Poland to that effect.

Mr Dolly, avoiding his family, spent a great deal of time alone in the shop, where he was surly with customers and seemed to shrink under the sausage-grove, which pointed down upon him, like a crowd of accusing fingers. He harboured no particular feelings about Kozlowski himself, beyond bewilderment and disbelief. His was not a mind that could have encompassed the strange passions and desperation that must have driven the young man. All he could think of, over and over again, was the uncleanness that he had brought to his wife.

Mrs Dolly hoped that it would pass, that things would get better in time; but in her heart of hearts she feared that they never would. Sorely in need of a friend, she drew closer to Mrs Fairhazel, and an understanding grew up between them that was much deeper than before. It was, however, an understanding that could only be expressed obliquely, as they never talked openly of intimacies.

Naturally they discussed David Kozlowski and the Russian woman; and they both blamed her far more than the young man. Him they were inclined to pity rather than to condemn; and, although censorious, they found it hard to keep all tenderness at bay. For the woman herself they had no pity; she was the personification of wickedness and death. Even so, even as they vilified her, they could not help wondering, secretly, if they themselves possessed, deep in their hearts, a little of that terrible power that Katerina had so fatally exerted.

But these were thoughts that remained buried deep, and only revealed inklings of themselves in sighs and knittings of the brow. Maybe they possessed that power. It was not impossible. But even if they did, neither could have brought herself to use it.

The arrest of David Kozlowski was very much in the air also in shady Gray's Inn. There, in the room in Raymond's Buildings where Mr Leviticus's grandchildren peeped and smiled down from the walls, and peeped and smiled up from Mr Leviticus's watch-chain, Mr Leviticus himself was much inclined to peep and smile at his minion, Mr Clarky, who, respectfully, peeped and smiled back.

There was about the mountainous old lawyer and his dried-up clerk, just as there was about the delicately depicted grandchildren, a sense of innocent delight. They were both rather childishly pleased over Mr Clarky's success. They did not, of course, feel that they were kings of the castle and that Inspector Groom was, in any way, the deposed dirty rascal, but it was impossible not to feel that they had got the better of him. Although the inspector had taken full credit, that credit had been extended to him by Gray's Inn; and it was not likely that he would ever be allowed to forget it.

There was also another pleasure expressed by the clerk's and lawyer's smiles; but it was not quite so innocent. It was the pleasure of knowing that their unspoken doubts and fears need never now be spoken; their noble client in Gloucestershire had not been in any way involved. They had done well. They had served both the law and the family. They had been the bringers of happiness.

'I will write and inform him,' said Mr Leviticus. 'Perhaps, Clarky, you would like to enclose a few words?'

Mr Clarky demurred. His own effusions would be put so much in the shade by Mr Leviticus's measured prose, that he felt his best wishes to the gentleman and his daughter would be more happily conveyed by his employer.

'As you wish, Clarky, as you wish,' said Mr Leviticus; and set about composing his letter.

'My dear Sir Robert,' he began. 'It gives me very great pleasure to inform you that—'

He paused. A sensitive mind—an over-sensitive mind—might easily read into the expression, *very great pleasure*, a certain feeling of relief; as if the writer had harboured suspicions that had now mercifully been proved groundless. Mr Leviticus judged shrewdly that the gentleman was in a delicate state of mind, and that such an inference, if drawn, would be deeply disturbing to him.

'My dear Sir Robert,' he began again, 'I am pleased to inform you that the inquiry you requested Mr Clarky to undertake has been successfully concluded. A young man by the name of David Kozlowski has been arrested and committed for trial. There is not the slightest doubt about his guilt.'

He paused again. That last sentence. There was altogether too much of an air of reassurance about it. A sensitive mind might easily read into it more than was intended. He sighed and shook his head; and began once more. This time he overcame all difficulties and skirted all pitfalls. He praised Mr Clarky highly and then passed on to less delicate ground.

He trusted that all was well with Sir Robert and his pretty daughter—who, he hoped, might be persuaded to sit for Mrs Leviticus—and that they had settled down to family life. He was sure that the air of Gloucestershire would prove beneficial to the child; and, although he, Mr Leviticus, would always be at Sir Robert's service, he did not doubt that Sir Robert's life would henceforth pursue a prosperous and untroubled path.

He thought a great deal about the last portion, and wondered if a sensitive mind might not read into it certain misgivings on the part of the writer. But he decided otherwise; and the letter was at last dispatched.

A prosperous and untroubled path! Mr Leviticus need have had no misgivings on that score!

Sir Robert and his pretty daughter were a nine days' wonder in Gloucestershire. Tenants, neighbours and country folk alike could not smile at them, raise their hats to them, run to windows to wave at them, and find any pretext to call upon them and stare, enough to satisfy their affectionate curiosity; and the servants were unstinting in their praise. Miss Perdita in particular enchanted them. With one accord they declared her to be as pretty as a picture, a sight for sore eyes, and able to charm the birds down from the trees—which was an ability, however, not much prized by the family who preferred to shoot them down instead—and Miss Perdita blossomed like the apple trees and the pears.

The vicar dined; pronounced it to be not inappropriate that Sir Robert had returned at Eastertide (the restoration of Our Baronet tactfully compared with the resurrection of Our Lord), and preached an impromptu sermon on the subject so movingly that he wept unashamedly into his soup; and neighbours drank wholesomely to times remembered and times restored.

Halcyon days; and, to all intents, halcyon nights. The returned wanderer, with shaded candle, would pass along gallery and passage, move up and down secret stairways, in search of the kingdom of childhood. Once a startled servant took him for a ghost; and indeed he was an uncanny sight, in his dead brother's dressing-gown and his huge shadow brooding along the wall. He would drift down into the Great Hall, raising his candle as he descended the stairs, till the glass eyes of the stoats and weasels and foxes and birds glimmered down upon him like dead stars in a dead sky. There he would pause, but not daring to look up. He knew the swan was there. He could feel the chill of its outstretched wings. He had found, not the kingdom of childhood but its hell.

A prosperous and untroubled path. Mr Leviticus's letter arrived when the family were at breakfast, in the five-sided little room that resembled a casket that had once held something of value. There were three tall windows, and the sunshine streaming through them made the table heraldic with the shadows of lattices.

Sir Robert read the letter. He exclaimed aloud at the shock of Kozlowski's arrest for the crime. The family, sitting in a gaol of shadows, looked up curiously. Sir Robert began to explain, when Perdita, her eyes enormous with amazement, broke in with a furious condemnation of the youth. She had hated him from the very first. He was evil—

'Will they hang him, Pa? Do you think they'll hang him?'

Sir Robert did not know. Hanging was a terrible thing—

'But he killed her! They'll have to hang him for that!'

Her voice was shrill, and with an edge to it. Lady Standfast, pouring tea through, as it were, a black crucifix, nodded and said it must have been very disagreeable for her brother-in-law and niece to have been acquainted with such people, but that sort of thing was all behind them now; and Aunt Augusta, who, despite her decrepitude of mind and body, never missed the first meal of the day, remarked quite audibly that she also was acquainted with some disagreeable people who, far from being behind her, were in front of her at this very moment—

'I did not say that the *people* were disagreeable,' corrected Lady Standfast coldly; and there ensued a brisk exchange, to the accompaniment of toast, eggs, pork chops and mustard, which was terminated by the old lady's beginning to cry and appealing to her beloved Robert for protection.

She really needed it. The wretched law suit had ruined her and she was wholly dependent on the family's goodwill. She ate voraciously, like a bird that was stuffing itself prior to migration; and, considering her precarious position, doubtless the same instinct was at work.

Lady Standfast's sons, William and the dispossessed Charles, who were suffering from the effects of a heavy dinner the night before, sat with glazed, stuffed heads, very like the glazed, stuffed heads in the Great Hall, but lacking the veiled thoughtfulness of dusty glass eyes. Shadows bordered them, like the anniversary of a sad event. Charles was a tragic figure. The loss of the title had severely undermined his intellect. He drank heavily to drown his grief; going down, so to speak, three times under a crimson tide, and emerging only twice. He had nothing to look forward to in life but the death of his uncle; and he could see no way of hastening it.

'Why do you not take your cousin for a ride, Charles?' said Lady Standfast. 'It is such a fine morning for it.'

Perdita looked expectant; but there was no response. Charles only stared dully at the hurtful window through which could be glimpsed a sunlit prospect of lawns, trees and gentle slopes; and mourned the absence of treacherous bogs and precipitous ravines into which his uncle and cousin might happily be plunged.

Perdita frowned, and fidgeted behind a bar sinister. The letter from Mr Leviticus was still in her father's hand.

'Is there anything more, Pa? Does he say anything else?'

Her father consulted the letter again.

'He hopes we are all well, and he sends his kind regards to everyone. And—and he says that Mrs Leviticus would like to paint your portrait, Perdita.'

Perdita gave a little bounce of pleasure and urged her father to close with the offer at once—there being nothing more delightful than the interest of an artist (however unskilful) in one's person.

Lady Standfast smiled indistinctly; and said that Mrs Leviticus had once expressed a wish to paint Charles and William, but nothing had come of it. One must understand that such offers were only made out of politeness . . .

'Please, Pa, please, write back and tell Mrs Leviticus that she can paint me as soon as she likes! Wouldn't you like to have a picture of me?'

He would indeed. The notion of a portrait, a likeness of Perdita as she was now, before she became something different, appealed to him strongly. He would write to Mrs Leviticus without delay—

'Will I have to go to London, Pa?'

He thought it likely, as Mrs Leviticus was an old lady—

'She's younger than me!' interposed the ancient aunt, extending a claw towards the pork chops as she was still ravenous.

'You might be in London when they hang that fellow with the queer name,' said William thoughtfully.

He was somewhat better disposed towards his uncle and cousin than was his brother. After all, they had deprived him of nothing. He could never be *Sir* William until Charles kicked the bucket.

'Old Leviticus might get you decent places to watch,' he said, without the smallest idea of being offensive, and meaning only to make a helpful suggestion as to passing an interesting morning.

Perdita stared at him. Her eyes glistened; and smiled incredulously. She did not know whether to laugh or cry.

Sir Robert put the letter in his pocket and rose abruptly from the table. He said he had to go into Gloucester. As he left the room, he glanced back at the breakfast company. The sun had shifted and the confusing shadows had changed. Across the table there lay now the unmistakable black outline of a gallows. Everyone was looking at him and smiling.

His business in Gloucester took him to a jeweller's shop. Mr Leviticus had heaped such praises on Mr Clarky's head for his skill and devotion that Sir Robert felt that he ought to make some personal gift to the little man to mark his gratitude. He chose, finally, a gold watch and asked for it to be suitably engraved. Mr Clarky would appreciate that. He might even be reminded of that time when he and a certain poor language teacher had looked in a shop window in Shoreditch, and how Mr Clarky had urged the poor teacher to buy gold when he could scarcely afford silver. He smiled to himself and, recollecting Mr Clarky's words on that occasion, asked the jeweller to add to the engraving: 'The young lady would have liked the gold object better.' The jeweller looked uncertain. Would not such a sentiment cause the recipient to suppose that the watch itself was not gold? No. The recipient would understand quite well what was meant.

The jeweller duly recorded the sentiment and said that the watch would be ready in about a week. Sir Robert said he would return.

As it was still morning and the weather was fine, he dismissed the coachman who had brought him into the town and said he would walk back. The man courteously pointed out that it was a fairish stroll, even for a lad. Sir Robert nodded and said, rather oddly, 'Yes—yes . . . you are right. I may not be as old as I look, but I am certainly not twenty any more. Thank you . . . but I would prefer to walk.'

The distance was between five and six miles; but the way was green and gentle. He set off briskly, but once out of the town, his head began to droop and his pace to lapse into a shuffling, aimless trudge. He would continue thus for about a quarter of an hour, and then, as if suddenly realising that he had fallen into a bad old habit, he would straighten up and stride on energetically. Then he would sink again and his left arm would rise and his fist clench, as if he was still carrying over his shoulder a stick and a bundle.

But all this was purely instinctive, and doubtless brought on by his walking along a country road for the first time in God knew how many years. His thoughts were with the young murderer, David Kozlowski. He tried to bring him to mind, but could recollect no more than an impression of pallor and of dark, clever eyes. He had not particularly liked him, but nevertheless he felt a kind of terrified pity for him; and the calm, unconcerned attitude of the family angered him.

The idea of going to watch the young man being hanged had been repulsive. In his mind's eye he could still see the smiling faces. Even Perdita's! How quickly, how very quickly she seemed to have become one of them! When she talked (as she rarely did) of the good people in Shoreditch and Bishopsgate Street, it seemed to him that it was with a growing indifference; and he could feel a gulf between himself and the child. The nightly ritual, by which they had both set such store, had been abandoned. Perdita had been frightened that they would be overheard. She seemed content to let the secret—so long kept alive between them—die.

He walked on; and presently whiffs of a faint but unmistakable smell informed him that he was not far from the house. It was an odd smell and was only apparent for brief moments. An earlier Standfast, in the reign of Charles the Second, had provided the mansion with a moat, apparently under the impression that the restoration of the monarchy heralded a return to happier feudal times. But the moat had proved excessively inconvenient and had been filled in. Unfortunately the ground had always stayed soft and moist; and, at certain times of the year, smelled stagnant.

His aunt was waiting for him. She must have seen him approaching and had tottered and hobbled to meet him in the Great Hall. She stood, supporting herself on a silver-handled cane and attired in a shrubbery of agitated black. Above her the dark swan swayed and glared greedily down, as if wondering if the morsel below had blood in it.

She beckoned, rather slyly; and informed him that everyone was out. Plainly she wanted to confide in him. He waited. She looked rapidly about her and then, as if suddenly overcome by tender recollections, reminded him that he had always been her favourite, that she had always taken his part, and defended him, and interceded for him when he had been little. Trembling with emotion, she drew his attention to countless occasions on which she had protected him from punishment and wrath.

Patiently he listened. The punishments and wrath he remembered very well; but could, not, immediately, recall any intercessions on his behalf. However, he nodded amiably; and thought that, at the first opportunity, he would have the monstrous swan taken down and burned. He had always hated it.

'You are not listening, Robert!'

'I am indeed, aunt. You were talking of those times when you used to take my part.'

'Yes—yes! *I* used to take *your* part! *I* did everything for *you*! But you! You do nothing for me! Out into the street with them, Robert! That's what you should have done! Thrown them into the street!' And there followed an endless list of her griev-

ances and the petty cruelties that had been visited upon her . . .
The wire that was supporting the swan was attached to a circular
skylight. It would need quite a long ladder to reach it . . .

'You are not listening, Robert!'

'I am indeed, aunt.'

'No—no! You care nothing about me! You think only of your
child! Well, let me tell you, Robert, it will all happen to her! Oh, I can
see it! When you are gone, they will treat her just as they've treated
me! That woman and her sons! They are as hard as iron. And you
won't be there to protect her, Robert. There will be nobody to
protect her. She won't be able to run away, as you ran away. You
were a young man, and it was different. They will grind her down,
Robert, and take everything from her—just as they have from me!'

She paused, breathing noisily and shaking in every filmy black
leaf. She could see, from the look on her nephew's face, that she
had struck on a vulnerable spot and eagerly pressed home the
advantage by repeating her grievances and concluding with her
oft-expressed wish for her enemies to be cast into the street. She
would have brandished her cane for emphasis, but wisely refrained as she suspected that, without its support, she would
topple over sideways onto the floor.

'Well, Robert! What will you do?'

Confusedly he stammered that he had had so little time, but that
he would see about restoring her rose garden—

'You are a weakling, Robert!' interrupted the old woman bitterly. 'You are as weak as your brother, as weak as your father, as
weak as water! Why did you ever come back?'

30

The rose garden's grave was found, and plans were made for its
resurrection. Also some small but treasured items of furniture that
had wandered, like lost children, about the house were taken back
to the old lady's two dark rooms.

These trifling acts of restitution went a good way towards
rehabilitating Sir Robert in his aunt's eyes; and, to a certain extent,

in his own. But they were performed with such mildness and tact that one might have supposed that this Odysseus would have despatched the suitors with gifts rather than with arrows. He was terrified of provoking any resentment in the hearts of the family that might be stored up and, sooner or later, visited upon Perdita. He wanted to do everything possible to prevent the old woman's terrible prophecy being fulfilled.

With this very much in mind he had written to Mr Leviticus; and, after asking for his gratitude to be conveyed to Mr Clarky, and expressing a pleased interest in the idea of Mrs Leviticus painting Perdita's portrait, had said that he wished to make his will and would come to Gray's Inn at the lawyer's earliest convenience. Mr Leviticus had replied, suggesting a date some three weeks hence.

Three weeks! Why so long? The delay was unnecessary, intolerable! He became angry with the lawyer—who could not possibly have known the anxious torment he was inflicting on his noble client. Three weeks! What if something were to happen to him during that time? He became obsessed with the idea of dying before he had been able to secure the child.

When he went to collect the engraved watch from the jeweller in Gloucester he thought about going to some local attorney, then and there. But of course it was out of the question, as all his affairs were in Mr Leviticus's hands, and he had no idea what were his rights of bequest.

To make matters worse, the old woman kept nagging him. The restitutions he had already made, he discovered to his cost, were only a beginning. She flapped and crowed after him, making more and more demands; making them openly so that he did not know where to turn. Having found out his weakness, she harped upon it, never failing to predict that Perdita would end up like herself— ground down by that woman and her sons. Unless he was strong. And by strength she meant, of course, redressing all her grievances, real and imagined.

She got it into her head that she was entitled to her father's shaving-stand and mirror. It had long since been appropriated for the use of son and grandson, and there was no earthly reason for her to have it. For God's sake! She didn't shave—although, in Charles's irritated opinion, she would have been improved by it. She wanted it because her father had looked into the glass every morning of his life. It suggested a scene of terrible loneliness and desolation: the ancient daughter gazing into a mirror for the imprint of a phantom face.

This and her grim little bag of earth. The idea of Perdita being reduced to such pitiful reminders haunted him; so that, at times, he wished he could vanish as if he had never been.

'But thou shalt wait till I return.'

The curious expression came into his head irresistibly. He had come across it only the other day in a journal in which there had been an account, by a correspondent, of meeting with a mysterious individual in the vicinity of Hyde Park, who had claimed to be that legendary personage, the Wandering Jew.

The correspondent—an antiquarian—had naturally been sceptical, but conceded that the individual appeared to have been very old and to have travelled extensively. The correspondent who, fortunately, was acquainted with the legend, had questioned the individual closely; and that personage, who had given his name as Mr Ahasuerus, admitted to having been in Newcastle in 1790 and in Stamford during the previous century. Also he confessed to having visited Madrid in 1692 and Poland in 1838. These claims were in accordance with known previous appearances of that footsore wanderer.

He was described (it had been dark at the time) as being bearded, melancholic, and having the haunted expression of one who is accursed. Remarkably, he was able to recall quite clearly the occasion on which he had urged Our Lord to hasten on His way to crucifixion; and the words that Christ had uttered in reply: 'I go; but thou shalt wait till I return.'

The correspondent, by no means convinced, offered the account as a curiosity of human nature and an interesting example of the variety of people and incidents to be met with in the great city.

Although the absurdity of the individual's claim, and the rather obvious credulity of the correspondent had caused Sir Robert to smile, the article had, nevertheless, made a deep impression; and the words, 'Thou shalt wait till I return,' kept recurring in his thoughts.

Doubtless this was because, like all legends, the tale of *The Eternal Jew* had arisen out of profound fears and desires, and therefore was able to awake an uncanny sympathy in every heart; but whether he had been stirred by its aspect of redemption, or of damnation, or of eternal life purchased at a high price, remained obscure.

The appointment in Gray's Inn was for a Friday early in May; and Sir Robert, thinking very much of Mr Dolly's Friday nights, wanted Perdita to come to London with him. Lady Standfast, however, was opposed to this. Surely it was not a good idea for the child, who was settling down so well, to visit, so soon, people and places that she had put behind her? She was a warm-hearted girl and might easily be upset by meeting people for whom she might well have formed attachments, but whose station in life was now so far below her own. Perdita was summoned.

'You don't want to go to London, my dear, do you?' inquired Lady Standfast kindly.

'No, aunt, of course I don't!' said Perdita, who was frightened of Lady Standfast and anxious to placate her in every way.

Sir Robert frowned, but did not press the point as his sister-in-law seemed so well-disposed towards the child.

It was plain that Perdita had won, if not Lady Standfast's heart, then certainly her interest, which was probably the more valuable prize.

That the girl was generally admired did not unduly harm her in Lady Standfast's eyes—just so long as she flattered the noble lady by being easily influenced and led into an imitation of her aristocratic ways. Lady Standfast took what she considered to be a great deal of trouble with Perdita.

She advised her on dress and deportment, wrote away for possible governesses, and patiently explained to the child those subtle distinctions between persons that were conferred upon them by birth—distinctions that not even Death could erase, as they lived for evermore in the pages of Burke's *Peerage and Baronetage*.

That august volume, which listed the principal accomplishments of the British nobility (getting born, getting married, getting buried), was produced and a page and a half of Standfasts pointed out, with the assurance that Perdita herself would be added to their company in the very next edition. Then, as a matter of interest, Lady Standfast turned to her own family, the Westleys, who had a page and three-quarters.

Long and hard Perdita stared at the entries, until the print danced before her eyes; and she wondered in what manner her own unknown birth could be recorded—and worried about it greatly.

It was partly because of this that she shrank from the old nightly ritual, with its insistence on the mystery of her origin; but only partly. There was another reason, and possibly a more important one. Although it distressed her, she could not help feeling a reticence in the presence of someone she thought she had always known, but who had now turned out to be someone quite different. She felt herself to be quite unchanged.

On the night before the visit to London, the vicar and two neighbours came to dinner, and afterwards sat down to whist. The vicar drew Lady Standfast as a partner, and promptly dedicated whatever he might win to the poor-box. Lady Standfast shrugged her shoulders, and the two neighbours followed suit. They began to play.

Lady Standfast was a passionate player of the game, and played with relentless concentration. Although she looked fearfully grim, hunched over her cards and scowling, she was, in point of fact, enjoying herself immensely; particularly when she was winning, which was usually the case. It was remarkable that, in spite of being a singularly stupid woman, she was an excellent card-player—but then skill at cards is rarely indicative of anything more sensible than a desire to get the better of others. Her late husband—Sir Robert's brother—had also been partial to the game, and she recollected him tenderly when trumping, as if his ghost was standing behind her.

'There, Richard! Was that not clever of me?'

'You cheated!'

The accusation did not proceed from the discomfited neighbours, but from Perdita. She and her father were sitting apart at a small table. They had begun by playing 'Beggar-my-Neighbour' while Lady Standfast beggared hers, but Perdita's shrill exclamations had distracted the whist-players, so that they were now engaged in the silent occupation of building rival houses of cards.

Or it would have been silent had not Sir Robert proved the better architect and had not Perdita's elaborate structures always collapsed at the very moment of triumph.

'You cheated! You shook the table, Pa!'

'Not so, not so! I swear it!'

'You did—you did, Pa!'

'Never! On my word of honour! Here, take mine! Look! It's quite firm! There's two floors already!'

'No, thank you! I don't want your house. *That* would be cheating!'

She swept all the cards on the floor, and, with the most peremptory of goodnights, she left the room and went to bed. After a moment's indecision, her father followed her. The whist-players played on.

Perdita was sitting on her bed. She had been expecting him. Her room was large, large enough for two of the rooms in Shoreditch to be lost in it; and very possibly they were. Her bed was an ancient oak four-poster, with flowered curtains in which she enclosed herself at night. They were almost drawn now, as if, at any moment, she was prepared to retire within them.

He remembered that once, long ago, he had promised her that she would, one day, sleep in such a bed, in exchange for another he had left in a street; and now she had come to it. Well; he had kept one promise, at least!

She looked up at him.

'Why did you break your word of honour, Pa? You've never done that before.'

He did not answer. It had been stupid of him to break his word of honour over such a trifle as the shaking of a table, when there were other lies that needed his word far more desperately for their support.

'Why did you?'

It was hard to explain that he'd only wanted to provoke her into one of her old tempers after which there had always been warm reconciliations.

'I'm sorry. Please forgive me.'

'I'll think about it; but I can't promise anything.'

'Shall we talk . . . as we used to?'

'If it pleases you.'

How cold she was.

'Perdita!'

'I know—I know! You want me to say, "What a silly name! Why did you give it to me?"'

'Because it means "lost girl"; and you were lost and I found you.'

'I didn't mean you to go on, Pa.'

'Perdita. What is wrong? Why are you like this?'

'Like what, Pa? Like Perdita Standfast? Because I am Perdita Standfast. Because my—my father is Sir Robert Standfast. Because my aunt is Lady Standfast. There! Is that enough?'

He fancied she was smiling. How bitter it was to see her so eagerly embracing a way of life that he, in his heart of hearts, despised.

'I asked you, Pa, is that enough?'

'Yes—yes. Quite enough.'

She looked momentarily taken aback. What should he have said?

'Then good night, Pa.'

'Perdita!'

'Yes, Pa?'

He fancied that for a moment she had been about to soften, and ask all the old questions. But she only looked at him inquiringly.

'Shall I give your love to our friends in London?'

'My regards, Pa. You may give them my regards. My love—my love is something only I can give.'

'Very well, Perdita; your regards . . . if you are sure you can spare them.'

'Good night, Pa.'

She drew the curtain sharply; and vanished from his view. He walked to the door and turned the handle.

'Pa!' A disembodied voice from within the curtains.

'What is it?'

'You can give them my love, if you like.'

'I'll do that, Perdita, gladly.'

'Will you be seeing Mr Clarky?'

'Yes, of course.'

'He is very clever at finding out things, isn't he?'

'Yes.'

'Do you think, Pa, he could find out something for me? Do you think he could find out where I really came from?'

'I—I don't know, Perdita. I don't think so.'

'Will you ask him?'

'I—I will think about it.'

There was a long pause, during which the curtains seemed to

tremble; then the disembodied voice once more, sharp with tears: 'I hate that horrible tramp who stole me! I hate him—I hate him with all my heart!'

He left the room and went downstairs into the Great Hall. There was an ache in his heart and a burning pain in his head. The foxes, weasels, badgers and stoats snarled down at him, and the monstrous swan swayed and glared. He could hear, from the drawing-room, Lady Standfast loudly claiming honours and the vicar's high-pitched laugh.

31

He had, of course, written to Mr Dolly explaining that he was coming to London and that he looked forward very much to seeing his old friends. His letter contained enough tender recollections for the genuine warmth of his feelings to be apparent.

He had written, in much the same vein, to the Streamers and to Mrs Fairhazel—although he had hesitated over the latter. Their last meeting had not gone well. There had been constraint on both sides, and he regretted it. He would very much much have liked to surprise her; but she would almost certainly have heard of his letter to the Dollys and so would have been hurt by his supposed neglect. The letter cost him some trouble in its composition, as he was particularly anxious that no condescension should be read into it. He valued Mrs Fairhazel highly.

The Streamers had replied with distracted pleasure; and Mr Dolly had inevitably invited him to dine on the Friday night. The invitation had been couched in stern imperatives and the impression conveyed that, were he not to accept, then Bishopsgate Street would be desolate and Famous Pickled Herrings be laid to waste. Mr Dolly had mentioned his cousin, Mr Dolska, and it was not hard to read between the lines—Mr Dolly was not very clever at concealment—that he looked forward to a little harmless boasting by having a baronet to dinner. Mr Dolly's letter was of such simplicity, openness and affection that beside it Sir Robert felt his own to have been cool and calculating. Mr Dolly, he decided, was the best man he had ever known.

Mrs Fairhazel had not replied; and he did not know what to make of it. It could have been due either to indifference or strong feeling. He dressed himself with care; he wanted to look his best.

At first he had toyed with the idea of wearing his old clothes— to impress on everyone that he was unchanged—but he soon realised that it would have been an absurd affectation that would have exposed him to the accusation of stooping to his company. He wore a fine grey coat, a silk hat and stupendous trousers (the creation of a tailor in Gloucester), and looked every inch the baronet. He was, all in all, in an agreeable and expectant state of mind.

He arrived in London at one o'clock and went directly to the inn off Gray's Inn Road where Mr Leviticus had taken a room for him. He deposited his luggage, dined and presented himself at the lawyer's office at two o'clock.

Mr Leviticus had everything in readiness: a sea of papers, a pint of ink, a great black deed-box like a baby's coffin, and a warmly welcoming smile. Delighted to see Sir Robert looking so well, et cetera. The good air of Gloucestershire plainly agreed with him. Did not Mr Clarky think so? Mr Clarky, hovering at his employer's elbow, thought so. Sir Robert looking every inch the baronet. Courteous inquiries after the family and, in particular, Sir Robert's pretty daughter. A pity Sir Robert had not brought her. But then the business of making a will might be distressing to a child. One must temper the wind to the shorn lamb.

Sir Robert agreed, having tempered that wind himself almost to the death of it. A few more kindly remarks to put the client at his ease, for there must always be a certain gloomy apprehension in the making of a will, and then: 'Shall we begin, Sir Robert?'

'I would like to leave everything that is in my power to bequeath to my daughter Perdita. That is all.'

'Everything?'

'Everything.'

The lawyer pondered. Pointed out that, although the title and the estate could not be alienated away from the male heir—they would have to go to Charles—there was still a considerable personal fortune. Were there no small bequests that Sir Robert might care to make? Was there no one else he would like to remember in his will?

('Thank you kindly. I'll remember you in my will.' Sir Robert recollected a dead old woman and a dead boy to whom he had once made that promise.)

'No one. I want everything to go to her. I want it secured so that she cannot be deprived of it.'

The lawyer wrote. His pen scratched as if there was a bird somewhere, trying to get out. Sunshine chequered the walls, and books and grandchildren played hide and seek . . .

'Very well, Sir Robert. I have it all down. I will notify you when the document is ready for your signature.'

More delay. Why?

'I would like something done right away, Mr Leviticus. Cannot it be done?'

The lawyer frowned. Why the haste? Would it not be better to wait until the will was properly drawn?

'I want to be easy in my mind that the child is secured. Anything might happen to me . . . one never knows . . . '

Even so, the lawyer pointed out, even if something unforeseen were to happen, Sir Robert's personal property would go to his child. Did not Sir Robert understand that? Sir Robert understood. Then, pursued the lawyer, was there any reason for Sir Robert to fear otherwise? There was. The lawyer rubbed his pen against the side of his nose, as if to sharpen either one or the other. And what might that reason be?

'I am not her natural father,' said Sir Robert, staring hard into vacancy. The confession cost him an enormous effort, but there was no help for it. He waited for the exclamations of amazement. They did not come. Neither the huge old lawyer nor his spry little clerk seemed unduly perturbed. Doubtless they had heard more momentous revelations in their time.

'The child knows this?' said Mr Leviticus quietly.

The child knew. Had known since earliest infancy.

'Her natural parents? What of them?'

Unknown. Almost certainly dead. Time of war and confusion.

The lawyer nodded. Gazed meditatively at his client.

'And you found her—?'

The client hesitated; then told his strange romantic tale. The tramp, the cart, the purchase . . . and then the many hardships of the return to England.

He told the tale he had told to the child. It was the only way in which the lie could become the truth.

'So . . . so,' said Mr Leviticus, breaking into an immense smile, to the measureless relief of the client, 'you have cared for her all the time, and now she has become as your own. Quite a fairy tale; don't you think so, Clarky? Quite a fairy tale!'

'Like a story in a book!' responded the little man, who had read nothing more marvellous than affidavits and summonses since he was a child, and consequently was apt to dream of actions for trespass on the domain of magical beanstalks and of instituting proceedings against dragons.

He beamed at Sir Robert, and Sir Robert smiled back; and all was kindness and sentiment. The sunshine seemed brighter, the air warmer and the world a better place. The matter was settled, and there remained only to decide upon the child's guardian (Herbert Joseph Dolly of Bishopsgate Street), and the will's executor (Mr Leviticus of Gray's Inn). The lawyer wrote, the bird scratched, and at last flew free. The document was signed and witnessed, and no power on earth could take away from Perdita what her father had given her. The document was buried in the black deed-box, and a key turned in the lock.

What had been buried? The lie, or the truth?

Sir Robert rose. Put his hand in his pocket and took out a leather jeweller's case. It contained the gold watch. Begged Mr Clarky to accept it as a mark of his gratitude for the little man's help in the affair of the murder. Mr Clarky absolutely overwhelmed. Did not know what to say. Had always dreamed of possessing a gold watch. Would pension off his silver one without delay. Could not get over Sir Robert's kindness. Showed the watch to Mr Leviticus. Mr Leviticus whose letter had ingeniously prompted the gift, beamed delightedly as if *he* had given his minion the watch. Sir Robert felt warm, noble and generous. Not a cloud in the sky.

'The young man—Kozlowski—has been found guilty, you know,' said Mr Leviticus contentedly. 'He had no defence. Mr Clarky has received a letter of commendation from Inspector Groom.' Mr Clarky nodded. 'The sentence is to be carried out on Monday.'

'The sentence?'

'Yes. He is to be hanged.'

Sir Robert felt a little less warm, a little less noble, a little less generous. A chill struck at his heart as he remembered the pale young man with clever eyes; and a vision of unutterable dread clouded his mind's eye. Then he managed to shake it off, and he left the lawyer's office for the bright sunshine of the May afternoon.

The season bedecked and bedewed the London faces, and brought them out in pinched smiles. An eager day. He walked briskly in the direction of Shoreditch, meaning to call upon the Streamers. He did not particularly relish the visit as he was not staying in his old rooms, and he feared that the Streamers would be offended; but the thought of being there without Perdita had been curiously dismaying. Nevertheless it was a visit that had to be paid, both out of courtesy and for another, more pressing reason.

He wanted to collect the old trunk from the loft and dispose of its contents once and for all. Now that he had secured Perdita, now that she was safely locked, so to speak, in Mr Leviticus's black deed-box, he felt that he had to rid himself of the last traces of the secret he had kept for so long.

Previously he had always meant to tell her about it . . . when she was grown up and married, and with strong new roots that would sustain her for when he was no more. He had even thought of writing everything down in case, when the time came, he lacked the courage to come out with it. He had really thought that the truth ought to survive. He had looked forward to her forgiving him for the deception, and understanding the reason for it; and even being moved by the extraordinary effect that she—the tiny nameless baby—had had upon him.

But he knew it was impossible. The sound of her voice, shrill and tremulous from within the bed-curtains, still echoed inside his head.

'I hate that horrible tramp! I hate him with all my heart!'

That horrible tramp. Himself. His heart contracted. Her hatred had lasted too long, and had burned too deep for there to be any forgiveness this side of the grave.

He would take the trunk and throw it, with its damning contents, into the river. The decision, which he ought to have taken long ago, afforded him enormous relief. He had, after all, reached journey's end; though whether that end had been in his heart from the very beginning, he could not say. He smiled, a trifle wryly. His had been the journey; hers the end.

The fruit and vegetable market was somnolent in the afternoon's warmth. The shouts were dreamed, the air drooped with drowsy odours, and the marauding children darted and stole like sleepy butterflies. The aged flower-seller on the corner, having outlived the daffodils (how pitiful and unnatural that they should have died before her), was now entombed in red and purple tulips. As he passed her, the smart baronet inclined his head in recognition . . . perhaps a shade more deeply than the shabby language teacher might have permitted himself to do.

The Streamers were both at home. Mr Streamer had not yet set out for the theatre, and Mrs Streamer was giving a lesson. Sounds of sweet melancholy floated; and effort stumbled unwillingly after, turning melancholy into horrid despair. However, on being informed of the presence of the visitor, Mrs Streamer despatched her pupil with a briskness that was deeply gratifying to both, and welcomed Sir Robert into the music-room.

The good lady was honoured, was proud, was really flattered that Sir Robert should think of visiting her so soon after his arrival. She beamed, Mr Streamer beamed, and even the piano seemed to stretch its keyboard in a wide, ivory smile. Sir Robert blushed inwardly as he thought of the reason for the promptness of his visit.

Mr Streamer, being in his usual state of guilty obligingness, rushed to bring in the tea things, while Mrs Streamer inquired about Perdita and hoped that she was practising regularly . . . such a shame to neglect her talent! Then Mr Streamer returned, rattling and steaming like a china engine, laden with thin bread and butter, cakes, and a tottering cathedral of cups. Mrs Streamer poured, and Mr Streamer gushed . . . about concerts and pupils, the latest piece in the theatre, and all the absorbing things that had happened since Sir Robert had gone away. Like most people who meet a friend who has prospered above them, they were eager to talk of their own concerns, as if anxious to assure the elevated one that the world had not stopped because he had risen above it.

Patiently Sir Robert listened until the flow of the Streamers' news dwindled into a trickle, and was reduced at length to such trifles as confiding that Mr Streamer's violin had been repaired and sounded as sweetly as ever, and that the instrument that Sir Robert had kindly lent him was now back in the loft.

'Perhaps you would like to take it back for Perdita?' suggested Mr Streamer. 'Now that it has been restored and restrung, it has a very pleasant tone.'

The violin in the loft. An excellent idea. Perdita would be pleased. Sir Robert rose. He would go up at once and fetch it; and, at the same time, he would collect the old trunk he had left there.

Mrs Streamer demurred. She did not think it right for the baronet to be climing up into such a dusty place. Mr Streamer could go. Mr Streamer bobbed and beamed. Twisted his ram's horns fetchingly. Mrs Streamer's word was his command. Vanished. Sir Robert insisted on following.

He left the room and began to climb the familiar stairs. At every step, pangs of memory assailed him. 'Perdita Walker', at varying heights, and in varying stages of spelling and calligraphy, still embellished the wall; and the doors of the old rooms looked lost and forlorn. 'Perdita, I'm home, my dear!' he whispered to himself, as if the child was inside, waiting for him again.

Mr Streamer ascended the ladder like a trousered angel, and vanished into the black hole of the loft. Sir Robert placed his foot on the bottom rung, and waited to receive the trunk. As he stood, he fancied he could still smell, even after so long, Katerina's scent. It seemed to have got into the very interstices of the house.

The trunk came down, then Mr Streamer, clutching the violin that was wrapped in cloth, like a baby. They went downstairs and into the music-room. Mrs Streamer exclaimed over the state of the trunk; said Mr Streamer ought to have carried it. Mr Streamer was overcome with guilty remorse—absolutely genuine, but not on account of the trunk. He unwrapped the violin, which gleamed with new varnish. He tapped it with the bow.

'You must let me play something for you!' he said eagerly; and placed the instrument under his chin, where it nestled like an affectionate cheek. Mrs Streamer sighed; but so deep was her love of music that she seated herself at the piano and struck a note. Mr Streamer tuned. Then, with a nod and a rolling of his moist eyes at his ever-injured spouse, began to play a very soulful air.

Mr Streamer played skilfully. The notes he produced were full and vibrant; and the listener seemed properly affected. His head was bowed, his eyes closed and his lower lip thrust forward, as if in admiring appraisal.

It was the first time he had heard the instrument played upon; and, just as the sentimental violinist's bow awoke the sleeping notes, so those notes awoke sleeping memories and ushered them before his inward eye. The shattered cottage . . . the dead boy in the window . . . the awkward wrenching of the fiddle from his fixed grasp . . . the sigh of clothing as he fell, as if the last gasp of life was escaping . . . the pointing hand . . . 'Thank you kindly, young man! I'll mention you in my will.'

The playing ceased. Mr Streamer said, 'It might almost be an Italian instrument, don't you think? But it was made in Poland. The restorer thought it was probably by one of those village craftsmen. Often they're the best. They make few instruments, but each one is a labour of love.'

'A labour of love!' echoed Mrs Streamer mournfully, and exchanged glances with the pallid bust of Chopin.

'It's the new varnish that has made all the difference,' went on Mr Streamer hastily. 'The old varnish had been damaged by fire. Did you know that, Sir Robert?'

Sir Robert knew.

'It was quite blackened in places,' explained Mr Streamer, turning the instrument this way and that in his delicate Italian hands. 'The maker's name was quite obscured. But one can see it now. It's engraved on the back plate. There's some writing in Polish, which, I suppose, says, "*This violin was made by*—" and then the name: "*Stanislaw Kozlowski*".'

'*Kozlowski?*'

'Yes. The same name as that terrible young man—our murderer. But I'm told it's a common Polish name. I knew a Kozlowski once who played the 'cello—'

'*Kozlowski?*'

'Yes. There it is. If you hold it towards the light you can see it plainly. And the writing . . . '

Sir Robert took the fiddle and turned it till the light illuminated the engraved words: '*Stanislaw Kozlowski*'. He stared at the writing above, which Mr Streamer had supposed to say: '*This violin was made by*—' It was not quite that. It said: '*This violin was made for David by his father, Stanislaw Kozlowski.*'

230

'My own instrument is an Italian one,' prattled on Mr Streamer. 'My family are originally Italian ... my name, you know— Giovanni—is Italian ... '

'I gave it to him when we were married,' said Mrs Streamer. 'The violin, I mean ... '

David Kozlowski!

' ... Made in Cremona ... a beautiful tone ... '

David Kozlowski had been there! But where? The dead boy? Had he really been dead? Think! The ashy staring face, the outstretched arm, the pointing fingers. Had they stirred? He should have looked more carefully. No. The boy had been dead. And anyway, he would have been much older than the other one. Then where—?

' ... We were married here, in Shoreditch Church ... a wonderful organ ... '

The glowing embers in the night! Had they been eyes?

' ... Quite the envy of my colleagues in the orchestra ... the violin, I mean ... '

Look everywhere! In the blackened, smoky corners ... and back along the road. Turn quickly and look!

' ... We used to play a great deal together ... duets ... '

Nothing! This is madness! Kozlowski's a common Polish name. There must be thousands. Why him? Because of Katerina! She had known him. He had told her. He was the *other one* who had been there. Her threat had been the truth! The young man had been interested in him, had questioned him closely. And what had he said? Yes. Children sometimes remember strange things. A strange thing indeed to see a battered tramp crooning over a cradle!

' ... I have a short solo, with the soprano, in our present piece in the theatre ... '

The Streamers' voices buzzed and fumbled as Sir Robert held the fiddle in his shaking hands. Suddenly Mrs Streamer's clock (which told, in tutelary terms, the passing shillings) emitted a doll-like chime. It was five o'clock. With a start he awoke from his frightful reverie, apologised for God knew what, and left the house distractedly. He could hardly manage, even, to say goodbye.

As he stumbled back through the dying market, he presented a most curious sight. A gentleman, elegantly attired, clutching, as if his life depended upon it, a shabby, worn-out trunk by the rope that secured it, and holding under his arm a fiddle wrapped up in a

231

sheet. Every inch the baronet; and every foot and every yard the haunted, terrified man.

The nameless, solitary baby he had found in that place of death and desolation, the baby whose faint spark of life he had blown upon and whose slowly flowering existence had caused his own to flower anew, had been neither nameless nor alone. Her name was Kozlowski; and she had a brother who was to be hanged.

This dreadful conclusion sprang upon him with irresistible force, and drove everything else from his mind. Curiously the worst of it was, not that she had a brother, but that she had a name. It seemd to cut her off from him, and make her a stranger.

He cursed the violin and his own greed in stealing it; and above all he cursed the irony of having carried away, and lovingly preserved like a poisoned seed, the instrument of his own and the child's eventual destruction.

'Thank you kindly,' he had said. 'I'll remember you in my will!' No need for that any more. The dead had remembered *him*.

He wondered if the young man had said anything, had confided in anyone? And he wondered, very desperately indeed, if the young man would be willing to carry his secret to the grave. This thought was uppermost in his mind; and over and over again he framed passionate requests and pleadings, that were, he knew, as unseemly as they were hollow and false.

32

The prison lurked in the innermost part of the town like a dark, unwholesome thought; a thought obscured, a thought hidden, a thought confined behind immense, grime-blackened walls.

These walls, pierced at intervals by mean, barred windows, were constructed of great stone tablets—as if God had taken legal advice and handed down, for the defence of the Realm, not ten, but ten thousand Commandments. Never were there so many 'Thou shalt nots'.

But to no avail. The prison and the narrow street outside it stank of failure; failure of heart, failure of soul, of love, of faith, of understanding; and, most disagreeably, failure of bowels.

At first there had been some obstacles in gaining admittance to the condemned cell; but the gentleman's appearance, title and a small sum of money soon overcame them; and he was conducted along passages of stone and iron that echoed and re-echoed with the curious sound of hard laughter.

He had left his baggage (the trunk and the fiddle) in a small, stuffy room beside the entrance. He did not want to take them with him and perhaps needlessly betray himself. It was possible that the young man knew nothing after all. At most he could only have suspicions.

'Not much further, Sir Robert.'

He had been on the point of giving a false name (Mr Ahasuerus had irresponsibly occurred to him), but had realised that such a subterfuge was really as unnecessary as it might have proved hazardous. After all, he was acquainted with the prisoner. It was quite reasonable for him to visit the young man in his last hours. If the visit were discovered, it would be taken as an act of charity and compassion, an act of Christian virtue. The baronet was known to be strong on Christian virtue. Had he not once spurned riches to tread the pilgrim's path? But the path he trod at the moment was very different.

'It's kind of you to take the trouble, Sir Robert,' said his guide, an elderly man with a limp and a gnarled face, like a stricken tree. 'I'm sure the prisoner will be glad of it.'

'I—I feel so sorry for him.'

'It wouldn't be human otherwise,' said the gaoler, pausing before a turning, and shaking his ugly head. 'I don't hold with it, sir. I'm afraid I don't hold with it.'

'Hanging?'

'That and other things.'

'Then it must be hard for you to work here. Why do you do it?'

'It's a living, sir. I've grandchildren to provide for. No—no! I didn't mean that, sir!' (Sir Robert had put his hand in his pocket.) 'I want to leave 'em something. Which makes me as bad as anyone. Property's the cross we all have to bear, sir. It wasn't the Tree of Knowledge that brought us down, it was the Tree of Property.'

A younger colleague of the gaoler came sauntering by. He grinned.

'You don't want to take notice of 'im, sir! 'e fancies 'imself as Jesus Christ!'

The elderly one shook his head good-humouredly; and resumed his journey through the gaol. Presently he halted outside a
heavy, iron-studded door, such as might have guarded something
of immense value—a king's ransom, perhaps. He nodded and,
lowering his voice, murmured discreetly, 'This is it, sir. He's
inside here. He's very frightened, you know. He don't show it,
but he's shaking to his very heart. One doesn't know what to do
for the best, when one knows everything must come to the worst.
But he'll be glad of the visit. There's only been a couple come to
see him so far; and there's little enough time left for more.'

'He's had visitors then?'

'There was a gentleman from Bishopsgate Street who brought
him a basket of food and a bottle of wine. And then there was a
lady who brought him a book—not a religious volume, but a
book of poems. Shakespeare and suchlike. A very fine person.
One of those ladies you'd think were too nervous and gentle to
come inside a place like this. But you can never tell. Often there's a
great deal more to them than you'd guess. A Mrs Fairhazel—'

The baronet started. He'd not counted on such a thing happening.
He wondered if Kozlowski had already betrayed him? Such was his
state of mind that he did not even feel ashamed of his own purpose
compared with the kindness and compassion shown by his friends.

'Here's someone come to visit you, David, my boy,' said the
gaoler, unbolting and opening the door. 'Here's Sir Robert Standfast.'

The room was small—wretchedly small—with whitewashed
walls and a little window set too high to reach. It was sparsely
furnished, with a bed, a table and two chairs. It might have been a
monk's cell, but it lacked calm; there was too strong a feeling of its
being the last place on earth.

The prisoner, who had been crouching on his bed with a grey
blanket round his shoulders, as if he was bitterly cold, jumped to
his feet in excitement. At first glance, his face looked dirty; but it
was due to a shadowy smudging of youthful beard that resembled,
more than anything grown-up, a Christmas of burnt cork and
made him look unnaturally young. His eyes were sunken as if
from the pressure of knuckles and thumbs.

He expressed delight at being visited; clapped his hands and
peered with almost painful expectation at his visitor. His at-

titude—his way of staring at his visitor's hands, then past him to the gaoler as if to see if that personage was carrying a parcel—so strongly suggested the eager hopes of a child, that the visitor felt wretched for not having brought a present. The gaoler withdrew, murmuring that he would wait outside until the visitor wished to leave.

'It's almost certain, you know,' began David, as soon as the door was shut, 'that nothing will happen. At least, not for another week!'

'That's good—that's good!' It was impossible not to share the young man's excitement.

'It's because they have to build something outside. And if anything was really going to happen, they would have started by now. There was nothing outside, was there? I've been told there was nothing. And I'm sure they would tell me if there was. It has to be by Debtor's Door, you know. They haven't started, have they?'

'No. They haven't started. There was nothing there at all.'

'You see? You see?' cried David, clapping his hands triumphantly. 'They can't possibly do anything in time! They would have started—'

'Of course they would have started. You are quite right.'

'Because it has to be properly done. People will be standing there. The governor and the sheriff, and—and—What a thing it would be if everything collapsed under them! Imagine that! They wouldn't dare to risk it! I suppose that when they do it, when they really do it, they have to start at least a week before! Don't you think?'

'At least a week.' Surely false hope was better than real despair!

'And one would be bound to hear it. There'd be a great deal of hammering and that sort of thing.'

'Oh, yes. I'm sure there would be.'

It was hard to think that the childish young man was a murderer. It was hard to think of anything except that he was going to be hanged on Monday.

'And—and they say that someone comes to see you first. He would have been by now, don't you think?'

'Yes—yes. I'm sure you're right!'

So this was David Kozlowski. So this was Perdita's brother. Look at him closely if you dare. Remember him, so that you can trace his features in Perdita's for ever.

'They don't keep me in here all the time; and that's another thing! I can walk in a passage outside. They wouldn't let me do that if—if anything was going to happen. After all, where would be the sense in it?'

'There would be no sense in it at all!'

The young man, who had been walking about the tiny room, paused and nodded thoughtfully. Then he glanced at his visitor with a quick, rather sly smile.

'You—you didn't bring me anything, did you? I wondered if you had—and if you'd forgotten about it. Did you bring me anything?'

'No. I'm sorry. It was bad of me . . . but I didn't think of it.'

'Will you come and see me again?'

'If you want me to.'

'Oh, yes! But only if you bring me something.'

'I'll come tomorrow. What would you like me to bring?'

'Oh, I don't know. But, yes! I do know! Can you imagine what? I want a violin! I had one once, but it was stolen. Come tomorrow and bring me a violin!'

He left the prison, taking with him his ungainly baggage. The meeting had decided nothing. The young man had so concentrated his mind on the fragile hope that nothing was going to happen that he had been incapable of speaking, or even thinking, of anything else. His whole existence had shrunk to the solitary consideration of whether or not any preparations had begun outside Debtor's Door.

But he had not forgotten the violin. Perhaps, in another day, even that would be gone. Perhaps it would be better not to go back to the prison. It was, as the gaoler had said, hard to know what to do for the best when one knew that everything must come to the worst.

The baronet returned to his inn off the Gray's Inn Road. He went directly up to his room and lay down on his bed; and fell asleep so suddenly that it was as if a black bag had been put over his head.

When he awoke, it was pitch dark and quiet. God knew what time it was. He remembered, with a start, that he should have gone to the Dollys for dinner. They must have gone to bed hours ago.

They would be angry with him. He felt terribly unhappy; and lay still, crushed beneath the weight of endless lies and deceit. He waited until it was light and he could hear people about, and went out again, taking his burdens with him. He walked about the town for he did not know how long, trying to make up his mind whether or not he should go back to the prison.

He was frightened that Mr Dolly or Mrs Fairhazel might be visiting again, and he shrank from the thought of meeting them there. Nor did he really want to see the young man, whose horrible preoccupation distressed him immeasurably. He caught himself wishing that it was all over; that he, rather than the victim, should be spared any further suffering.

He walked past the prison several times, hiding himself like a thief. He saw that there were still no preparations outside Debtor's Door. He felt almost light-headed with relief; and decided that he would keep his word. The old gaoler received him with surprise and pleasure.

'It's good of you to come again, Sir Robert. David will be pleased. It's a great kindness you are doing, sir.'

'I've brought him something. It is all right, I suppose?'

'So long as it's not a knife, or a pistol, or a file . . . or poison, or even a length of rope. I have to ask, you understand.'

'It is a violin. He wanted it.'

The instrument was unwrapped and examined. Nothing fatal could be discovered in it; so the gaoler nodded and limped on ahead.

The prisoner was in much the same state as before: crouched on his bed with a blanket round his shoulders as if he was bitterly cold. Perhaps his beard was a shade more defined, and his eyes a little more thumbed and knuckled; but otherwise he was unchanged. As before, he jumped excitedly to his feet and welcomed his visitor. Then, as soon as the gaoler had withdrawn, he confided eagerly that he had heard no hammering yet; which was an infallible sign that nothing was going to happen. He went on about this significant absence of hammering and did not appear to have noticed the violin at all.

Then he saw it. He smiled appreciatively at the bringer and picked up the instrument from the table on which it had been laid. He turned it over, read the inscription on the back plate, and seemed about to say something. Then, apparently changing his mind, he took up the bow and scraped it across the strings, making a most disagreeable noise.

It was plain that he could not play it. He could not, as Mr Streamer had done, awaken any sense of melody from it. It was, to all intents, quite useless to him. It was no more than a toy, an idle possession, a piece of inanimate property.

He made one or two more painful flourishes with the bow; then put the instrument down and seemed to forget all about it. He returned, with increased animation, to recounting the various reasons he had devised for hoping for the hopeless, for believing in the unbelievable. His visitor did everything he could to support him in this as he could see no reason for doing otherwise.

The violin and everything it signified seemed to have slipped from the young man's mind altogether. Surely this was a cause for rejoicing—if it was possible to rejoice in such a place! Surely this was a moment for blessed relief, if it was possible to be relieved in such a place! But there was neither rejoicing nor relief. Instead there was a most perverse desire to probe and press, like one exploring an aching tooth.

'Do you remember, David, that you once said to me that children sometimes remember strange things?'

'Did I?' said the young man coldly; as if he was angry with this visitor for daring to mention anything outside his present preoccupation.

'Yes . . . yes. You said that. Why?'

'I don't know.'

'You have forgotten?'

The young man was silent. The raucous noises of the prison filled in the vacancy. The old gaoler's eye appeared at the Judas hole in the door. Was the visitor ready to leave? The visitor looked undecided. The eye deepened its inquiry. The visitor stirred in his chair.

'I saw you there, you know,' murmured the young man. 'I was watching you . . . '

The visitor slightly shook his head. The eye went away.

'Where were you?'

'In the street . . . in the houses . . . in the shadows. I watched you all the time.'

'Why did you hide?'

'I was frightened of you.'

'But afterwards . . . when you saw me again. You knew it was me?'

'I was not sure at first. But then I knew.'

'But you were not frightened then?'

Again the silence. Again the Judas eye.

'I was only a child—' A shake of the head. Judas blind again. 'I could not understand . . . I didn't know. I had been punished, you see.'

'When—when?'

'At that time. Just before the soldiers came. My father had beaten me and I'd run away into the woods. For ever. And it was for ever, too!'

'But why? What had you done?'

'The violin. I'd given it to my friend . . . for his pocket knife. My father was angry . . . '

The visitor started. He trembled; tried hard to control his excitement. *His friend*! He had given it to his friend! The dead boy in the window! *He* had been the brother! Kozlowski had been nothing to that house. Only a friend. He was nothing to Perdita. He was nothing . . . nothing!

'The soldiers came and I heard the screaming and shouting,' continued the young man, frowning heavily; 'and I could see the fires. I was frightened. I was only a child, you know. When the soldiers had gone, and it was quiet, I came down from the hillside. I was thinking of my violin. I wanted to get it back. But I saw the—the tramp . . . and he took it. I waited all that night. I hid in our house. The walls were burning hot. I never looked at my father and mother. But they were looking at me. And all the time I only thought about the violin.

'The tramp went off in the morning . . . and I followed him, hiding in ditches all the way. You didn't see me, did you?'

The visitor, who had been utterly absorbed in his own feelings of relief, was momentarily bewildered by being asked a question. The young man looked at him reproachfully and repeated the question.

'You didn't see me, did you?'

'No—no. I was looking only at—at—'

'Yes—yes! I know all that. I saw you. Then in the town people caught hold of me. I was crying, I suppose. They wouldn't let me go. It was out of kindness, of course. Kindness. But the tramp went on . . . and I lost him . . . '

'Did you—did you tell anyone?'

'I told them about the violin . . . and they were angry with me for crying about a toy instead of for my father and mother. But I was only a child . . . and I didn't really understand about their being dead. So I never talked about it again . . . until—until that woman. But even then I never said it was the violin. I told her about the old man . . . and everything. Of course, she thought it was the baby. I never told her. I was frightened she would think I was a child . . . and I didn't want her to think that. You can see that I didn't want her to think that! I've never told anybody before. But you can understand, can't you, about being a child . . . and being frightened . . . and not wanting to think about it . . . ' He paused, and stared at the violin. 'I'm glad you kept it . . . and brought it for me. Did you see anything of *hers*?'

'No. There was nothing there. Everything was burned.'

'There was a little doll, I remember. It was made of knitting. My mother made it for her—'

'It was burned—burned!'

'She would have liked it, you know,' said the young man, rather wistfully. 'It's good to have *something*.'

He plucked idly at the violin strings. There was a sound from the door. The Judas eye peered in. The visitor rose, somewhat stiffly, to his feet. The young man looked at him with some anxiety.

'Will you come and see me again?'

'Yes. Tomorrow.'

The door opened. The young man suddenly seized his visitor by the sleeve.

'When you came—when you were outside,' he whispered rapidly, 'you saw nothing? They were not doing anything at Debtor's Door?'

'Nothing! Absolutely nothing! I swear it!'

As he left the cell he thanked God that he had been able to give such comfort truthfully. It was, as it turned out, the last thing he ever said to David Kozlowski.

On the next day, the prisoner refused all visits. He had heard some sounds in the night and early morning, and did not want to be told what they signified. In particular he refused to admit any member of the clergy. He had convinced himself that, by doing so, he would prevent anything happening. He believed devoutly that, without Absolution, he could not be hanged; that it would be unlawful to destroy his soul as well as his life.

He was so convinced of this that he went so far as to stuff his ears with fragments of cloth torn from his shirt so that he would not be able to hear any priestly words that might be uttered. He believed that no man on earth had the right to deprive his soul of salvation.

He was hanged at eight o'clock on the Monday morning.

33

Monday. The morning train from Paddington arrived at Gloucester at twenty minutes past one o'clock. Some dozen miscellaneous passengers alighted, sniffed deeply, praised the country air, and filtered away attended by laden porters, after the manner of explorers. Sir Robert Standfast had not been among them. A breathless running and staring into every carriage, in case he had fallen asleep, confirmed that he had not been on the train. The coachman and Miss Perdita, who had been waiting for half an hour, mutually concluded that he had missed the train and would be arriving on the next one, some three hours later. The coachman was philosophical; the daughter was exceedingly wroth.

It was the first time that she and her father had been parted from one another for more than a day. He ought not to have missed the train. He must have known that she would be waiting for him. It might even have been pouring with rain—it was not—and she would have got soaked. It was irresponsible of him, and she would tell him so.

The coachman, a kindly man with daughters of his own, who read perhaps more distress than anger in the child's indignation, suggested that the master might have been delayed by looking for a suitable gift to bring his daughter. Although the daughter declared, in no uncertain terms, that her father ought to have thought of such an important matter before, and not left it to the last minute, it was plain that she was partly mollified.

Following on the supposition, which had now become a certainty, that Sir Robert would be arriving at twenty minutes past four, a short debate ensued as to whether they should return to the house or wait in Gloucester. The coachman was for returning, as Lady Standfast would wonder what had become of them otherwise; but Miss Perdita was overcome with a tender consideration for the horses, to whom a double journey might well prove injurious.

They waited; and filled in the time with glum refreshments from the station and agreeable conjectures as to the wondrousness of a gift that could have caused Sir Robert to miss the first train.

The next London train—the whisper of its smoke sighted a good five miles off!—arrived, panting with anxiety; and disgorged a motley cargo of travellers, who, by their ugly faces, vile voices and tawdry attire, ought to have stayed at home. Sir Robert was not among them.

The coachman supposed that the master had, very understandably, decided to take luncheon in London rather than risk eating at Swindon, where the food was notorious rather than celebrated. There was a convenient train leaving Paddington at half past three which would arrive at Gloucester at ten minutes to seven. He said, rather more firmly this time, that they must return to the house and tell Lady Standfast. After that, they could come back again. The horses wouldn't mind in the least.

Although he was quite matter-of-fact in his speech, he felt some slight qualms of uneasiness that he did not want the girl to sense. She was so very bright and quick that he did not trust himself to hide things from her for long.

Miss Perdita agreed that he should go back; she, however, was going to wait. She would be perfectly all right with the stationmaster; and she had enough money to regale herself in the refreshment room like a queen.

The coachman, intimations of royalty notwithstanding, demurred. He protested that he would certainly get the rough edge of Lady Standfast's tongue if he left Miss Perdita behind. To no avail. Miss Perdita was unmoved; and, it was clear, unmovable. Accordingly, and with a heavy heart, the coachman entrusted her to the stationmaster (distinguished from humbler railway servants by the wearing of a kind of black silk smoke-stack, like a Sunday engine) and returned to Standfast House with his disquieting news; while the stationmaster diverted Miss Perdita with a thousand instances of harmlessly missed trains ... all of which were known to him personally, and to the truth of which he could swear. For example: the London traffic. Where was Sir Robert staying? Gray's Inn? Well, well, the stationmaster knew of a gentleman who had taken three hours to get to Paddington from Gray's Inn! Then again, there'd been another gentleman who'd chanced to meet a friend arriving in London just as he was about to leave; and he'd stayed and talked away three trains before he'd looked at his watch. And speaking of watches, well, they were no more reliable than their owners. Only the other week a gentleman had been worryingly late because it turned out that his watch had stopped and he'd passed a whole day fixed at nine o'clock!

At half past six, the coachman returned. Mr Charles came also, but riding on a bay gelding, the present apple of his eye, as he had a natural antipathy for wheels which, in his own extraordinary fashion, he connected with craftiness, making things too damned easy, and, above all, with the Town. He had been quite excited when he had heard that his uncle had not arrived; and, it must be admitted, was human enough to hope that something had happened to him. Here it must be said that the young man was exceptionally well-endowed with those qualities of being human that are peculiar to mankind and are not shared either with animals or angels.

He clattered about in the station yard until the train arrived, with a shriek and a gasp and a mighty exhalation of steam that frightened his horse. Then, perceiving from his young cousin's wild and distraught manner that her father had not been on the train, he raised his hat and trotted smartly back to Standfast House, where he was inexplicably berated by his mother for not having waited for Perdita. This seemed to him to be very unjust; and he protested that there was nothing he could have done other than to point out the obvious, which was that either the old boy had dropped down dead somewhere, or that he had run off again.

Naturally these thoughts had occurred to Lady Standfast, possibly even before they had occurred to her son, as she possessed an intellectual quickness that he had not inherited; but she chose to keep them to herself ... at least until a reasonable time had elapsed. It was quite possible that Robert's business with Mr Leviticus had extended until the Monday, and that there would be a letter in the morning explaining everything.

The child, of course, was absolutely impossible. She would not eat her dinner; she wanted to go straight to London that very night, and when told that it was out of the question, she had a screaming fit that would have disgraced a child half her age. Charles and William wanted to give her a good strong dose of brandy, to quieten her down and send her off to sleep; but fortunately it turned out to be unnecessary as she calmed down of her own accord and went up to bed quite quietly, thank God! She even remembered to wish everyone goodnight, and asked that nothing should be said to her father about her being so angry and upset just because he was a day late.

After she had left the room, the family waited for a decent interval of about a minute in order to allow time for the girl to have got upstairs and into her own room, before opening their minds to one another and displaying the treasures therein.

Sir Robert was dead. There could not be the slightest doubt about it. Either he had been run over, knocked on the head, or had just dropped down in the street. After all, people of his age were dying like flies everywhere. Old Leviticus would let them know in the morning ...

'Not so loud, my dears, not so loud!' warned Lady Standfast. 'We don't want to upset the girl again!'

Obediently the sons moderated their naturally robust voices to discreet shouts and went on to discuss their expectations which rose, Phoenix-like, from the presumed ashes of Sir Robert; while the remaining member of the family, the ancient Aunt Augusta, pecked ravenously at morsels and darted venomous glances at each speaker in turn.

The talk turned to the child. What was to be done about her? She would come into money, of course. Why the devil should she?

Because she was his daughter. What the blazes had that to do with it? It was the law, and Mr Leviticus would—To hell with old Leviticus! He can't live for ever! Must wait until—Wait? Wait? Hasn't there been enough waiting? Damned old fools!

Thus the family debated and discoursed over the skeletal remains of the evening feast, while a pair of early flies crept inside a bony carcass like black souls in a ruined church. Although the consensus of opinion remained firmly in favour of Uncle Robert's death, from time to time, by way of devil's advocacy, the possibility was advanced that the morning might yet bring unwelcome news and it would be learned that he had been detained on business and not by death. But this was never seriously entertained, as it was obvious to all that the father's obsessive regard for his daughter would have overcome all obstacles short of the grave.

So they had really seen the last of him; and they were left with the child. What was to be done about her?

'Why don't you kill her like you've killed him?'

The suggestion, in a hoarse, rather jeering voice, emanated from the venerable lady who, having devoured everything within her reach, now gave vent to her feelings by accusing her relations of having made away with her beloved Robert, presumably by way of employing the services of a hired assassin. One did not have to seek far for the motive as, had he lived, he would undoubtedly have turned them out into the street. They had killed him; and in support of the colourful contention, she pointed her fork at the sideboard and said that she had seen Robert's ghost standing there and viewing his murderers with terrible eyes.

Involuntarily the family turned; the flies flew out of church, and there was a moment's silence. But the ghost had gone. Presumably it had gone to comfort the child. If so, then it was not a moment too soon.

Perdita's door was open, the curtains of her bed were tightly drawn; but they enclosed emptiness. Yet her clothes were strewn in their usual disorder, partly over a chair and partly on the floor. So she was undressed and in her nightgown. But not in the room. She could not have gone far.

She had gone no further, in fact, than a very modest distance to a point halfway down the stairs, where there was an alcove in which stood a marble figure in a marble gown that bore some faint resemblance to her own. She was crouching behind it, like its frightened spirit, and listening to the voices from the dining-room.

Dead animals glared down upon her from the walls, and the black swan swayed menacingly aloft as she heard her fate debated, as if her father was really no more.

Sick with grief and terror and lonelines she stared up into the glass eyes as if for some sign of melting pity in them. Nothing. Sick with longing and forlorn hope, she stared across the hall to the great front door as if, at any moment, it would burst open and her father would be standing there. Nothing . . . nothing; only the murmuring voices:

'The child . . . what is to be done with her?'

'Not so loud . . . not so loud . . .'

'His daughter . . . the law . . . old Leviticus . . . daughter . . . daughter . . . dead . . .'

At last, quite worn out, she sank down into a dazed sleep. She lay huddled behind the marble figure whose cold limbs obscured her and whose draperies mingled cunningly with a wayward fold of her nightgown. Only the dead knew she was there.

There was no letter in the morning; and that silence of the heart that follows on the blankness of no news, on the passing of the hands of the clock beyond the time of the postman's calling, fell upon the house.

The girl wanted to go to London on the very first train. She had money, she said. She wanted to go to Mr Leviticus and Mr Clarky.

It was pointed out to her, quite kindly, that it might turn out to be a foolish journey. Her father might easily arrive that day, and she would have missed him.

No matter! She would learn of what had happened from Mr Leviticus, and so would come straight back again.

But would it not be more sensible to wait, say, until the afternoon, in case her father arrived during the morning? Surely it would be better to wait, and then to talk about it again?

No. She had to go at once. She had already packed her night things and some shoes. If no one wanted to help her, she would walk all the way to Gloucester station by herself. She knew the stationmaster—

What nonsense she was talking! Why, she sounded as if she meant to run away! Her father would be very angry—

His daughter *was* very angry!

His daughter should remember that she was still a child; and that children were sometimes locked in their rooms—

And sometimes jumped out of windows!

That was no way to talk to people who loved and cared for her!

A silence; from which it might have been inferred that, had the circumstances been as proposed, then the conversation might indeed have taken a different turn.

After this, no further obstacles were put in the girl's way, and she left the house within the hour, fiercely clutching her bag. The coachman who drove her to Gloucester station was instructed to accompany her to London and to see that she reached Mr Leviticus's safely. He was then to return with whatever news he had been able to obtain.

The coachman (he who had daughters of his own, all in service now), did everything he could during the journey to keep up the girl's spirits, to encourage her to hope for the best, while at the same time, gently preparing her for the worst. A hard task for any man; and not made easier by dark eyes that kept fixing upon his own and catching him out. Nevertheless, he must have done well enough: when at last they got to Gray's Inn, and Mr Leviticus's, and the time had come for him to go back, he was most unexpectedly rewarded by a sparkling of tears and a kiss. This gratified the coachman (whose own daughters had long since grown out of such impulsive gestures) out of all proportion; and he felt that he would not be going back to Gloucester empty-hearted as well as empty-handed.

There was no news at the lawyer's. Mr Leviticus had seen Sir Robert on the Friday, when their business had been concluded. There had been no further appointment.

The lawyer was as perturbed as everyone else over Sir Robert's failure to come home; he did not, however, as the coachman and the stationmaster had done, put forward a host of comforting possibilities to account for it. Doting as he was upon children, and always ready to make his person ridiculous for their delight, he was not prepared to do the same for his intellect. He was too good a lawyer, in the very best sense, to perjure his heart for the sake of obtaining a temporary injunction on grief. He had the gravest doubts about his client; and when the child announced her intention with a trembling determination of not going back to Gloucester, he nodded sombrely, and agreed that she should remain in London, under his care, until more was known.

He wrote a brief but courteous letter to Lady Standfast explaining his decision and trusting that it met with her approval, and despatched it with the coachman. Then he regarded the child who sat before him, so unsuitably in the client's chair.

She seemed dwarfed by it. Its back and arms engulfed her. Worry had shrunk her, had hollowed her eyes and pinched in her cheeks so that the plump, smiling innocence that peeped down from the walls and up from his watch-chain seemed to mock her with a superior confidence. Mrs Leviticus would not have cared to paint her as she was.

'We will do our best, Miss Perdita,' he said. 'We will find out what has happened. Mr Clarky will attend to it; and Mr Clarky is a very clever man.'

He raised his eyes and stared at Mr Clarky, who sat beside the door. Mr Clarky stared back. Although their natures were quite different, being united only in a profound respect for the law, long association had given their thoughts a similar turn. They were both thinking of Sir Robert's visit on the Friday, and his anxiety to have his will drawn up and signed. His urgency in the matter now assumed a disturbing aspect, and his meticulous provisions for the child's future took on a grave significance.

'Before we proceed any further,' said the lawyer quietly, 'I would be obliged, Mr Clarky, if you would go to the establishment in Gray's Inn Road where Sir Robert has been staying. It is possible that there might be some news of him there . . . although, had anything untoward happened, I fancy that the proprietor would have notified me by now. He will not be gone for long, my dear,' he said to his small, pale client as Mr Clarky departed; 'and while he is away I want you to try very hard to remember if your father said anything to you before he left that might be of help to us.'

The huge old gentleman shut his eyes expectantly; partly to sharpen his powers of attentiveness, and partly to relieve his young client of the embarrassment of his gaze.

The young client, awed by the venerable room, the legal aroma, the size of her chair and the lawyer's suddenly sightless bulk, recollected, in the smallest tones, that her father had engaged to give her love to Mr Dolly, to the Streamers, and possibly to Mrs Fairhazel—

'Mrs Fairhazel?'

'Oh, she's an old friend.'

'Old, you say?'

'Oh, yes! She must be nearly forty!'

'Old indeed!' commented the lawyer. 'Quite a graveyard case!'

The young client blushed; but, as the old gentleman's eyes were still shut, she wasted her sweetness, so to speak, on the legal air, and blushed unseen.

'He spoke of no one else?' resumed the lawyer.

'No one . . . except, of course, you, Mr Leviticus, and Mr Clarky.'

'So you knew he was coming to see me?'

'Yes. He told me.'

'Did tell you why?'

'He said it was on business.'

'It was to make provision for you. He wanted to secure your future. As you are not his natural daughter—Oh yes, I know that!' said the lawyer, not opening his eyes but hearing the young client's sharply indrawn breath.

He mentioned the fact because he believed she would feel easier with him if she knew he was party to her secret.

'I—I never thought of that,' whispered the young client, very tremulously indeed.

'And why should you?' inquired Mr Leviticus. 'It is for grown men and lawyers to think of such things. Children should be thinking of birthdays, and sweets and butterflies and—' He broke off, and then resumed in a more businesslike manner. 'Your father has made certain provisions for you; and, until I hear otherwise, it will be my duty to carry them out. Your affairs, Miss Perdita, are in my hands. You are, of course, at liberty to question my decisions; but not to go against them. I will listen to any objection you might care to put forward, and will give it every consideration. But until your father, or some other competent person, says otherwise, I will represent you. In effect, Miss Perdita, you are my client and I am your lawyer. I hope that is satisfactory to you?'

The old gentleman would dearly liked to have opened an eye to judge the effect of his carefully measured words upon the young client; but he refrained and was rewarded by a rather fearful confession that it *was* satisfactory to her. It was plain that the magnitude of being a client had succeeded in lifting her, however briefly, from the wretchedness and uncertainty of her position.

'Very well, Miss Perdita; now that everything is on a proper footing, we may talk with one another as lawyer and client.'

'We—we had an argument,' admitted the young client at length.

'About what?'

'I—I don't remember. Yes; I do! He wanted to talk to me about when I was a baby, and I wouldn't let him. I think he was angry about that. I wanted him to ask Mr Clarky to try and find out about my real mother; and he didn't want to. Then I got angry and told him how much I hated the old tramp who'd stolen me. You—you know about him?'

'Yes. I know about the tramp. I know about everything. Remember that I am your lawyer. It is my business to know—'

'Then where is he? Where is he, Mr Leviticus? What's happened to him? Please, please tell me! Please—please—'

At this point the old lawyer opened his eyes and saw that his client was in tears; and all his books, and all his learning, and all his vast experience of litigation could supply him with no more useful precedent than gently to stroke his client's soft dark hair and offer her the use of his pocket handkerchief.

Mr Clarky came back. It turned out that Sir Robert had slept in his room at the inn on the Friday and the Saturday nights. He had gone out on the Sunday afternoon and had not returned.

'Did he say that he would not be returning?'

'No, Mr L. He never mentioned it,' said Mr Clarky, with a finality that suggested to Mr Leviticus that more might have been said, but not of a hopeful nature.

He was right. The proprietor himself had been worried as Sir Robert had left some things behind and had not settled his bill. Mr Leviticus shrewdly suspected something of the kind, and did not press Mr Clarky further. Instead he turned his attention to the young client's immediate future. Bearing in mind her father's expressed wishes, he said that he himself would take her to Mr Dolly's, in Bishopsgate Street, where she was to stay until more was known.

'Do you think you will find him? Please, please find him! Mr Clarky—Mr Clarky—will you find him?'

34

Clarry Dolska, man of business, man of substance, man of ever-impending generosity, with a large capital sum in the bank (Fox and Hankey of Lombard Street, no less!), continued to oppress Mr Dolly and to hang over the household in Bishopsgate Street like an expensive silver lining, fearfully full of cloud.

Even Jonathan Dolly, ordinarily the most optimistic of youths, no longer felt hopeful of obtaining the great man's patronage. Like most optimists, he swung to the other extreme, and could be heard confiding bitterly to the herrings as he eviscerated them in the basement that Clarry Dolska, far from seeing what could be done about things after he had looked around, would be with them for ever and would end up by leaving all his money to the family in Poland.

In truth, Clarry Dolska didn't seem to do much looking around; he was more inclined to hover in the shop, like a shadowy Board of Management, murmuring, 'Noo?' at intervals, in tones of well-intentioned criticism. As a result of this, Mr Dolly developed an anticipatory wince, which Mrs Dolly in the privacy of the bed-chamber tried hard to discourage.

The disappointment of Friday night had made matters worse. The absence of the promised baronet had furnished Clarry Dolska with yet another opportunity for demolishing his cousin's pretensions; and Mr Dolly was sure he had written home about it.

Consequently Mr Dolly was very angry with his old friend, who, he felt, had slighted him and made his harmless boasting look ridiculous. There had been no letter, no word of explanation or apology; so Mr Dolly had been driven to imagine that some grander invitation had intervened, and his old friend's accession to a title had made him think twice about dining with a poor Jewish shopkeeper.

Thus resentment entered Mr Dolly's soul; which would certainly have found no place there in the old days. In the old days he would have jumped to the conclusion that something had happened to his friend, and he would have been beside himself with worry. As it was, he laboured among his cheeses, and chopped liver, and Ali Baba barrels, with maggots gnawing at his heart.

Then Mr Leviticus came into the shop, holding Perdita by the hand; and in a moment, Clarry Dolska and all the maggots were blown to the winds.

'Princess!' cried Mr Dolly, instantly restoring Perdita to Dolly's *Peerage*, from which she had earlier been banished. 'What a surprise! How good it is to see you! How very kind of you to come! Everybody!' he shouted delightedly. 'Everybody! You will never guess! Our princess is here!'

'Noo? A princess?'

'Come upstairs, my dear! Please—please—I'll shut the shop—'

'Noo? He shuts the shop when there is still trade about? Is this the way to make a success?'

'You must come upstairs! Mrs Dolly will be so pleased! And Jonathan and the girls, of course! Such a surprise! Please—you will let me kiss you?'

He skipped towards her with open arms and quite engulfed her.

'But, princess! What's this? You are crying! Come—come! No more tears! What is wrong? What has happened? Your father—'

Mr Leviticus, mountainous amid the hanging gardens of sausages, stooped, made himself known, and gravely explained the reason for the visit.

'Noo? Other people's troubles? Doesn't he have enough of his own?'

Mr Dolly was incredulous, aghast! He had to lean back against the counter.

'But this is terrible—terrible! My poor child! Jonathan! Jonathan!'

Jonathan came running from the basement, shining all over with herring scales like a knight in threadbare armour. Saw Perdita, saw the lawyer, saw his father; saw their faces. Wished he had washed himself and put on a coat.

'Jonathan! Our princess . . . her father . . . our good friend! Such terrible news! He has not come back! Nobody knows what has happened to him! This is Mr Leviticus, Jonathan. The lawyer. He has brought our princess here. Mr Leviticus . . . if you would be so kind, sir. Please come upstairs . . . Mrs Dolly, you know . . . I can hardly believe it! But one must hope for the best! One does hear of such things . . . and—and it is not yet two days! I'm sure everything will be all right! I am so glad you came to us! Our princess is quite one of the family, Mr Leviticus! That's right, Jonathan, that's the way!'

The threadbare knight, smelling powerfully of Famous Herrings, had taken Perdita's bag and was helping her up the stairs. Most likely she could have managed on her own, but he put an arm round her to be on the safe side.

'There! You see, Mr Leviticus? Already she is beginning to smile!'

Although the smile was frail and uncertain, like a butterfly in winter, it went a long way towards reassuring the lawyer that his young client would be in good hands; and he followed her up the stairs, borne on the tide of Mr Dolly's anxious eloquence.

Imperial Mrs Dolly was taking tea with her friend, Mrs Fairhazel, and the Dolly girls had put in an appearance, bearing such articles as hairbrushes and rather ostentatious sewing and embroidery. Having heard only their father shouting to announce the princess's arrival, and knowing nothing of the tragedy, they were fully prepared to be off-hand and condescending towards the princess, as they thought it very likely that she would be unbearably condescending towards them.

Then Mr Dolly broke the news, and a frightened chill swept through the cheerful, lively parlour; eyes widened, breath was drawn in, and everyone felt suddenly unsuitable . . . as if they should have been in black instead of in garish pinks and blues and greens, and the couch and chairs in black, instead of in their petticoats of foolish flowers, and the mirror covered up, and the blinds down . . .

'Perdita! Perdita! My poor child! Come! Take off your bonnet! Come and sit with us—'

Mrs Dolly and her daughters and her son gathered round the white-faced, desolate child, comforted her, tended her, spoke words of hope . . . and yet, at the same time, seemed almost frightened of her, as if grief made her formidable and cast a huge shadow that made everything seem small and false. Uncannily Mr Leviticus was put in mind of his grandchildren gathering round a bird the cat had caught . . . breathlessly watching its tiny breast fluttering . . . tending it with timid concern . . . telling one another that it would be sure to get better . . . The bird had died in the night, he remembered. He shivered slightly, and drew Mr Dolly to one side.

'I will, of course, communicate any news to you directly,' he murmured.

'That is very good of you Mr Leviticus.'

'I will continue to act on behalf of my young client—'

'Client! How strange that sounds!' murmured Mr Dolly, glancing towards the child, as if he felt that that particular dignity ill became her.

The lawyer nodded understandingly; and continued: 'Although you, sir, as her legal guardian—'

'Legal guardian? How is that?'

'Did not Sir Robert inform you?'

'No. But—but naturally I am very pleased . . . I am very honoured that my old friend should have thought of me so!'

'I am surprised, Mr Dolly, that Sir Robert did not tell you.'

'But we have not seen him—'

'Did he not come to you on Friday night? I understand he was to have dined with you.'

'No—no. We were very surprised. We expected him . . . but he did not come. We should have guessed that something was wrong. It was not like him . . .'

The lawyer frowned, looked puzzled; but made no further comment.

'Then I may take it that my client will be domiciled with you, sir?'

'Domiciled? Oh, yes, yes! Of course! Mrs Dolly—Mrs Dolly!' Mrs Dolly came rustling to her husband's side. 'Mrs Dolly, our princess is going to stay with us!'

254

'Yes . . . yes!' said Mrs Dolly, somewhat flustered. 'She—she will sleep with the girls . . . until—until your cousin has made arrangements. Then she can have his room . . .'

'Would it not be easier if she came to stay with me? Please, forgive me, I couldn't help overhearing.'

Mrs Fairhazel, prettyish, in soft, wispy green—like a recollection of Spring—stood with frightened eyes and tightly clenched hands.

'It's all right, it's all right, my dear! We can manage,' said Mrs Dolly hurriedly. She would very much liked to have availed herself of the offer, as the girls were already crowded in their room and Perdita would have been far from comfortable, but she knew it was hopeless as there was such an antipathy between the child and Mrs Fairhazel.

'I would like to take her, you know,' persisted Mrs Fairhazel. 'After all, I am not very far away. I have my own house,' she explained to Mr Leviticus, 'in Stepney. Perdita would be very comfortable. She would have her own room. Would it not be more sensible?'

Mr Leviticus looked doubtful; not because he was concerned for his young client's security—the lady was, in his opinion, obviously a gentlewoman and not likely to neglect her duties—but because he was aware of strong feelings in the matter. Tactfully he suggested that his client should be consulted so that her preference might be known.

'It is a hard time for her,' he said; 'and although you and I may think we know where her best interests lie, none of us can answer for her feelings.'

'Then I will ask her,' said Mrs Fairhazel, with a quick look at Mrs Dolly and a smile at the legal guardian; 'that is, if Mr Dolly will give me leave to do so!'

Mr Dolly, wearing his unexpected dignity like a hat that was too big, blinked unseeingly. Mrs Fairhazel approached the couch on which Perdita sat, surrounded by eager kindness, with plates of cake, bread and butter and chopped liver to tempt her; so that Mr Leviticus was again put in mind of the injured fledgling.

Perdita looked up, saw Mrs Fairhazel about to say something to her, instantly imagined that it was going to be something terrible arising from the murmuring of the grown-ups.

'What is it? You know something! What is it?'

'Nothing . . . I promise you. I wanted to ask you—to ask you—'

Mrs Fairhazel faltered. Her courage began to fail her. Everyone was looking at her. She must have been out of her mind to approach Perdita! But she felt so strong a kinship with the child, so great a need to be with her, that—that—

'This lady would like you to stay with her, Miss Perdita,' interposed Mr Leviticus, with his client's best interests in mind.

He regarded Mrs Fairhazel carefully; and judged, on the basis of his immense experience of plaintiffs and defendants, that the lady was inclined to undervalue herself. Had she been his client, he would have advised her, within the limits of propriety, to be a little bolder with the world. He would have said to her, 'Everyone, on his own accusation, stands in the dock, my dear; and must, in the end, give evidence on his own behalf.'

Perdita stared at her lawyer; then back to Mrs Fairhazel.

'Is that what it was?' she demanded, still not convinced that nothing was being withheld from her. 'Was that all?'

Mrs Fairhazel managed to withstand the child's anxiously probing gaze.

'Yes, Perdita. That was all.'

It wasn't, of course. Perdita could see that quite clearly. She could see that behind the offer lay a fear and a loneliness quite the equal of her own. She could see that the offer had been made as much for Mrs Fairhazel's sake as for her own; and she was, in the strangest way, comforted by it. Nonetheless she was still sufficiently the princess to remember her dignity, which she suddenly clutched about her, like a garment.

'Then why didn't you say so?' she demanded.

Mrs Fairhazel smiled apologetically, and shook her head. Perdita went on with increasing importance, 'I must ask my lawyer if it will be all right. My affairs are in his hands, you know. Mr Leviticus! Will it be all right if I go and stay with Mrs Fairhazel?'

Mr Leviticus turned aside to cough into his hand; and glanced inquiringly at the legal guardian. Mr and Mrs Dolly were both taken aback by Perdita's response, but were not displeased by it. They nodded.

'It will be quite all right, Miss Perdita,' said the lawyer solemnly.

'Then I will come and stay with you, Mrs Fairhazel,' said Perdita, 'until my father comes back.'

'Until—until your father comes back,' agreed Mrs Fairhazel, with a warmth in her voice that convinced the lawyer that his young client had made a wise decision.

Soon afterwards Mr Leviticus took his leave; but not before Mr Dolly's cousin, wearied of being so long on the periphery of events, had pushed himself forward as the head of the family and made the lawyer acquainted with his moral and financial standing. He apologised for his cousin's modest circumstances and cramped accommodation that had given rise to the inconveniencing of the young lady, and said that he would certainly see what could be done about them when he had settled down and had had time to look around.

So Perdita went back to Stepney with Mrs Fairhazel; and when she had gone, the Dollys stood in the shop and watched the jostling, hastening crowds swirl past their window along Bishopsgate Street, homeward bound.

'That poor child!' murmured Mrs Dolly, reaching for her husband's hand.

'Our poor princess!' he sighed.

'Poor—poor—poor!' whispered the child to her old companion, the glazed, ever-astonished doll, as they lay side by side in a strange bed in a strange room that smelled of ironing and lavender.

The brothers Wilkinson, delighted to see her again, had overwhelmed her with kindness; and Mrs Fairhazel, her hair loose about her shoulders and in a dressing-gown that was all over leaves and flowers, had sat with her, reading her stories of caliphs and merchants till her head swam with wonders, long into the night. But now the candle was out, and the room was huge with darkness.

'We are poor! Now we are really poor, my darling!'

The glazed one, dim in starlight, stared at her high-born mistress as if unable to take in the terrible words.

'Or in reduced circumstances. That sounds better, doesn't it! Do you remember that? Do you remember that's what Pa said to me? Not poor but in reduced circumstances. But I was right. We weren't poor them. Only *now*. Oh, Pa, Pa! He's left us and we're alone! Nobody knows us . . . nobody, except—*him*!'

Desperately the child clutched hold of her doll and listened to the vast, empty night. Clink—clink—clink! she seemed to hear, somewhere in a street nearby. But the sound no longer frightened her. That nightmare was ended. Her dread of the horrible tramp had been supplanted by one that was far, far greater.

'Oh, my darling!' she whispered to the doll. 'Do you think Pa is dead?'

Clink—clink—clink! went the tinny little banging in the night, passing unheeded along the street.

35

'A curious thing, Clarky,' said Mr Leviticus, as he returned from Bishopsgate Street to his chambers in Gray's Inn. 'A very curious thing.'

'Relatin' to the matter in 'and, Mr L.?' inquired Mr Clarky, standing on tiptoe to help his employer out of his coat.

Mr Leviticus nodded and passed ponderously into the inner room where he seated himself at his desk. Mr Clarky, having disposed of his employer's hat and coat on something that resembled a mad old tree, followed and stationed himself at the lawyer's elbow. They formed a strange pair: like an elderly enchanter and his elderly sprite, still formidable even in the evening of their days. For several moments neither spoke; then the enchanter looked up from a prolonged contemplation of his fingers, and the sprite inclined his ear as if for news of a spell.

'Had I been asked for an opinion, Clarky, before I had visited Bishopsgate Street, on what had become of our client, I would have expressed the gravest misgivings.'

He paused. Mr Clarky waited patiently.

'But now I am not so sure,' concluded Mr Leviticus.

'The curious thing, Mr L., if I might make so bold?'

'Exactly so. It seems that our client did not, as was expected, dine with his friends on the Friday night. Nor did he communicate with them. Yet I understand that he slept at the inn on both the Friday and the Saturday nights?' Mr Clarky nodded. 'Is that not curious, Clarky?'

Mr Leviticus laced his fingers over his watch-chain and waited, while his minion's conjectures caught up with his own.

'Curious indeed, Mr L.,' agreed Mr Clarky, after a brief pause.

Mr Leviticus continued: 'The young lady—our young client —places great faith in you, Clarky.'

Mr Clarky modestly bowed his head.

'And so do I, Clarky.'

Mr Clarky was quite overcome.

'Our young client is, at present, residing with a certain Mrs Fairhazel, who is domiciled in Stepney—'

Mr Clarky was fully acquainted with the lady and the premises. Both were beyond reproach.

'I had already judged them to be so, Clarky; otherwise I would not have been party to the arrangement.'

Mr Clarky was abashed. He had not dreamed of thinking otherwise.

'If the news turns out to be bad, Clarky,' continued the lawyer, when his minion had finished apologising, 'you will inform me before anyone else.'

'Understood, Mr L. Perfectly understood.'

'But if it is good, Clarky—'

Mr Clarky looked inquiring.

'If it is good, Clarky, then you may use your discretion. All I ask is that you remember that I am an old man. I doubt if I could withstand the shock of hearing good news first. I think, perhaps, that you might tell our young client yourself.'

Mr Clarky beamed.

'Understood, Mr L. Perfectly understood.'

The news from Bishopsgate Street was certainly curious, and Mr Clarky pondered it carefully. It suggested that something had happened on the Friday itself that had affected Sir Robert so powerfully that he seemed to have forgotten the very existence of his old friends. It suggested that, whatever it was, might well have had a bearing on subsequent events. So Mr Clarky, who had previously intended to wait until the morning before making the melancholy round of hospitals and mortuaries, thought it might be worth paying a visit to Shoreditch that very evening. He thought it quite possible that Sir Robert had called at his old lodgings on the Friday afternoon, and that the Streamers might have news of him. Accordingly, despite the lateness of the hour—it was long past eight o'clock and the day seemed hardly able to keep its eyes open—Mr Clarky crammed his hard round hat on his head, and set off for Shoreditch.

Mrs Streamer, since the loss of her tenants, had employed a living-in servant: a Welsh girl with a sweet voice and a sweet face (Mrs Streamer knew the risk, but could not help giving in to beauty), who took Mr Clarky for a bailiff and loyally tried to shut the door on him. Then the lady herself appeared, expressed astonishment at seeing Mr Clarky on a Tuesday night instead of on a Saturday morning; said it was late anyway and she had an understanding with neighbours that there were to be no lessons after eight o'clock; and put a stop to the continuing skirmish with the door.

Mr Clarky, disencumbered, confessed that, although he pursued the art with undiminished ardour, he had come on an errand unconnected with 'the forty'. Mrs Streamer looked apprehensive; and more so when Mr Clarky intimated that it was on a matter inconvenient to broach in the doorway. A thousand fears assailed her, each of which involved Mr Streamer. Mr Clarky was drawn inside and shown into the parlour and the loyal Welsh servant totally excluded.

'I was wonderin', ma'am,' said Mr Clarky, having courteously inquired after Mr Streamer and been told, palely, that he was in excellent health, morally irreproachable and, at present, playing the violin in the theatre, 'I was wonderin' if our friend, Sir Robert Standfast, 'as called 'ere?'

'Why no, Mr Clarky!' exclaimed Mrs Streamer, much relieved. 'We have not seen him since—since —'

She worried at her fringe and Mr Clarky's spirits declined.

'Since Friday!' she came out with finally, apparently having extracted the information from her fringe.

Mr Clarky's spirits rose.

'Did 'e mention another appointment, ma'am? Did 'e confide where 'e might be goin'?'

Mrs Streamer applied to her fringe again; but to no avail. She shook her head, and wondered why Mr Clarky was asking. Mr Clarky explained. At once Mrs Streamer was aghast. Her eyes grew enormous with tears, and her plump hands became a bewilderment of unravelling fingers. She recollected, in a torrent, their dear friend's entire history, she remembered the day he arrived with his little angel and his sad old trunk and fiddle—and *this* should be the end of it all! She spoke of his unfailing gentleness and courtesy, his regularity with the rent, his love of the child, his ceaseless efforts to better himself, his mild successes, his happiness when his angel was happy, his grief when she was out of sorts. Then there was his kindness, even to the poor soul who had been murdered . . . and then, when everything seemed set fair for him and his angel—*this!* Here was a tragedy that made Mrs Streamer's little distresses seem like joys by comparison! Mr Streamer would—

'Then 'e said nothin' that might be of 'elp, ma'am?' interposed Mr Clarky.

'No—no! He went off without a word! So unlike him. But then he was upset, you know—'

'Upset, ma'am? Distracted, would you say?'

Mrs Streamer consulted with her fringe and agreed that Sir Robert's state might well have been described as distracted.

'And could you, ma'am, without prejudice, 'ave put a cause to it?'

'The violin, Mr Clarky. I'm sure it was the violin. He came to visit us—we are, after all, old friends!—and we suggested, Mr Streamer and I, that he should take it with him for Perdita. Such a talented child! One hopes that she keeps up with her music, Mr Clarky; but she is inclined to be self-willed and—'

'The violin, ma'am. I believe you mentioned the violin?'

'Yes—yes, I was coming to it, Mr Clarky. It was in the loft and Mr Streamer was just going to fetch it when Sir Robert remembered his old trunk. Such a shabby old thing, tied up with rope, would you believe! It was a wonder he bothered with it. It had been up there for years. But he would have it, so Mr Streamer—'

'The violin, ma'am—'

'Yes, yes, Mr Clarky, I was just coming to it. Mr Streamer had been using it while his own was being repaired. An unfortunate accident, Mr Clarky, but one must make allowances! Of course, it was not so fine as Mr Streamer's own, which is an Italian instrument. A wedding gift, you know. A remarkable tone. Mr Streamer often plays solos—'

'The violin, ma'am . . . Sir Robert's—'

'I was just coming to it, Mr Clarky. A Polish instrument. Mr Streamer had had it re-strung and re-varnished. It had been damaged by fire, I understand. Of course we didn't ask Sir Robert to pay. Mr Streamer bore the cost himself, as was only right . . . Not that Sir Robert would—'

'Ah, yes! Sir Robert, ma'am. You mentioned Sir Robert and the violin. You mentioned that 'e was upset by it.'

'I was just going to tell you, Mr Clarky. It was the maker's name. The varnishing had brought it up. Mr Streamer drew his attention to it; and he was terribly shocked! You could see it at once. Like a ghost!'

'The name, ma'am. Do you recall it?'

'Indeed I do! It was, Mr Streamer said, quite a common Polish name, like Jones or Smith, but in Polish, of course. But it was such a coincidence. It was the same name as that poor young man who has just been hanged. Kozlowski—'

Mrs Streamer, amiable as she was, could not help feeling mildly irritated as, for a second time, she found herself hastily abandoned following the pronouncing of that name.

Mr Clarky to the dark prison came. A heavy sense of wickedness in the dwindling air. A narrow street; a public house whose windows gleamed watchfully on sundry shabby individuals loitering round its flickering doorway, like moths with mouldy wings. Mr Clarky was suddenly, unaccountably oppressed. He reflected, as he approached the great gaol, that this was the house the law built. He walked along in the shadow of the piled-up tablets of stone, and could not help thinking that here was the wall that guarded the house the law built; and wondered where might be the door that led through the wall that guarded the house the law built; and having so begun, went on in the way of the nursery rhyme, with particular reference to the maiden all forlorn and the man all tattered and torn . . .

He gained entry at last through a small door set within an immense one; a pickpocket of a door, as if for the admission of little crimes, while the larger one was for the welcoming in of Murder.

A noisy, stony place inside; full of stony shouts, stony songs, stony laughter, and, in between, little stony silences. This was the house the law built . . .

Mr Clarky, making free with his employer's name, which meant nothing, and Inspector Groom's name, which meant a great deal, applied to a prison dignitary for information relating to visitors to one David Kozlowski.

The dignitary responded to the effect that D. Kozlowski's existence had recently been terminated, which might be regarded as the end of the matter. He spoke defensively as the legal connections of the spry little inquirer made him fear that there might have been a miscarriage of justice that would reflect badly on the establishment that provided him with a livelihood. Had there been any irregularity, he said, he could not be held responsible; and he could do no more than to refer the inquiry to the underling under whose Judas eye D. Kozlowski had passed his last hours.

The underling was summoned. He came, gnarled and limping, with a face full of shadows out of which his eyes peered searchingly, as if through Judas holes in his head. Mr Clarky, sensing the solemnity of the man, forbore to inquire, admiringly, into the mysteries of his trade. Though he did not doubt that there was an art in it, it was not an art he wished to acquire. Instead he stated his business plainly. Had a gentleman, a well-dressed gentleman, most likely in a grey coat and handsome trousers, visited David Kozlowski in his cell?

'Sir Robert Standfast, do you mean?'

'The very gentleman! The very gentleman!'

'He visited David twice. He came on the Friday, and again on the Saturday—'

'And the Sunday?'

'He called, but David would not see him.'

'A disagreement? A quarrel?'

'With the world, sir. David would see no one on that day. Your gentleman came back, and back again. But it was no use.'

'But 'e was 'ere on the Sunday, you say?'

'All night, I fancy. Why do you ask, sir?'

'The gentleman 'as disappeared.'

'I am sorry to hear it. He was very kind to David.'

'All night, you said?'

The gaoler glanced at the prison dignitary, as if an answer would involve him in a clash of views with his superior, which he would rather avoid. He shrugged his shoulders; and then, as if suddenly recollecting, said, 'But I'm glad you called, sir. There's what you might call an *effect* of David's that you might know how to dispose of, sir. I'll fetch it for you . . . if you don't mind waiting on the displeasure of a lame leg.'

Mr Clarky expressed concern, and offered to accompany the lame one, to save him the labour of a double journey. He guessed that the man had been unwilling to speak freely in front of his superior, and had offered him the opportunity of a private exchange.

The dignitary, uneasiness now dispelled, nodded approval; and the old gaoler limped and puffed Mr Clarky through the little world of stone and iron to his cubby-hole that adjoined the condemned cell.

Strange apartment! A crowded little windowless repository of pastimes, like a cupboard. Chess, draughts, playing-cards, cribbage, backgammon, dice, and boards with mysterious pins and hooks and numbers on them, were piled up everywhere in profusion . . . as if a huge family of children had, under the eye of a strict governess, put their games away and gone to bed.

Which, in a grim sense, Mr Clarky reflected sadly, was the case.

'When the world shrinks,' murmured the gaoler, 'there's nothing left but games.'

Mr Clarky's eye fell upon a chessboard with the pieces deployed in an unfinished game. The gaoler, divining his visitor's interest, explained: 'An old one. A long time ago. I keep it like that as it was his move.'

Mr Clarky did not inquire further.

'Your gentleman, sir,' said the gaoler. 'I think I saw him on the Monday morning. I'm not sure—there was such a crowd, you understand—but I think it was him. I was surprised as I did not think he was the sort of gentleman to come and watch. I think it was him . . . by the public house opposite. Perhaps he went inside afterwards?'

'Thank you. I will ask there.'

'The *effect*, sir, David's effect. Will you take it with you? Perhaps you might know where it belongs?'

'I would be 'appy to oblige.'

The gaoler reached up to a shelf and took down the violin.

'It was from your gentleman. He brought it for David on the Saturday. It was very kind of him.'

Mr Clarky received the instrument into uncertain hands.

'There's David's name on it,' went on the gaoler. 'It was his own. His father made it for him. He lost it when he was a child, and had always dreamed of it. He was very happy when your gentleman brought it for him. I understand your gentleman found it a long time ago, in the place where David came from. It was the only thing left for him.'

'Did 'e ask for it to be returned to Sir Robert?'

'No. He seemed to forget all about it at the end. But I thought that your gentleman, having had it for so long, might like to have it back again.'

'My gentleman! Yes—yes. Between you and me, I would like to 'ave my gentleman back again! Did 'e mention anythin' that might 'ave been in 'is mind?'

The gaoler shook his head.

'He was a very confused and distressed gentleman, I thought. David told me that there had been some misunderstanding about a child—a baby—but that had all been cleared up. And indeed, when your gentleman went away on the Saturday, he seemed a changed gentleman . . . until, that is, on the Sunday, when David would not see him.'

'And then?'

'A very confused and distressed gentleman all over again. He wanted to ask David something—something important; but David would not see him.'

'Did 'e mention what it was?'

Again the gaoler shook his head; this time with a touch of severity, Mr Clarky thought—as if he felt that Mr Clarky had no right to ask that question, as if it was enough that David had been stripped of his life; as if David's secret, whatever it was, ought to remain inviolate; and that no one ought to be emptied and reduced to nothing.

Little Mr Clarky, perched on a narrow stool, quite surrounded by games and pastimes, like childhood's latter end, felt uncomfortable in both body and mind. The gaoler's obvious affection for David Kozlowski made him feel awkward as he reflected haplessly on his own part in the young man's fate; and the gold watch he had received as a reward for his efforts weighed heavily as he took it out to consult it.

'If you hurry,' said the gaoler, taking note of his visitor's concern for the time, 'the public house opposite might still be open. I am sure it was your gentleman standing outside it on the Monday morning. I thought he was trying to shout something up to David. But then, all the world was shouting, too.'

Mr Clarky left the dark prison; and with it, he left a little of his spryness. He found himself thinking, most unfamiliarly, that the house the law built might be, after all, a somewhat imperfect piece of architecture; and he shrank within himself as he thought of the games and pastimes that lay at its stony heart.

The public house opposite—a famous establishment, whose upper windows overlooked the scaffold and were always in great demand—was on the point of closing when Mr Clarky entered.

The publican, a fat man in shirtsleeves, wearing what appeared to be a gigantic turban, none too clean, looked sourly at the newcomer, pointed accusingly at the violin he carried under his arm, and drew his attention to a notice highly detrimental to itinerant musicians. Courteously Mr Clarky explained that his connection with the offending instrument was legal rather than musical, asked for a glass of port, and wondered if the good publican could assist him in his inquiries? He was interested in a gentleman, a well-dressed gentleman in a grey coat and handsome trousers, who might have patronised the distinguished establishment on Monday morning, after the hanging. Mr Clarky was quite aware that many gentlemen of high degree must have been the publican's guests on that morning, but—

'Carrying a dirty old trunk was he, by any chance? And holding on to it by a dirty old rope was he, by any chance?'

'The very gentleman!'

'The very murdering bastard you mean! Look! Look at this!' He pointed at his turban with an outraged finger. 'Do you take me for a bleedin' Turk or something? There's injuries under there! Horrible injuries! Scarred for life, I'll be!'

'For God's sake, what 'appened?'

For answer, the good publican summoned his wife, a waiter, the potboy and a customer who had also been witness to the scandalous assault. So what had happened? Tell him—go on, tell him!

Well, it was like this. The gent had been sitting for two hours and more, drinking down brandy till it was coming out of his eyes. So up goes the waiter to him and asks, very thoughtful and considerate, if it was his first hanging, as it often turns the stomach, but not to worry as it happens to the best of us. To which the gent responds with something very offensive. So naturally the guv'nor takes a hand and asks the gent outright if he happens to be one of them dirty stinking Abolitionists, of which there's always a few about, trying to spoil folks' fun.

'What your sort needs,' says the guv'nor, calm as anything, 'is a damn' good hiding!'

On which the gent, without a single word, fetches the guv'nor a fourpenny one with the brandy bottle.

You should have seen it! Shouts? Screams? The lot! There's the guv'nor, bleeding like a pig ('No offence, guv'nor!'), with bits of broken glass ornamenting the top of his bonce, like a wall; and there's the gent, out of the door quick as a fart, and off down the street swinging his trunk and his legs going like clappers!

'And now I'd be obliged,' said the publican, with three little bonfires burning in his countenance, one in either cheek and one at the end of his nose, 'if you'd furnish me with that gent's name. There'll be an action, I can promise you! An action for attempted murder!'

But it turned out that Mr Clarky was unable to help. It was with the greatest regret that he came to the conclusion that the gentleman was not his gentleman at all. Most unfortunate, but a total stranger. His gentleman was nothing like that.

Mr Clarky went outside. He peered along the dark street, which vanished into blackness. Beyond lay chaos and confusion. He leaned against the wall. He felt weary, weary unto death. He could go no further. The trail he had followed so rapidly and eagerly had ceased. It had ended in a thunderclap of violence that had obliterated everything.

36

Mr Clarky a wanderer in the night.

'The young lady places great faith in you,' Mr Leviticus had said. 'And so do I.'

A double burden; and the heavier part was the child's. Faith at her age was a life-sized affair and not, as with the declining man, a somewhat shrunken article weighing little more than a word.

The night was starless and beginning to leak with rain. Mr Clarky, coat collar turned up, hard round hat shining with wet, investigating street after street, alley after alley, court after court. . .

'Beg pardon—beg pardon, but 'ave you seen a gentleman, well-dressed, in a grey coat and carryin' a trunk tied up with rope? On Monday it would 'ave been . . . '

There was a storm somewhere, a long way off. Faint flashes made the streets grisly, and distant thunder kicked and banged, like a temper shut up in a box-room. Mr Clarky thinking to himself that surely he had come back to where he had begun; for was not that the prison again, looming in the sky? *But the young lady places great faith in you* . . .

'Beg pardon—beg pardon, but 'ave you seen a gentleman . . . ?'

Mr Clarky off again, feeling, rather metaphysically, that he was lost in a night of the soul; and wondering how it would have been with the daughter and father had he never entered their lives. But *the young lady places great faith in you* . . .

'Beg pardon—beg pardon, but 'ave you seen a gentleman . . . ?'

The burden grew heavier as the night wore on; and the spry little man began to bend under it, and threatened to snap, like a dried-up twig. But *the young lady places great faith in you* . . .

A coffee-stall somewhere, a lamp-lit cupboard in the night, a kind of Punch and Judy, with Punch in a dozen mufflers and a woollen hat, leaning out for money, and Judy presiding over a large funereal urn. Mr Clarky cuddling his mug and watching the rain make a pin-cushion of his drink; while round about hard, hungry faces floated in the yellow murk.

'Beg pardon—beg pardon, but 'ave you seen a gentleman, well-dressed, in a grey coat and carryin' a trunk tied up with rope? On Monday it would 'ave been. No . . . no? Much obliged anyway. . . much obliged.'

A long night; and the hours stalked, stiff as corpses, round the dial of Mr Clarky's fine gold time-piece. At last, by dint of staring at it, the darkness faded from the sky; seeming to drain down into the chimneypots and fill them up till they stood, black as ink against the grey. The lamps of the coffee-stall turned wan and sickly; and Mr Clarky bent his steps towards Pentonville Road.

He walked slowly; not because of weariness, but because, no matter how watchful the household, a quarter past five in the morning was still too early to call.

'Why, it's Mr Clarky, ain't it? What a surprise! Well, I never! Mr Clarky, of all people!'

Mrs Groom, in a shrubbery of curl-papers, stared at the little gentleman from Gray's Inn who stood forlornly on her doorstep at ten minutes past six o'clock in the morning.

'Come inside, Mr Clarky, do come inside out of the wet! I'll go and tell Mr Groom that you're here!'

She ushered Mr Clarky into the parlour and hurried upstairs, while her children, angelic in nightgowns, kept the visitor under close surveillance in case he stole the spoons.

Presently Inspector Groom appeared; an imposing figure in a yellow dressing-gown with a black design which Mr Clarky took to be a pattern of handcuffs, suggesting sunshine in custody. He greeted Mr Clarky warmly, expressed concern for his damp condition; and, producing his immense bunch of keys, inquired if it was too early for his visitor to partake of sherry. However, before Mr Clarky could reply, the inspector raised a warning finger, moved quickly to the door, opened it, and dismissed the little eavesdroppers with an indulgent smile. Then he returned to Mr Clarky, who declined the sherry but was prevailed upon to take a glass of rum which the inspector strongly advised as being a sensible precaution after any exposure to the elements.

'Well now, Mr Clarky,' said the inspector, seating himself and smoothing down the back of his head, 'what is it that you have come to tell me?'

He crossed his legs and brought into prominence a large bedroom slipper, such as might have patrolled the very limits of dreamland. His brow was smooth, his face benign and he radiated the assurance of a calm soul.

'In what way, Mr Clarky, can Scotland Yard be of assistance to Gray's Inn and Chancery Lane?'

'If it is agreeable to you, Mr Groom,' proposed Mr Clarky humbly, 'I would be obliged if we could proceed on a more personal footin'. With respect, Mr Groom, I would sooner think of it as Mr Groom bein' of assistance to a young lady, Miss Perdita Standfast—'

'*And*, of course, to my friend, Mr Clarky?' hazarded the inspector.

Mr Clarky, conscious of his damp, forlorn appearance, was unable to deny it, and the inspector expanded.

'Very well, Mr Clarky, it shall be as you wish. We shall leave Scotland Yard out of it; and Chancery Lane too. We are two gentlemen together. Come now—the trouble!'

'The young lady's father, Sir Robert Standfast, 'as disappeared, Mr Groom.'

'When?'

Mr Clarky told him.

'You have, I take it, pursued some inquiries yourself before coming to me? Come, come, Mr Clarky! It would have been unreasonable of you not to have done so! You have, for example, inquired at the hospitals and mortuaries?'

'Not so, Mr Groom . . . at least, not yet.'

The inspector pursed his lips.

'I take it, then, that your suspicions have been aroused in another direction?'

Mr Clarky nodded, and, on the inspector's invitation, related how he had heard of Sir Robert's curious absence from the Dollys'

Friday dinner, which had prompted his own subsequent inquiries at the Streamers, the prison and the public house.

The inspector listened carefully as Mr Clarky divulged every detail of his encounters; praised his memory, commended his perspicacity, and commiserated with his fruitless search in the night. It was, he said, a circumstance with which members of the Force were all too well acquainted, and he was sorry, really sorry, that a representative of Gray's Inn should have experienced it too.

'I 'ad 'oped,' said Mr Clarky, with an air of mild reproach, 'that we were on a personal footin', Mr Groom, and that Scotland Yard and Chancery Lane would be 'eld in abeyance.'

'Indeed they are, Mr Clarky, indeed they are! Mine was but a passing observation. No criticism was intended. So let us continue to put our heads together,' said the inspector, leaning forward as if to draw attention to how much larger his head was than Mr Clarky's, and that any putting of them together could only result in Mr Clarky's cranium being totally eclipsed. 'What you have told me is of great interest, and possibly of value, too. There are details that certainly whet the investigating appetite—'

'The violin, Mr Groom?'

'And other things, Mr Clarky. One would like to know, for instance, what it was that Sir Robert was so anxious to ask the unfortunate young man on the Sunday; and one would like to know why the old trunk was so important that he remembered to take it with him even when he fled from the scene of the assault. These matters may well have a bearing on what has become of him; but before we can say that, we must know more, Mr Clarky, much more.'

'I am in your 'ands, Mr Groom. You 'ave but to ask.'

'I would like you to tell me everything you know about the gentleman, Mr Clarky; every detail, no matter how unimportant it may seem to you. You must let me be the judge, as what might seem a trifle to Chancery Lane might be of the greatest significance to Scotland Yard.'

'On a personal footin', Mr Groom, if you would be so kind.'

'A passing observation, Mr Clarky, no more than that. We are, as I promised, two gentlemen together. Now, tell me about Sir Robert Standfast; for if we are to discover where he has gone, it is of great help to know where he has come from. Generally speaking, Mr Clarky, in moments of sudden fear, panic or distress, men are inclined to rush where instinct drives them. They do not fly to such a refuge as you or I might choose. Often they take a course that you or I would think to be mad; for we do not know the pursuer, and therefore the refuge is something we cannot understand.'

'I need 'ardly say, Mr Groom,' murmured Mr Clarky humbly, ''ow much I admire the art.'

'Then let us put it to the test, Mr Clarky,' returned the inspector, smoothing down his head. 'Tell me about the gentleman . . . and the child.'

So Mr Clarky told him, omitting nothing, however trifling; and, so far as he knew, adding nothing, no matter how perspicacious it might have seemed. He told of Sir Robert's early history: the theft of money and the subsequent flight. He told of his own first meeting with 'Mr Walker', and that gentleman's reluctance to claim his inheritance. He told of Sir Robert's passionate attachment to the child—

'That is opinion, Mr Clarky. Please be so good as to keep to facts.'

Mr Clarky ventured to say that it was an opinion borne out by fact, as Sir Robert had, on the Friday, made a will leaving everything in his power to the child; on which the inspector withdrew his objection and invited Mr Clarky to proceed. So Mr Clarky continued, and confided the true relationship of the father and daughter to one another, and the curious history of how they had come to be together. He told of the strange transaction with the tramp—

'A tramp? That is very remarkable, Mr Clarky.'

'Quite a fairy tale,' agreed Mr Clarky.

Inspector Groom studied his prominent slipper, revolved it as if to disentangle his foot from something distasteful.

'It is remarkable,' he pursued, 'on more counts than one, Mr Clarky. It is remarkable because, had the unfort'nate individual stolen the child with the idea of ransom in his mind, he would not have parted with it so readily. On the other hand, had he found the child and, as an individual of sentiment and feeling, taken it with him out of pity, he would have left it in the care of a family rather than dispose of it to a wandering foreigner. Being an individual of sentiment and feeling, he might well have made some effort to rear and nurture the child himself. Do you take my drift, Mr Clarky? Do you follow me?'

Mr Clarky did; and expressed a sincere admiration for the inspector's powers. Although he and Mr Leviticus had arrived at the same conclusion—that both the tramp and Mr Walker were fictitious aspects of the same man—it had taken them several minutes longer.

'An individual of sentiment and feeling,' murmured the inspector, indicating, by a smoothing down of his head, that his powers were fully wound and ready to strike. 'But not an honest individual, not a straightforward individual like you and me, Mr Clarky. It would seem that we have an individual who makes up a story for a child for the purpose of deceiving her and deceiving himself. Why he did this, we cannot know. Individuals tell lies for many reasons. Lies, Mr Clarky, are very like that flight from pursuit; and unless we understand the nature of the pursuer, we cannot understand the refuge.

'Let us suppose that, in the first instance, the lie is kindly and well meant, and is merely a means of protecting the child from something disagreeable. But then, by persisting in it, it becomes something else. It becomes a means of removing the child and the tramp, of separating the child and the tramp from their origins. Thus our individual of sentiment and feeling, Mr Clarky, in thinking of the child is really thinking of himself.'

'But is that not so with all of us, Mr Groom?' interposed the little man, curiously depressed.

'Indeed it is, Mr Clarky! I don't deny it! But you and I— Chancery Lane and Scotland Yard—are servants of the law. We uphold something greater than ourselves. Not so the individual of sentiment and feeling. Not for him submission to statute and precedent. He knows better. He makes his own law and upholds his own lies. Such individuals are dangerous, Mr Clarky. Such individuals provoke riotous assemblies with the aim of over-throwing governments. However, in the present instance, I fancy that the individual has only overthrown himself. The discovery concerning the violin undoubtedly suggested to the individual a connection between the child and the condemned murderer. The

273

shock must have been terrible. Forgetting all his obligations, he rushed to the gaol for confirmation. But he received no satisfactory answer. So there follows a great desperation to communicate once more with the condemned; for he must ask that interesting question. Even at the foot of the scaffold—if we are to believe the gaoler—he shouts it out. But it is too late; so there is violence and flight. A little more rum, Mr Clarky?' inquired the inspector, breaking off in order to refill his visitor's glass.

The inspector's brow was still smooth and his countenance benign; but his yellow gown seemed to have a little more black in it, as if the sunshine had received a life sentence.

'So, now that we have some idea of the nature of the pursuit,' resumed the inspector, returning the bottle of rum to its gaol and locking it up, 'we may make a guess at the nature of the refuge. We have an individual urgently seeking the answer to a question whose origins are most likely in Poland. So I suggest that we direct our attention to the docks and inquire about anyone seeking to board a vessel for Poland. Furthermore,' went on the inspector, raising his hand as if to prevent Mr Clarky rushing off to the docks at that very moment, 'I suggest that we abandon our inquiries for a well-dressed gentleman in a grey coat carrying a trunk. The violin has told us a little; but the trunk, tied up with rope, tells us a great deal more. I think we might hazard a guess as to its contents. An individual of sentiment and feeling, Mr Clarky, likes to keep things—things that you and I might well discard. Therefore I suggest that we think in terms of a ragged individual, with a rope around his middle and tin articles hanging from it. Yes. I fancy that will be the case,' said the inspector, with a satisfied nod. 'Or I'm a Dutchman.'

Mr Clarky rose to leave; but once more the inspector delayed him.

'There is no need for you to do more, Mr Clarky. I will set my men to the task. I would not like to see Chancery Lane doing work more fitted to Scotland Yard. Even on a personal footing.'

37

Soon after nine o'clock on the Friday morning, a person in plain clothes called at Raymond's Buildings, Gray's Inn, and inquired, with unmistakably constabular discretion, if he might have a word in private with a gentleman by the name of Mr Clarky. He said that his business with the gentleman was on a personal footing. His manner was sober, his expression bland; he was a person who might have carried news of an earthquake or a resurrection with equal imperturbability.

Mr Clarky glanced apprehensively at his employer. Mr Leviticus frowned. The little man was looking poorly. He had disregarded Inspector Groom's excellent advice and had been searching the wastes of dockland each night on his own account. Consequently spryness had quite gone out of him, and greyness and doubt had crept in at every seam and crack. Mr Leviticus nodded; it was a very small nod for so large a man.

'Remember, Clarky, if the news is bad, you must tell me at once. But—but if it is good, then you must use your own discretion.'

Mr Clarky nodded and conducted the constable into the outer office, and closed the door.

'Well? What is the news?'

The constable cleared his throat.

'Inspector Groom has directed me to ask you, sir—ahem!—if you would be good enough to accompany me—ahem!—on a personal footing, to where he is awaiting you. Ahem! At your earliest convenience, sir.'

''as 'e found 'im, then? 'as 'e found 'im?'

'Ahem! It being on a personal footing, sir, Inspector Groom did not see fit to—ahem!—confide in me.'

Mr Clarky put on his hat with an unsteady hand. He stared round the office as if bidding it farewell. He looked hard at the closed door; he hesitated, then knocked on it, opened it and poked his head inside the room. Mr Leviticus was reclining massively in

275

his chair. His eyes were shut. To all intents he was taking a nap.

'Understood, Mr L. Perfectly understood,' murmured Mr Clarky; and went off with the constable without further delay.

Inspector Groom was to meet him in the private room of The White Cross, a gaunt and dismal public house in Shadwell that stood upon a corner of which nothing more remained but the corner and the public house on it—everything round about having fallen into ruin and decay. Mr Clarky waited while the constable went off to fetch his superior.

There was a wind blowing and bits of dirty paper kept fluttering against the window, like crumpled birds trying to get back into the Ark with the news that there wasn't much doing outside. 'It is with the deepest regret that I have to inform you,' Mr Clarky began to read, as the torn-up fragment of a letter flattened itself, momentarily, against the glass; when Inspector Groom arrived.

''ave you found 'im, Mr Groom?'

Inspector Groom nodded; and smoothed down the back of his head . . .

'In a manner of speaking, Mr Clarky; if you take my meaning.'

Mr Clarky took a cab; and, agitation getting the better of thrift, kept it waiting outside Mrs Fairhazel's house in Stepney. Mrs Fairhazel herself opened the door, and Mr Clarky, without any courteous preliminaries, demanded, 'The young lady, ma'am! Miss Perdita! Is she at 'ome?'

'No—no, Mr Clarky. She is out walking with the gentlemen from upstairs. But she will not be long—'

'Might I wait for 'er, ma'am?'

'Of course, Mr Clarky! Please come inside! But your cab—?'

'Let 'im wait, ma'am!'

'Then there's news?'

Mr Clarky, inside Mrs Fairhazel's shining little hallway, looked round as if for eavesdroppers; and nodded.

'Is he—is he alive?'

Mr Clarky investigated the hall again, paying particular attention to a hat-rack, before nodding again.

'Thank God—thank God!'

Mr Clarky, with a devout look to the ceiling, concurred; then exclaimed, 'Is that 'er outside, ma'am? I 'eard something!'

Mrs Fairhazel went to the door.

'It is only your cab-driver, Mr Clarky.'

Mr Clarky passed a hand across his brow. Mrs Fairhazel trembled. It was apparent that the little man was deeply troubled.

'What is it, Mr Clarky? Please—please tell me! Is he ill?'

Mr Clarky did not answer. Instead he wondered again if some noise outside signalled the young lady's return. Mrs Fairhazel looked, and said no, it was only a child playing in the street. Mr Clarky begged pardon, but—

'Is he ill, Mr Clarky? For God's sake, is he ill?'

'It's not that, ma'am. It's just that I 'ope I'm doin' the right thing. The young lady . . . I 'ardly know 'er, ma'am.'

'She has great faith in you, Mr Clarky.'

Mr Clarky, far from being comforted by the information, looked exceedingly depressed. Instinctively Mrs Fairhazel laid a hand on his sleeve, where it rested with all the reassuring power of a butterfly. Mr Clarky glanced down at it gratefully.

'If I might trouble you, ma'am, for your opinion . . . Mr Leviticus, you understand, 'as left matters in my 'ands . . . It makes it difficult, ma'am . . . I do not wish to go be'ind the young lady's back . . . obligation to a client, you know . . . But I would appreciate a word with you, ma'am . . . bein' a disinterested party—'

'Disinterested, Mr Clarky?'

Mr Clarky reddened under the woman's suddenly incredulous smile.

'Beg pardon—beg pardon! Understood, ma'am, perfectly understood! But . . . Is that 'er, ma'am? Did I 'ear 'er just now?'

Mrs Fairhazel investigated yet again, only to discover that Mr Clarky's abnormally sharp ears had detected a neighbouring boy holding a conversation with the cab-horse. She suggested it would be easier to watch for Perdita's return from the front room than to remain standing in the hall. Mr Clarky, after some agitated debate with himself (which appeared to involve his hat and, mysteriously, the contents of his pockets), submitted to being led into Mrs Fairhazel's parlour, where the noonday sun came through the lace curtains in a hundred bright slices. But under no circumstances could he be persuaded to sit down. He went to the window and hovered at the lace curtains like a large black fly. Mrs Fairhazel watched him with a deep fear in her heart.

'You wanted my opinion, Mr Clarky? Please—please tell me what it is that is worrying you so much?'

'It's the child, ma'am . . . our young client. The gentleman—well, 'e's another matter . . . but the child, ma'am. She's the one. In the end, everythin' comes down to 'er. 'as she—'as she told you anythin' about 'er 'story, ma'am? 'as she said anythin' about 'erself and—and 'er father, ma'am?'

'Yes, Mr Clarky. She has told me. She has told me about how she and her father came together.'

'And what did you think, ma'am?'

'It was a great surprise to me. And yet, not altogether. There has always been something—something anxious about their feelings. I often thought that they were both frightened for each other. He showed it more, of course; but it has always been in Perdita, too. If anything, her fear was the greater.'

Mr Clarky gazed at the woman in some admiration for her understanding; and felt that here was yet another art in which he was a mere infant.

'So she's told you everythin', ma'am. She's opened 'er 'eart to you.'

'We—we have become friends, Mr Clarky.'

'Then she'll 'ave need of you, ma'am,' muttered Mr Clarky, peering anxiously through the curtains.

Mrs Fairhazel went very pale, and helplessly remembered the feelings she'd had, long ago, when someone had come to the door to tell her that there'd been an accident in Holborn . . . a cart . . . her husband . . .

'But—but you said he was alive! You said he was not ill!'

'The gentleman,' said Mr Clarky quietly, 'is in very poor circumstances. At this moment, 'e is in Shadwell. Inspector Groom 'as 'im under observation—'

'The police?'

'On a personal footin', ma'am, no more than that. Inspector Groom is very discreet. The gentleman does not know. But 'e is in very poor circumstances indeed. More than that, it would not be proper for me to say, as it would be goin' be'ind our young client's back. But it will come as a shock to 'er. To be honest with you, ma'am, Inspector Groom was very much against my fetchin' 'er before anythin' was done; but I thought that—that—Do you

278

think I'm doin' the right thing, ma'am? You see, I take it to be a matter of truth, if I might put it that way. I would be obliged, ma'am, if—ah! That's 'er! That's our client!'

This time he was not mistaken; and a moment later a bombshell in muslin, with black curls streaming like a fuse, rushed inside the house and exploded in the parlour.

'Where is he? Where is he?'

She had seen the cab waiting outside, had guessed instantly that there was news; and had left the brothers Wilkinson halfway down the street, amazed, with nothing but air between them.

'Where is he?'

She stared round the room in frantic inquiry.

'Miss Perdita—' began Mr Clarky.

She turned on him. Her eyes were huge and wild.

'He's dead! I know it! That's what you've come to tell me! That's why you're looking at me like that! He's dead! I hate you for coming to tell me that! I hate you, I hate you!'

'But Miss Perdita—Miss Perdita—'

Mr Clarky, shaken, bewildered, tried to make headway against the storm; found himself assailed by fists and bright new shoes.

'Miss Perdita—'

'He's alive, he's alive, Perdita!' cried Mrs Fairhazel, trying to hold the girl. 'Mr Clarky has found him! He's alive—'

At once Mr Clarky found himself in receipt of a gratitude that was as fierce as the previous despair. He staggered under a thousand arms and kisses. Then the young client fell back. She stared from face to face, suddenly overcome by doubt.

'Why isn't he here? There's something wrong, isn't there? I can tell! There's something wrong! I want to go to him! Please take me to him, Mr Clarky! Take me to him now!'

'The cab's waitin', Miss Perdita. It's waitin' to take you now!'

By the time the brothers Wilkinson, sure but slow of pace, had caught up with their young charge, she was already in the cab, with their pretty landlady and the little lawyer's clerk from Gray's Inn.

''e's been found, gentlemen!' called out Mr Clarky as the cab drove off. ''e's been found!'

The journey to Shadwell was a great torment to Mr Clarky as he sat, jerking and jolting in both body and mind, opposite Mrs

279

Fairhazel and his palely excited young client. He tried to catch Mrs Fairhazel's eye, in private, for her support; but the confinement of the cab and the sharpness of the young client (she watched every flicker of his eyes), put anything like that out of the question.

He dreaded that he was doing the wrong thing, that he was misusing the discretion he had been told to use, and that he was about to destroy what he most hoped to build. He kept having second thoughts, and third thoughts, and more thoughts than his head could contain; and wishing he could take counsel's opinion on behalf of his young client. ('In your view, sir . . . in your view . . . what does the law have to say on this point, sir?' And so surrendering all human responsibility to the great mechanical master.)

Over and over again he leaned forward, fully intending to prepare the young client, (in accordance with counsel's opinion); and over and over again he fell back . . . not so much out of fear, but because Mr Leviticus's words kept dinning in his ears: 'The young lady places great faith in you.'

In the end he took counsel with himself and felt, in his heart of hearts, that the only way in which he could be worthy of that faith was to accord it the dignity of trust.

The cab halted. They had reached Shadwell. Mr Clarky took a bag of sweets out of his pocket and offered it to Mrs Fairhazel and the young client. They refused; so he ate one himself.

38

The young client felt a sense of the deepest importance that accorded very well with her most elevated dreams about herself. The concern and even deference displayed towards her seemed to set her apart and to demand of her a calmness and dignity that were not, inconveniently, integral parts of her nature.

Mr Clarky had left her sitting in the cab with Mrs Fairhazel while he had gone into a public house. It was a dismal premises with dirty stained-glass windows downstairs, as if it had been a church in its infancy but had grown out of it. She wondered what her father could be doing there, and she longed to jump out and go inside; but a gentle shake of Mrs Fairhazel's head reminded her of calmness and dignity; so the young client waited and wondered what she would say to her father.

Mr Clarky came out. Her heart fell down a hole. Mr Clarky was alone. She wanted to scream and cry; but a slight pressure of Mrs Fairhazel's hand reminded her again of calmness and dignity; so the young client clenched her fists till her nails must have drawn blood.

Mr Clarky handed the ladies out of the cab and told the driver to wait. He wanted to know for how long? Mr Clarky said, crossly, Why! until they came back, of course! The driver said he'd heard that one before; so Mr Clarky gave him some money and promised he would have the rest in a little while.

It turned out that her father was not far away, and they were going to walk to meet him. She wanted to run, to fly . . . but Mrs Fairhazel's arm round her shoulders reminded her yet again of calmness and dignity; so the young client behaved admirably and walked between her companions as if she was going to have her head cut off.

She was terribly frightened of what might be awaiting her. She wondered if it was something about herself; that her father had taken her at her word and had asked Mr Clarky to find out about her, and he had done so, and she was going to be confronted by a mother so extraordinary that no one dared to tell her. She wanted to plead and beg: 'What is it? Please, *please* tell me!' But a deeper feeling stopped her. She was more frightened of finding out than of not knowing; so the young client bit fiercely on her lip, and calmness and dignity triumphed.

'Careful, Miss Perdita, careful!'

They were walking in a terrible place: worse, even, than what she could remember of the part of Whitechapel where they had lived before the Streamers. It was like the end of the world: a wilderness of fallen walls, broken chimneypots, bits of rusting iron with sharp edges ('Careful, Miss Perdita!') and heaps of smelly rags that had once been coats and gowns and pretty bonnets that had all become caked together into mere outlines, as if they'd been pressed in a Bible, like flowers. She looked down and saw that her shoes had got dirty and that she'd torn the bottom of her dress. Suddenly she thought that, sooner or later, her own most treasured possessions would end up in a place like this, and she felt profoundly sad.

She wondered why they had come to such a place; and comforted herself by thinking that, whatever the reason, it wasn't the worst thing. Her father was not dead. Perhaps he'd lost all his money? Perhaps it had been found out that he wasn't Sir Robert Standfast after all, and they would have to go back to the Streamers, and pinch and save and be poor again? If so, then certainly calmness and dignity were the order of the day, thought the young client, raising her head and scowling in the face of the threatened reversal. If her father had really lost everything, then she'd be a great comfort to him. It would be in her power to remind him that, whatever misfortune might have befallen him, whatever people might have found out about him, *she* was still the elevated mystery she had always been: Perdita, the lost girl, the stolen princess . . . so everything was not lost after all. 'Pa!' she would say to him, 'You are not to worry—'

'Careful, Miss Perdita, careful!'

It was a dead cat, all heaving with flies. She had almost trod on it, and she cried out in involuntary disgust. Mrs Fairhazel drew her away, and Mr Clarky said, 'Careful, Miss Perdita!' as some rags, piled up in a hole, stirred and mumbled, and turned into an old man, snoring his head off. There was a cracked saucer lying beside him, and she wondered if the cat was his, and if he knew it was dead.

As they hastened away, Mrs Fairhazel put her own shawl round Perdita's shoulders, even though she'd said nothing about feeling cold. It was just like Mrs Fairhazel to do a thing like that, without asking . . . in case you said, No, thank you. Mrs Fairhazel's first name was Barbara, she'd found out. She ought to tell her father that; and also that Mrs Fairhazel—Barbara, rather—was a very good sort of person when you got to know her, and that they had had some quite interesting conversations together. She might even mention that Mrs Fairhazel—Barbara—looked very pretty when her hair was down and when she laughed . . . All these things she would tell her father in a great rush. She would tell him about the stationmaster at Gloucester and her time with him, and her journey to London on the train—practically on her own. And the Dollys ... and the excellent brothers Wilkinson ... and how she'd seen the cab waiting outside, and had guessed! And then Mr Clarky, and ... and ...

So the young client chattered frantically inside her head, nineteen to the dozen, as the desolation all round her, the fallen-in houses, the heaps of stinking rubbish, the busy nets of flies—who were the only ones who seemed to take a pride in their appearance, being smart and shiny while they fed off filth and death—an endlessly barking dog, and the hopeless derelict of a man who crouched by a wall in the sun, suddenly chilled her heart so that she shook and trembled as if she would never get warm again.

He was sitting there; and the sun, staring down on his ancient black hat, cast his face into the deepest shadow so that all that could be seen of his countenance was a faint shine of tears, like snail-tracks in the dark. But she knew him. He was wearing a horrible old coat, threadbare, torn and stained; and it was tied round the middle with a rope from which hung a saucepan, a kettle and a tankard, all battered and dented into faces like demons from a nightmare. His hands were clasped round his knees and he was rocking himself to and fro; and the kettle, saucepan and tankard kept banging together: clink—clink—clink!

39

Think of the old Jew who once chided Christ, waiting for forgiveness. Think of him wandering down the centuries, watching the world grow worse and worse till it must seem too late for Christ ever to return: the sky yellowing, the green grass shrinking, the trees dying, and only the sour bricks growing, growing everywhere into a dull crowding of prisons; and, worst of all, the monstrous madness of the office growing greater than the man.

Think of the old Jew dragging his crime (that had been so small and unthinking at the beginning) through all this thickening gloom, till it grows so heavy ,with the gathering corruption of years, that he can hardly move any more; so he sits and rocks himself to and fro, and wonders hopelessly what size of forgiveness would be needed now for a crime that has grown so huge.

So dreamed the tramp, as he squatted in the rubbish and slowly rocked himself to and fro, while a dog barked and ceaseless flies buzzed and widowed the stagnant air.

He was a fugitive. He had, in a moment of drunken madness, committed a violent assault—for all he knew he had killed the man!—and had fled to escape arrest. He had thrown away his good clothes and put on his present wretched rags in order to hide himself—a ruin among ruins.

But that was not the worst of it. He remembered the repugnance he'd felt when he'd taken the ancient rags out of the trunk, how he'd shrunk from them . . . and then, when he'd put them on, how they'd enveloped him in a dreadfully welcoming familiarity, so that he had become loath to abandon them, even though every hour, every minute he delayed made his situation worse.

He had watched a hanging, a murderer being murdered; for if the grand criterion of murder be malice aforethought, what could be more malicious, more carefully thought out, than to take a man outside and hang him?

Young David Kozlowski, trussed like a chicken, had jumped and jerked at the end of the rope for almost a minute, while the black bag put over his head for decency's sake had bulged most horribly, as if with bursting blood. Yet it was only the day before—no! The day before that, as David wouldn't see him on the Sunday—that he had agreed with David, had assured him and comforted him that nothing was going to happen. So in that last minute of incredulous agony, what must David have thought of the kindly liar who did not even have the courage to prepare him for what he knew must happen? What hatred and contempt he must have felt for the emptiness of the lie and the emptiness of the liar! Then it was over, and David hung, limp as mutton.

Yet even that wasn't the worst of it, because that, at least, was over; the worst was still living on. There was another kindly lie he dragged about with him, ever gathering other lies to support it, till it had become so large and heavy that he could hardly take another step. It was the lie he had told the child.

Again, not the worst of it, he thought as he rocked himself back and forth, clinking softly, and lost in his painful memories. The worst was surely that he had lost the truth for ever. Perdita's name. He might have found it out when David had talked of his mother making a doll for the baby. David would have known her name. But he hadn't asked, and had been thankful when David himself had not told him. He hadn't wanted to know her name because he had been frightened to give up any part of Perdita that he himself hadn't made. He was frightened to destroy the lie he had put inside her, even though there had always been times when he'd looked at her, when he'd crept in to watch her sleeping, and had thought that her deepest dreams, the secret companions of her sleep, were as vain and empty as the man who had put them there.

It had only been afterwards that he'd repented of what he'd done, and tried to move heaven and earth to undo it, even at the foot of the scaffold; but David never heard him, and then David was dead.

There was a ship sailing for Danzig on the following night. A Polish sailor in the public house, glad to find someone who spoke his language, had told him and had advised him how best to get aboard. He would go back to the village, which must have been rebuilt by now. There must have been some survivors of the massacre—people who'd been out of the village at the time— who'd come back again. *They* would remember the name. He would find it out and somehow get it back to Mr Leviticus, so that when he died he would not be leaving Perdita as a kind of lonely phantom with nothing inside her but his lies.

The tears ran down his cheeks as he realised that the course he had determined on meant that he could never return, and would never see Perdita again. Yet, he reflected (and anyone looking at him would most heartily have agreed), she would be better off without him, as his presence was only destroying her. At least he had secured her financially and left her in the care of a guardian who was far better than himself or any of his kind.

So the tramp brooded as he rocked himself to and fro, so that his saucepan, kettle and tankard clinked together like the links of a heavy chain; and his thoughts reverted to the old Jew, waiting for a forgiveness that could never be enough, because his crime had grown too large. Clink—clink—clink!

Someone was watching him! He did not look up as he had had such a feeling several times before, and had seen no one. Most likely the watcher was inside his own head, as the sensation of being watched was the natural companion of guilt.

The sensation grew stronger, acutely so. He scowled and examined his knees. He was not, after all, the only inhabitant of the wilderness. Others, as ragged as he, sometimes trudged and scavenged there. He heard a sharp intake of breath. He raised his head, and saw smart black shoes with pretty paste buckles; and trembled. He saw a muslin skirt, flowered like a garden, and gathered up into a young girl's waist; hands, tightly clenched, and a silver bracelet round a young girl's wrist . . . and so upward until he met with a face, pale as death, looking down at him with eyes that were filled with incredulous tears.

Although his heart rejoiced to see her again, he shrank in shame at her seeing him; and there was no kindly lie that could hide the truth any more.

She thought he said something, but it was hard to hear as the dog was barking all the time. It might have been, 'Perdita—Perdita, my darling!' but it sounded more like a moan. She tried to think of all the things she had been going to say to him; but nothing would come. Her head was empty of everything, except that the one she had feared and hated most in all the world was also the one she loved most.

He looked terrible. She hardly knew him. He hadn't washed or shaved for several days, and he looked a hundred years old. His eyes were thick with crying, and he tried to wipe them with his fingers, just like a baby. She gave him her handkerchief; and two ragged children, who had been exploring the rubbish, observed the transaction with interest and wondered if the smart young girl was in the business of distributing good things to all and sundry. They scrambled towards her and, shrilly and tearfully, made her acquainted with the sadness of their lot. She gave them her purse and they ran off with it before she could come to her senses and realise what she had done.

The handkerchief, having been put to good use, was offered back. She shook her head. It was dirty now.

'I—I gave you a handkerchief once,' he mumbled, frowning

and squinting up at her. 'Not as fine as this one . . . it was only a
rag, really. I gave it to you when *you* were crying.'

'Did you, Pa?'

'Yes—yes. It was when I found you.'

'Was it, Pa?'

'It was in a place like this . . . no! It was worse, much worse!'

'Was it, Pa?'

'Everyone was dead . . . they had been killed by soldiers. You
were the only one left alive. I found you in a wooden box,
underneath a table.'

'Did you, Pa?'

'I gave you some wine to keep you quiet. It was all I had. I told
you that you couldn't expect anything more from a fellow like me.
You sucked it and got drunk. Then you went to sleep.'

'Did I, Pa?'

'You woke up, and I sang you a lullaby . . .'

'Did you, Pa?'

'Then in the morning, I put you in a cart and took you away
with me.'

'Did you, Pa?'

Her responses were dull and uninterested. It was impossible to
guess if she believed what she was told, or not. It was as if she had
been made to listen, against her will, to something that did not in
the least concern her.

'The rest—the rest you know.'

'Do I, Pa? Do I really know? Why are you here, Pa? Why did
you run away? Are you going to tell me that, too?'

He did not answer.

'Did you change your mind about me, Pa? Were you tired of
being my father?' Although she spoke in the same, indifferent-
seeming voice as before, there was no mistaking the terror that lay
behind the question.

'Was that why you ran away from me?'

'No—no! Never that!'

'Then tell me . . . tell me why you are here. Tell me why you are
dressed like this. Tell me everything that you've never told me
before.'

He told her. He told her everything, sparing her nothing, as if he
actually wanted her to hate him with all her heart. He told her that

she was no more than the orphaned child of obscure Polish villagers who had been horribly murdered and left lying, like dogs, in the open street. He told her what he himself had been when he'd found her: a man who'd lost everything through his own weakness and folly; a thief, a scavenger, with nothing in his heart but a few shreds of mocking vanity that he liked to think of as pride.

As he spoke he watched her for signs of bitterness and anger as she learned of the deception and the necessary overthrow of her dreams. But there was only gravity in her look, and a certain dignity in her manner as she stood in front of him, listening intently to his story. It was as if she wished him to know that there was something else inside her other than false dreams.

He told her why he'd made up the tale about buying her from the tramp and so encouraging her to imagine that she was better than she was. It had been to spare her the knowledge of the murdered village and to give her something of the inner sense of importance that he had himself, and which he believed had helped to keep him alive. He told her how once begun, the story had taken so deep a hold that it had seemed to kindle a kind of radiance in her that he had been frightened to extinguish; and that her hatred for the tramp had increased his fears that she should ever find out.

Yet he had always kept the old rags, dangerous though they were to him, because, in his heart of hearts, he knew that he must not destroy the truth entirely. He told her about David Kozlowski, and his fear that the murderer was her brother, then his relief when he learned otherwise . . . a relief so great that he let slip the chance of finding out her real name. Let slip? He shook his head and confessed that he hadn't wanted to know.

This last confession was most painful for him; and he waited for the girl's contempt. But her gravity was unshaken, and she made no movement except to brush away the flies. He told her of his repentance, and that he was going to Poland—

'Are you, Pa?'

Her voice was remote; and all her radiance seemed to have been quite put out. The dog's barking rose to a sudden yelp as a child threw a stone with shrewd success; and Mr Clarky from his vantage point a little way off, with Mrs Fairhazel beside him, watched his young client with painful anxiety.

288

'I 'ope, ma'am,' he muttered, 'I sincerely 'ope I've done the right thing!'

The young client seemed so aloof and unmoved as she stood in front of her father; and he, poor man, seemed to shrink as if he was all shadow.

It was indeed a strange meeting in the wilderness between the false father and the false daughter; yet, in a way, it was not very different from their first meeting . . .

'Perdita—Perdita—Perdita, my love!' murmured the false father, hopelessly.

'I wish, Pa,' answered the false daughter, her voice catching a little, 'that you wouldn't call me that. It sounds so common.'

Then, to Mr Clarky's ineffable relief—he had been miserably contemplating Mr Leviticus's just wrath!—he saw the young client suddenly kneel down and put her arms around the old client's neck.

'Oh, Pa, Pa!' she whispered. 'Did you really think there was nothing at all inside me? Don't you know how much I love you? Don't you know that we've always kept each other alive? When you gave me the wine, Pa, when you sang to me, when you took me away with you, you kindled both of us, Pa . . . and you can never, never put that out!'

To Mr Clarky's further relief, which was accompanied by hearty self-congratulation, which he found to be a reward far beyond a gold watch, he saw his young client taken into her father's arms. Mr Leviticus, he felt, would be well pleased.

'Tell me again, Pa, tell me how you found me. It's so much better this way. I like it much better that you found me than that you bought me. I always thought you gave too little! So tell me . . . tell me from when you first heard me crying. Tell me about the wooden box again, and how I got drunk . . .'

He told her; and she listened to him with such intentness that the very wilderness became absorbed. The dog grew quiet, the tumbledown walls seemed to lean towards the pair in profound interest, the broken chimneypots became ears, and the mouldering rags remembered their glory and grew colourful in the sun, and jewelled with flies.

When he had finished, she said to him, 'The name, Pa . . . do we want it? After all, Pa, we could never find out for sure. Nobody could really know. A baby in a box under a table? That baby might have come from anywhere. I might be anybody, really, Pa; I might even be the princess that Mr Dolly calls me. Don't you think so, Pa?'

He looked at her. Her face was serious. It was impossible for him to tell if she meant what she said. He smiled, a little ruefully, as he understood that beyond the truth there must always be another lie.

'Don't you think so, Pa?' she repeated. 'Don't you think so?'

He nodded. To nail the lie would be to crucify the truth. The old Jew must have his forgiveness . . .

So they went back together; and, with Mr Clarky and Mrs Fairhazel, they returned to Mrs Fairhazel's house in Stepney; and Mr Clarky had to give the driver a small fortune for the fare.

40

Although he was a strong man and had, in the past, slept in many places far worse than the squalid shelters of the last four nights, had been cold, hungry, buffeted and despised, he was, nevertheless, utterly exhausted and could hardly stand upright. He was put to bed in Perdita's room while she moved in with Mrs Fairhazel. A doctor was sent for who prescribed pills and rest; the pills were to satisfy his own professional dignity; the rest was for the good of the patient.

He came to see him on the following day, and found him to be greatly improved; but not sufficiently to get up until at least the Wednesday. The patient was, he said, in a state resembling recovery from a fever.

He was not much mistaken, although the illness was more a fever of the spirit than of the blood. It was a fever that had been caught long ago; and, as the patient had carried it about with him, it had taken many different forms. But behind each one of them lurked the black swan of his childhood, which was Death.

Perdita and Mrs Fairhazel—Perdita insisted that he call her

Barbara—nursed him, and rarely left him alone. When they did, one or other of the brothers Wilkinson kept him company and talked to him about their campaigns. It was as if they were all frightened he would run away again.

Sometimes Mrs Fairhazel—Barbara, rather—read to him; not because he was unable to read for himself, but simply because it was an agreeable thing to do. He slept well (sometimes, he was ashamed to discover, while he was being read to), and almost dreamlessly; which was a great blessing and helped in his recovery.

He had visitors of course, who brought him warmth, smiles and grapes. And chopped liver in handsome jars. Mr Dolly was the very first to call. He was overjoyed to see his old friend alive and nearly well. Not that he'd ever doubted it would happen. He'd said as much to Mrs Dolly. Mark my words, he'd said, one day, you'll see, he'll come walking back, as large as life! Gladly Mr Dolly gave up his guardianship of the princess; although, he said, it had been a great honour while it had lasted. He would dearly liked to have known what had happened to his friend, but as no one told him, he concluded this was something very personal, so he was content to let his natural curiosity wait upon his natural delicacy and good manners. All in good time, he thought, all in good time. And then, aloud, he wondered if his friend would be well enough to come to dinner on Friday night?

Mr Leviticus came, huge and creaking and almost too large for the little house. He sat with him for about half an hour; was grave and rather severe, but relented in the end when he realised how severe his client had been on himself.

'My dear young man,' he said, '—and you must pardon me for calling you a young man, but all the world is young to me. My dear young man, this is twice you have run away. You must not make a habit of it, you know. Your pretty daughter thinks the world of you; you must not take away that world. It is not yours to take.'

Mr Clarky visited on the Tuesday, with new clothes for him, which he had bought in the Strand under precise directions from his young client. He brought good wishes (and a pineapple) from the Streamers whom he had seen on the Saturday morning as he still resolutely pursued 'the art'.

There was, in addition, one other visitor; an unexpected one but curiously welcome nonetheless: Inspector Groom. He chatted quite cheerfully about the merry chase Sir Robert had led him and mentioned, in passing, the wounded publican, but did not think a complaint was likely to be lodged. As he rose to go, he remarked, smoothing down the back of his head, that, although the ways of Gray's Inn and Chancery Lane were reasonably wise, it was, in the end, Scotland Yard who did the work.

So little by little the invalid came out of his darkness and, on the Wednesday morning the doctor pronounced him well enough to get up. Great were the rejoicings when he came downstairs; and the sun shone brightly when he strolled a little way outside.

'Do you think, Pa,' asked Perdita anxiously, 'that you'll be well enough on Friday to go out to dinner?'

'I think,' said he, seriously, 'that if there is not a flood, or an earthquake or anything else like that to stand in my way, I might just manage to go!'

Just as the warmth of the evening brings out the scent of honey-suckle, sweet william and stock, so it brought out the aroma of Mr Dolly's stock . . . and so overpoweringly that the door of Famous Pickled Herrings was kept open and all Bishopsgate Street smelled cheesy.

Mr Dolly, perspiring gently, sat on a barrel under the sausage-grove, which had come out in a seasonal flowering of fly-papers, and waited for the last of his Friday night guests. Seven o'clock already. Outside, the Amalekites streamed past the window, but at a more leisurely rate, as if King David had given up the chase; and Mr Dolly wondered why Mrs Fairhazel was always late.

He wondered how it happened that someone as mild and gentle and anxious as Mrs Fairhazel could always be so unpunctual. He wondered what chain of little calamities could always manage to trip and delay her, and what doubts and confusions could always contrive, last-minutely, to assail her. Or was it just the difficulty of deciding between one hat and another? How foolish, thought Mr Dolly; she looks charming whatever she wears!

At last a cab stopped outside. The driver descended, let down the step, opened the door and stood aside with an outstretched palm. Out came the princess, out came Mrs Fairhazel, with an incautious flash of stocking, and, thank God, out came his old friend. To be honest, Mr Dolly had really been worrying that his friend might have disappeared again.

He jumped off the barrel and hastened to greet his guests.

'So good of you to come! So kind—'

'I'm sorry we're late, Mr Dolly,' said Perdita, accepting her tributary kiss. 'But—'

'I know, I know!' cried Mr Dolly mischievously. 'It's your father's fault! Like a tortoise, eh?'

'Why, no, Mr Dolly, nothing of the kind! Pa's been ready all day! It was Barbara—I mean, Mrs Fairhazel! She took ages!'

They went upstairs and Mr Dolly shut the shop door, saying to himself, 'Twelve at table again, thank God!'

Twelve at table: six guests and six—no! Five guests and seven Dollys, as one had to count Clarry Dolska as one of the family. Just as at every christening there has to be a bad fairy, so at every table there has to be a Clarry Dolska.

Mr Dolly, in the midst of his overflowing pleasure, kept catching sight of his cousin; and felt, intermittently, something of the indignation of Macbeth. Well might he have asked: '*Which of you have done this?*'

Shadows crossed his heart as he answered the question. The perpetrators had really been the poor woman who had been murdered, and the tragic young man who had been hanged only the other day. It was, after all, they who had brought about the breaking of old Mr Dolska's heart and his dying of it . . . and so Clarry Dolska's coming to London. It was a true saying that every man's death diminishes me; for old Mr Dolska's death had certainly diminished Mr Dolly. But on the other hand, with a man like Mr Dolly, it was probably better to say that every man's life enriches me; and there was no doubt that his old friend's presence at his table enriched Mr Dolly mightily.

'My good friend, *Sir* Robert,' he kept mentioning proudly, and watching for the effect on his cousin. 'My good friend *Sir* Robert has a great estate in Gloucestershire, you know. My good friend *Sir* Robert comes from one of the best families in the country. Such people! You can have no idea, cousin!'

All things considered, the dinner was a great success. Everybody ate and drank enormously, the children didn't quarrel, the two admirers of the older girls for once opened their mouths and managed to come out with sensible things, and the empress— Mrs Dolly—sat shining resplendently beyond the Sabbath candles without ever giving any of those quick, incredulous looks at her flushed and beaming husband that denoted that all was not well somewhere and hadn't he noticed; while the maidservant within the Dollys' gates—Brandyella—fetched and carried, fetched and carried, and, whenever she could, took a brief respite from her labours in the public house next door.

'And when,' inquired Mr Dolly, when dinner was over and everyone was sitting expansively in the parlour, 'are you going back to your mansion in Gloucestershire, *Sir* Robert, my friend?'

Sir Robert thought hard. Looked to Mrs Fairhazel and his daughter for support. Mrs Fairhazel examined her shoes; Perdita found an interest in the ceiling. Sir Robert shook his head. He was not sure. He really hadn't made up his mind. In fact, he had been thinking of settling in London again.

Everyone expressed pleasure at this; it would be good to have their friend among them again. Jonathan Dolly thought it an admirable idea, and remarked wisely that a child like Perdita, a child at the very threshold of life, would undoubtedly benefit more from the cultural advantages afforded by the capital city (which he himself felt well qualified to display) than from the company of simple peasants and ignorant villagers.

'And what is wrong with villagers?' demanded Perdita, with an odd smile at her father. 'I might be a villager myself at heart, for all you know, Jonathan Dolly!'

'Oh, no!' said Jonathan, shocked. 'You're a princess, Perdita! We all know that!'

'London,' said Mr Dolly pensively. 'Hanover Square, perhaps . . . or Kensington? The best parts of the town, cousin,' he informed Clarry kindly. 'Or what about Park Lane?'

But no. Sir Robert did not think so. He had a great fondness for the older parts . . .

'Greenwich, then? Or Dulwich? I believe that there are some wonderful old houses there.'

'No . . . no. Somewhere a little nearer to the heart of things.' Another glance at Mrs Fairhazel, who was examining her fingernails. He thought of somewhere more like—more like Stepney. But he would look around . . .

'Exactly so!' said Clarry Dolska. 'That's what I always tell my cousin. One has to look around before one settles down. And then one can see what can be done! Noo! I happen to be doing the same thing myself!' And Clarry Dolska, without further delay, went on to make the titled gentleman with the large estate fully acquainted with his own situation in life and the fact that he had a large capital sum deposited with Fox and Hankey of Lombard Street; and that when the baronet had decided upon a suitable premises, he, Clarry Dolska, might well be interested in becoming his neighbour.

'Noo?' said Clarry, with the air of bestowing an inestimable benefit on his cousin's important friend.

'Didn't you notice?' said Mrs Dolly to her husband that night, in the privacy of the bed-chamber. 'Didn't you see?'

'See? Notice? What should I have noticed, my dear? Everybody was getting along famously! Weren't they?' he added, overcome by a momentary doubt.

'Didn't you notice Mrs Fairhazel . . . and our dear friend?'

'What was there to notice?'

'Good God! Do they have to fly into each other's arms across the tablecloth before you see anything?'

A pause. A widening of Mr Dolly's eyes. A glinting of watch-chain, and then a great, broad expanse of it.

'No! I don't believe it! Never! Not really?'

Mrs Dolly sighed. Her beloved husband was not the most perceptive of men. He had other qualities, yes; wonderful ones. But not perception. She remembered that he hadn't even noticed her own feelings for him when he had presented himself, such a fine young man, at her house, burdened with flowers so you could hardly see him. She'd had to tell him herself, though it had cost her quite an effort. And even then he had found it hard to believe that he had made so good an impression!

Mrs Dolly's perceptions were not unfounded; and in due course, and by special licence, there was made another Lady Stand-fast—to the unutterable confusion of Burke's *Peerage and Baronetage*. Mrs Fairhazel's antecedents were minutely inquired into, and her first husband's name spectacularly misspelt. But there was rejoicing in Bishopsgate Street and Mr Dolly's brother-in-law sang an aria from *The Barber of Seville*, to Hebrew words.

At the suggestion of Mr Leviticus, the marriage was published in *The Times* where it was read with interest and pleasure by Mr and Mrs H. H. Bloggs of Reading, who remembered the gentleman on the train very well. But it was read in Gloucestershire with anger and dismay.

Although the family did not think it likely, they were haunted by the awful possibility of a natural-born son who would inherit the title; and the hatred for Uncle Robert knew no bounds. There was no pleasure in anything any more; even the horses had longer faces than usual. The Standfast family crouched in the great mansion while the dead animals on the walls and the great black swan above brooded over them, as if to remind them that they were mere tenants, owning nothing but what they had brought into the world, and able to pass on nothing but what they had given to the world.

Nor was this the only tragedy to record, for it rarely happens that everything turns out well for everybody, without a single blot. Doubtless for the best of reasons, a statesman in Bosnia was blown up by a bomb. He left behind him a widow, five children and a scandal that toppled his government. Debts were dishonoured, loans called in, and many innocent people were utterly ruined. Among the victims was Fox and Hankey of Lombard Street, with whom Clarry Dolska had deposited his large capital sum. Every penny of it was lost. Clarry was a broken man.

'I tell you what, Clarry,' said Mr Dolly when he had heard and digested the news. 'Just give me a little time and I'll look around and see what can be done. Noo?'

Clarry Dolska stayed on in Bishopsgate Street for a few more weeks as his cousin's pensioner; and then, with funds provided by Famous Pickled Herrings, he went grimly back to Poland. There, safely in the bosom of his family, he heartily abused his cousin, his cousin's gates . . . as anyone would after such a reversal of fortune.